THE LINK
A Victorian Mystery

THE LINK

A VICTORIAN MYSTERY

a novel by

ROBIN MAUGHAM

McGRAW-HILL BOOK COMPANY
New York · St. Louis · San Francisco

TO FRANK

AUTHOR'S NOTE

THOUGH THE IDEA of this novel was suggested by the Tichborne Case and by my father's book on it, I have not made use of any of the characters who appeared in that strange Victorian mystery.

For various reasons, I wanted to set my novel in the same period, so I spent a year—1967/1968—travelling in Australia and Mexico to find the background material I needed. But not one of my characters is based on any person alive or dead.

While I have tried not to use any expression which was not current in those Victorian years, I have deliberately avoided 'period' phrases or dialogue. However, when I now read novels and travel-books of the eighteen-fifties, I am surprised how little the vernacular differs from our language today.

R.M.

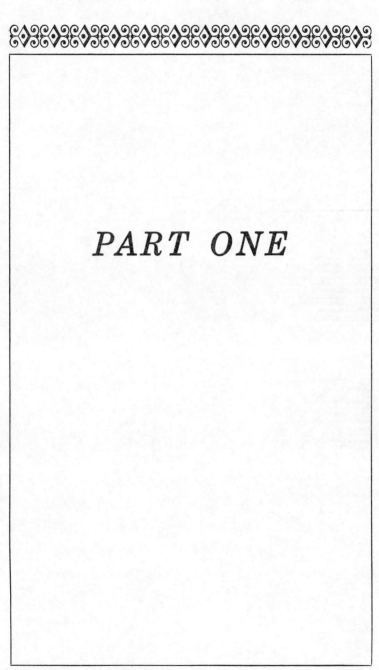

PART ONE

From an advertisement in *The Times*, March 20, 1862.

"A handsome reward will be given to any person who can furnish such information as will discover the fate of James Edward Steede. He sailed from the port of Acapulco, Mexico, on the twenty-third of April, 1852, in the ship *Clara*, and has never been heard of since. But a report reached England to the effect that a portion of the crew and passengers of a vessel of that name was picked up by a ship bound for Australia—Melbourne it is believed. It is not known whether the said James Steede was amongst the drowned or saved. He would at the present time be thirty-two years of age. He is the son of Sir William Steede, Bart., now deceased, and is heir to all his estates. All replies should be addressed to The Dowager Lady Steede, The Dower House, Steede, Nottinghamshire."

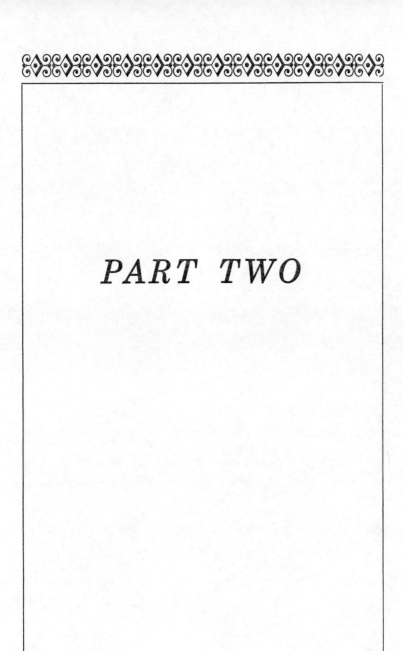

PART TWO

I HAD no need to be deceitful when I was a child, for I was happy. I loved my mother; I loved my pony, Midget, and my nurse, Agnes, and my mother's old friend, Colonel Savage, with his grizzled whiskers and gruesome tales of Waterloo, who used to give me riding lessons. And I was fond of my father, because on the few occasions when he returned from the Orient he brought me fantastic presents. For instance, when he came home for the Queen's coronation in 1838, I can remember native drums and plumed hats, a hundred wooden toy soldiers with black faces and crimson tunics, a set of dominoes made of jade and ivory, a leopard skin, and a small stuffed crocodile which glittered strangely in the light of the gas-lamps and made Agnes shudder each time she looked at it. I was rather awed by my father's extreme height and sallow, fashionably Byronic, melancholy face, but I was attracted by the smell that emanated from him—a mixture of a heavy gardenia perfume and peppermints, overlaying a reek of tobacco and the stale odour of rum.

My mother seldom went to London in those days, so I spent almost all the time at Steede—riding in the park with Colonel Savage, learning my lessons with Agnes, going for walks round the garden with my mother, and amusing myself without a moment's boredom when I was alone—for Agnes had to spend some of her time with my brother Arthur who was then a baby; he was six years younger than myself.

My days were filled with happiness. Misery only began when I was nine years old and I drove with my mother in the new carriage she had ordered to Brierly Lodge near Leicester. There she left me in the school hall, standing beside my play-box with my name, James Steede, painted on it in curling black letters. It contained a miniature Hindu temple with little bells that tinkled and a lacquered handkerchief box—my father's latest gifts—and a pair of boxing-gloves which my mother had bought the previous week in Nottingham in the hope that the school might make a man of me.

When I think of myself at the age of nine I can only see my physical appearance as it was portrayed in a family group by Sir Francis Grant, which used to hang in my mother's sitting-room at Steede. I was small for my age and very slim. My pale hair and pale skin and light-blue eyes, which always seemed over-large in the painting, were certain, I now realise, to have excited the instinct for cruelty which smoulders in most schoolboys. That first afternoon at Brierly Lodge there were no lessons. The boys gathered round me in the classroom, examining me in a silence only broken by brief titters.

"Can you speak?" the tallest boy asked me.

"Yes," I answered. I could feel myself blushing.

"What's your name?" the boy asked.

"James Steede."

"Can you repeat a sentence you hear, Steede?"

"Yes."

"Then repeat this after me. 'I one my mother, I two my mother.' Go on, repeat it."

I hesitated. I looked round at the rest of them. They listened in silence, waiting. Obviously I was expected to repeat the meaningless words. "I one my mother. I two my mother," I began.

"Go on," the boy said. "'I three my mother.' Go on."

In confused embarrassment I continued, uncertainly, until I heard my voice saying. "I six my mother." Then I stopped.

"Go on," the boy said.

"I seven my mother," I continued. "I eight my mother."

And at that all twenty of them broke out into a wild yell of triumph. "He ate his mother," they screamed in derision. "Steede ate his mother, Steede ate his mother!"

As I listened to their laughter, I tried to smile. But even as I made the effort, I felt that in some terrible way I had made a betrayal of my mother's confidence in me. But it wasn't the feeling of guilt which disconcerted me. It was the expression on the boys' faces as they stared at me. For I suddenly became aware that, for some reason I could not understand, they disliked me. They were all hostile to me, and I had never met with hostility before. At Steede they were all fond of me—even Jenks, the head gardener, whose peaches I stole. The realisation that without any bad behaviour on my part I was disliked filled me with a kind of sick bewilderment. I was somehow so dazed by my wretchedness that I scarcely minded when later they tore my Hindu temple to pieces, bit by bit, trampling flat the little tinkling bells. I watched unmoved as they scraped the lacquer off my wooden box and then wrenched off the lid and snapped it in two.

Misery hung around me like a fog, muffling my emotions. Only now and then would the fog lift in gratitude for some unexpected trivial act of kindness, and then, with the first act of subsequent brutality, the pain would become unbearable. My second term, I ran away from school. I walked seven miles into Leicester, took the train to Nottingham, and walked from the station to Steede. My mother saw me limping up the drive, and I ran to her. Then she hustled me up to my room on the top floor, using the back staircase, because my father and Colonel Savage were in the house and she didn't want them to find out I'd run away until I'd had time to calm down and rest. That evening after supper she came up to my room and sat down on my bed, and she told me she'd persuaded them to let me stay at home for a week, and she listened. . . . But in the light of what happened later I can't bear to write down any more about that evening—though I know I'm apt to talk about it when I'm drunk.

It rained that next day at Steede, so I didn't go out. I read a book of fables my mother had brought me. One of the fables I read was about the oak and the willow, and as I thought about the story it occurred to me how stupid the oak was to be proud it didn't bend before the storm. For the oak was torn down, but the willow survived the tempest.

When I went back to Brierly Lodge, I was told it was a school rule that any boy who ran away must be caned. I had never been caned before, for I had enough enemies among the boys without adding to my troubles by giving offence to the masters. But I now heard my enemies say that the headmaster caned hard—sometimes whipping a boy until he cried. And then, they said, he would press the boy against him and comfort him as if he were not the same person who had inflicted the boy's pain.

After prayers that night I was summoned to the headmaster's room. I walked along the yellow-coloured corridor and pushed open the door which led to his study. He was a large, heavy man with a solid, round-shaped face. Usually when I looked at him I could not avoid staring at the thick black hairs which sprouted around his nostrils, but that evening while he lectured me on my wickedness in running away from school, I could not take my eyes away from the long cane which lay on the table beside him. It was made of bamboo, and it had a curling handle.

"So I want you to promise me, you won't run away again," he said in conclusion. "Do you promise me?"

His voice was husky. For an instant I thought he would let me go.

"I promise," I said.

"Very well," he said. "But I'm afraid I must still punish you, because it is a school rule. So you must take down your trousers."

I tried to make myself think of Steede as he took hold of me and pushed my head under the table. The first lash of the cane on my flesh was more startling than painful, and there was such a long pause after it that I wondered if I'd got off lightly. But the second stroke came, and it seemed harder. And then, after another pause, came the third which made me wince. I cried out aloud with the next heavy swipe, and at the fifth I gave a sob of pain. But the punishment, I soon realised, had only just begun. The cane continued to fall, and now its lash seemed so hard that I was sure it was cutting deep into my skin. In my anguish I gave up counting the strokes. My whole being seemed concentrated in a dread of the cane's next lash. I was still determined not to break down into tears. But suddenly—I find it hard to describe—suddenly something inside me snapped as thoroughly and completely as the lid of my lacquer box, and I began to cry. And then the headmaster stopped whipping me. He took hold of me, and he began to comfort me. And when he pressed me tight against him, I didn't try to wriggle away from him. I stayed with him. Because I wasn't the oak, and perhaps I never had been. I was the willow which inclined with the wind.

From that moment, when such pride of spirit as I possessed had snapped in two like my box, I became deliberately pliant: I copied the willow in the fable. I taught myself to smile when I was angry; I learned to please those I feared and detested; I inclined gracefully before the prevailing wind. I led a life of carefully planned deceit. Only in the holidays could I be myself again, and I could be completely at ease now only when I was alone. I would go for long rides on the little mare called Blossom which my mother had bought me for my tenth birthday; I would take some food in a knapsack and stay out all day till nightfall, and no one seemed to object, though my mother was sometimes annoyed if I didn't get back till an hour after dark. For as those years dragged by, I had noticed that my mother seemed to have become fonder of me—and more possessive, because I was now the only person in the family on whom she could fix her devotion. She had never appeared to care much for my younger brother Arthur, and I had already become aware that she no longer had any affection for my father. In fact, on my father's rare visits to Steede my mother seldom even spoke to him.

By the time I was twelve, my willow-like behaviour had made life at Brierly Lodge at least bearable. But I left the school without any regret, and I calmed my apprehensions about the prospect of life at Eton by remembering that I had learned to avoid trouble by making myself gracefully pleasant. I had already found out something about life at Eton from a boy who had left Brierly a year previously. With my kind of looks and with my shyness he warned me I was in for it. Unfortunately he would be able to do little to help me once I arrived at Eton, for he was two years older and in a different house—which would make it almost impossible for us to meet.

My first night home at Steede I undressed and stood naked in front of the long looking-glass in my bedroom. I was still small for my age and very lightly built, and though the pale wheat-coloured hair was clustered thick on my head, I still had hardly a hair on my body. That night I cursed my wide-set, light-blue eyes, my delicate features, and my smooth skin. But at least, this time, I would know what to expect, and I would know how to deal with it.

———

At Brierly Lodge the oldest enemy I had had to deal with had been a boy thirteen years old. But at Eton there were boys of seventeen and eighteen, and of course I had known this before I arrived at Jackson's house where I boarded—just as I'd known that each boy had a small room to himself. Yet for some reason it gave me a shock to see that two or three of the older boys in the house were the size and height of fully-grown men. The Captain of the house was a torpid, spotty-faced lout, almost nineteen, who was nearly six foot tall, and Burdock, the Captain of Games, though he was not quite eighteen years old, had the muscles of a wrestler. Burdock was large and thick-set. His rather bony nose jutted out from beneath the thick ridge of his brows. His narrow lips were set, straight as a matchstick, in his mouth. His expression was enthusiastic yet grim as he urged on the 'lower boys' of the house at football practice.

When Burdock was coaching us in the Field Game, I soon noticed that it was always my side of the scrum he would choose, and it was next to me that he would wedge himself in. Soon I began to dread the feel of his tough sweating body pressing against me. One of my duties as a lower boy was to cook the sausages and eggs for Burdock's tea in the evening, and I'd been warned not to burn them, for Burdock, they said, had a large collection of canes. Burdock's grim red face and heavy limbs began to haunt me. But as yet he was my only worry. I had been wise enough to put up with the usual bullying with an appearance of fortitude. When the lower boys of the house invaded the little cell-like room in which I slept, and they tore up the shirts my mother had bought me, I had neither complained nor lost my temper. But I was aware that all of them resented me, for with the oddly accurate instinct of the herd they knew I was not one of them. But, so far, I had done nothing in particular to arouse their desire for cruelty. So far I was safe, and Quackie Jack, as we called our distracted but apparently benevolent housemaster, seemed to be pleased with me, because my weekly reports from my form-masters were generally good. At least I could avoid getting into trouble from idleness.

I counted each day to the half-term break which we called Long Leave, so I can remember it was at the end of my fifth week that Burdock sent a boy to fetch me to his room after prayers.

"You're for it," the boy said, grinning at me. "He's taken out one of his canes."

I walked slowly down the narrow, dark corridor which led to Burdock's room. I knew what it was about. I knocked at the door.

"Come in," I heard Burdock say in his deep voice. He was standing in front of the fire in his room with his hands thrust deep into his pockets. He had taken off his tail-coat, and he was wearing a blazer which was much too tight for him. His lips seemed to vanish into his red face as he glared at me. Lying on his wicker armchair was a long cane. "I'm told you've been shirking games' practice. Is that true?"

I nodded and stared down at the floor.

"Now that I'm busy with the house-side," he continued, "I suppose you thought I wouldn't find out. Is that it?"

I shook my head.

"Then what is it?"

"I've not been feeling well," I answered truthfully. "I've had a pain. I've still got it."

Burdock glowered at me suspiciously. "Where have you got a pain?"

"In my shoulder," I answered.

"Which shoulder?"

"My left one," I said.

"Take off your jacket and show me where it hurts," he ordered.

I took off my jacket and put my finger on the end of my left shoulder bone. Suddenly he stretched out his hand and gripped my shoulder at the point I had touched. I winced.

"That's genuine enough," he said. "Does it hurt badly?"

"Fairly badly."

"How long have you had it?"

"Over a fortnight."

"Do you know what caused it?"

"I knocked it in a scrum at practice."

"You may have cracked the bone. Take off your shirt and let me look."

As I pulled off my shirt he scowled as if I had done something to annoy him. "You've got a skin just like a girl," he said, frowning. "Now show me again where it hurts."

I pointed to the place. He put his hand on it very gently—and began kneading it lightly with his fingers. "I don't think there's anything much wrong," he said. "There's certainly nothing broken. Anyhow, I'll let you off practice for another week. Come to me in a week's time, and I'll have another look."

His examination was finished, but his hand still remained on my shoulder. "Were you at a preparatory school?" he asked.

"Yes, Brierly Lodge."

"Did you get bullied much?"

"Quite a bit."

"Weren't there any older boys to look after you?"

"They bullied me as much as the rest of them."

"I'd have thought some older boy would have taken you up as a friend?"

I shook my head. His warm hand seemed heavy on my shoulder.

"Poor little Steede," he said. He was staring at me steadily now. I could hear the sound of his breathing. "I like the name Steede," he added. "Your people live near Leicester, don't they?"

"Near Nottingham."

"I expect you're looking forward to the holidays already, aren't you?" he asked.

"Very much," I answered.

"You haven't made any particular friends in the house yet, have you?"

"Not yet," I answered.

His hand began to stroke my shoulder. "You ought to find a friend," he said. "At any rate you ought to have someone to look after you."

I was silent. His hand slid down from my shoulders on to my back. "You'll need someone," he said. He was now standing so close to me that I could see the sweat shining on his forehead. He was breathing heavily. I glanced up at him. Suddenly I was frightened. He was trying to smile, but his face looked dark and swollen. His whole body was tense and quivering. "You'll need someone," he repeated. "So if you don't want to get into trouble, why not let it be me?"

I said nothing. I felt sick. I was determined not to give in to him unless I was forced. There must be some way in which I could manage to escape. But even as I tried to work out ways of getting away from him I somehow knew it would be impossible. Then, without any conscious volition on my part, I felt my head droop slowly forward until it was touching him. And at the instant my head touched him, his arms seized hold of me.

In my innocence I had supposed that Burdock's attitude towards me would change noticeably the following day. But when I came into his room the next afternoon to bring him his tea, he was as gruff and harsh to me as ever. Ten days went by before I was sent for again.

When I came into his room this time he was sitting in his shirt sleeves, hunched up in the wicker armchair. "How's the shoulder?" he asked.

"A bit better," I answered.

"You went to practice yesterday."

"Yes, because you'd only let me off for a week."

"But you didn't go to practice today."

"Because my shoulder was aching."

"Come here," he said. But I did not move. "Come here," he repeated. "I promise I won't hurt you."

"I'll stay where I am, if you don't mind."

Slowly he got up from the chair and stretched his arms and walked over to me. "What's wrong?" he asked.

"I think I'd better go," I said.

"No, don't. Please don't. Tell me what's wrong." He put out his hand and ruffled my hair. He was trembling. "You didn't mind last time," he muttered. "So tell me what's wrong?"

"You said we were going to be friends," I said.

"We are friends," he replied.

"No, we're not."

"Why do you say that?"

"Because people are kind to their friends," I answered.

For a moment he stared at me in silence. "How do you want me to be kind to you? You can't expect me to go about with you. I'm over four years older than you are. I'd be sacked before a week was out. So what do you want?"

"You said you'd look after me," I said. "You said you'd stop me getting bullied, so why don't you let them all know you won't stand for it? You saw they were going for me in the corridor last night. But you just walked straight by."

"Right," he said. "The next boy who lays a finger on you will get it hot from me. Now, anything else?"

"Yes," I said. "They take it out on me in the scrum. I get hurt every time. So if you want me to go with you and be your friend, then let me off games. Tell them you've found out I'm not well. Tell them the doctor's said I've got a bad heart. Tell them anything—but get me off games."

Burdock's hand was stroking my neck. "If I keep my side of the pact," he said slowly, "do you promise you'll keep yours?"

"Yes," I answered. "I promise."

"And you'll never tell anyone?"

"I promise."

"Right," Burdock said. "Then we'll be friends." Slowly, still gazing at me, he began to take off his shirt. "So now let's see you keep your part of the bargain."

Burdock must have had a word the very next morning with the head lower boy, because from that moment I was never bullied again, and without anything being definitely stated, from odd remarks and stray glances I realised that most of the other boys in the house knew Burdock had adopted me and that for the time being, at least, I was under his protection.

I knew I wasn't the first boy he had taken under his care. I wasn't the first of his willows. Others had inclined when prudence demanded it. But as the weeks passed by and the fierce possessiveness he now displayed towards me remained unaltered, I decided that perhaps the others hadn't inclined quite so gracefully and completely. And my reasoning must have been accurate, for I remained Burdock's friend until the day he left the school. By that time, thanks to Burdock's training, I was better fitted to look after myself. For during his last term—during the last few weeks of the Easter half, when we met almost every evening now that he had found a way for us to get out of the house after lock-up—Burdock became worried by what might happen to me after he left. So he insisted on giving me long and arduous lessons in wrestling and boxing.

"I couldn't bear to think of you going with anyone else," he told me.

"I couldn't bear it either," I replied.

Burdock put his heavy arm around my neck. We were walking back together after a very cold moonlight swim at Cuckoo Weir.

It was our last evening together. "Promise you won't," he said. "Promise."

"Don't worry," I answered with a laugh.

Suddenly Burdock stopped and gripped my shoulders and swung me round so I was facing him. Then he gazed at me in silence for a while, peering at me intensely in the light of the full moon. I believe, now, that he was trying to fix me in his memory, so this would be the portrait of me—standing there in an old shirt and flannel trousers with the moon shining on my damp tousled hair. This would be the engraving which he would carry with him, willingly or unwillingly, for ever.

"You're a slacker and you're a shirker," he said. "You're a little runt in many ways. But you're the best of the lot of them." He nodded his head solemnly several times. I noticed there were tears in his eyes. "Remember this," he continued. "You'll always be my friend. So wherever you are and wherever I am, if you're in trouble and need me, I'll always come to your help." He paused and gave a long sigh. "You see, little Jamie," he whispered, "I'll never forget you."

I remember I stared up at him in wonder, for in all the time I had known him I suppose his little speech was the nearest he ever came to making a declaration of love.

John Clive Burdock: now married to an Admiral's daughter; father of three children. I wonder what he'd do if he received a letter from me saying, *I'm in Berrima, New South Wales, and I need your help urgently.* And I wonder if he's been able to push to the back of his mind the portrait of a damp-haired boy in the meadows, staring up at him in the moonlight.

———

When I try to recall the next few terms after Burdock had left, I find they are wrapped in the vague mist of unhappiness which always surrounded me in those days. I survived. That is the only way I can sum up that period. I did my work well enough not to get into trouble; I still shirked games—except in the summer half when I would row on the river. And gradually I managed to make a few friends with boys of my own age, who now tolerated me because I could sometimes make them laugh, and because I was well supplied by my mother with pocket-money, so that I could afford to buy them 'sock' in the form of cakes, sweets, and fruit which we would purchase from a mysterious old man who appeared daily at the Long Wall with a portable store.

I survived. But I felt guilty, for I knew somehow that survival was not enough. From hearing as a child the talk of my father, who had played cricket for the school at Lords, and from hearing the talk of Colonel Savage, who had been Captain of his house, I had somehow been forced to realise that Eton was more than a famous school which had produced prime ministers and governors and bishops and generals. Eton was a way of life. For in a sense, Etonians never left Eton; they merely changed into being Old Etonians. One could see it in their endless conversation, over the port and brandy, about their days at school. One could see it in their enthusiastic attendance at cricket matches, or at Founder's day, or on the Fourth of June. One could read it in the tedious books of sentimental reminiscences which were bought so eagerly. One could hear it in the anxiety with which they discussed Eton's chances in the boat-race against Westminster, or the match at Lords against Harrow. But it was not only a way of life which implied a continual looking back at the school they had left; it was a religion which enforced a continual duty to conform to a fixed pattern of behaviour, and to lend every assistance to co-religionists —provided they had not lapsed in their faith. It was a club in which your standing depended not on what you were doing in your life as an adult but on what you had done in your years as a boy at Eton. By that behaviour and by that reputation, rather than by subsequent success or failure, you were judged.

And I was failing. Each day, each week, each half—I was establishing the reputation of being a shirker. I knew it, yet I made no effort to mend my ways. Perhaps even then I was aware that however hard I tried I would never be able to conform to the rules of Society. I would never be accepted in the club—probably because they guessed I didn't care for them or their code of rules. I would be the one whose name would be passed over quickly—if it ever cropped up in their talk over the nuts and wine. I would be an outsider. And even at the age of fifteen I was resigned to it.

While I had been under Burdock's protection, I had noticed that a boy called Adeney seemed—to use Burdock's expression—"interested" in me. If I looked up from my plate in the dining-hall he would always seem to be staring at me. In chapel he sat across the aisle opposite to me. When the evening prayers were being read out and we were kneeling, I would watch him secretly from between my fingers and see him gazing at me. Adeney was only a year older than I was, but he was far taller and sturdier. His appearance was unusual because of its contrasts. His hair was thick and dark, almost jet black, and it looked coarse in texture, but his skin looked smooth and as white as ivory. His body, though lean, was powerful, yet he moved lightly and easily. His face with its thick brows and fleshy nose and wide mouth had something rather brutal about it, yet a shy, timid, sensitive person seemed to be staring out of his light-brown eyes. It was as if a fawn had put on the head of a bull.

At the beginning of the summer half, after Burdock had left, I noticed that although Adeney lived on the first floor of the house he had taken to lingering in the corridor on the top floor near to my room. Each time I appeared he would pretend to be surprised to see me—he would call out some greeting, then walk away. But as the days passed by, he became less timid. He would sometimes stay and talk to me. Once or twice we walked down the High Street together to drink a glass of cider at the Christopher, and we soon became casual friends. When I had been to his room several times—to talk or to borrow a book—and he had been to mine, I decided I had been wrong in supposing he was "interested," though I was aware he always seemed constrained when he was alone with me, while he was talkative and noisy when he was with his older friends. Then came the present from him.

At that period the craze in school was for cross-bows. A man called Towers specialised in making them, and he sold them in his shop which was just beyond Barnes' Pool Bridge. At the back of his shop was a garden where he allowed boys to practise if they had bought one of his bows, which cost eight shillings. One of Adeney's older friends had lent him his cross-bow, so Adeney and I had spent a hot summer's afternoon using it in Towers' garden. A few days later at the end of some peaceful hours on the river after 'absence,' as roll-call in School Yard was called, when I came back to my room I found a parcel on my little table. I unwrapped it and discovered to my surprise that it was a new cross-bow. There was a note tied to it which read: "For J. Steede with best wishes from P. Adeney". I was delighted. I examined the bow. It was beautifully made. I put it down on my table and rushed downstairs to thank Adeney. His room was on the first floor at the far end of the dark, twisting corridor. I flung open the door and walked in. Adeney was standing in a circular tin bath such as we all used, and it was a quarter full of water. A large brown can was on the shelf beside him. He was soaping his shoulders.

"Thanks for the present," I said. "Thanks enormously."

"That's all right," Adeney replied. He was obviously embarrassed by my sudden appearance, for he began to blush. I could see the redness spreading across his body.

"I'm really tremendously grateful," I said, and I turned to go. But somehow I found myself still standing there. In silence I watched the flush covering his pale white skin. I could see his muscles growing taut as he gazed at me. For a while we stared at each other in silence. I could now see his desire, and I could see the brutality in his face. I was afraid of him. But I couldn't move.

"Can you throw me the towel?" Adeney said, breaking the silence. "It's on the chair."

I picked up the towel and walked over to him. I could smell the soap and the strange smell of his body. When I gave him the towel, he turned abruptly away from me. He began to dry himself with brisk, rough tugs at the towel. Now that his back was turned to me, his confidence returned a little, and he started to talk, uttering anything safe that came into his head. So he talked of Towers' shop and his garden and the targets used for practice and the length of the arrows. But all the time my eyes were fixed on a small muscle at the back of his thigh which was quivering incessantly. Then as he lifted the towel, I saw there was a wet patch of skin at the base of his lean, smooth back.

My voice sounded odd to me when I spoke. "You haven't dried your back properly," I said. "Give me the towel and let me do it."

He said nothing, but he clenched the towel in his hands. Then he shook his head, which was still turned away from me.

"Why not?" I asked.

Suddenly I saw his body begin to tremble. With a violent jerk of his hands he dropped the towel into the water.

"Please go," he said. "I'll see you later. But get out now, I tell you. Get out."

I hesitated for a moment. I felt sick. But this time it was neither from fear nor disgust. I could feel my heart beating. I was so dazed that for a few seconds I couldn't move. Then I turned and left the room, closing the door very softly behind me as if my visit to him had been secret.

Adeney did not come up to my landing for the next few days. I told myself I was glad. I remembered the sessions I had been forced to endure in Burdock's room, and I shuddered. For the time being, at least, I was safe, and in my own lonely kind of way I had begun to enjoy my freedom. Now that I was older I had no need of a protector, I told myself. Those days of fear were over.

But during the next few warm summer nights in my airless little room when I lay awake in bed searching restlessly for sleep, an image of Adeney would slide into my mind. He would be standing in the tin bath, soaping his heavy shoulders. I would observe the contrast between his milk-white skin and his coarse black hair. I would notice the power of his limbs, and sometimes I would think of their brutality. Then I would begin to breathe faster, and I would turn in my bed, thrusting my face into the pillow to obliterate the image.

The following Saturday, I decided to spend the whole afternoon on the river. The sun was shining from a pale sky. There was not a breath of air. I took a towel in case I wanted to swim, and I left my room. Leaning over the staircase on the landing was Adeney.

"Hullo," he said, noticing my towel. "Going on the river?"

"That's right."

"Is there anyone you could get to answer your name at absence?"

"I daresay. Why?"

"If you get someone to answer for you at six-fifteen, and you wanted to come, we could get a skiff. We might get as far as Bray."

I hesitated. I had finished all my work, and I had made no particular plans. "All right," I said. "Just wait while I get a stand-in."

The river was as still as a lake. We rowed in silence, listening to the splash of our oars, watching the water rats scurry into their holes among the roots of the overhanging trees, passing beneath banks which were white with hawthorn blossom, rowing steadily and silently, sometimes seeing the blue gleam of a kingfisher in the bushes, sometimes meeting a solemn line of swans. The air was very still. The elms in the far meadows stood like masts. Presently, after we had been through a lock, we reached a part of the river that was deserted. Here would have been the place to swim. But neither of us spoke, and we rowed on. And as our journey continued and we moved into quiet backwaters and shaded reaches, I realised that we had no fixed objective such as Bray. Our objective, I began to feel, lay not on the river but in our minds, and we were rowing towards a destination which perhaps both of us dreaded but to which we were nevertheless inexorably bound, just as already we were so closely linked together that it was as if we rowed with one body and thought with one mind. Thus when I turned my head and saw the island, I knew Adeney had turned and seen it too, and we rowed towards it without speaking.

A rotting platform extended for a few feet into the water. We tied up the boat to it and walked up a flight of broken stone steps which were covered with moss and which led through a wild tangle of undergrowth. Suddenly in a clearing we saw the ruins of a summer-house.

The roof had fallen in on one side, but the walls were still standing. The paint had peeled away from the cracked wooden panels of the front door, which was fastened by a rusty padlock. Then we saw that the hasp was broken, so we took off the padlock and opened the door and walked in. There was one main room, and in it the shutters were closed and locked. But by the light of the open door we could see frescoes on the walls and on the ceilings, and as our eyes became accustomed to the dim light we saw that the frescoes were all of monkeys, and the monkeys were not portrayed as wild or mischievous but as stern and as thoughtful as senators.

I turned and looked at Adeney, and at the same moment he looked towards me. His lips were open in a smile. For once the expression of his face was gentle. But then I saw his eyes, and I suddenly felt afraid, because there was nothing gentle in his gaze. Before, it had been his face which gave an impression of brutality, while his eyes stared out shyly from the animal's mask. Now, it was the lines of his face which seemed soft and harmless, while his dark eyes gleamed with fierce excitement in which I sensed that cruelty rather than passion was the stronger desire. For a while he stared at me in silence, and slowly it seemed as if the force which was controlling his eyes gained mastery over the rest of him, for the smile left his face and his body stiffened. He had begun to sweat.

"It's stifling hot," he said. "We could go for a swim."

I wanted to get away from the decayed house with its damp smell of rot and its grotesque monkeys which now seemed evil and threatening as they spied down on us. "Yes, let's swim," I said. I moved towards the door which was open. But Adeney was standing in the way, and he didn't move.

"We can take off our clothes here," Adeney said. He took off his shirt and dropped it on to the tiles of the floor. He stood bare-chested, watching me.

I knew that if I walked out of the door now he would let me go, and I knew what would happen if I stayed. I took a step towards the door. Then I stopped. He was now only a few feet away from me. I could see the ivory-white skin stretched tight over his strongly-muscled shoulders and deep chest. Once again I was aware of the strange smell of his body. Suddenly as we stared at each other, I realised that this moment was the objective to which our long afternoon had been directed. This was the end of our journey, and it was as inevitable as the flow of the river we had rowed along. This was the instant of meeting towards which the two separate channels of our lives had joined and flowed together.

I stopped still for a while. Then I took off my shirt. As I dropped it on the floor, Adeney turned and closed the door. The room was now in darkness, but some light came in from between the shutters. The monkeys now seemed horribly alive. Adeney took a few paces towards me. I could hear him breathing. His trembling fingers now began to undo the buttons of his trousers while he kicked off his shoes. Then he wrenched his trousers down from his thighs and pulled them off, so that he stood before me completely naked, his white body glittering before the frescoes on the walls, as if the artist who had painted the monkeys had decided to paint an obscene example of another species. And this time Adeney did not turn away. He gazed at me in silence as I undressed. Then, when I was naked, he moved towards me steadily and very slowly, with his shoulders bent, as if he were carrying a heavy weight.

That night I couldn't sleep. I stirred restlessly, trying to understand the new and odd emotions Adeney had aroused in me. Suddenly as I lay staring at the moonlight filtering in to the room between the curtains, I heard a board creak in the passage outside. Then my door opened softly and Adeney crept in. He was barefooted, and he was wearing a cotton dressing-gown. I gaped at him in surprise. One could be expelled for being found in another boy's room after lights-out. Adeney closed the door quietly behind him.

"I came because I was worried," he whispered. "I was worried about this afternoon. Are you sure it's all right? You're not angry with me?"

"No," I said. "I'm not angry."

"And you're all right?"

"Yes. But I'm pretty tired."

"As long as you're all right," he said, and stood by my bed, in silence.

"Did you think I'd get in a panic and tell old Quackie Jack?" I asked him.

"No, it wasn't that," he answered. "Besides, I wanted to see you. I wanted to tell you how much I hope you'll come to the island tomorrow."

"I'm not sure," I said.

"Please do," he whispered. "Please come there with me."

"I'll think about it," I answered.

For a while he was silent. Then he bent down and took hold of my hand and drew it to him. He stood there without moving, as if the physical contact were a plea in itself. Perhaps at that stage of his life he was so intensely animal he could express his feelings more simply in movements and gestures than in words.

"Please say 'yes.'"

I was silent. I could feel the strength of his desire flowing towards me in the darkness of the little room.

"Please," he urged.

"I'll let you know in the morning."

"No," he answered. "You've got to say 'yes' now. Otherwise I'll just stand here waiting all night."

I laughed. "All right," I said, "I'll come with you tomorrow to the island."

He gave a long, shuddering sigh. "Bless you," he whispered. "Bless you."

"But now you must go."

"Can't I stay just for a little while?"

"No," I answered. "It's too dangerous."

"Just for five minutes?"

"Wait till tomorrow," I said.

"Promise?"

"I promise."

"Goodnight then," he muttered, and moved silently towards the door.

When I saw the door close behind him I suddenly felt a sense of disappointment. Then I realised that I wished he had stayed. I shifted uncomfortably in the darkness. I began to recall each event of the afternoon from the moment we had seen the island. And as I recalled the image of Adeney standing facing me, naked beneath the frescoes, and as I remembered him moving, crouched like an animal, towards me, I felt a violent surge of desire sweep over me like a great wave, leaving me dazed and gasping for breath. Then at last I became aware that in the summer-house I had not only shared in Adeney's passion and his wild brutal ecstasy, I had experienced a new fulfilment of my own. I had reached a new destination along the road of experience. And some instinct told me there was now no way of returning from it.

I had been right in supposing a second visit to the island would make our relationship permanent. As the weeks passed by, a close friendship grew from our passion. Adeney was only a year older than I was, so we were allowed to go about together. We saw each other every day, and when custom had blunted the edge of the guilt which Adeney had confessed to me he felt, he became less brutal and more affectionate. He was now jealously devoted to me, and I flourished in the security of his protection. I had always resented my slightly-made, soft-looking body. But now I began to be proud of my slender limbs and smooth skin. And as if in response to my pride in it, my body seemed to glow and to become stronger. Even my work improved. I was still—by school standards—a failure. I won no colours for games; I won no prizes for work; I drifted contentedly through the days, gliding peacefully along the stream of Adeney's devotion, warmed by the affection which I now felt for him. And whereas before I had lived through each day at school in longing for the peace of Steede, now when I was at home—except during the weeks that Adeney came to stay —I would count the days until the new term began.

Adeney was going into the Army when we left school, and I was going to Trinity College, Cambridge. We planned to leave at the same time, at the end of the summer half. Adeney had arranged to come and stay at Steede for a few days during the short Easter holidays before the term began, but at the last moment he had written saying he couldn't leave home because his parents—his father was a General and his mother came from a military family—had made plans for him to attend the local Corps manoeuvres.

Adeney was now Captain of Games in our house, so he could have his pick of rooms, and he had chosen a room on the top floor at the end of the corridor opposite mine. As soon as we met that first day of the new half I felt uneasy, for I could see his greeting was strained. That night after lights-out when he came into my room, I was almost certain his attitude towards me had altered—even though he was sitting on the side of the bed and his arm was round my shoulder. For a while we talked about the holidays, then about the weeks that lay ahead of us.

"It's wretched to think it's our last half together," Adeney said.

"But even when you're in the Army we'll be able to meet fairly often," I said. "Unless you get sent abroad, you'll be able to come and stay with me at Cambridge."

"Yes," he answered, "I expect so. But it won't be the same thing."

Suddenly I was afraid. "Why not?" I asked.

Adeney took in a deep breath and expelled it in a sigh, as his hand held my shoulder. "When we leave school we'll have to stop all this."

I stared up at him in silence.

"What we do now," he continued, "we do because we need it so badly we can't help ourselves. But when we've left school it'll all be different. For one thing, there'll be girls who are available."

He paused, but I still remained silent. He was frowning now, and he spoke slowly but steadily as if he were making a speech he had rehearsed several times.

"We won't be schoolboys any longer," he said. "We'll be men, so we'll be expected to behave as men. And for men to do what we do together is not only all wrong, it's a crime. One can go to prison for it for seven years. Besides, when we've been with girls we'll lose the desire for it. People do. That's how it happens. People forget about it when they're grown-up. Their only interest is in girls."

As he spoke, I remember that Adeney had an elder brother who was already in the Army.

"You've been talking about all this with someone," I said. "Was it with your brother?"

"Yes," Adeney answered. "We just happened to discuss it."

"And it was your brother who told you about going to prison for seven years?"

"Yes, he did."

"What else did he tell you?"

"He said that so far as grown-up men were concerned it was a vile thing. I mean, for instance there was an officer in his regiment when they were out in India who did it with a native servant and got found out, and he killed himself."

"What else did your brother say?"

"Well, if you must know, he said that even here at Eton one ought to be very careful. It's not only a question of getting caught, he said. One's got to be careful not to get a reputation for it, because that kind of reputation can follow you beyond the school walls. It can harm you for life."

"Do you think either of us has got a reputation?"

Adeney hesitated. "I hope not," he said. "But I don't think it would do any harm if it got around that you or I had been with a girl and was mad about her."

Then I understood why Adeney had put off coming to Steede to stay with me. "So you've had a girl," I said.

Adeney nodded. "My brother knows a girl in a village not far from Guildford where we live," he answered. "And this girl produced her young sister. She was seventeen, and it was really wonderful."

"So now you're a man," I said.

"I didn't say that," Adeney protested. "I was only telling you because I thought you'd want to know."

"And you thought the rest of the house ought to know," I said. "Why don't you make an announcement after prayers to-morrow night?"

"Don't be a fool," Adeney replied. "Can't you understand I'm telling you all this not only for my own sake but for yours? At the end of this half, we're both leaving. We're both going out into the world. I don't want you to make any mistakes. You've got to grow up, Jamie. That's all there is to it. You'll soon learn. It's far too dangerous here. But when you get back home, why don't you go into Nottingham and find yourself a girl? They say Nottingham's famous for them."

"I'll think about it," I answered. "But in the meantime I'm feeling rather sleepy. I'll see you in the morning."

Adeney took my hand and drew it to him. "Let me stay," he said. "After all, it's our first time together for quite a while."

"And we're not men yet," I said.

Adeney laughed softly as he took off his cotton dressing-gown. "Not till the end of this half," he said, lowering himself on to the bed beside me.

Our friendship continued. We still saw each other every day, but I soon noticed that Adeney now seemed less keen for us to meet in public. The little sermon his brother had preached to him had affected him more than I would have believed possible. His sense of guilt had returned with increased power. He was now ashamed of his desire for me. When we lay in bed together he would begin to tell me about his girl in the village near Guildford, and I realised he was trying to convince me as well as himself that a girl could provide exquisite pleasure and was the proper companion for a man to love. Lying beside me, he would describe in detail the various ways in which he had made love to the girl on his secret visits to her, giving me an exact description of her body and of her actions, until, at the climax of his account of their love-making, he would seize me and take me roughly in his arms, as if the brutality with which he treated me excused the unlawfulness of his act.

Though we still seemed to be friends, I realize now that in fact I had lost Adeney. By means of using his brother as its missionary, the Etonian religion of conventionality had seized Adeney in its grasp. From now onwards in his life he would conform with a pathetic zeal to the rules of established society.

Our last Saturday together at the school, Adeney insisted we should row for the last time to the derelict summer-house on the little island in the Thames. Once again it was a hot day without a breath of wind. The sky was white with heat. We were both sweating heavily by the time we reached the small platform of rotting wood which served as a landing-stage. There was no one about. In silence we took off the rusty padlock from the peeling door of the summer-house and walked in, closing the door behind us. In silence we took off our clothes and lay down on our towels which Adeney had placed on the floor, side by side. I watched Adeney as he lay beside me. Because I saw him so frequently I had not noticed how much he had grown. But as I looked at his heavy limbs I realised he could now indeed claim he was no longer a schoolboy, but a man. Then Adeney spoke.

"This is where it all began," he said. "And this is where it's going to end." Then he took my hand. "I want you to make me a promise, Jamie. I want you to promise that after today you'll never do this again."

I shook my head. "Why should I promise?"

"Because I don't want you to get into trouble."

"Or is it because you can't bear to think of me with someone else?"

Adeney flushed. "I told you. So far as I'm concerned I intend to do what others have done—forget all about this sort of thing. I want you to do the same. That's why I want you to make me the promise."

I hesitated. It would be easy to make the promise in order to satisfy his conscience, but I resented the idea of lying to him.

"I can't promise," I said.

"Why not?" he asked suspiciously. "Is there someone else?"

"No. But if you leave me, if you don't want me any more, how can I be certain there won't be?"

Adeney scowled. "You're making it horribly difficult," he said. "Can't you see I'm fond of you? I feel responsible for you—can't you understand?"

Suddenly I thought a way of clearing his conscience. "I tell you what I will promise," I said. "I promise you that when I get home I'll go into Nottingham, and I'll sleep with a girl, and I'll do my best to forget about this island."

Adeney gripped my hand. "Do you swear it?" he asked.

"Yes," I answered, smiling at his anxious face. "I swear it."

Adeney's grasp relaxed. "Good. That's made me feel a lot happier, because I'm very fond of you. I really am." Then he leaned over and put his arms round me. "And now," he said in a muffled voice, "please, Jamie—please let's make this afternoon last as long as we can."

Memory is oddly selective in the periods it chooses to remember. For a time I used to think the more intense the experience the deeper the groove in one's memory. But during the years I spent at Cambridge my experiences were no less vivid than at Eton. Yet those years are curiously vague in my memory. One reason for this may be that when I reached Cambridge I began to drink quite heavily.

I began to drink the very first afternoon I arrived at Trinity. I can remember only too clearly the reason for it.

I had moved into my rooms in College which looked over the Great Court. I was unpacking my things when there was a knock at the door, and a plump young man of about twenty walked in.

"Are you James Steede?" he asked.

Suddenly my mind swung back to my first days at my preparatory school.

"Yes," I answered, smiling at him nervously. *"Can you repeat the sentence?"* I now expected him to say. *"I one my mother."*

"You were at Eton at Jackson's house, weren't you?" he asked. With his heavy, florid face and prominent nose he reminded me of a statue of a Roman senator.

"Yes," I answered.

"I thought so. My name's Edmond Parker. My rooms are across the passage opposite your door. I was at Repton myself, but I find most of my friends here in College come from Eton. So I've heard a little about you already."

He nodded his head solemnly. Then he sat down on my sofa, crossed his legs, and leaned back comfortably.

"Can I get you a drink?" I asked.

"Thanks," he said. "Brandy preferably."

For a while there was silence while I poured out the drink.

"Your family live in Nottinghamshire, don't they?" he asked.

"That's right."

"My family's just bought a place near Nottingham. It's called Foss Grange. You may have heard of it."

I had indeed heard of it. Foss Grange had been built ten years previously by a building speculator from Newark. With its turrets, battlements, and gables, it was vulgar and pretentious. I handed the plump man his glass. "Yes," I replied. "It's about ten miles away from where we live."

"So we'll be neighbours," he said, swilling the brandy round in his glass. Then to my surprise he gave a little titter. "So I suppose we ought to make some effort to be friends."

"To be sure we should," I answered. I was smiling at him, but I noticed he did not smile back.

"If we're friends," he said, sipping his drink, "I think there are various things you should know."

"Such as?"

"Well, to begin with—perhaps you ought to know you've already got a bit of a reputation."

I swallowed some brandy. "A reputation for what?" I asked, still smiling at him.

"You didn't have many friends of your own age, did you?"

"Not many," I answered cautiously.

He took another sip from his glass. "At the risk of offending you," he announced, "I'd better tell you straight out you've got the reputation of being rather wet and effeminate."

"I'm sorry to hear it," I answered. My smile was still there.

He gazed down at his glass. "I hope it's all completely wrong. You see, they're pretty tolerant in this college. But there are some who don't like eccentrics, and they don't like fancy-boys."

"So I've heard."

"The odd ones are apt to get rather a rough time," he continued. "So I thought I'd better warn you."

Even as I drank down my drink I made up my mind what I should do.

"Please tell me," I said, "where's the best place to dine in town?"

"At the Bull, I suppose. But I usually dine in Hall."

"Why not make an exception this evening?" I asked. "Won't you be my guest at the Bull for dinner tonight?"

For a moment he hesitated. "Very well," he said, after a pause.

Then he gave another nervous titter. "After all, we are neighbours," he added.

Before coming up to Cambridge I had not decided on any definite rôle to play. I had been optimistic enough to hope I could afford to be myself. Obviously I was wrong. And as I walked along the street to the Bull that evening with Edmond Parker I decided on the kind of character I would pretend to be while I was at the University. Three factors would enable me to assume the rôle I had chosen. First, my parents had given me a large allowance; I had plenty of money to spend. Secondly, even when I was a child my father had let me drink wine at meals and I had a good head for liquor. Thirdly, I had kept my promise to Adeney; I had gone into Nottingham, I had drunk a great deal at various pubs, I had picked up a little street girl of fifteen, I had taken her to an hotel, I'd gone to bed with her, and because she was so young and attractive and because she was both eager and experienced, I had—to my surprise and satisfaction—enjoyed myself not only that night, when I was drunk, but also the following morning, when I was sober.

As soon as Edmond Parker and I sat down to dinner I launched myself into the part I intended to play by ordering the most expensive champagne on the list and the most expensive food on the menu. I could see that my guest, son of the new owner of Foss Grange, was impressed. Over the second bottle, I began to talk about girls. Over the port I found out that my guest knew of a good brothel in the town. Over the brandy, I persuaded him to take me there. At the brothel, which was above a tobacconist's shop in the back street, I chose a girl of seventeen with red hair called Doreen, because she was both attractive and flamboyant. After we had slept together I suggested that Doreen should leave the brothel and become my mistress, and she agreed with pleasant enthusiasm. I then helped Edmond back to College.

"You're a fine lad," he announced as he clambered up the stairs to his room. "I shan't let anyone say a word to the contrary."

I had made a good start.

Looking back on those days at Cambridge, I wonder why I bothered to put on the elaborate act that I did. Perhaps it was because the success of my night in Nottingham had almost persuaded me to believe that Adeney might have been correct in what he said about love-making with a girl. Or perhaps it was because I resented being thought "wet and effeminate" when I knew I was as virile as the rest of them. Or perhaps there was a childish streak in me which made me wish to show off. Whatever the reasons, within a few weeks of arriving at Cambridge I had gained a very different reputation from the one I had started with, and I was soon accepted by the so-called fast set, of whom a young man called Michael Fairley was the leader.

I first met Michael Fairley in a gambling club, formed by a group of undergraduates who met in a private room on the first floor of the Bull to play cards and dice and drink. With his thick auburn hair, straight nose, and large, dark-blue eyes, Michael was absurdly handsome. He was tall and slender and he dressed in very sombre clothes as if to atone for his rather flashy good looks. As he played dice with a handful of friends at a table in the corner, I noticed that the smile of contentment never left his face —whether he won or lost. When I was introduced to him he greeted me warmly. Then he gave me an amused look which was at once friendly and secretive. His slight smile immediately seemed to suggest that in some way we were fellow-conspirators, so I was not surprised when later in the evening he suggested we should go back to his digs in Market Square for a night-cap.

I was almost certain from the way he looked at me that Michael Fairley was "interested"—to use Burdock's pet expression. But after I had spent half an hour in his poorly-furnished little attic room I began to be less sure, for his talk was mainly concerned with girls—he knew all about Doreen—or racing at Newmarket. His next favourite topic seemed to be the aristocracy, with whose members he appeared to be intimately connected. His mother, he confided to me, was the daughter of the Earl of Prescot, and his father was descended from a Scottish Chief. Then he began to speak about life at Cambridge.

"You want to join the right club," he told me. "Not the stuffy ones—the ones with plenty of excitement. I'll take you round a few of them, so you can decide for yourself. I'll be delighted to propose you for any one of them you choose."

"Can you dine with me at the Bull tomorrow night?" I asked. "Then we could do a round of the clubs afterwards."

"Delighted, my dear man," he said. "I'm entirely at your disposal." He finished the port he was drinking and poured us both another glass.

"By the way," he said casually, a little later in the evening, "I'm just slightly short of cash till my next allowance comes in. Could you be awfully kind and lend me a bit? I can pay you back in a fortnight. But at present my wine merchant's being a little awkward."

Then I understood the sense in which we were fellow-conspirators. We were both acting. I was pretending to be a reckless lover of girls; he was pretending to be a rich young spendthrift—when, in fact, he probably came from a very poor and very respectable family.

"Of course," I said. "I'll bring along some cash tomorrow night."

"That'll be just splendid," he replied with his warm, conspiratorial smile. "Isn't it simply maddening in life how the best of everything costs by far the most—from girls to port wine?"

Several months later I discovered I had been right in my guess about Michael's family. His father was a doctor in Bath; his mother was the daughter of a country parson. Michael's aristocratic pretensions were completely false—and this I found endearing, for by then I found most things about Michael endearing. The truth, which I tried to conceal from myself for quite a time, was that while I enjoyed going to bed with Doreen, I felt no emotion towards her, whereas when I saw Michael smile I found that my heart stirred quickly. And as the weeks of that third term passed by, Michael seemed aware of my feelings towards him. When we were now alone together, he would often put his arm round my shoulder or take hold of my hand half-jokingly—even when he didn't need to borrow money. My interest in Doreen had grown rather stale in the months since I had first installed her above a confectioner's shop on the Trumpington Road, and as Michael's outward displays of affection towards me seemed to grow warmer and more frequent I began to wonder if we were also fellow-conspirators in another form of deceit. So I invited him to stay for a week at Steede during the summer vacation.

When I returned home at the end of that term at Cambridge, I confessed to my mother that I was badly in debt. She scolded me severely, not only for my extravagance but for neglecting my work—about which my Tutor had complained. However, I had a feeling she was secretly pleased I had approached her with my trouble rather than write to my father, who had returned to India. The tradesmen and money-lenders were settled; my next quarter's allowance was paid in full; and in gratitude I spent even more time than usual at home with my mother.

Arthur, my rather awkward and highly-strung younger brother, was there at Steede for the first fortnight. He was pleasant enough in his nervous way, and I tried to find subjects in common to discuss with him. But his main interests were in postage stamps and shooting, neither of which appealed to me, so our conversations together tended to languish. I was not sorry when he left Steede to stay with a family in Provence to learn French, and I could see that my mother was delighted to be alone with me. But while I wandered round the lake with her, or sat on the terrace by the orangery having tea and listening to her long complaints about my father's neglect of the estate, my mind was absorbed with Michael Fairley. I could see the oddly amused smile on his face; I could recall the lines of his lithe body. I was counting the days to his arrival. I had already made arrangements for him to be given the room next to mine on the top floor. But I knew I would be taking a risk if I let him know what I felt about him, for I had made enquiries from an undergraduate who had been at school with him at Tonbridge, and his reputation there had been blameless. Perhaps my suspicion about him might be wrong. However, I was prepared to wait until I was certain.

The moment occurred on his third night at Steede.

After dinner that evening we rode into Nottingham and made a round of some of the pubs where young girls were to be found, for Michael had seemed to be excited by my description of the fifteen-year-old prostitute I had discovered. It was a warm night, and a full moon made the yellow street lamps of the town look pale. Though there were plenty of pretty girls in each place we visited, Michael seemed strangely restless. After drinking a couple of brandies at the bar counter beneath the flaring gas-jets, he would suggest moving on to some different haunt. By midnight he was obviously drunk.

"I've had enough," he muttered. "Let's leave."

By the time we had ridden back he was almost sober.

"What about a final drink up in our rooms?" he asked.

I picked up the brandy decanter and soda water which old Lucas, the butler, had left in the hall, and together we walked up the stairs, turning out the lamps on the way.

"It's terribly close tonight," Michael said when we reached the landing. "I'll just slip off my clothes and put on a dressing-gown. Then I'll come and join you."

I poured myself a drink. I undressed and got into bed and sipped my brandy as I waited for him. I tried to force myself to remain calm by reminding myself that my instinct about him might prove to be wrong. Presently the door opened, and Michael came in, wearing a white silk dressing-gown. As he closed the door behind him I saw that for once the smile had gone from his face. His hands were trembling as he poured himself a drink. Then he crossed the room towards me and leaned against the brass rail at the end of my bed. For a moment he stood in silence, staring at me. Suddenly he tilted back his head and finished his drink in a few long gulps. Then he took a step closer to me.

"I suppose you're the best friend I've got in the world," he said.

"Certainly you're the only person I can turn to. You see, Jamie, the fact is I'm in a bit of trouble."

"What kind of trouble?" I asked.

Michael put down his glass on my bedside table beside the flickering candle. "I've written a cheque for a hundred pounds," he said. "It's payable on the first of next month, but the money isn't there in the Bank to meet it. I can't tell my father, because last time he paid my debts he threatened to take me away from Cambridge if I ran up bills again."

His face was puckered with anxiety as he gazed down at me.

"Don't worry," I said gently, "I can let you have a hundred pounds."

Michael moved forward and grasped my hand. "Do you really mean it?"

"Yes," I said. "To be sure I mean it."

"Jamie, you can't imagine how grateful I am!" he cried. "I've been fretting myself silly about it. Now I don't have to worry any more."

"So why don't we both have another drink to celebrate?"

"Don't you move," he said, crossing to the table in the corner where I had left the decanter. "I'll get them."

When he returned with a glass in each hand I saw him shiver. "You're cold," I said.

"I am a bit," he answered. "I expect it's just excitement."

As he put the glasses down on my bedside table he shivered again. "I can't think what's wrong with me," he said.

"You don't want to catch a chill," I said, casually moving to the far side of the bed to make room for him.

"The air was quite stifling when we got back," he muttered. "But it's quite cold now." Then he kicked off his slippers, and without looking at me—and it seemed without any embarrassment —he got into bed beside me.

For a while there was silence. I could feel my heart thudding against my chest. Then he leaned over towards me and put his hand on the back of my neck. "Jamie," he whispered. "You've no idea how fond of you I am."

"Perhaps you've no idea quite how fond I am of you."

"I hope so," he said. "I do hope so."

His hand was warm against my neck, and he lay very still. He was so close to me I could feel the heat of his body.

"Dear Jamie," he whispered.

I stretched out my hand and slipped it between the folds of his dressing-gown. Gently I slid my hand down from his chest across the flatness of his skin until it came to rest at his groin. For an instant he did not move. He might have been asleep or unconscious, for there was not a flicker of response. Then I felt his right hand slide away from my neck. Suddenly his left hand plunged down between the sheets and grasped hold of my arm and thrust it away from his body. With a violent wrench he scrambled out of the bed. Abruptly he turned and stood glaring down at me, his face twisted in disgust, his eyes cold and narrow with contempt. For a while he stood there, panting as if he had run a race. Then, when he had recovered himself, he thrust forward his face, and the words came hissing out of him.

"I ought to have known," he said. "I ought to have guessed long ago. Doreen always said you never really wanted her except when other people were about. I should have guessed you hadn't really changed. They warned me about you when you first arrived, but I wouldn't believe them. I couldn't believe anyone like you could be so vile. But I see now I should have listened to them."

He pulled the dressing-gown tight round him and strode across the room. At the door he turned. "I suppose you thought you could buy me with your money," he said. "Well, you made a mistake. But don't worry—I'll get my hundred pounds just the same. I know someone else who'll lend it me. He's not a cheap fake, and he's not a filthy, rotten sodomite."

Then he left the room. An instant later I heard him closing the door of his bedroom next to mine. I heard the key turn in the lock. Quickly I drank down my brandy. Then I poured myself another. Several drinks later I got back into bed and tried to sleep.

When I awoke in the morning it was late. I was almost certain he would have left. I opened my bedroom door and looked out onto the landing. The door of his room was open. His clothes and luggage had gone. I dressed and went downstairs. In the hall I found out from Lucas that Michael had appeared over two hours previously. He had declined breakfast. He had asked Lucas to bring down his luggage and to ask the groom to drive him over to Foss Grange.

For several weeks after Michael left Steede I could not bear the prospect of returning to Cambridge. By now I had become quite expert in the lies I told my parents. I had invented for their benefit a wonderfully plausible excuse for Michael's departure. I could easily invent reasons to avoid returning to Cambridge. But I was more afraid to admit my own cowardice than to face Michael and his friends. Moreover, when I met Edmond Parker at a dinner-party at a neighbour's house, I discovered to my surprise that Michael had not told him the exact reason for his abrupt departure from Steede: he had merely said we'd had a serious quarrel, and he had let Edmond guess the reason. Perhaps, I reflected rather cynically, perhaps Michael remembered he still owed me money and I still held the promissory notes. Or could there be a different reason? Why had Michael started to shiver when he came back towards my bed with the drinks? "I expect it's just excitement," he had said. Was it merely excitement because he had got his loan—or had a part of him been excited by another prospect? I would never know. Certainly his passionate denunciation of me had been genuine enough. He had without any doubt persuaded himself that my behaviour was vile and rotten. From now onwards he would be my enemy, and I must do my best to avoid him. Edmond, however—as I had rather expected—was only too anxious to believe the trivial reason for the quarrel which I invented for him, because Edmond and his parents were determined to shine triumphantly in the society into which they had now moved. But Edmond had already realised that to buy a house in the county was one thing, but to get accepted by the county was another. Edmond wanted his family to be invited to dine at Steede. And after some difficulty I persuaded my mother to invite the whole lot of them: Edmond, his pompous father, his loud-voiced mother, and his sharp-eyed little sister Maude.

When I returned to Cambridge I moved in a different set. My companions were now even more rowdy, boisterous, and drunken than before. One evening a few of us were walking along King's Parade when, advancing towards us along the pavement, I saw Michael Fairley in the centre of a group of his friends. They had probably come from forming some new club at the Bull, for each of them wore a dark red carnation in his buttonhole. Michael was laughing at a joke. His head was thrown back; a strand of auburn hair had fallen over his forehead. Then he saw me. At once he stopped laughing, and his face took on an expression of grim defiance. As he drew closer he gave me a hard stare. Then he passed by me. My companions knew he had been my friend, but not one of them made any remark.

At dinner that night I ordered more wine than usual, and over the port we began to make stupid wagers. Could one of us stand on the edge of his chair without over-balancing? Could another drink a pint of ale in a single draught? Could a third lift a heavy chair from the ground, holding only one of its legs? But after we had left the private room I had taken in an hotel, the wagers grew wilder. There were races round Market Square; there was a bet who could be the first to climb into College. It was at two in the morning, when we had reassembled in my rooms in Great Court, that the final wager was made. I was bet fifty pounds I couldn't climb to the top of the Chapel and hang my cap and gown on one of the spires.

"Bet taken," I cried immediately.

I was not drunk, but I had been drinking since lunch-time, and my nerves were completely deadened. Otherwise I'm sure I would have given up the attempt in terror. Even now I can't imagine how I managed the climb, for it's all vague in my mind. But I can remember the College Proctors coming out with lights as I made my descent to the drunken applause of my companions.

Even before I was summoned to appear before the Senior Tutor I had packed my bags, because with my record of idleness and other misdemeanours it was obvious that my days at Trinity were over. I was certain to be sent down, and I was certain to be scolded by my mother. But at least I left in a faint flicker of fame —or notoriety. I was not sorry to leave Cambridge.

I had given Doreen as large a present as I could afford when I had said goodbye to her, and we had parted good friends. But now that I was back at Steede I had begun to miss her expert embraces. Once or twice a week I would ride into Nottingham to drink in the various haunts I now knew quite well. But if I spent the night with one of the girls off the street I was always afraid of catching some disease. Gradually this fear, which was probably increased by a sense of guilt, grew so strong that I became determined I was already diseased and—like a fool—went to see Millward, the family doctor, who was an old friend of my parents. Millward examined me very carefully. Then, after a long delay while he peered through the microscope, he told me that I had caught no infection. But he warned me sternly against "exposing" myself "to any further risk."

A month or so later, some friends of Colonel Savage—a Major Anstey and his wife—rented Normanton, a house some five miles to the west of Steede. In his kindness, Colonel Savage, who had recently returned from service abroad and given up his commission, insisted on taking me to call on them. And on that grey afternoon of early spring I met their daughter.

Margaret Anstey was a fragile-looking, pale, fair-haired girl of sixteen. I suppose the first thing which attracted me to her was not so much the charm of her appearance as the fact that she was obviously frightened. Her grey eyes seemed wide with fear, and there was a very slight tremble around her lips. She moved uneasily. Terror seemed to be waiting behind her shoulder. At first I thought it was her father she was afraid of. He was a red-faced, bull-necked officer who had served in the Hussars. But then I noticed the girl's expression as she watched him while he talked with Colonel Savage, and I saw from her admiring gaze that she was devoted to him. Certainly it could not be her gentle, unobtrusive mother with her faded looks and simpering smile who inspired fear in her. Then of whom—or of what—was this slender little girl afraid?

I did not find out the answer until two months later.

Colonel Savage had suggested that for two or three days I should take Margaret Anstey riding to show her the countryside, and she had been such a pleasant and undemanding companion, so unashamedly grateful to me, that I had ridden over to Normanton several times to show her new rides along the Trent hills. These rides had now become a habit, and I had made such friends with her parents that they allowed us to go out without a groom. That particular afternoon I had taken Margaret to see a shooting-lodge my father had built in the woods when his Oriental mania first seized him. The lodge looked like a cross between a pagoda and a bungalow. It was now deserted. The day was warm, and after I had shown her the inside of the weird place with its walls lined with cedar-wood and its carved beams and painted ceiling, we sat out on the porch in the sunshine. For a while we were silent. We could hear the birds rustling in the thatch of the roof behind us and rooks cawing in the tall beech trees. Bees were humming in a hedge of wild dog-roses. Then I put my question.

"Who are you frightened of?" I asked. "Or what are you frightened of?"

Margaret put her hands to her cheeks. "Does it show so much?"

"Not always. Perhaps I'm the only one who notices."

"I hope so," she said. "It's getting better now anyhow."

"Can you tell me about it?"

Margaret stared at the ground beyond the wooden steps we were sitting on. "You'll think me stupid," she said. "Because it happened over two years ago."

"What happened?"

She hesitated. "I've never told anyone," she muttered, twisting her hands together.

"Then perhaps you should," I said gently.

She sighed. "I expect you're right," she whispered.

"I'm four years older than you are," I said, smiling at her. "Of course I'm right."

"Very well," she answered nodding her head solemnly. "I'll try."

As I listened to the story Margaret Anstey told me I found it curiously simple to imagine the scene she was describing. I could see the old house in Devon with its slate roof and stone walls, where her parents had lived before they came to Nottinghamshire; I could see the ploughed fields beneath the rolling hills and the small farm-house, some three miles away from them, which belonged to a Devon farmer called Craig, a widower with two children. For some reason I felt I could imagine even more details than she was telling me; I had no difficulty in piecing together from her halting sentences and pauses and occasional silences a fairly accurate picture of the event.

Margaret was an only child. By the time she was fourteen she had come to enjoy her solitude. She would go for long walks over the moors. Each day of her summer holidays was precious to her. One afternoon as she passed close to a barn which lay about half a mile away from Craig's farm she heard the sound of someone crying. The door of the barn was open so she looked in. Lying on a heap of straw, half naked, was Craig's younger son, Davie. Even though his face was partly covered by his hands, Margaret recognised him because he often came over to their house with the milk. Davie was only a little older than she was, and she had often tried to get into conversation with him, but he seemed shy and nervous. Then, as Margaret gazed down at the boy, he twisted round on to his side, and to her horror she saw that his back was covered with the livid red weals of a whip.

"Davie!" she cried out.

His hands sprang away from his eyes, and he looked up at her trembling. She now saw there was a heavy bruise on his cheek. As he recognised her he began to whimper.

"Davie," she said, kneeling down beside him. "What have they done to you?" But even as she spoke, Margaret could guess exactly what had happened. The boy's father was known in the neighbourhood for his cruelty when drunk; there were rumours of a horse that had to be shot after he had beaten it.

"Was it your father?"

The boy nodded. He made an effort to control his tears, and presently he told her what had happened. "I was playing about in the dairy," he said slowly. "I knocked over a milk-churn, and all the milk ran out to waste. And he came into the yard on his way back from the village and saw it. And he got his whip and took me here."

Then, as the memory of the savage whipping came back to him, the boy began to weep again with short little sobs. Margaret had already decided she would tell her parents as soon as she returned home, so that someone—the local magistrate, perhaps—would go and see Craig. But her immediate concern was to comfort the boy, so she took him gently in her arms and began rocking him to and fro as if he were a small child, and he clung to her while his sobs came faster.

"Don't cry, Davie," she murmured. "Please don't cry."

"I thought he'd never finish," he gasped.

"Don't worry, Davie. I promise you it won't happen again."

"Curran was there," the boy said, and she remembered that Curran was the lout of eighteen who was his brother. Dark hair was thickly clustered around Curran's heavy head, and his clothes always seemed too tight for him. "Curran saw him taking me away," the boy said. "And Curran knew he'd been drinking. But he didn't even say a word to stop him."

"Never mind," she said, cradling him. "Never mind."

Presently the boy's sobs grew quieter, and after a while his tears stopped. He lay so quietly in her arms that she began to think he had gone to sleep. But then he lifted his face and put his lips against her cheek and kissed her. Already Margaret, by holding him in her arms, had put herself in the place of an elder sister or even of his dead mother, so she did nothing to stop his pathetic little kisses, nor did she prevent the boy from pressing himself closer to her, and for a while they remained, clasped together, without speaking. Suddenly the silence was abruptly rent by a sharp laugh. With a start, Margaret looked up and saw Curran. He was standing a few paces away from them, staring down at them. His lips were parted in a leering grimace, his eyes were glittering.

"You've begun young," Curran said. Then he grabbed hold of his brother's arm and wrenched him up from the ground. "Now you can get out," he said to the boy. "You can leave her to someone that knows what to do. And don't let Dad or me see you again this evening." As he spoke he gave a sudden twist to the boy's arm. Davie screamed out in pain. "Now clear out," Curran cried, flinging the boy's arm away from him. Davie stumbled, then ran out of the barn.

Curran took a step towards Margaret. Then he stopped. For a while he was silent as he stood there watching her, with his hands on his hips and his thick legs well apart, as if he were straddling a horse. "If you want it," he said after a pause, "you shouldn't go for a boy, you should go for a man." He parted his lips again over his tight clenched teeth. "For a man," he repeated, "if you want it."

He moved no closer to her, and his wild eyes still watched her. His hands now began to fumble at the buttons below his belt.

Margaret tried to cry out, but no sound came.

"I was so frightened I couldn't scream," she told me. "I was horribly afraid. I felt I was going to faint. Somehow, if he'd moved forward, it might even have been better, because then I could have tried to fight against him. But he didn't move. Yet I knew it was going to happen. There was nothing to prevent it. I was alone with him, and I could see from his eyes he was mad. I kept trying to scream, but I couldn't. I couldn't do anything but stare at him. His mouth was open wide now, and his face was almost black. But still he didn't move. It was then I looked down at his hands, and I saw what they were doing. Quickly I turned away. But I could still hear him, and I could hear him breathing. Then he gave a short laugh. I glanced up at him. With an abrupt kind of jerk of his shoulders he swung round, and he walked out of the barn. My legs were trembling so much I could hardly move. When I got to the door, he'd gone. I ran most of the way home."

The keys that can unlock desire are varied and oddly made. I had at first listened to her story with interest, but also with complete detachment. Gradually, as her awkward phrases continued, I found to my surprise I could imagine the scene so vividly that I might even have been present. And as soon as she began to describe Curran's arrival I felt that in some way I had become curiously involved. I was there with them in the barn. I could smell the bales of hay; I could smell the sacks of barley and oats. I could see Curran as he stared down at her; I could see his fingers as they fumbled beneath his belt. But in my mind it wasn't the farmer's son, aged eighteen, who stood there in his gross virility; it was another boy of the same age. It was Adeney the last time I had seen him naked. I could see Adeney with his heavy limbs staring down at her. And when he turned away with a quick jolt of his shoulders, I could smell the odour which would forever remind me of the island.

But from watching Adeney, suddenly my thought switched to the fourteen-year-old girl, crouching in the barn on a heap of sacks, motionless, transfixed by her fear like a butterfly on a pin, her grey eyes wide with horror and disgust at Curran's obscene display.

Then I blinked and turned my mind away from the barn, and I looked at Margaret, now aged sixteen, sitting on the wooden steps beside me in the sunshine. And gradually I began to feel a stirring of desire which seemed to grow more intense the more I stared at her, and in a haze of bewilderment I understood its cause. I realized I wanted the girl. I wanted to hold her and to make love to her. I wanted to pinion her to the ground. I wanted to be the one that took her.

Margaret glanced towards me. The tremor around her mouth was now quite noticeable.

"But surely you haven't told me the end of the story," I said.

"Yes, I have. When I got home, I told my parents that Craig had whipped Davie, but I didn't say anything to them about Curran."

"Why didn't you?" I asked.

"Because I didn't dare. Because somehow I couldn't."

"Curran didn't follow you on your way home?"

"No. At least, I never saw him if he did."

"But you met him again, I suppose."

"Never. I never even saw him again."

"When he lived only three miles away?"

"I never left our home grounds again if I was alone. I've never since been out for a walk alone."

"But you've been out for a ride alone."

"Never."

"I mean, you're alone here now with me," I said.

Her lips trembled into a smile. "Yes, that's true."

"And you're not frightened?"

"No, I'm not."

"Why aren't you frightened alone with me?"

"Because we're friends, Jamie. Because I trust you."

"Why are you so sure you can trust me?" I asked.

She smiled again. "Because you're gentle. You'd never do anything to hurt a person. I was sure of it the day I first met you. I could see you were quite grown-up, but I never thought of you as a man."

Then I realized she had somehow formed the same idea of me as Burdock had, and Adeney, and the rest of them. Margaret was only sitting beside me alone on the steps of the empty lodge because she didn't consider me a man. Suddenly, with a complete certainty, I knew what I must do to break that picture finally— not only in her mind but in my own.

"You shouldn't trust me," I said. "You shouldn't. Because I'm as much a man as Curran was."

She stared at me. I think it was the tone of my voice more than my words which made the tremor round her mouth more apparent.

"I still trust you," she answered, but I could hear a trace of fear in her voice.

"Because you don't think I'm a man?"

"No, Jamie," she answered, moving a little.

I seized hold of her arms. "You won't try to run away this time," I said.

"Please, Jamie," she said. "Please let me go."

She was trembling now, and her arms were struggling to escape from my grasp. But I was scarcely aware of her struggles and her cries. I was conscious only of the intensity of my need and of a throbbing which was so painful I could hardly breathe. Her face was turned away from me. But now she moved her head and stared into my eyes as if hoping to find there some hope of escape. But as she gazed up at me, she must have seen the promise of my fierce determination, for she gave a little cry. Her arms stopped writhing in my grasp, and her head fell back limply. I thought that the pain I forced on her had stifled any response. But when it was all over I felt her hands stroking my neck.

I realise now that our friendship had started because of our affinity. We had both of us been victims. The affair arose from my desperation and from her fear. My having her removed both. For when I had slept with a prostitute I had always had a suspicion that my status of being the master in the act had only been bought with cash. But there was no doubt now that with Margaret I had achieved complete dominance by my own virility, so I no longer felt myself the subservient, weaker partner. I had proved my manhood. And once Margaret had known what it was that she had dreaded since the afternoon in the barn, her fear left her, so that after a few days I was even able to persuade her to meet me secretly at the lodge. And very soon, because we were already fond of each other and because we were both young and passionate, we entered a phase of happiness in which we found we could obtain contentment only when we were alone together and in which we could examine the future only in the light of our remaining together.

I'm aware, now, that I had motives for flinging myself so eagerly into this state of happiness—motives which were probably hidden from myself. Certainly I was proud to be in love with an attractive girl, and I was proud she loved me with a startling devotion which even her sense of guilt at deceiving her parents could not disturb. Although we had to keep our meetings secret, there was no reason to conceal our affection for each other, because we had already decided that when Margaret was seventeen I should ask her parents' consent for us to become engaged, and we had no doubt of their answer, for both Major Anstey and his wife had made it clear they liked me. My mother's attitude, however, towards both Margaret and my obvious interest in her, was ambiguous.

"What charming people," she had said, the first time she had met the Ansteys. "And what a delightful little girl. We must invite them to dinner one evening next week."

But when I began to call at Normanton almost every day, her attitude changed towards the parents—though not towards Margaret, or so it seemed to me.

"What an entrancing little girl Margaret is," she said after the Ansteys had dined at Steede. "But I can't pretend I'm impressed by her father. Did you notice the amount of claret he swilled down? Weren't you bored to despair by those long stories of his? No wonder that dreary simpering wife of his is as silent as a mute. Obviously she's never allowed to speak, poor woman. Let's pray dear Margaret doesn't grow up like either of them."

My mother appeared to be sincerely fond of Margaret. But though she must have known I was going for rides with Margaret almost every afternoon, she never made any reference to our relationship. Colonel Savage, however, seemed to understand our affection and to approve of it.

"You're drinking less," he said to me. "You're looking far fitter than you did. And I suspect I know the reason for the change."

I was as wonderfully happy during those summer months as I had been when I was a child.

The blow was as abrupt as it was unexpected. That hot August afternoon I had ridden over to Normanton as usual. I got off my horse in the drive in front of the red brick façade of the old house and pulled the front-door bell. Vaguely I noted there was a longer delay than usual. Presently Cope, their butler, opened the door. I saw at once that he seemed embarrassed.

"Afternoon, Cope," I said. "I've come for Miss Anstey."

"Sorry, sir," Cope answered. "Miss Anstey's gone out."

"Gone out? Where to?"

Cope flushed. "I don't know, sir."

I knew then that something terrible had happened. Perhaps her parents had somehow found out. I was determined to discover the worst. Was I now being deliberately denied entry into the house? "Then perhaps I could see the Major or Mrs. Anstey?" I asked.

Cope hesitated. "They're not in, sir."

I knew he was lying, and I knew he didn't like to do so. I smiled at him. "Thank you, Cope," I said casually. "Please let them know I called, will you?" I smiled once again. Then I rode away.

The letter reached me late that evening. Old Lucas, who had been the butler at Steede for as long as I could remember, had been retired with a pension; he now lived in a little cottage on the outskirts of Nottingham, where I visited him occasionally. Denham, a man of about forty who had been in service in London with some friends of my mother, had taken his place. He was bluff and solid-looking, with a deep voice and a rather shy smile, and I was soon on as friendly terms with him as I had been with Lucas. It was Denham who brought me the letter a few minutes after my mother had retired to bed. I did not recognise the writing, for Margaret had never written to me. But I could guess from the copper-plate handwriting on the envelope. I tore it open.

"Dear Jamie," the note read. "I must see you. I can get away tonight when they're asleep. I'll meet you at the lodge. Margaret."

"Who brought the letter?" I asked Denham who was still standing by the door.

"One of the maids from Normanton," he answered. "Is there any reply, sir?"

"No, thank you very much," I said. "Goodnight, Denham."

When the door closed behind him I looked at my watch. It was eleven o'clock. Quickly I finished the wine in the decanter. Then I walked down to the stables. It was a clear night and the moon was almost full, so Margaret would have no difficulty in finding her way through the wood. As I rode along the glade I decided there was only one explanation. Somehow her parents must have found out. But how? Then I recalled that after the first occasion, when we had been lying quietly together in the darkness of the shuttered lodge, Margaret had told me that the fear which then disturbed her was that she would have a child. So on all subsequent occasions I had taken precautions, and gradually Margaret's anxiety had ceased. Had she now discovered she was with child and in a panic told her parents? I dreaded the scene which lay ahead of me at the lodge. But I was glad I had drunk two bottles of wine during the evening, as I needed all the courage I could muster; and I was glad I had taken the precaution of filling my saddle-flasks.

There was no one at the lodge when I arrived. The pagoda-shaped roof looked grotesquely beautiful in the moonlight. I found two oil lamps and lit them. Then I sat down on an old leather-backed chair with my two brandy flasks beside me, waiting for her.

I had finished one of the flasks by the time Margaret arrived. I had heard the sound of hoof-beats so I was there waiting for her in the porch.

"Jamie, thank heavens you're here!" she cried.

As I kissed her forehead and her lips, I felt her flinch away from me. "Please don't," she said. Her eyes were full of tears.

"What's wrong?" I asked. "What's happened?"

She gazed at me desperately. I saw she was close to breaking down. I led her inside the lodge and made her sit in the low leather chair while I crouched beside her. "Now tell me. What's happened?" I repeated. I could see the tremor around her mouth had returned.

"Your mother called at Normanton this morning," she answered.

I stared at her. "But she can't have done. This morning she said she was driving into Nottingham to see about some lace she wanted to buy."

Margaret shook her head. "She came to Normanton. I was there with them in the drawing-room. But she said she wanted to speak to my parents alone. So I left." Margaret's hands were trembling and she clasped them together. "Half an hour later I heard her carriage drive away, so I came down to find out what it was all about." Margaret paused. "At first they wouldn't tell me what it was. But they told me I must promise never to see you again."

I was dazed. "But why mustn't you?" I asked. "Why? What's wrong?"

"You must know why," Margaret replied.

"I swear to you I don't."

"Please don't force me to tell you."

"But I must!"

Margaret turned away from me and stared down at the ground beyond her feet. "When my parents refused to give me the reason, I told them that in that case I wouldn't promise not to meet you again. Then they turned on me. They said I was disobedient and ungrateful and shameless. But I still wouldn't give in. So then at last they told me."

"Told you what?" I asked quietly.

Margaret lowered her head. "When she was alone with them, your mother said she knew that a close friendship had grown up between us. And she was in favour of this friendship, so long as it developed no further—because marriage was out of the question. For two reasons. The first was that we were both far too young. . . ."

Margaret hesitated and then was silent.

"And the second reason?"

Margaret still hesitated. In the silence I could hear the moths hurtling themselves against the lamps. "The second reason," she said slowly, "your mother told my parents in secret. She made them promise they would never tell anyone else—not even me. But at last I got it out of them."

My mouth felt very dry. "What was it?" I asked.

"The second reason," Margaret said in a dull tone of voice, "was because you were sick. You went to see the doctor two months ago because you were afraid you'd caught a sickness from a girl when you were in Cambridge. The doctor made some tests, and then he told you that you were diseased. He said you mustn't think of marrying until you were cured."

I was so dazed with astonishment that I gaped at her in silence. Then Margaret turned and looked at my flushed, bewildered face.

"What I have to know is this," she said. "If I have a child, will it be born deformed?"

What followed, I now see, was almost inevitable.

I told Margaret that it was a lie, and I wasn't diseased. I confessed to her I had been to consult Dr Millward. I repeated the exact words he had said. I explained to her that the reason my mother had gone to visit the Ansteys was that she was extremely jealous and abnormally possessive. She was determined not to lose me. So she had determined to stop me marrying. My mother had used what Millward had told her in confidence and distorted it to suit her own ends. Finally, I told Margaret I loved her. I tried to persuade her to leave with me for London to get married. But even as I spoke I knew I was making little impression. Perhaps I was too desperate and too drunk. For I was very drunk indeed. I could hear my slurred voice stumbling as I tried to explain my mother's deceit and treachery.

"I'm not staying at Steede any longer," I said. "I refuse to live in the same house with her. I'll never forgive her for this. Come away with me, Margaret. I swear I'll do all I can to make you happy."

"No, Jamie."

"Why not? I can get money from my father. I can borrow from Colonel Savage until he comes back from abroad. I'm twenty-one in a few months' time, and then I get possession of quite a big property at Ruston. I could sell it easily enough to raise some cash."

"I couldn't leave my parents," Margaret said. "Not after what's happened."

"But what *has* happened?" I asked. "My mother's told a horrible lie—*that's* what happened!"

"Can't you see?" Margaret cried. "If I left with you now, they'd never believe the truth. They'd think I'd married a man who was diseased."

"Dr Millward could tell them different," I said. But even as I spoke I knew I was failing to persuade her. With each instant that passed I could see that my only hope of leading a normal life with a girl I loved was being wrenched away from me.

"They wouldn't believe him," Margaret answered. "They'd think he'd been bribed."

I made a last effort. "I can't stay at Steede any longer. "Surely you can understand?"

"Yes," she answered. "I can see you must go."

"Then you must come abroad with me. That's our only hope."

"I can't leave my parents," she said. "They'd never forgive me."

I began to despair. I unscrewed the top of the second flask and took a long drink. "They'd forgive you in time," I said.

I saw her eyes turn towards the flask in my hand. Suddenly I felt sure she was thinking, "He'll turn out to be a drunkard like his father."

"But I might not forgive myself," Margaret answered.

Then, as I looked at her face, set in embarrassment and misery, I saw an expression of obstinate determination in her eyes, and I knew it was hopeless. I had lost. My only desire now was to get away from the whole lot of them.

"I'm leaving for London to-morrow," I said. "I shall catch the evening train. Can you meet me here at six in the afternoon?"

Margaret sighed and unclasped her hands. "Wouldn't it be best for both of us if we didn't meet again?"

"I'd like to say goodbye to you when I'm calmer. Besides, I must give you the copy of a letter I shall be writing. It's important. I must give it to you myself."

Margaret hesitated. "I can meet you at six," she said after a pause. "But not here."

"Why not here?"

Margaret rose from the chair and moved to the door. "This place has too many memories," she said. "I'll meet you in the little orchard below the wood."

I was so drunk I can't remember riding back to Steede that night. When I woke up in my bed the following morning, for a while I thought it had only been a nightmare. Then with a lurch of misery I realised it was true. For a moment I thought I would be sick, so I went to the basin and splashed my face with cold water until I recovered. I looked at my watch and saw it was noon. After I had shaved and dressed I sat down at my desk and wrote out two copies of a letter. One copy I would seal and give to Elliott, our solicitor in Nottingham. The other copy I would give to Margaret.

"I, James Edward Steede," I wrote, "do hereby request my executors in the event of my death and in the event of Margaret Anstey becoming with child to give her the house at Ruston and one thousand pounds a year and to make suitable provision for our child."

When I had finished the second copy I began to pack.

At one o'clock there was a knock at the door. It was Denham, so I let him in.

"I came to see if you were all right, sir," Denham said with a slight smile. I wondered if I had made a noise on my return from the lodge.

"I'm fine, thanks, Denham," I answered.

"Her ladyship asked me to tell you she's spending the day at Lower Farm with Colonel Savage. She'll be back in good time for dinner."

This suited my plans. "I'm going up to London for a few months," I told Denham. "Will you be very kind and see that my luggage is taken to the station? I'm catching the evening train."

I noticed that Denham did not look surprised. Perhaps I already had the reputation of an eccentric.

"Very well, sir," he said. "Anything I can do now to help?"

"No thanks, Denham," I answered. "I'll see you before I go."

I had told Margaret I wanted to say goodbye to her when I was calmer, and in a way, when I appeared in the orchard, I was calm, for I was almost dazed with drink. I had feared an emotional scene. I needn't have worried, for in our own minds we had each of us already said farewell. We had already parted, so it was a ghost from the past that each of us now greeted.

I handed her the letter. I had left the envelope unsealed. "I want you to read this," I said to her, "because it concerns you. Then you must seal up the envelope and keep it hidden in a safe place."

Margaret examined the letter slowly and carefully. I noticed for the first time that her lips moved as she read. Then she put the paper back in its envelope. "I'll keep it carefully," she said. "I'll keep it for the child's sake, . . . if there is one." Then she stretched out her hands towards me, and I took hold of them. "Goodbye, Jamie," she said. "I'd like you to know that I realise I was partly to blame. I don't expect we'll meet again for quite a while, if you're going abroad. By the time you come back, I hope I'll have forgiven you."

I stared at the slim, pallid, grey-eyed ghost facing me. I had not thought of our parting in terms of her forgiveness. Suddenly she withdrew her hands and turned away. I felt that even our farewell meeting was going wrong.

"Let me kiss you goodbye," I said.

Margaret shook her head.

"Why not?" I asked.

She did not turn back. "It's safer I don't touch you," she said quietly.

Then I knew that at our meeting in the lodge she had not believed in my protests. My mother's words had taken root in her mind. Nothing I could say now would remove them. I watched her in silence as she walked slowly away along the path. Then I could no longer see clearly, for my eyes were full of tears.

When my mother returned to Steede that evening to discover that I had left for London, she must have guessed that the Ansteys had not kept their promise and I had found out her treachery, for she followed me to London the next day. But I had foreseen this possibility, so I stayed at a dingy little-known hotel in Kensington. Each time I visited my club I would find frantic, hysterical notes from my mother beseeching me to come to the house in Belgrave Square where she was staying. I did not answer them.

In the port of London I found a ship bound for Cuba, and I took a passage on her. Cuba seemed as good a starting-point as any for a voyage of despair. I sailed in September, 1850.

My recollection of my first days in Cuba are shrouded in a haze of drunkenness. I can remember Havana, with its harbour full of merchant shipping and vessels from every part of the world, and small boats frisking like dolphins amongst them. I can remember untidy streets and faded houses painted pale blue or pink and the oddly uninhabited appearance of each dwelling, because there were no glass windows. I can remember gardens full of flowers and fountains; the vivid green of the sugar-cane and orange groves; and the entrancing coffee plantations, with long, single-storeyed wooden huts, and the huge torn leaves of the plantains, rustling in a faint breeze so that it sounded like rain.

At that stage of my existence, the part of me that wished to survive was still quite strong, and as the weeks passed by and I could examine my life with some detachment, I realised I had two problems. The first was the nature of my sexual inclinations. The second was drink. I decided to make an attempt to lead a calm, sober, and normal life. I avoided meeting any Europeans; I rented a cabana on the outskirts of Havana close to a sugar plantation, and presently I found myself a young girl, for at that stage girls if they were small, young, and slim could still attract me. Ina's parents, to whom I'd given a large present, claimed she was fifteen, but I suspected she was younger. She had a mischievous, rather simian face, and she was already surprisingly experienced. And for a while we lived a carefree, sensual existence. I congratulated myself on my escape from the confines of my life in England. I was feeling far healthier; I was drinking less; and Ina seemed fond of me. Almost every day she would manage to discover some new means of intensifying our pleasure. The girl certainly appeared to enjoy her life. Each present I bought her was a new excitement, and her gratitude was undisguised and rather pathetic. Evidently her previous lovers had been either very mean or very poor. I tried to find out about them, but Ina was always evasive. "I don't care for the other men," she would say. "I only go with them because they give money, and my family is poor and needs it." Then she would slide her arm onto my chest. "But I go with you, because I love you," she would say as her hand began to glide across my body. "You are a very young man. Not an old one. And you are very much of a man."

Our life was pleasant in its routine. In the morning we would go for a swim. Then we would return to the cabana and drink rum and pineapple juice until two or three, when we would lunch. Then in the heat of the afternoon we would retire to our bedroom for a siesta which either began or ended with lovemaking. After a bath we would sit on the terrace, watching the long blue shadows stretching over the grass until it was time for a drink before dinner in the candlelight. The idle months slipped by.

I never noticed the approach of boredom, though I had un-easily observed that each evening the blue shadows seemed to take longer to cross the stretch of grass in front of our low, wooden bungalow. I now seemed to need more drink to sustain me through the hours from sunset until we went to bed.

One morning when I woke up with Ina curled as usual beside me and contemplated the day in front of us and could see in it more weariness than pleasure, I was dismayed. I pushed the thought firmly to the back of my mind. But a few days later it returned. After another week I began to confess the truth to myself. I was bored, and immediately my whole existence took on a different aspect. I was very fond of little Ina, but I now became aware that over the months she had become more demanding, and her constant desire to be entertained or admired or taken to bed had grown wearying. I enjoyed the act of love-making with her. After I had stretched myself out in bed, exhausted with the pleasure of fulfillment, for a while I would stare at the child lying beside me and remind myself how fortunate I was to have found such an entrancing, eager companion to sleep with. But then, a few minutes later, a sense of uneasiness would creep over me, and I would turn onto my back and gaze up at the ceiling, op-pressed by a feeling of dissatisfaction. Very soon I would become disquieted, because I knew the reason for my restlessness. I had begun to think about the past again. But my memory had in some strange way avoided Margaret or Michael Fairley, and had found its way back to the island on the Thames. It had reached the summer-house in which Adeney moved slowly towards me as if he were carrying a heavy weight.

I now began to crave for Adeney. But Adeney belonged very much to the past, I told myself, so it was useless to yearn for him. It was a long time before I would confess to myself that my yearning was more vague and yet more specific than it had once been. And when at last I admitted to myself exactly what I wanted, for a while a lingering self-respect kept me from pursu-ing it.

My excuse to leave Cuba came when I discovered that Ina had

started an affair with a boy of seventeen who worked on the sugar-plantation beside us. He was earning enough money for them to marry—or so she confessed to me between her rather exaggerated sobs of rage at having been found out. So I gave her a wedding present, and I gave her parents some farewell presents, and I moved to an hotel overlooking the harbour.

I took a passage to Mexico because there happened to be a ship in port which was sailing to Vera Cruz.

———

At that period I was so determined to evade the tentacles of the class from which I had escaped that I no longer went by the name of James Steede. At the hotels and bars I now frequented I was generally known as Jimmy, and if they asked me my surname, I would say it was Smith. I made friends with sailors, Indians, Mexican soldiers, half-castes, and peons as I passed through on my way across the country—Puebla, Mexico City, Oaxaca.

By the time I had been in Mexico for a few months, the part of me that wished to die had gained control. I had long since given up caring about conventions; I now gave up caring about the future. I immersed myself completely in the present. I drank heavily, and each day and each night I followed my inclinations. In my ignorant insularity I had imagined that my particular form of desire was only prevalent in a certain class of England. I was now amazed to discover that in every class and in every race—black or yellow or red or white or brown—there were to be found men who were alike inclined.

I think I was more attracted to the Indians than to any other people I met during those days. I was astonished by their beauty. I marvelled at their smooth skins gleaming like polished mahogany, and their graceful, slender limbs which concealed an intense strength, and their strange mixture of gentleness and virility. Their desire, I found with some of them, was as unimpeded by shame as was my own, and when I found one who seemed fond of me, I only wished that we could converse in words as fluently as we made love so I could form a permanent friendship with him. But when the session came to an end, we would smile, rather hopelessly, sadly even, and then we would part. As the drunken days passed by, I began to long for someone of my own age—someone who spoke English or French, the only two languages I could speak—someone with whom I could make friends, someone I could live with.

Even during the early period in Cuba when I was trying to lead a normal life, I had observed that large harbours such as Havana offered the best opportunity for the particular form of enjoyment from which I was then trying to escape. Sailors, I had noticed, on board ships and off them, were not governed by social conventions—particularly after a few drinks. I now began to wonder whether I might find the young companion I was looking for in a seaman's bar in some harbour. Even as a child I had always been fascinated by the sound of the words 'the Pacific', and so, when I left Oaxaca and my Indian friends there, I made my way to Acapulco.

After searching round the little town for a while, I found a pleasant room on the first floor of an hotel close to the Zocalo, overlooking the broad sweep of the almost land-locked harbour. The situation was perfect for me, because in the evening I could sit out in the corner of the wooden balcony outside my bedroom and watch the passers-by.

It was while I was sitting on that balcony in Acapulco at six o'clock one afternoon, with a brandy on the little table beside my chair, that I first saw Clint.

As the young man wandered along the street, beneath my balcony, I thought, when I looked at him, that he must be Mexican, for his skin was olive-dark and he had black hair which had grown so long that it curled at the back of his neck. He wore a very clean white singlet and tight black trousers. His slenderness and his slight stoop as he walked probably made him seem smaller than he was. Then I noticed a tattoo on his forearm, so I presumed he came off a ship, and for some reason I had a feeling he was English. As I stared down at him, he looked up. His eyes were large and very dark; his thick eyebrows almost met above the bridge of his surprisingly delicate nose. When he saw me gazing at him, he smiled, and his face which had been set in a stern, almost sullen expression, suddenly became alive and attractive. His teeth were very even and as white as his singlet, and his mouth was over-wide. Then, as I smiled back at him, he gave me a nod and a friendly wave of his hand, and he walked on down the street. I decided that if he stopped at the first bar he came to it meant he expected me to join him. But he passed the first cantina and the second. Outside the third, which was one of the largest cantinas in the town, he paused, and for an instant he looked back towards my balcony to see if I were still watching him. Then he walked inside.

———

He was leaning against the bar-counter finishing his drink when I came in. He put down his glass and smiled as I moved towards him.

"Are you Danish?" he asked.

I laughed. With my very light-coloured hair and fair complexion I was used to being taken for a Scandinavian. "No," I answered, "I'm English." By then I'd learned to assume a rough kind of voice as a form of protective disguise.

"Where do you come from?" he asked, staring at me. He spoke with a sort of drawl I could not place. His accent was neither American nor cockney, yet there were traces of both in it.

"From near London," I answered.

"What'll you drink?" he asked. His eyes seemed to be fixed on my hair.

"Brandy and soda, thanks."

Our conversation was perfectly ordinary, but somehow each word seemed to have significance. When he turned to the half-caste behind the bar to order the drinks I had a chance to examine him. He was a few years older than I was—about twenty-six, I reckoned. But the skin of his face was so soft I had the odd fancy that if I touched his cheek I would leave the stamp of my fingers behind. His head was still that of a boy, and his slender neck joined awkwardly with his heavy shoulders. He was quite slim, yet he gave the impression of unusual strength. His hands were broad and well-shaped and very clean. The tattoo of an anchor on his left forearm seemed out of keeping with his hairless skin.

"Where do you come from?" I asked him when we had settled down with our drinks at a table at the back of the cantina.

He grinned. "Since I was born out there, I suppose I can call myself an Australian. My name's Clinton, but they call me 'Clint'." He looked at me over the rim of his glass. "I suppose you're wondering how I come to be here in Mexico, so I'll tell you. I sailed to San Francisco on a ship that was going there last year—it was at the time of the gold rush. I worked in the gold diggings for quite a while, but I didn't have any luck. So then I took a ship down here to Acapulco. The ship's still in the harbour—the Captain's a friend of mine. She's a three-masted schooner, a bit over three hundred tons. The *Clara*, she's called. You've probably seen her at anchor. We may be sailing down to Lima in a few weeks' time."

I picked up our glasses and went to the bar to get us some more drinks.

"What about you?" he asked when I returned. "I don't even know your name."

"It's very dull," I said. "It's Smith. Jimmy Smith."

Clint winked at me. "Did you know that in Sydney, New South Wales, there are more Smiths per head than in any other city in the world?" he said. "And may I ask what you're doing in Mexico?"

I stared steadily into his dark eyes. "I got into debt in England," I replied. "Gambling and such like. So I thought I'd better go abroad for a while."

When Clint grinned, I saw he hadn't believed a word of it. "You ought to come to Australia. I think it would suit you fine."

"Perhaps it would. But what would I do there?"

Clint looked at me. He examined me carefully and without haste. Then he smiled. "You'd find plenty to do," he said, "of one kind or another." For a while he was silent. He had resumed his appraisal. Suddenly I felt uneasy. With some people, when they stare at you, the intentness of their gaze makes you wonder if they are trying to look into your soul. But then, while Clint was gazing at me, looking me over carefully, I had a strange feeling that he was examining the shape of my body so as to assess the quality of my strength of endurance. He was examining my features in order to form an impression of my force of character. But I felt that the complete examination was only being undertaken so that Clint could form an accurate judgment of my physical and moral power to resist him. As if he had seen my flicker of disquiet and wished to sweep away my uneasiness, Clint laughed, and the raucous sound was so joyful and innocent that I forgot my slight moment of fear in the happiness of watching him.

"You'll find plenty to do," he repeated as he rose slowly from his chair to carry our glasses to the bar.

I watched him as he crossed the room. He moved lightly and very carefully, as if each sinuous movement he made had some particular importance. He seemed intensely conscious of his own body and of the physical attributes of those around him, as if he were an animal moving amongst creatures of another species.

When he came back to the table he was carrying a half bottle of brandy. "To save us jumping up and down," he explained with a grin.

As soon as he had settled himself comfortably at the table he began to talk about Australia. I was beginning to get drunk, so I cannot remember all he said. I was watching his smile and the curve of his lips and the softness of his olive-dark skin.

"Out there," he was saying. "Out in Australia they don't care who you are. It's *what* you are that counts." He paused to pour us some more drink. "I'd guess you were fond of riding," he said, and I nodded. "You've got the build of a good rider. Out there, you'd find the best riding in the world. You'd love it, I'm sure. It's a free and easy country."

I smiled at him. "Free and easy in what kind of way?"

Clint laughed. "You can do just what you want, and no one

cares a hoot—so long as you don't get found out. In fact, you can do all kinds of things."

There was a pause. Clint's eyes were fixed on me.

"What kind of things?" I asked.

Clint leaned back in his chair and crossed his legs. His trousers were so tight I could see the muscles of his thighs. His gaze never moved from my face. "Well, for instance," he said in his slow, curiously attractive drawl, "the country's been short of women since the first settlers and convicts came out there. So the men have had to get used to making do without them. They've had to get along on their own." He took a gulp of his drink and smiled. "You can guess what happens," he said. "And that's been going on for years and years—inside the jails and out. In fact, you could say it's become quite a custom."

He was silent. He was now watching me closely, waiting for my reaction. I smiled. Then I finished my drink. Clint picked up the bottle to fill my glass. But I had already noticed the bottle was empty.

"Shall we go back to my hotel for a drink?" I asked.

"All right," Clint answered, as he uncrossed his legs and rose from his chair. "Let's go."

In silence we walked along the street to my hotel. I could feel my heart pounding with each step. There was no one in the shabby entrance hall. Four lamps hung from a rack beside the desk. I unhooked one of them.

"You lead the way," Clint said.

I could hear his footsteps following me up the creaking stairs. I took the key out of my pocket and unlocked the door. I put the lamp down on the wooden table in the centre of the room with the key beside it. Clint followed me into the room. He closed the door behind him.

"It's bloody warm in here," he said. For an instant he hesitated. Then with a quick smile of apology he stripped off his singlet. His shoulders were heavily muscled. His deep chest was smooth and hairless. The tattoo of the anchor was the only blemish on his gleaming skin.

"What will you drink?" I asked. "There's rum or there's local beer."

For a moment Clint was silent. He was no longer smiling. "I think we've both had enough to drink for the time being," he said.

Slowly his eyes moved round the shabby room with its high ceiling and long shutters and dusty wooden furniture. He stared down at the lumpy bed from which the stained quilt had been thrown back for my siesta that afternoon. Then he picked up the key from the table and walked to the door and locked it, sliding the bolt above it into position.

When he turned, his eyes seemed to glow in the light of the oil lamp. As he crossed the room he paused to examine himself for a moment in the spotted looking-glass above the wash-stand. Then he slipped off his shoes and lay down on the bed, his head leaning against the bolster, his dark eyes fixed on me.

When I awoke in the morning I wondered if Clint would be embarrassed or surly and threatening. With other sailors I'd had experiences of all three. Clint was lying with his head cradled in his arm, staring at me. When he saw I was awake he grinned. Slowly he stretched out an arm and cuffed me lightly on the back of the head.

"You're all right," he said. "You don't even snore. So now what about some breakfast? I'm starving."

Clint moved into the hotel that afternoon. He assured me he would not be sailing to Lima "for quite a while." I felt that at last I had found the companion I'd been seeking.

Though I believed I was lucky to have met Clint, I had two worries about him at the time. The first should not have surprised me, for I had seen a wild look in his oddly-smouldering eyes. I discovered Clint was dangerously violent when drunk. The first time I saw his violence displayed was in a cantina one night on the wharf-side. He had been drinking heavily, and he'd been eyeing a young Mexican girl who was sitting at the next table with an American sailor. Suddenly Clint beckoned to her, and the girl, who was obviously fascinated by him, left her escort and came over to us. But the sailor followed, and within a minute the fight started. I had seen plenty of brawls before, but what horrified me was the moment when it looked as if Clint was fighting to kill. He had thrown the sailor to the ground. He was kneeling on his chest, almost throttling him, when I dragged him away. After I'd got Clint outside—which wasn't easy, for I was half drunk myself— I cursed him for his behaviour. Clint glared at me.

"Let's get this clear," he said. "If you and I are going to be friends, I'm going after a girl when I like and how I like."

"Fine," I answered. "But not, I suggest, someone else's girl."

Clint grinned at me apologetically. "Let's go home and forget about it," he said. "I'm sorry, Jimmy. Please forgive me."

My second anxiety was caused by Clint's strange evasiveness about his plans to sail to Lima in the schooner. When he would return from one of his meetings with the *Clara's* skipper, Captain Leigh, he would be curiously reticent about the arrangements he had made. Clint had introduced me to Captain Leigh, who was a long-faced American of about forty. Leigh was affable to me in his way. But for some reason I did not trust him. His face was weak; his expression was rather sly. Dressed in his smart dark-blue jacket and white trousers, with his carefully trimmed sideboards and neat beard, he looked somehow too trim and spruce, too nautical to be the honest genial sailor he pretended to be.

One night, after an evening spent on board the *Clara*, Clint came back to the hotel drunk and oddly elated. I was already in bed. He sat down on a wooden chair beneath the shutters and grinned at me.

"You're all right, Jimmy," he said. "I'd rather have you as a friend than a girl any day. You can't go out for an evening round all the bars with a girl. You can't really talk to her. You can't really trust a girl with a secret either. But you're just beaut."

'Beaut'—meaning 'fine' or 'beautiful'—was one of Clint's expressions for high praise. I felt pleased. Suddenly he leaned forward in his chair. "Now if I tell you a secret do you promise not to tell anyone? And do you promise not to be shocked?"

I smiled. "I can safely promise both."

Clint nodded his head. "I know you can keep a secret, because you've never let on who you are or where you really come from. You're not just plain Jimmy Smith from near London—I'm certain of it. So if you can keep your own secret, you can certainly keep ours."

"Ours?" I asked.

"George Leigh, you, and myself," he answered. "Us and the crew, because they'll be in it as well. They've got to be. Every single one of them. But none of them will ever talk for fear of hanging—because it's a hanging offence."

I stared at him in bewilderment. Clint smiled. He was enjoying keeping me in suspense. "In a fortnight's time," he said, "you and I will sail in the *Clara* to Lima. I shall be Mate. And Lima's the direction we'll sail in—southerly. But when we're a few days out, on the night of the first storm that comes along, we'll lower the long-boat and spare rafts and life-belts—all of them with the *Clara*'s name on—and we'll cut them loose and let them drift. Something's bound to be picked up eventually. So they'll think the *Clara*'s been wrecked. And what'll make them doubly sure is that she'll never turn up again. Because the *Clara* will be seen no more. And the owners will be certain she's been lost with all on board her."

Clint got up from his chair and came to sit on the end of the bed. "Meanwhile a ship called the *Arabella* will reach the port of Melbourne," he continued. "But she won't be painted white like the *Clara*. She'll be painted dark blue. And there'll be various other differences about her. For instance, her papers will show that she comes from a different port of registry, and belongs to her Master, Captain Robinson—or shall we call him Jones? And the Captain, when he lands, will let it be known he's thinking of selling her. And in a week or two, he'll do so. All legal and aboveboard. But no one's going to know that he shares the proceeds with me and the rest of the crew."

Clint smiled. "Then we'll all scatter and make our own way to the gold diggings," he finished.

I gaped at him. I was still bewildered.

"Haven't you read any newspapers?" Clint asked. "Haven't you heard that gold's been found at Ballarat in Victoria in huge quantities? Fortunes are being made every month out there—every week almost. And we're going to share in the spoils—you and I. We're going to be rich."

I was silent for a moment while I examined his plan. Then I shook my head. "No," I said after a while. "I'm afraid I can't join you. I'm sorry, Clint. But it's not for me."

Clint scowled. "What's wrong with the plan?" he asked. "Or are you scared of the whole idea?"

"I don't think I'm scared," I answered. "Though I don't much like the prospect of getting involved with a fake shipwreck. My main objection is that I don't see where I'd fit in. I'd be no use to you in the gold fields."

"You'd be my partner."

"But what use would I be to you? What good could I do in the diggings?"

"At one time you said you liked the idea of going to Australia."

"So I do," I answered. "But not as a gold miner."

"As what then? What else could you do?"

"I can ride. I could get a job riding or training horses."

"I'd like to see you try to break in some of the wild horses we've got out there."

"I could always learn."

"But there's no money in horses. So what's the point?" Clint asked. "Why not admit you're scared and be done with it?"

His jeering voice irritated me. "You and Captain Leigh have thought up a hare-brained plan over several bottles of grog," I said. "You'll probably think better of it in the morning."

"Right then," Clint said. He sprang up from the bed and walked to the door.

"Where are you going?" I asked.

Clint glared at me. "To find myself a friend who's not a coward," he said. "To find myself a real partner." Then he left the room, and the door banged after him.

I had hoped that Clint's fit of temper would have blown over by the morning, so I waited for him in the hotel till noon, but he did not appear. Nor did I see him that night. By seven o'clock the following evening, when there was still no sign of him, I began to be afraid he had already found himself "a real partner," and I would never see him again. Then I had a sense of frustration and despair so intense I felt weak. With dismay I now confessed to myself the truth of my emotions. I needed Clint so badly that I could not endure to live without him. I dressed and left my room, without locking the door—in case Clint arrived while I was out. Then I began to search the bars and cantinas.

I found him shortly before midnight close to the wharf in a tiny bar which we seldom used because it was dingy and the drink was bad. He was slumped over a table with his head buried in his arms. A bottle of tequila stood beside him. I recognised him from his thick black hair and the olive skin of his delicate neck even before I could see the tattoo on his forearm. As I sat down at the table he looked up, peering at me through red-rimmed eyes. Suddenly he smiled. His face was drawn with exhaustion, his eyes were bloodshot from drink. But nothing it seemed could impair the charm of his rather apologetic smile.

"I didn't find a partner," he said. "To tell you the truth I didn't try to find one. If you won't come with me, then I'll go to the gold fields alone. Sit down and have a drink."

I smiled at him. "I'm sitting already," I said. "But I'll have a beer."

Clint grinned at me. "I'm sorry," he muttered. "I haven't slept for two days, and I'm a bit fuddled. Are you very angry with me?"

"I was angry," I answered. "But I'm not any more."

"Can I come back to the hotel?"

"Of course you can."

Clint propped up his head with his hands. "There's something I've got to tell you," he said. "I met George Leigh last night sometime, and he asked me what I was all upset about, so I told him.

And he told me I was a bloody fool. He said for a start you didn't have to be mixed up with the taking over of the ship in any way. All you'd have to do is book a passage on the *Clara* to Lima."

"But what am I supposed to do when the *Arabella* lands in Melbourne, and I'm on board her?"

Clint grinned. "You just say nothing," he said. "You needn't be involved. You wouldn't want to take a share of the proceeds of the ship's sale anyhow, because I gather you're not short of funds."

"If I was on board and knew what was going on, I'd still be an accessory. But what else did George Leigh say?"

"He said I was stupid to want you to go to the diggings with me. He said it would be far better for you to get a job somewhere breaking in horses, and let me go to the diggings and make my little fortune. Then we could join up later."

Clint raised his head in excitement. "Oh yes, and there was another thing George said which I completely forgot. He said if you take a passage, he'll move out into the Mate's cabin, so that you and I can share his one—the cabin we drank in the night you came aboard. Think of it, Jimmy. The crossing takes at least three months, so we'd be all that time together. Wouldn't that be beaut?"

I knew it was unwise: I knew the risks. But only a few hours earlier I had realised how tenuous was my desire to go on living. I was now aware how little I had to lose.

I smiled at Clint. "Yes," I said. "It would be beaut. When do we sail?"

Clint had cheerfully assumed I wasn't "short of funds." But in fact the letter of credit which Glyn's Bank in London had given me was running out. On the last occasion when I had called on their agents to collect money in Havana I had found several letters from my mother waiting for me. Strange hysterical letters they were, begging my forgiveness in one paragraph and accusing me of heartless ingratitude in the next. But every letter contained a long plea, beseeching me to return home. I left them all unanswered. I could not forgive her. But this time, I was certain that Margaret Anstey was not going to have a child. I had arranged for her to send a letter to Elliott, the solicitor in Nottingham, if she became pregnant, and Elliott had secret instructions to forward any letters to Glyn's agents in Mexico. No letter from Margaret had come. By now I had begun to think of Margaret less as a person and more as a symbol of the normal life which my mother had denied me. However, by the time I had reached Acapulco I found my memory had played an odd game. Instead of remembering the misery my mother had caused by destroying my happiness with Margaret, I began to remember her devotion to me when I was young; I recalled in detail, for instance, the afternoon my mother met me in the drive when I had run away from school. I remembered her smuggling me up the backstairs to my bedroom and sitting beside my bed until I fell asleep. So from Acapulco I had written her a letter which in effect was an overture of peace. I said I believed we should forget the circumstances which made me leave England; I told her I expected to return home—for a while at least—next year. In the meantime I begged her to lend me some money, with the lands of Ruston as security, and I asked her to send me the amount through Glyn's. By the same mail I wrote, without much hope, a letter to my father telling him I needed money. My letter to my father was never answered—so far as I knew. However, the day after I had agreed to sail with Clint on the *Clara* I went to see Glyn's local agent in Acapulco, and there, waiting for me, was another letter from my mother. It contained the usual excuses for her behavior —she had done it all for my sake—the usual complaints that the Steede estates were being mismanaged in my father's absence, and the usual hysterical accusations of ingratitude. But throughout the rambling pages one message emerged in clarity: I would get no more money from her until I returned to England.

My financial position was far from being desperate. I still had enough money left to last for several months, and at the worst I could write to Elliott and Baxter and ask them to sell the property at Ruston, which I came into when I was twenty-one. But this would take time. What enraged me was my mother's response to my letter of forgiveness. She had deliberately refused to lend me a penny, even with Ruston as security.

During the fortnight before we sailed from Acapulco, Clint had been so busy that I seldom saw him except late in the evening when he was tired and nervous. Both of us, during those evenings, took refuge from our anxieties by drinking to excess. With each drink, my rage against my mother increased. One night, when I was so drunk I could hardly hold a pen in my hand, I decided to write to her, for I had suddenly thought of a way of punishing her for all her wickedness. I wrote saying that I was sailing to Lima from the port of Acapulco on the twenty-third of April in the ship *Clara.*

Let her think I'd been drowned, I thought to myself. Let her mourn me. And in a stupor of alcohol I posted the letter.

Three days later, the *Clara* sailed.

We were carrying a cargo of coffee-beans, lentils, and phosphates. Only a day out from harbour I began to be afraid we were overladen. The ship seemed to lack the buoyancy which should have carried her over heavy seas. Whenever a large wave crashed against her bows, the *Clara* would strike it with the sound of a sledge hammer.

When the storm hit us on the sixth day out, I was terrified. Great waves struck down on us. Sheets of water were swirling over the decks, carrying away everything that wasn't secured; and the huge swelling waves, it seemed to me, were threatening to obliterate us. I went below to my cabin. I lay down in my bunk with a bottle of brandy, and as I drank I thought how ironical it would be if instead of faking a shipwreck we were truly wrecked. About two hours later, when I had almost finished the bottle, I fell asleep. So I wasn't—to use Captain Leigh's phrase—"mixed up" with the actual faking of the wreck, because by the time I had woken up, all that was necessary had been done. The long-boat had been lowered and set adrift; spare rafts and life-belts with the *Clara's* name on them together with packing-cases and other odd debris had been hurled into the sea; and we had set our course for Melbourne. With the first days of calm weather, planks attached to ropes were lowered over the side, and the repainting began while the ship wallowed in a gentle Pacific swell.

For the next fortnight I was wonderfully happy. By day I would sit in a chair on deck, reading a book or gazing at the endless haze of blue ocean spread around us, watching the dolphins leaping beside us, staring down at the foam rustling in our wake. At night, when it was Clint's watch, I would stand beside him by the wheel. The sea was so quiet and the breeze so steady that the sails, spread out high above us, were motionless and still as marble. The dark blue canvas of the sky was pierced by stars. Presently I would look at the chronometer and know that in an hour the second mate would appear to begin his watch, and then Clint and I would go below to our cabin.

I was happy. But as the days passed by, I became aware of a tension on board the ship. Now that all of us were accomplices in crime, the men treated the officers with less respect. Captain Leigh, for all his spruce appearance and brisk manner, was too weak to maintain any form of discipline. Gradually, he had begun to look towards Clint to keep order and to deal with any trouble-makers.

One of the most surly members of the crew of fifteen men was an American called Brody. He was a tall, thick-set man of about thirty, with a fine head. He would have been quite handsome but for his fleshy nose and close-set eyes. The other person who was always causing trouble, and who seemed to resent any form of discipline, was a young German nicknamed Fritz. Young Fritz was quite small, but his muscles seemed to stand out like rope from his sunburned skin, and his strength was astounding. He had once been a professional weight-lifter in a circus. His small bright blue eyes glared out defiantly from his hard, almost beautiful face. His fists moved fast when he lost his temper.

The first trouble occurred at the beginning of the morning

watch. The crew were washing down, scrubbing and swabbing the decks as usual. About twenty minutes before seven bells when all hands got breakfast, Brody, the large American, wandered across to the windlass, sat down and lit a cheroot. He did not move when Clint came up to him.

"Having a rest?" Clint asked.

Brody looked up at him in contempt. "Looks like it," he replied.

"It's not seven bells yet."

Brody spat, then settled himself more comfortably. "Isn't that interesting," he replied. There was a silence. Then a man tittered.

Clint's hands began to quiver. "Stand up," he said.

Brody glowered at him. "Try and make me," he answered.

Clint moved so swiftly that the fight had begun before I was aware of it. He seized Brody by the shoulders and pulled him up from the windlass. Then he smashed him to the ground. Brody scrambled to his feet. He was taller and heavier than Clint; he was confident of himself as he lumbered towards him, his large hands hanging ready at his sides. Then he rushed in. But Clint ducked the first two lunges of Brody's fists, and suddenly struck out at him hard, aiming low at the man's stomach. Brody gave a groan, and as he fell to his knees Clint hit him again. Brody toppled sideways and lay motionless on the deck.

Clint turned to the group of men who had been watching in silence. He grinned at them cheerfully. "Now get on with your work." Then he gave me a wink and moved down towards our cabin.

"I'm just waiting for the chance to deal with that other little bastard, young Fritz," Clint said, as he bolted the door of the cabin. His eyes were shining, and he was still trembling with excitement. "I've heard Fritz is having a good time with one of the young deck-hands." Suddenly Clint smiled at me. "Not that I'm quite in a position to complain," he added as he slipped off his singlet and lay down on the bunk.

During the next few days I noticed that Clint began to talk quite often about Fritz and his friend, the seventeen-year-old deck-hand who shared his watch. When the two of them were on deck together, Clint would glance at them from time to time, and his lips would move as if he were making a calculation.

"Fritz was shouting curses at the Captain in the fo'c's'le," Clint said one night when he came down into our cabin. "He's asking for trouble, is Fritz, and I'll see he gets it."

Later in the night I was vaguely aware of Clint getting up and leaving the cabin. A few minutes later I heard shouts from above on deck. Then a man began screaming for help. An instant later there was silence. I lit the lamp by the bunk. Presently Clint walked in and bolted the door behind him. His cheek was cut and bruised, and he was sweating heavily. But his eyes were gleaming with triumph.

"He was on look-out, Fritz was, and I found him asleep," Clint said. "Think of it! A look-out man asleep. The bastard, he just didn't care! When I shouted at him he had the nerve to answer me back, so we had a real fight." Clint smiled. "He landed a few smashers on me, but I gave it him back. More than he'd reckoned for. When I got him down on the deck I made him really sorry. You probably heard him screaming. I don't think he'll be having much fun with his young friend for a long time to come."

Clint stripped off his clothes. His whole body seemed inflamed and swollen with his success. He stood staring down at me for a while. Then he crossed over to the bunk.

After the fight with Fritz, when I was on deck with Clint I could see that he was hated by the crew, but his orders were obeyed. I now began to feel I was despised, not only for being a passenger who did no work, but because I was Clint's friend. However, when once we were below, with the door safely bolted, we could forget the world outside. Our world was confined by the teak bulwarks and fluted panelling of our cabin, with its gleaming brass lamps and polished table on which stood a set of broad-based ship's decanters which were always kept full. I had never shared such close quarters before, and at first the intimacy of it delighted me. Clint and I would play cards or draughts or dominoes. Some evenings he would try to teach me a little about sea-lore, for he was determined to make an experienced sailor of me. Sometimes we would read to each other from some book that had taken our fancy. The hours passed very pleasantly in the security of our little cabin.

One evening Clint fished out an old leather-bound book from the bottom of his trunk and threw it over to me. "Have a look at this," he said. I glanced at the title and saw it was called the *Stranger's Guide in New South Wales*. It had been published in 1838. With interest I turned the pages until I came to a chapter headed 'Hints to Immigrants'.

"'All immigrants'," I read out, "'should be particularly on their guard against drinking or gambling on their passage out, or after they land, which many are led into by frequenting or lodging in public-houses'."

Clint smiled. "What did I tell you?" he asked.

"'All immigrants'," I continued, "'ought also to be careful in forming hasty acquaintanceship in this colony, or with their ship-mates on the voyage hither'."

Clint laughed happily. "So you be careful, Jimmy," he said.

"'As soon as an immigrant is landed'," I continued, "'all dispensable cash should be placed, if above fifty pounds, in one of the public Banks, if under that sum in the Savings' Bank'."

"Australia was a wild, lawless land a dozen years ago," Clint said. "In some parts it still is. Now read out the page which gives the advice the author offers to convicts."

"'Hints to Convicts'," I read out. "'As the causes which have brought you to Australia have been in every case such as were discreditable to yourselves, the cause of grief to your friends, and of shame to your companions in the land from which you have been expelled, and as you have been landed on these shores as unworthy members of society, make it your endeavour, from the instant you set foot on shore, to give up those habits which have brought you into such a degraded condition'."

Clint sprang from the bunk. "Can you believe it!" he exclaimed. "Those words of advice are meant seriously. The smug hypocritical bastard! I'd like to see him trussed up to the triangle in Norfolk Island jail, ready for a flogging." His eyes were glaring, and his face was suddenly twisted in hatred. He was shaking and trembling as if he were suffering a fit. An instant later he recovered. He breathed more easily, and the wild look left his eyes. Suddenly I began to wonder if I could not guess the reason for his unusually intense bitterness. Then Clint nodded his head. "Yes," he said, as though answering a question I'd put. "My parents were convicts. Both of them. My father carried the scars of the lashes on his back till the day he died."

The hours I spent alone in the cabin with Clint passed quickly, without a moment's boredom, for not only was I intensely attracted by the lean, graceful body sprawling on the bunk beside me, not only was I obsessed by him, but I was constantly interested by the odd conflicts of his nature. At times his unexpected tenderness surprised me. A few days after the storm I had been ill with a slight fever, and he had looked after me with amazing care and gentleness. Yet he would punish the men savagely. In him seemed to be mixed both tenderness and cruelty, both softness and brutal strength, both a pliable mind and crude obstinacy. His attitude towards Australia contained equally mixed conflicts. He loathed the whole range of men—the police, judges, lawyers, administrators, prison governors, officers, and warders—who had been responsible for his parents' sufferings; he detested the colonists and property owners to whom his parents had been assigned as convict servants. For the assigned convicts were scarcely better off than slaves. His father had worked in a quarry near Sydney, his mother in a factory. Both of them had toiled in the hope that "their industry and good conduct" would prove them "deserving of receiving a ticket of leave which exempted them from forced labours." Clint's father had been flogged and lashed by the settler to whom he was assigned; his mother had been sentenced to the treadmill. Yet Clint was proud of his countrymen and fiercely proud of his country. For instance, if any product was mentioned, from wheat to wine, Clint would maintain that the Australian-produced kind was the best. Whatever type of scenery was mentioned, from mountain-range to desert, Clint would affirm that the ranges and the deserts in Australia were larger and grander. And no man, it seemed, could match an Australian in talent or strength or generosity. Nor would Clint's opinion be in any way changed by the criticism or banter of Captain Leigh or the second mate. Australia was "great"; Australia was just "beaut." We would see for ourselves.

At first I had been amused by Clint's dogmatic statements and firmly held beliefs. I had smiled at his obstinacy. But gradually I found I had begun to resent Clint's profound certainty that his opinion must be right about everything, his conviction that every act done by him must be perfect, and every command he gave must be obeyed. Clint's arrogance began to irritate me. One evening when I was almost drunk and he had pronounced some idiotic statement about forestry which he defended with his usual obstinacy, I became annoyed. When he persisted in his argument with an unusually contemptuous air of infallibility, I lost my temper.

"Can't you see I know a little about forestry?" I asked. "After all, you must allow me to know *something*. I'm not just a common-or-garden colonial."

Clint stared at me for a moment without moving, then he sprang forward and pinioned me down on the bunk. His face was dark with rage. He was trembling.

"Now just you listen to me," Clint hissed at me. "For all I know or care you may come from one of the grandest families in all England. My father and mother were convicts. But where we're going, it doesn't matter a tinker's curse who you are. It's *what* you are that counts. So don't go calling me a colonial ever again. Understand?"

Suddenly he hit me hard across the face. I struggled to free my arms from his grip, but he was far stronger than I was.

"Thank heaven I'll be able to get away from you as soon as we reach Melbourne," I cried out.

Clint smiled down at me. "Don't be too sure," he answered.

For a while he gazed down at me in silence. "I like having my little Jimmy around when I need him," he said quietly.

At first I had been amused by Clint's assumption of dominion over me. Perhaps a part of me had been excited by it. But I still had sufficient self-respect to resent being completely dominated. I therefore now tried to achieve an attitude of detachment towards him; I tried to care less about him; I forced myself to recognise the humiliations which my passion forced me to endure. But Clint was very much aware of the strength of his power to attract me. Every movement he made as he wandered about the cabin was calculated to display his physical charms. I would avoid looking at him; I would pretend to be reading a book. But it was as if he could exude the force of his charm across space, for while I turned the pages of my book I would be aware of him lying half naked on the bunk in his tight linen trousers, and presently the shape of his limbs would seem to cover the printed page. Then I would hear his quiet drawl.

"Come over here, Jimmy," he would say. "Come over." And as if he were dragging me with invisible ropes I would find myself moving towards him.

Though my will-power might well have been too weak for me to break away from Clint as I had threatened, the chaos of our lives when we arrived in Melbourne made our parting almost inevitable. The gold discoveries at inland places such as Ballarat and Castlemaine and Bendigo early in the eighteen-fifties had turned the town mad. Every hotel and boarding-house in Melbourne was full of newly-arrived immigrants. A hundred thousand people were living in tents in the suburbs. Houses were sprouting up everywhere like toadstools. Land-jobbers were gaining a fortune each day. The public-houses were crowded with merchants and shop-keepers who had made so much money they could afford to be idle and drunken for a while. The whole town seemed to tremble with excitement and disorder.

Clint and I found ourselves a room in a dingy lodging-house, and we were soon caught up in the bustle and nervous tension which pervaded every street. Clint was busy in helping Captain Leigh to find a purchaser for the ship. I was busy exploring the first Australian town I had visited—gazing at small shacks and huge mansions, wandering along streets of terraced houses, admiring the slender iron pillars which upheld graceful balconies with iron-work as delicate as lace; staring at the ladies in their white muslins and the men in their black coats and plaid trousers; gaping at the thickly bearded diggers who had returned rich from the goldfields and who now sat in the inns attended by flashy prostitutes in gaudy silk dresses, standing drinks to all within reach of them. I was amazed by the throng of carts, and cabs and private coaches; I was astonished by the vitality of the place and the feverish vigour of its inhabitants.

Both Clint and I became infected by the general excitement around us; both of us drank as heavily as most of the men in the bars we visited. Both of us became tired and irritable. The general restlessness had affected us like a disease. The symptoms were nervousness and a quick temper. We now began to quarrel frequently. Neither of us could control his impatience and annoyance at trifling mishaps or accidents. We had both lost our sense of proportion. Cracks in the façade of our relationship had formerly been filled in. Now they were left open.

Our final row took place a few days after the ship had been sold and the proceeds had been divided accordingly to the share-arrangement which had been planned. Clint intended to leave for the diggings at Ballarat, and he wanted me to go with him. If I loathed the life there, he said, I could leave him and find work with a stockman where I would be riding all day long. "But at least you must go with me as far as Ballarat," he announced firmly as we leaned against the mahogany bar-counter of a crowded public-house.

Something about his self-assured attitude annoyed me. "I'll think it over," I said.

"You won't think it over at all," Clint replied. "In fact, we'll leave for Ballarat tomorrow. I'm getting fed up with Melbourne. I've got all the kit we shall need, so we can leave first thing in the morning. So that's an end to it."

"You can leave," I answered. "I shall stay on here for a while."

Clint glowered at me. "You'll do as you're told," he said.

"We'll see." I gulped down my drink and walked out of the bar.

"Don't be a fool," Clint called after me. "Come back."

But for once my anger was stronger than my attraction to him. I walked into the street and turned quickly down a side-alley in case Clint tried to follow me. I hurried along the next street I came to. I went into the largest public-house I could find. Later that evening I picked up a young prostitute and spent the night in her room with her. I stayed there the following evening, and the next.

When I returned to the lodging-house, Clint had left. There was a note for me by the wash-stand. "This time I shan't be coming back to you," Clint wrote. "This time I've found myself a real partner."

I had wanted to escape from Clint. I was now free of him. But to my dismay I found my whole being seemed to ache with grief. For day after day I wandered in a daze around the grey and brown streets and squares and brightly coloured gardens of Melbourne. The strange thing about my wretchedness was that I knew I was probably well rid of him, yet it was this very knowledge which somehow made losing him seem all the more bitter. I now began to blame myself for various unpleasant rows we had had together in which formerly I had been certain Clint was to blame. My memory conspired with my conscience to make me forget his fits of ill-temper and his violence. I only remembered the olive-skinned, impudent face and the graceful body. I now lived from day to day—not daring to contemplate any future with Clint absent from it.

One afternoon, as I was wandering vaguely along a street on the outskirts of the town, I came to a yard in which some horses were being put up for auction. Since I had nothing better to do, I strolled into the yard and stayed there, watching the proceedings. Presently, a tall, heavily-built man of about fifty who had been glancing at me from time to time came up to me.

"Are you interested in horses?" he asked.

"Yes, I am."

"Are you a good rider?"

"Not too bad," I answered.

His sunburned face creased into a smile. "Do you want a job?" he asked. Then, before I could answer, he clapped me in a friendly way on the back. "Perhaps I'd better explain," he said. "My name's Dimmock, and I'm a stock-keeper. I've got a property to the north of Albury. The man who used to break in horses for me has got the gold fever. He's left for the diggings, and I'm short-handed as it is."

"I can ride well enough," I said, "but I've never had any experience of training horses."

"I could teach you," Dimmock replied. "I have a feeling you'd be good with horses. Do you want the job?"

I liked his deeply-lined leathery face and his very clear grey eyes.

"Yes," I answered. "I do."

"Great," he said. "We'll leave tomorrow, if that suits you. But now let's go and have a drink on it."

The night we reached Dimmock's homestead I was so tired I would have liked to have gone straight to bed. But his wife, who was a stout, pleasant-faced woman of about forty, insisted on preparing a huge meal for us. Afterwards, Dimmock and I sat at the kitchen table with a bottle of brandy between us, while he told me about horse-breaking.

"Horses can sense kindness in a man," he said. "When I was a kid I loved horses, and I just had that little flair—I can't think how else to describe it—so that horses liked me. A man's voice has got a lot to do with it. So has the smell of him. When I first go up to a horse, I always rub my hand under my armpits, then I stretch out the back of my hand and let him smell it. That way he gets used to me."

Dimmock filled his glass and pushed the bottle across to me.

"Another thing you must do is to fix your gaze on one of the horse's eyes," he continued. "Out in the pastures, if a wild horse stands on his hindlegs and looks at you—then that's a horse you can deal with, because he's got some regard for you. But if the horse won't lift his head from the pasture, if he ignores you, then he'll be difficult. And of course every horse has a different temperament—the same as human beings."

Mrs Dimmock had appeared in the doorway. "And this human being," she said, "has a temperament which tells her it's high time we were all in bed. Young Jimmy—if he doesn't object to being called by his Christian name—is dropping with exhaustion. So show him to his room and let the poor lad sleep."

The next morning I went out with Dimmock into the paddock and watched him at work in the breaking-yard, which was a round enclosure about forty feet in diameter. I watched him throw a rope round the neck of a horse which had been drafted from the mob in the paddock. I watched him as he waited for the horse to calm down a little, then stepped in front and threw a half-hitch over his nose. He slowly approached the animal's head, giving him the back of his hand to smell. Then slowly and gently I saw him run his hand up to the horse's eye and close it.

"It seems as if a horse has got two brains," he explained to me. "Because if you close one of his eyes, you just sort of confuse him. Now you run the half-hitch above his eyes and below his ears. You put another half-hitch on his nose, and then you take a blindfold." From his pocket he took out a piece of black cloth about thirty-six inches square which he folded in the shape of a triangle. Perhaps I watched him with such fascinated interest only because already I had an idea that this was going to be my profession for the rest of my life. "Now you roll the cloth in your hand and let the colt smell it and sniff it." It was odd to see that the colt, which at first had been nervous and restive, now seemed quieter. "You put one corner under the top hitch and the other under the bottom hitch so as to cover his eye." Dimmock turned back to the gate-post. "Now you get the bridle," he continued in his soft, deep voice. "You lengthen the cheek-straps to the full extent, you put the headpiece of the bridle over his ears, you buckle the throat-strap, then you stand in the same direction as the horse is standing, and using your forefinger and thumb, you put the bit into the horse's mouth and adjust the length of the cheek-straps so that the bit isn't pulling on the horse's lips, but so that it's not loose enough to injure his teeth."

Dimmock turned round and smiled at me. "The colt's now bridled," he said. "So now we'll start again, and see *you* have a go."

Dimmock's way of breaking in a horse took fourteen days from the moment the animal was brought into the paddock from running wild on the station property. He would have ten horses in the paddock, and with each he would go through the same stage of training for that day. He was wonderfully patient; I never once saw him lose his temper.

"The wilder the horse in the yard," he said to me with a grin when a colt had been giving him trouble, "the easier to control him in the end. It's the quiet ones you have to beware of, because they're the most cunning. But a horse has got an instinct. He knows about you from the word go. And I tell you this, young Jimmy, my guess was right. You've got the flair, and from today on you'll be on your own. I've other work to do."

Dimmock was right, I did have some kind of flair. At any rate I learned quickly, and the horses seemed to sense I was fond of them. The work was tiring, but I was pleased with myself. For the first time I was earning a weekly wage. I was proud that at last I was making a living on my own. And I delighted in the openness of the countryside and its inhabitants. I felt as if all my life I had been living in a stuffy room and I had come out at last into fresh air.

I suppose it was after I had been staying at the Dimmocks' homestead for two months that the idea of setting up in business as a horse-breaker first occurred to me. There were several advantages to the idea. At the homestead I had a room of my own. But even if I could have found someone at the inn at Albury to replace Clint—even for a few hours—it would have been impossible to bring him back, and I needed to find a companion, because I was convinced that it was only by becoming intensely attracted to another person that I could rid myself of my yearning for Clint. Also, I was growing fond of Jack and Sarah Dimmock. There was a kindness about them which I later learned was to be found in almost all Australians. Probably because of the anguish and hardship which the first settlers in the country experienced, and probably because of the mutual suffering of the first convicts, which Clint had told me about, in those prisons where a thousand bodies had been maimed and a thousand spirits broken—as a result of all this suffering it seemed to me that somehow Australians had learned the value of kindliness and friendship more than any other people I had known. The Dimmocks were warm-hearted; their kindness to me may have been all the greater because they were childless. Each day I could feel I was being treated more as a son than as a paid hand. Each day they seemed to grow more solicitous about my heavy drinking, when I'd visit one of the public-houses at Albury. Each day they had begun to suggest it was time I settled down. There would be room for a wife of mine at the homestead, they kept telling me. And I had begun to find their possessiveness and affection for me a little stifling. The longer I stayed, the more painful would be the parting.

The third reason for my wanting to leave the homestead was that in an old English newspaper which had somehow found its way to Albury I had read a small paragraph reporting the news of my father's death. The title had passed to my younger brother Arthur, the report said, because I had been presumed dead when the wreck of the *Clara*, in which it was known that I'd sailed from Acapulco, had finally been established.

I now realise how rash my letter to my mother had been. For only one passenger, Jimmy Smith, had sailed on the *Clara*. If any members of the crew or Clint or Captain Leigh happened to see that particular report in the papers they would at once guess that Jimmy Smith was James Steede, now a baronet and heir to the Steede estates. And though they were in no position to blackmail me, I had an uneasy fear of rumours spreading about my true identity, for I was now Jimmy Smith. I had made good as Jimmy Smith; I had proved to myself I could succeed without the help of a rich and titled family. I intended to remain Jimmy Smith until the day I died. For I never again wanted to see Steede and the conventional, staid, hypocritical society which surrounded it. The further, therefore, that I moved away from Ballarat the less chance there was of any rumour following me.

One evening, at a public-house in Albury, I happened to hear of a holding which was available near Berrima in New South Wales. I still had enough money left to provide the small amount of capital I'd need to start up business as a horse-breaker.

With sadness I said goodbye to Jack and Sarah Dimmock—and with gratitude. I'd told them I'd been offered a job running some stables in Sydney. I think they believed me. No one in the Albury district knew I was heading for Berrima.

I was lucky to have heard about the holding. The small two-storeyed shanty house was already built. The land was already cleared. I had only to fence in paddocks and a breaking-yard, and I was ready to start business.

I charged a pound a horse. At first I got little work. I was a stranger in the district, and they mistrusted me. But every evening I'd go into Berrima and make a round of the pubs, and I soon made friends. Gradually, stockmen began to send me their horses, and they were pleased with the results. Soon my little business began to prosper.

My holding was situated on the side of a gentle incline which sloped down to the Wingecarribee river where I used to go to swim in the shallows at the end of my day's work. In the distance I could hear the bleating of sheep and the lowing of bullocks. I felt a sense of peace and security. All around Berrima the land had been cleared, and the countryside was open and undulating with lone trees and wide stretches of grass between small thickets, presenting from a distance an endless expanse of ground far wider and more beautiful than the largest English park I'd ever seen or imagined.

It was only when you walked nearer that you observed marvellous differences. The thickets were of eucalyptus trees with mallee gums or ghost gums whose smooth white trunks were devoid of any bark. And flying around in the thickets were parrots with rose-coloured breasts, blue wings, and green heads. Snow-white cockatoos screeched in the tall trees, and sometimes you could hear the oddly haunting call of a kookaburra, known as 'laughing jack' by the settlers because of the bird's strange long chuckle with which his call ended. The country was still wild, although parts of it had been settled, and as I gazed at it from the window of my bedroom in my little shanty house, which I had now furnished quite pleasantly, I felt an odd elation, a kind of liberation of spirit I had never experienced before.

At times I was lonely, and then I would spend all evening going round the pubs. Berrima was only the size of a small English country town with a church and a grey stone Court House and a gaol. But it contained fourteen public-houses—small inns, mostly, each with a whitewashed parlour and a rickety staircase leading to some rooms above. And in one of the pubs I would sometimes find a young man of my own age who was as lonely as I was. Then I knew I had a chance of success if I played the game carefully and discreetly. I would get into conversation with the youth whose loneliness and aloof appearance had attracted me, and we'd begin to drink together, talking of crops and horses and cattle until our conversation became more intimate, and we'd talk of the prostitutes of Sydney or Melbourne and the absence of girls in Berrima. Presently I'd see my companion looking at my reflection in the mirror behind the bar. Then I'd know that the message I'd been so discreetly exuding for the last hour had got through. My companion would be examining my features in a new light; my pale hair and blue eyes and soft complexion had now taken on a different meaning, and I'd know his eyes were now examining my body as if he were undressing me. That would be the moment when I'd ask him casually if he'd like a bed for the night, and as casually he would accept, and we'd walk back together to my little house, still chatting about girls and horses. Still preserving the bluff façade, I'd offer him another drink when we got home, and I'd casually return from a visit upstairs to announce the spare bed was damp but mine was large enough for two. Without a blush my friend would nod his head in agreement, and we'd have another drink. Then, still adopting our hearty manner, we'd go upstairs into my bedroom. But still the pose of decent normality would not be dropped. It would last until the very last moment— until we had got into bed, sometimes even until after I had blown out the candle. Then, with darkness the pent-up desire in my young guest would suddenly be unleashed, and his passion would pour out—sometimes with a cruel brutality which terrified me by its violence, sometimes with a bewildering tenderness and gentle affection which would last until the first gleam of dawn slid through the curtains.

One evening when I had returned from a round of the pubs alone—because my companion had been unwilling to leave a girl who'd come in from a near-by homestead—I saw a man on my porch. He was sitting hunched up, with his head almost touching his knees. As I approached, the man looked up, and I recognised Clint.

"I'm back," he said with a kind of apologetic smile. "I'm back, and I'm broke. Are you going to throw me out? Or are you going to let me stay here for a while?"

Perhaps he looked older because he was tired. Certainly he had lost weight, and I noticed that the smooth skin of his forehead was now marked by a scar above his left eye. He was definitely leaner and a little older. But his dark eyes still gleamed with alertness as he examined the expression of my face with the same intent gaze as he had stared at me the first night we had met, assessing my physical and moral power to resist him. But I knew, now, that I could indeed resist him. For I had proved I could get on without him. The proof lay in the paddocks around me. Yet as I stared back at him, I also knew from the heavy thudding of the left side of my chest that my emotions hadn't changed.

"Come in," I said, "and let's have a drink—before I get you something to eat."

"Thanks," he replied. "I don't mind telling you I'm starving."

When Clint had settled down with a glass of grog, I went to the tiny room at the back of the house which I used to smoke the meat I bought. I cut him a hunk of beef and made him a kind of damper of bread and some tea, which I brought into the room beside the kitchen where I ate. While he gnawed at his meat, I asked him the question which had been troubling me.

"How did you find me here?" I asked.

Clint grinned. "Luck mainly. I knew you'd made up your mind to get some job riding or breaking in horses. After I'd gone broke at the diggings, I got a job at a homestead at Broken Hill. One night in a pub, a man came in from Berrima. We got talking, and he mentioned that a youngster from England had started up as a horse-breaker in those parts. He'd met him one night at the Surveyor-General Inn, he told me. So I made him give me a description of the youngster, and then I knew for certain it was you. So here I am."

"I thought perhaps you might have heard some rumour about me," I said.

Clint looked at me suspiciously. "What rumour? What have you been up to?"

I was certain then that he hadn't read the newspaper report. I laughed. "I've been up to nothing, worse luck," I said. "But tell me about yourself. What have you done with your partner? Murdered him?"

Clint smiled. "Near enough." He raised his hand to touch the scar above his left eye. "He wasn't much good anyway. I only went off with him because I was angry with you for being so obstinate." Clint shook his head. "But I'm glad you didn't come with me all the same," he said. "Because it was pretty good hell." Clint finished his tea, and I poured him a brandy.

"It was all right to begin with," he said. "We got a licence to dig in an area along a creek where all of them seemed to be making a fortune. For the first few months we did fine. Some of the small nuggets we found were only covered by a few inches of soil. But that in the end proved to be the whole trouble. It was all on the surface, and the surface alluvial was soon exhausted. But we still struggled on."

Clint took a gulp of his drink. "We lived rough. Our home was a bark hut. Our furniture was just two boards covered with canvas for our beds and a block of wood stretched across a broken pail for a table. But it was the dirt I hated most. Fresh water cost a shilling a bucket—if you could get it. And when you went to wash at a muddy waterhole, little stinging flies would settle in swarms all over your body. I've heard men cry out in agony from the pain. But I could put up with all the filth and the flies so long as there was a chance of making a fortune. Then came the time when I realised there wasn't a chance any more. We'd come too late. All the big nuggets had already been picked up. The gold on the surface was exhausted. The day of the individual gold-digger was over. And it *is* over, I can promise you. Already mining companies are moving in both at Ballarat and at Bendigo—because to get at the gold now you need deep shafts and machinery. Already some of the companies are employing as many as a hundred men at a fixed wage. Soon they'll be employing thousands. I got to Ballarat a year too late. That's the truth of it. So there was nothing for me to do but to leave while I could."

Clint finished his drink and smiled at me. "You were right all along, Jimmy," he said. "We should have gone in for horses in the first place."

Then he stood up and came over to me and put his arm on my shoulder. "But if you want a partner here in Berrima," he said, "it's still not too late."

———

The next few weeks were the happiest I spent with Clint. He worked hard, and he seemed wonderfully contented. Now that I had a partner we could break in more horses. Soon we could afford to buy wild horses ourselves and break them in and sell them at local sales. Clint built stables and a second breaking-yard. I began to think that at last he would settle down. I knew there were dangers. He sometimes got drunk in one of the village pubs, and then there was always a chance he would be embroiled in a fight. He sometimes left me and went to spend the night with a girl in the village who doted on him. He was sometimes moody and restless. But I had learned to put up with his moods—just as I had learned to tolerate his arrogance and obstinacy. Only one thing disturbed me during that period. Clint had no patience with the methods of horse-breaking I'd learned from Dimmock. He maintained they took far too long. Clint's way was to throw a lasso over a horse's neck and tie him, half-suffocated, to a thick snubbing-post in the yard. Then he would put a heavy halter round the horse's neck, and leave him tied up all night without any feed. When the horse was exhausted, he'd saddle him and ride him round the yard until he'd broken him into submission. There were two obvious disadvantages to Clint's method. It was cruel, and it produced a nervous or a vicious animal.

"But I only take three or four days to break in a horse," Clint said to me when I tried to argue with him. "You take a fortnight."

"The horses I turn out are far better trained," I answered. "They're better in every way."

"Who cares?" Clint answered. "I sell mine just the same."

I wanted to point out that to succeed in our business a reputation of producing sound horses was essential. But I knew it was useless to argue with Clint. As usual, he was convinced of the rightness of his own opinion. As usual, he was certain his own way was infallible. So I kept silent. But I would no longer go anywhere near the lower paddock where he worked, because I now knew the kind of thing I might see. Once, seven weeks or so after Clint had appeared in Berrima, I had wandered down to the paddock to ask him about some trivial matter, and Clint had not noticed my arrival. He was galloping a colt round the paddock. The colt was in a lather of sweat and exhausted. But Clint was digging in his spurs and slashing its flanks with his whip. Suddenly I shuddered. For I could see from the excitement of Clint's flushed face and from his glittering eyes that he was enjoying himself.

That afternoon, as I walked back to the house, I had known I should make an effort to stop his cruelty. Yet I had known I would say nothing to him. And I was aware of the reason for this. It was because, secretly, I was afraid of him.

In the warm summer evenings when my work was over I would no longer go down to Berrima with Clint to wander round the pubs, for I felt a need to escape from him for at least a while. I would climb up the hillside to the wild, dense woods of eucalyptus, strolling vaguely in the half-light of the forest while I tried to regain the peace of mind I had known before Clint's arrival at Berrima, but which I had lost from the moment I acknowledged to myself the fact that I was afraid. Above me the rosella parrots would flash among the stiff leaves of the gum trees, and I would feel a sense of oldness in the wood with its thick undergrowth and eucalyptus trees, taller than masts, towering sombrely above me. Presently I would begin to wonder if the fear which had now invaded me was not only a specific terror of the cruelty I could feel inherent in Clint but part of a more general fear which might come from a sense of the vastness of the country I was living in—a land whose depths and mysterious emptiness had still remained untouched by men. The whole district of Australia where I lived was just a small plot in the immensity of the huge continent whose fringes only had been explored. Berrima, in fact, was merely a little paddock which had been carved out of the wilderness. Yet even here in the stillness of the early evening I had a feeling that as a human being I was an intruder in the forest. For these dense forests belonged to the pale ghostly trees and to the strange creatures that were hidden in them. Then, suddenly, I would jump as if a gun had been fired close to me, as the silence was rent by the piercing din of a kookaburra, screeching and screeching from the branches of a tree above, until the menacing sound changed to a mocking laugh. The low, hoarse laugh would seem unending. Abruptly it would finish in an obscene, deep-throated chuckle, which had an odd quality of knowingness and familiarity, suggesting an intimate awareness of the stark fear of the man walking through the undergrowth below, and a malicious pleasure at the prospect of some inevitable and terrible doom.

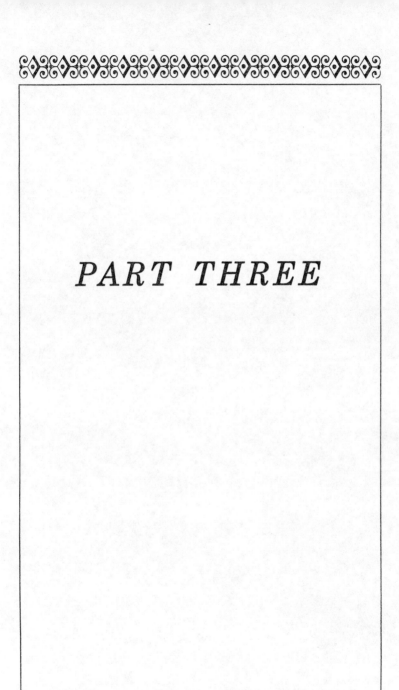

PART THREE

MARCH 20, 1862. It now seems certain that a lawsuit of some kind will arise from the events which occurred this morning. If the matter reaches Court, I am sure to be called as a witness. So I must write down this account.

––––––––

I awoke this morning very late, feeling ill and with a slight head-ache—which was unusual, because my constitution is excellent for a man of seventy. Then I remembered I had attended our regimental reunion in Nottingham the previous night, and had drunk a great deal. It is the custom to get drunk on such occasions, and I am a conventional person. Besides, I must confess I was moved by the fuss they made of me. When I was a young Ensign we wouldn't have bothered much with a retired Colonel. Perhaps, I reflected as I shaved myself, the young men of today have better manners than we had at the beginning of the century. Certainly the young labourers I employ on my little farm treat me in a most friendly manner, without any unnecessary deference but with sur-prising respect. (I notice I have written 'my' farm, but in fact I hold only a lease from the Steede estate—and that only through the good will of Charlotte, who is now the Dowager.)

By the time I had dressed I was feeling so much better that I even looked forward to my ham and eggs as I walked into the small dining-room. *The Times* was lying beside my breakfast plate and, as I unfolded it, suddenly I remembered what Charlotte had said when I'd dined with her at the Dower House three or four days previously. She had just returned from a fortnight's visit to her London house. Over dinner she had leaned forward to me, with one of her sudden impulses which made her interrupt even her own conversation, and she had asked me to make sure to read the Personal Column of *The Times* on Thursday. And then she had refused with her usual obstinacy, bless her, to appease my curiosity as to the reason. So this morning I scanned the column with care. Then I came across her ill-advised advertisement. I will transcribe it, word for word.

A handsome reward will be given to any person who can furnish such information as will discover the fate of James Edward Steede. He sailed from the port of Acapulco, Mexico, on the twenty-third of April, 1852, in the ship *Clara*, and has never been heard of since. But a report reached England to the effect that a portion of the crew and passengers of a vessel of that name was picked up by a ship bound for Australia—Melbourne, it is believed. It is not known whether the said James Steede was amongst the drowned or saved. He would at the present time be thirty-two years of age. He is the son of Sir William Steede, Bart., now deceased, and is heir to all his estates. All replies should be addressed to The Dowager Lady Steede, The Dower House, Steede, Nottinghamshire.

I sighed. I now understood the reason for Charlotte's mysterious little speech at dinner. Obviously she had realised that if she had consulted me about the advertisement I would have tried to dissuade her from inserting it. Equally, she had known I would have been offended if she had said nothing at all about the matter. Hence her strange behaviour. However, I was not surprised. I had known Charlotte long before she married William Steede—I had even been half in love with her myself for a while—so that by now I was aware she was a strange woman. I could forgive the latest manifestation of her almost insane conviction that her son Jamie Steede was still alive, but I very much doubted if Maude and Edmond would forgive her so readily. Maude—I must explain here —is the young widow of poor Arthur Steede, Charlotte's younger

son, who inherited the title and the estates when Jamie was presumed dead. Edmond Parker is Maude's brother. He moved into
the big house after Arthur's death to keep his sister company and
to help her manage the Steede estates which now bring in some
£30,000 a year. Edmond's family arrived in the county quite recently—only some fifteen years ago. But I'm afraid the Parkers
cannot by any standard be considered of much distinction. Nor
can their offspring. Edmond is a plump, nervous, unhealthy-
looking man of about thirty-four—a little older than Jamie if he
were still alive. He lacks poise and confidence; he is constantly
imagining that he's been slighted by some neighbour or by the
servants at Steede; and his nervous laugh is as irritating as his
arrogance. However, I must admit that for the last few years, since
Arthur's death from pleurisy, he has managed the estates shrewdly
and meticulously. It was to discuss matters concerning my farm
that I had been invited to the big house at noon this morning.

I looked out of the window. The pale sun of early spring was
shining from a clear sky. I decided to walk across the park, and
half an hour later I set out. It was a splendid morning. A light
breeze was ruffling the surface of the lake and stirring the clumps
of daffodils at the water's edge. As I gazed at the vast stretch of
park-land that rolled upward towards Steede Hall I wondered why
William Steede, my old friend, had been content to spend so
many years of his life abroad when he could have stayed at home
in the perfect beauty of his own property. I well know that he
used to quarrel with Charlotte. But after their two sons had been
born, husband and wife had contrived their life at Steede so that
they seldom met alone. How could William abide the heat and
vexations of life in India, when he could live so pleasantly at
home? Even during his years at Cambridge, William had always
proclaimed an interest in Oriental philosophy. But was that interest sufficient to make him neglect his wife and children and
allow his estates to fall into disorder while he travelled extravagantly in eastern lands? Or was it because—as he had once confided in me—he had in middle age grown tired of his adventures

with barmaids in the back streets of London and had developed a taste for young girls with dusky skins? We shall never know.

The house was now stretched out before me on the horizon. Steede Hall is an attractive though rambling building. The main block dates from 1700. However, the descendants of the second baronet who built it had added to his work according to their tastes. William's grandfather had joined an elegant pavilion to the west wing; William's father had built on a huge billiard-room beyond it; and William himself, on one of his few visits to Steede during the last ten years of his life, had constructed a vast conservatory on the east side of the house. Beneath that tall dome of glass he would sit in the damp heat which emanated from a complicated furnace below, admiring the tropical plants he had imported from the Orient which he now appeared to love more than his own home and family. His younger son, Arthur, even as a child had been moody, unassuming, and rather sickly. But in Jamie, with his fine looks and high spirits and grace of manner, he had an heir of whom any man should have been proud. But William displayed no more interest in Jamie than he did in his ill-managed estate. In fact, I probably saw as much of Jamie in his childhood as William did. And now both of them are dead.

Denham, the butler, must have seen me walking across the lawn, for he was waiting at the front door to greet me. He is a stout, good-natured man, with a brick-red, gleaming face. He greeted me warmly, and showed me into the morning-room. The room which had once been pleasant and unassuming was now, I considered, over-furnished. Heavy oil paintings in thick gilt frames hung over the ochre-painted panelling. The wing-backed chairs were covered in stiff brocade. Yellow velvet curtains, with deep-folded swags and massive gold tassels, drooped above the long French windows.

As I expected, Maude and her brother Edmond were sitting on either side of the fire-place and, as I feared, *The Times* lay unfolded on a table between them. Maude crossed the room to greet me. Once again I noticed how gracefully she moved and how well she wore her plain, well-cut dress. At twenty-five Maude was a handsome woman, but her charm was spoiled in my opinion by a peevish, rather disdainful expression.

"Have you read it?" she asked, pointing to the newspaper as we sat down. I nodded. I had hoped to be offered a drink before they began to discuss the advertisement. I was feeling very thirsty after my walk.

"She must have gone mad," Maude announced. "The *Clara* was wrecked ten years ago. All they found was a boat and some rafts. There wasn't a single survivor. Besides, if James is still alive, where does she think he's been these last ten years? And why has she only started advertising now?"

"I can see why—at least I think I can," Edmond said, raising his plump hand to stroke his cheek. "Even while Arthur was still alive she could only just bear to admit the possibility that her precious James might have been drowned. But now Arthur's dead it's very different. She's lost her power. So what does she do? She tries to make herself believe that James wasn't drowned. Why? Because if he were alive—if he came back from the dead—he'd be the baronet. He'd own this house and all the estates. And we'd be out."

Maude turned to me. "Can you believe for one moment that if James Steede had been alive, he wouldn't have come back to England when his father died?"

"I'm sure Jamie's dead," I answered. "There's no doubt of it in my mind."

"No doubt," Edmond repeated, fidgeting with his watch-chain. "No doubt whatsoever."

But I could sense that the advertisement had made them both slightly nervous, and I could sympathise with them. After all, if Jamie did "come back from the dead," Maude would lose a great deal. For a moment there was silence. Then I turned as the door opened and Charlotte came in and advanced with quick, light steps towards us.

Charlotte has kept herself very slim. The women of her generation were taught how to move with an appearance of naturalness which can be so graceful. This morning, however, Charlotte's bearing seemed deliberately stiff, and she seemed to be holding her head and shoulders unusually erect. Her white hair doesn't make her seem old—perhaps because it's so luxuriant. Only when you look at the wrinkles around her neck and when the light falls on her features do you remember she is over sixty-five years old.

Charlotte greeted the three of us with apparent cheerfulness, but I observed she noticed the copy of *The Times* on the table by the fire-place. Perhaps it was that—together with Edmond's openly sulky expression—which made her decide to be the first to put in her attack. She turned with a slight smile to Maude.

"Why have you been fussing poor Denham by telling him he should announce me each time I call here?" she asked. "Surely that's unnecessary?"

"I prefer Denham to announce all visitors," Maude said, smiling back calmly at her mother-in-law.

"Quite," said Charlotte. "However, I presume I can still visit my own son's house without being announced?"

Edmond cleared his throat. "With deference," he said with a nod of his large head, "I'm afraid I must point out that in fact and in law, of course, this is no longer your son's house. For both your sons are dead."

"Poor Arthur's dead," Charlotte answered. "But Jamie's not. I've never believed he was dead, and you know it."

Edmond picked up *The Times* between his finger and thumb, holding it away from him as if he was afraid he might be contaminated by its contents. "Is that the reason for this advertisement?" he asked.

"Exactly," Charlotte answered firmly.

Battle had now begun, and I yearned for a drink. My head had begun to ache again. Edmond advanced towards Charlotte.

"Didn't it occur to you," he asked in his soft voice, "to consult us before advertising to the world the fact you consider that Maude's child—your own grandson—has only a doubtful right to the title?"

"You'd never have put in that advertisement while Arthur was alive," Maude added.

"But I did," Charlotte answered. "Not in *The Times* certainly. But as soon as I heard the rumour that some survivors from the *Clara* had been rescued by another ship I advertised in the Australian papers. And Arthur knew I was doing so."

"Then why didn't he tell me?" Maude asked.

Charlotte flung back her head in surprise. "Tell you!" she exclaimed. "Why should he?"

"Because my husband told me everything," Maude stated.

Charlotte gave a little laugh. "My poor girl! How little you must have known Arthur to believe that! When he was ill who nursed him? Did you? No. I did—because you told him that he revolted you."

"I've always had a horror of drunkenness," Maude replied, her eyes glittering as her animosity to Charlotte began to kindle. "I couldn't control it."

"Arthur had a weakness for drink," Charlotte said, staring at Maude with her large, dark eyes. "But if you'd tried to understand him, you could have helped him. Instead, on your very wedding night you pushed him away. You said his reeking breath made you want to retch. Those were your words." Charlotte allowed herself a brief smile of triumph. "You see, Arthur did tell *me* everything."

"With respect," Edmond said, stroking his flabby cheek again, "I must suggest that Arthur showed you the side of him he wished you to see. Others were less fortunate. I'm certain you have no idea what Maude had to endure."

"Arthur was always gentle," Charlotte said quickly.

Maude shook her head. "I could have shown you proof of the contrary."

Charlotte turned to me. Her face was very white under her black bonnet. "Look at the pair of them, Ned!" she said to me. "Just look at them, glowering at me in disapproval. And why? Is it merely because I've put an innocent advertisement in a respectable paper? Of course it's not. Then why are they both so angry? I'll tell you. It's because they're afraid Jamie will appear one day to claim what belongs to him."

"No," Edmond replied, "we've no fear of that. We fear an intrusion of our privacy. Already Denham tells me that yet another man has been staying at the Bear, asking the landlord questions about the family. He can be expected to turn up here at any moment—or so I gather. And after your advertisement this morning I'm now afraid we shall be pestered by a series of impostors attracted by your advertisement like wasps to a pot of jam."

"I could deal with an impostor," Charlotte said. "Do you think I couldn't tell a fraud? Why—I'd recognise Jamie the instant I set eyes on him."

"One can change a lot in a dozen years," Edmond murmured.

I decided it was time to show Charlotte that even though I couldn't share her belief that Jamie was still alive, I was still on her side. "But the shape of your head and the shape of your hands don't change," I pointed out. "Your eyes, your voice, your smile —your whole personality—your expression and gestures, the way you stand, your tricks of speech and general mannerisms—they don't change."

"Besides," Charlotte added, "I believe I'd know him by instinct. If Jamie were in the same room—even if I couldn't see him—I believe I'd know."

Maude made an effort to control her irritation. "If you're so sure he's alive," she said brightly, "why do you think he hasn't come back?"

Charlotte's hands entwined as if each hand could find consolation in the other. "If only I knew!" she cried with a little moan of despair. "He could have lost his memory. He could be ill. If only I knew!"

Suddenly she rose from her chair, and I saw the grief in her eyes as she moved towards me. "Ned, call and see me at the Dower House on your way home, will you? There's a dear." I nodded, and she turned back to Maude and Edmond. "I'm sorry I can't stay," she said in a voice which sounded strangely bright. "I only called in to make sure of seeing Ned. It does me good to see a friend for a change." Then she turned and walked quickly from the room.

For a moment there was silence. Maude turned to me as the door closed. "Please, can't you help us? You're an old friend, and I know she respects you. Can't you use your influence to see she never puts in such a stupid notice again?"

"If I'd had any influence over your mother-in-law," I said, "I suppose I'd have married her forty years ago. But she'd set her heart on William Steede, and she's always got what she wanted."

"Without being able to keep it," Edmond added. "She couldn't keep her husband—he fled to India. And having lost him, she became so insanely possessive over her children she drove James abroad, and then she drove Arthur to drink. So in the end she lost them all."

His ill manners in attacking Charlotte in my presence enraged me.

"Talking of drink," I said, "I must confess I've a raging thirst."

"What can we offer you?" Maude asked, smiling at me with stiff lips.

"Could I have a brandy-and-soda?"

Maude crossed and pulled the bell-rope by the side-table.

"How's your son?" I asked.

Maude's face softened as I hoped it would. "He's growing out of all his clothes," she said. "I shall have to take him into Nottingham to buy some new ones next week."

"When are you going to let me teach him to ride?"

"Surely he's too young yet," Maude protested. "He's only eight."

"I had my first lesson when I was six," I said, and I began telling them about my early days in London when I was taken out by my father's drunken groom into Hyde Park. But I could see that neither of them was interested. And after Denham had brought in a decanter of brandy and some soda and I had been given the drink I had been longing for since I arrived, I was not surprised when Edmond interrupted my reminiscences to discuss the affairs of the Lower Farm, which, as I have said, I held as tenant from the Steede estate. During the period of bad management while William was living extravagantly in the Orient, the farm had been mortgaged; steps were now being taken to pay off the debt. I have no liking for Edmond, but I must confess he has a clear head for business matters. As a young man he studied law, and he was called to the Bar. But he has never practised—some say because of idleness; others believe it is because he's too conceited to risk failure. However, his legal training was useful this morning, and we soon completed our discussion, which I admit was rather one-sided, for Edmond did most of the talking and didn't trouble to disguise his conviction that though I may have had some ability as a soldier, I am neither a good farmer nor an an intelligent businessman—which I suppose is true. Presently we began to talk about public schools. The discussion arose from their uncertainty as to whether Maude's son, young Richard, should be put down for Eton. Here, of course, I knew my ground.

"It depends what house he goes to," I said. "In some houses where the tutor's a bit old or lax, the boys undergo bullying and privations far worse than any cabin-boy. Cruelty's infectious, and I've known some lads ruined for life by it."

"Isn't that the same in any public school?" Edmond asked. "I was at Repton, and the bullying was quite savage. I was once even made to eat a tallow-candle as a sandwich," he added with a giggle.

Once two men begin to talk about their schooldays, the conversation never falters. Time slipped by as we spoke of masters and sixth-formers we had known, and I was finishing my third brandy-and-soda and preparing to leave when the door opened and Maude's maid Harriet came in, looking even more mournful and haggard than usual.

"There's a gentleman waiting downstairs in the hall to see you, m'lady," she said to Maude.

"What does he want?" Maude asked.

"He says it's a personal matter and it's most important he should see your ladyship."

"Can't Denham find out his business?" Edmond asked.

"Mr Denham has gone to deliver a parcel for her ladyship," Harriet answered in a tone of disapproval.

"Gone to get himself a drink at the Bear more like," said Edmond. "What's the man's name?"

"He wouldn't give his name," Harriet replied.

"It's almost certain to be this person who's been staying in the village," Edmond muttered.

"In that case," I said, "I think that perhaps you should see him."

Maude turned to her brother. "Do *you* think I should see him?" she asked.

"I consider it would be most unwise at this stage," Edmond answered.

But we had no chance to discuss the matter. For as Edmond spoke, a young man appeared in the doorway behind Harriet and stood looking in at us for a moment before walking into the room. His clothes were clean but shabby, and although the style of his coat and waistcoat and trousers was quite ordinary, there was something foreign in his appearance. The man was in his early thirties, I reckoned. He was slender yet he was strongly built. But it was his face that held my attention. The pale hair and very light blue eyes set well apart, the short straight nose and the mouth that curled up at the ends—the likeness to Jamie was obvious, and I stared at him in amazement. For a moment there was silence. Harriet was still lingering by the door.

"Thank you, Harriet," Maude said in a voice pitched higher than usual. "You may go."

As the door closed, the stranger moved towards Maude with a smile. "Lady Steede?" he asked quietly. "Yes, that's right. You must be Arthur's widow—you were only a young girl when I left, so I don't suppose you'd remember me. Good morning to you."

Immediately I noticed the slight twang in his accent. As Maude stared at the stranger in silence, he turned towards Edmond. "But I know your brother quite well," he said, giving Edmond a brief nod. Then he advanced towards me with a warm smile of recognition. "Colonel Savage," he exclaimed; "I didn't expect to find you here. I'm so glad. How are you, sir?"

I examined him in silence. I was unwilling to speak because at that particular moment, for reasons which I now find it hard to explain, I was convinced I had never met him before. Perhaps it was his accent, perhaps it was some instinct. The young man was gazing at me in surprise.

"Don't you recognize me?" he asked. "But you must. I can't have changed so much." Then, as I continued to watch him in silence, he began to speak in his quiet, easy voice. "Don't you remember teaching me to ride?" he asked. "What was the pony called? Midget—that was the name. Remember when I fell off in the drive and you were afraid I'd broken my leg? And then, when Midget got too small for me, do you remember driving into Nottingham and buying that mare? What was the name now? My memory's completely gone to pieces, but I can remember she jumped wonderfully and always shied at anything white. Blossom. That was the name. And you used to ride a chestnut called Nestor."

He may have said more. I have put down what I can remember. The important thing to record here is that every single detail he gave *at that stage* was correct. However, for some reason I still remained unconvinced. Perhaps it was because he seemed to be a stronger, heartier person than Jamie had been. Yet life abroad might well have coarsened him. I must have shaken my head, for he gave me a smile as if I had spoken.

"But certainly I am," he said. "I've come back at last." Then he turned round to Maude. "Allow me to introduce myself," he said. "I'm your brother-in-law. I'm James Steede."

Maude put her hand to her mouth, which was quivering. Then she looked desperately towards her brother. Edmond shook his head. "No," Edmond said after a pause, "you're certainly not James Steede."

"You were quite pleased to be able to call me your friend a dozen years ago," the man answered.

"I have never seen you before in my life," Edmond announced firmly.

"Don't you remember begging me to get you invited to the

ball at Flintham?" the man asked. "Can't you remember how excited you were the first time I took you to dine at Greville House?"

Edmond's face was now swollen and flushed. "I dine there frequently," he replied angrily.

"During the last few years—perhaps," the man answered in his placid voice with its faint twang. "But *then* you hadn't. You'd only just moved into the county, and you were anxious to get accepted."

Edmond winced. "I can assure you that I didn't need the help of James Steede or anyone else to get accepted, as you put it," he said.

The man looked at him contemptuously. "Then your memory must be even worse than mine." He smiled. "And you haven't had a head injury."

Edmond raised his head and drew in his stomach as he always does when he tries to assume dignity. Then he lifted his flaccid hand. "I am afraid I must ask you to leave," he announced.

The man did not move. He remained standing at ease, with his weight nicely balanced on his two feet. "But you don't seem to realise," he replied. "Now that I'm back, this house doesn't belong to your sister. It belongs to me." Suddenly he swung round and faced me. "Colonel Savage," he said, "for reasons of his own Edmond Parker doesn't wish to recognise me. But you can, can't you?"

I looked down at the carpet as I tried to recall the young man of twenty-one who had left England a dozen years ago—a young man with a pale complexion and absurdly pale hair, a young man who was almost girlishly shy at times with strangers, and who was always reserved and secretive, even with his family and friends. Then I looked at the wiry, sunburned, confident young man who was gazing at me hopefully. The features were alike. But still I hesitated.

"I'm sorry," I answered. "But I'm afraid that as yet I can't say I do recognise you."

"But aren't I the same height?" he asked. "Aren't my eyes the same? And my hair and forehead? Aren't my hands the same?"

"If you're Jamie Steede," I answered, "you've changed a great deal."

"But everyone changes in twelve years," he pointed out. "You've changed, sir—if you don't mind me saying so. Your hair's gone grey, and you've begun to stoop. Edmond Parker's changed. He's lost nearly all his hair, and he's put on weight. But I'd still recognise him—the fat slug."

I saw Edmond move towards the bell-rope. I decided the time had come for me to exert some authority. "One moment," I said to Edmond in what Charlotte calls my parade-ground voice. Then I turned to the newcomer. "I admit that if you're James Steede, you've cause for annoyance at not being recognised as such. But as you must realise, rudeness won't help. So listen to me. I'm in no way disposed against you. However, I can't say you've convinced me. For one thing, your voice is different."

The man smiled at me cheerfully. "But I've been in Australia for the last ten years," he said. "Naturally during that time I've picked up a bit of an accent."

"The fact remains I don't recognise you," I continued firmly. "But obviously you must be given a chance to justify your claim —as I'm sure Lady Steede and her brother agree. If we find your claim to be James Steede is false, if you're an impostor, you must be aware that our only course will be to hand you over to the police. If you're in truth James Steede, then it's for you to prove it."

"But how can I prove it?" the man asked. "I've no birthmark. I've no deformity, no scar from any operation. I can only swear to you that I am James Steede. Look!" he cried suddenly. "I can give you this proof." And he held out his left hand towards me. On his little finger was a signet ring. "Do you recognise that?" he asked. "You must."

I examined the ring. It was an obsidian set in gold, and on it was an engraving of a Roman gladiator which I recognised immediately. The ring had belonged to Jamie's grandfather, who had left it to the boy in his will.

"That ring certainly belonged to Jamie," I said.

"But what proof is that?" Edmond asked, peering with disappointment at the ring. "James might have lost his ring or even sold it."

"You still don't believe me," the man said. "You think I'm a fraud?"

"At the moment I'm not sure," I answered quickly, before Edmond could speak. "But I'm willing to be convinced, and it's not very difficult. If you're James Steede, you'll obviously be able to answer questions about your life here in this house before you left England."

"Of course I will. In fact, I'll answer any questions you care to ask me," the Claimant—as I shall now call him—replied. "The more, the better."

So then my cross-examination began. I will put down my questions and the Claimant's answers as best as I can remember them.

"Where did you go to school?" was my first question.

"Brierly Lodge," he answered without hesitation. "When I was nine."

"In your second term did anything unusual happen?"

"Yes," he said with a smile. "I ran away from school. But I was sent back after a week, and I got a caning."

"After Brierly, what school did you go to?"

"Eton, when I was twelve."

"What was your house?" I asked.

"House?" he repeated vaguely.

"What was the name of your housemaster?"

"Jackson," he answered promptly. "We called him Quackie Jack."

"What colours did you get?"

"None," he said. "As you know, I was never much good at games."

"How old were you when you left Eton?"

"Seventeen. Then of course I went to Trinity, Cambridge."

"What was the name of your best friend there?"

"Michael Fairley. I heard he died of pneumonia the year after I went abroad."

"What was the name of your tutor?"

"My tutor?" he repeated, once again looking blank.

"Your tutor at Cambridge," I explained.

"Let me think," he said. "Was it Crawford? No, I'm afraid I can't remember."

"Surely you can remember the name of your tutor?" I asked.

"I've been hit on the head, I tell you," he replied. "My memory's hopeless."

"Yet you could remember Michael Fairley," I pointed out.

"That was different," he explained. "I could never forget a friend like him."

"What was the name of your first hunter?"

"Punch," he replied—once again correctly. "He was a black gelding, and a fair bastard. He bolted with me first time out."

"Did you win any steeplechases with him?"

"No. But I came second in the Grantham Cup," he answered. "You ought to know because you came first," he added, smiling.

"Look at me," I ordered.

The Claimant walked up and stared straight at me. His expression reminded me of Jamie, but at close range his complexion seemed darker and coarser. Yet I suppose ten years beneath the sun of the Antipodes could account for the change.

"If you're not James Steede, you know a lot about him," I said. "You've certainly got the same eyes."

"Are you still not sure?" he asked in surprise.

I hesitated. It's a shock when a person you've thought was dead ten years ago suddenly walks into the room, and I was confused. "I may be doing you a great injustice," I said. "But I'm not sure, though I can't imagine why. You must give me time to think."

"Would you remember my writing?" he asked.

"I think I could remember Jamie's writing," I replied cautiously.

The Claimant strode across to the writing-table, pulled out a pen and a piece of paper and scribbled on it. Then he brought the paper back to me. I examined it carefully, and then handed it to Edmond. "It's very like Jamie's signature, I confess," I said.

Edmond was silent.

"Why do you hesitate?" the Claimant asked.

"I don't really know," I answered. "I admit I may be doing you a terrible wrong."

Edmond had once again raised his head and pulled in his stomach. He now moved towards the Claimant. "Do you mind if I put you a few questions?" he enquired.

"No," the Claimant answered. "Provided I don't think they're insolent."

"Are you the person who's been staying for the past two days at the Bear?" Edmond asked.

The Claimant hesitated. "Yes," he answered after a slight pause.

"You spent a long time alone with Blaker, the landlord, didn't you?" Edmond asked.

"Yes," the Claimant admitted.

"The Blakers have lived over thirty years in this village, I believe," Edmond continued. I could see he fancied himself as a Counsel—even though he had never practised. "Is that correct?" he asked.

The Claimant nodded.

"So they would have known James Steede as a child?"

"They know me very well," the Claimant answered.

"Mrs Blaker is dead," Edmond continued.

"I was sad to hear it," the Claimant said.

"Did Blaker recognise you?" Edmond asked casually.

"Not at first," the Claimant replied. "In fact not until this morning."

"But I daresay he finally did recognise you," Edmond continued in his smooth voice, "after you'd prompted his memory and helped his conscience along with a little money." And he turned to Maude with a smug smile.

"I think that's enough," the Claimant said, glaring at him. "I'll have no more questions from you."

Maude had been examining the Claimant with a constant intensity from the moment he came into the room, noting each movement he made, each turn of his head, each flicker of his hands, as if a slight gesture might betray him. She now moved graciously towards him. "Will you answer me a question?" she asked. "Why did you stay two days at the local inn? Why didn't you come straight to this house?"

"I wanted to see how the land lay," the Claimant answered with an odd flash of amusement.

"You mean you wanted time to pick up every piece of information you could get hold of," Edmond said. Then he turned round to me. "Don't you see that he could have found out the answers to all your questions from that garrulous old fool Blaker?" he asked.

"Could I have found out about Michael Fairley?" the Claimant asked.

"Why not?" Edmond said. "Fairley came here to stay, didn't he?"

"And Quackie Jack?" I asked.

"Obviously James made no secret of the nickname," Edmond answered.

Suddenly I thought of some more questions to put. "Why did you come here this morning?" I asked the man. "Why didn't you go first to the Dower House to see your mother?"

"I did go to see my mother," he answered. "But when I called at the Dower House I was told she'd come up here."

I now came to my most important question. "The ship *Clara* on which James Steede was a passenger sailed from Acapulco on the twenty-third of April, eighteen-fifty-two," I said. "A week later one of her long-boats and some rafts were found floating derelict. That was ten years ago. Since then we've had no news of any definite kind from any survivor. How do you explain that not a single survivor has appeared in all this time?"

The Claimant—as I shall continue to call him—smiled at me with a look of surprising gratitude. "I've been waiting to explain all that," he said. "But you haven't given me much chance. You see, I was the only passenger. We were bound for Lima. There was a crew of about eighteen. She was a three-masted schooner of some three hundred and fifty tons. She was old, but she'd looked sound enough to me as she lay in harbour. All went well until the fifth night after we'd left harbour—when a storm blew up. I've never known anything like it. One moment it was calm, though she was rolling a bit. The next moment great waves were crashing down over us, and the whole ship was shaking. I was in the wheel-house having a drink with the Captain when it started. It was like some terrible nightmare. I can hardly remember anything more that happened that night."

"Why can't you remember?" I asked him.

"To be quite honest, because I was drunk," he replied. (I should state here that of course I'm now putting down his words as well as I can remember them.) "I have a perfect horror of the sea," the Claimant continued. "I was half drunk even before the weather started getting bad. When the storm broke, I finished another bottle. I was in a haze. I can remember the Mate coming in and saying that the ship had sprung a leak and was filling with water —and the Captain ordering all hands to work at the pumps. Then I was on deck, and they were lowering the boats. The *Clara* carried a long-boat on deck and two smaller boats slung from davits on either side. One of the smaller boats was stove in and useless. The Captain took charge of the long-boat. He ordered the Mate to get me into the smaller one. I was clambering into it, when a spar broke loose and came crashing down on my head. I was knocked out. In fact, I was unconscious for over twenty-four hours."

"Conveniently enough," said Edmond. But the Claimant did not appear to hear him. His mind seemed far away in the darkness and storm of the Pacific—or in a world of his own imagining.

"When I came round," he continued, "I was in the small boat with four members of the crew. They told me that the Mate had gone down with the ship and the long-boat had been lost in the storm. We were drifting with the wind. We'd enough provisions, but we were running short of water. One of the kegs had leaked in the night. We were getting frantic with thirst. On the morning of the fourth day after the *Clara* had sunk, one of the crew spotted a ship on the horizon. He was wearing a red shirt. He tore it off and tied the sleeve to an oar and hoisted it as a signal. I shall never forget the suspense as we waited and prayed the ship would see it. At last they changed course and made towards us. I was pretty weak by the time we were rescued, and for a time I was seriously ill on board the ship that saved me. You see, I had bad concussion. That's why my memory's so poor."

"What was the name of the ship you say rescued you?" I asked.

"The *Clio*," he said. "She was bound for Australia. We landed at the port of Melbourne early in July."

"With the four members of the crew from the *Clara?*" Edmond asked.

"No," he replied. "One of them had died. He was only seventeen too, poor devil."

"And what happened then?" I asked him.

"The three of them caught the gold mania," he answered. "They went off to the gold-diggings. Around eighteen-fifty in Australia whole crews used to desert from their ships and go off inland to make their fortune or die of starvation," he explained.

"Are the three men still alive?" Edmond asked.

"I don't know," he answered. "I suppose so."

"Then why didn't one of them answer the advertisement which was inserted in the papers out there?"

"What advertisement?" the Claimant asked.

"Lady Steede inserted a notice in various Australian papers offering a reward to anyone who could give information about her son," I explained.

"We seldom got papers where I was," the Claimant answered. "And I wager they seldom read one at the gold-diggings. You obviously don't know what the country's like. But there's another reason why none of the three men of the crew would have answered the advertisement. Only the Captain of the *Clara* knew my name. I'd had to leave Acapulco in a hurry because I was in debt. I was short of ready cash. In fact, when I landed at Melbourne I'd almost nothing except the clothes I stood up in."

"Why didn't you communicate with your family?" I asked. "They'd have sent you money quickly enough."

Once again he gave me a grateful smile as if I'd done him a favour. "Well, that's just it," he said. "Now comes the part I realise I'm going to have a hard time making you believe. You see, there I was with almost nothing but the clothes I was wearing—nothing in Australia, I mean. And no one knew—or cared—that I was James Steede. And suddenly I thought to myself, 'If I'm really worth anything in life, if I'm really a man, I'd make good on my own—without wealth and a title eventually and a great estate, and all the trappings that go with it.' Well, I was walking round the the town at the time, and I'd strolled into a yard where a lot of horses were being sold. Presently a man came up and asked me if I was interested in horses. I said I was. He asked me if I was a good rider. I said I wasn't too bad. Then he told me he was a stock-keeper, and his name was Dimmock. And then and there he offered me a job breaking in horses. He explained that the man who used to work for him had gone off to the gold-diggings. So I took the job. I left with him for Albury the next day. And that was the beginning of it all."

"You lived all this time without communicating with your mother?" I asked.

The Claimant stared down at his feet and sighed. At that moment he reminded me very much of Jamie as a child. After he had been scolded, Jamie would stand with his head lowered in the same way, his expression half-contrite, half-defiant.

"You'll never know how often I longed to let her know I was all right," he said. "But what could I do? I knew that if my mother found out I was alive, she'd never rest until she got me back. And she'd have spared no expense or effort to do it. I suppose I was selfish—I don't know. Somehow, out there, when I looked back on my life in England, it was like looking through the wrong end of a telescope. It all seemed so small. It just didn't seem to matter."

"Did you 'make good', as you put it?" I asked.

"No," he said, "but I've had some wonderful years."

"Why did you suddenly decide to return?" Maude asked. "Because you'd been a failure, I presume."

"I came back because I wanted to see my mother before she died," he answered. "And I was homesick."

"You realised, of course, that you'd be presumed dead and that the title would pass to your brother," I said. "Did you know Arthur had married and got a son? Did you know that he'd died and the title had passed to young Richard?"

"Not until I got here," he replied.

"And how did you find that out?" Edmond asked.

"From Blaker at the Bear, to be sure," the Claimant answered.

Immediately the phrase caught my attention. Until now the way he spoke had prejudiced me against him. His sentences and terms of speech seemed far less polished than Jamie's had been. However, the phrase 'to be sure' had been one of Jamie's pet expressions. He would add it to the end of a sentence so often that we used to tease him about his affectation. I now began to believe I had been mistaken in believing the man was an impostor. The expression of his face was like Jamie, and so were his gestures. Suddenly I thought of a test which I knew would satisfy me. It was something that occurred in Jamie's childhood which only his mother and I knew about.

"If you're James Steede," I said, "tell me what happened on the morning of your ninth birthday."

"My ninth birthday," he exclaimed. "That's quite a time ago!"

"It's something you never could forget."

"I've had a bad head injury, remember."

"Then let me help you a little," I said. "What was the name of your nurse?"

"Agnes, but I used to call her Aggie," he answered—again accurately. "She was quite young—less than thirty. She came from London, I remember. She had wonderful hair."

"What colour?"

"Dark."

"Can you remember something to do with Agnes and your mother's room and something yellow?" He looked quite blank. "At the end, your mother and I had to apologise to you," I added.

"No," he said after a long pause. "I can't remember. It's my wretched memory."

"You'd just come back from riding," I continued slowly. "You came into this very room we're in now. Your mother and I were having tea."

For an instant he raised his head, and I was delighted and thankful, for by now I had taken a liking to him, and I wanted to be convinced he was Jamie. But then he looked away in defeat.

"No," he said. "I give up. I've completely forgotten whatever it was."

I was now confused, and I felt it my duty to confess as much to Maude and Edmond. "I don't understand," I said. "He gets most of it right—Agnes with her black hair, for instance. Yet he can't remember the essential event."

"What did happen on his ninth birthday?" Maude asked me.

"Lady Steede discovered that five sovereigns were missing from a purse she had left in her room," I explained. "Jamie had been there earlier in the day. Five pounds was the price of a small rifle he'd seen in a shop in Nottingham. His mother had refused to give him the money to buy it because she was afraid he'd hurt himself. We accused Jamie of stealing the money, and he was beaten. Later it was discovered that Agnes had stolen it. She was dismissed and sent straight back to London. She died a few years later."

The Claimant, who had been standing silent by the French windows, gazing at the park spread out in the spring sunshine like a green cloth, now swung round.

"Heavens, but I remember now!" he exclaimed. "Poor Agnes! I remember how I cried when she left."

"But you couldn't remember a thing about it just now," Maude was quick to point out. "How could James Steede possibly forget such an incident?"

"I can't remember everything," he protested. "I've told you so. My memory's been patchy ever since I was hit on the head. I can remember some things but not others."

Edmond pulled in his stomach, which had begun to bulge

again. "Colonel Savage," he said, "unless you have any further questions you wish to put, I intend to ask this man to leave."

The Claimant came up to me. He tried to smile. "You can't let them throw me out," he said, forcing his voice to sound casual.

I decided it was wiser to plead with Maude than with Edmond, who was now frowning impatiently and fiddling with his watch-chain. "Surely we should wait?" I suggested to her gently. "If he's James Steede there's obviously one person who'll be certain to know him, and that's his mother." I turned back to the Claimant. For the first time since he had arrived he now seemed uneasy. "What message did you leave at the Dower House when you called there?" I asked him.

"I told the maid—she's some girl I've never seen before, incidentally—I told her to say a man had called who'd just come back from Australia with news of her son. You see, I didn't want the shock to be too sudden. So I didn't give my name, but I left a message with the girl saying I'd gone up to the big house."

"Then you can be certain Lady Steede will come back here," I said. "Do you believe she'll recognise you?"

"Recognise me? Of course she will," he answered. "The instant she sees me. Before I've even opened my mouth. I'm sure of it. She's my mother. She must."

"Before you've even spoken?" Maude asked him. "Before you've told her who you are?"

"Certainly," the Claimant replied.

Maude was sliding her hands together, as she does when she has a decision to make. Then she crossed the room and pulled the bell-rope. "If Lady Steede is coming back, we need warning of her arrival," she explained. "I don't want him talking when she comes into the room. I don't want her recognition to be prompted. He's said she will recognize him before he even speaks. Then let him be silent, and let's see what happens."

As she finished speaking, the Claimant took a step forward. His eyes were gleaming; he seemed to have regained his confidence. "I can tell you something I could only know if I were

James Steede," he announced. "That bell you've just pulled rings in the butler's pantry. The bell hangs above the sink."

"Even there you're wrong," Maude said. "It rings in the servants' hall."

The Claimant examined her face for a while in silence and smiled. "Excuse me, but I really don't think so," he began. Then he paused as the door opened and Denham came in. Immediately the Claimant sprang forward in greeting. "Denham!" he cried out. "How are you?" Denham looked at him in consternation and was silent. "Don't you recognise me?" the Claimant asked.

"No, sir," Denham said. "I can't say I do."

"You came as footman a few months before I went abroad," the Claimant said. He now spoke quite slowly, and his forehead was wrinkled. Each sentence he spoke was obviously an effort for him. "Old Lucas was butler then. You'd had a place in London but your chest was bad, so you came north to get out of the fog. Do you still not recognise me?"

"No, sir."

"Don't you remember bringing me an extremely important letter one night?"

Denham stared at him for a moment longer, then he gave a small gasp and rushed forward to the Claimant and clasped his hand. "You're back," he blurted out. "You've come back after all this time! Forgive me for not recognising you first go, sir. But I just didn't think I'd ever see you again. We'd all given you up for lost."

The Claimant swung round to us. His face was now radiant; he had scored at last. He flung out his arm in excitement, then smiled apologetically and turned back to Denham. "It's fine to see you again," he said. "How's life treated you? Are you married?"

"Not yet, sir," Denham answered, grinning fondly at him. "But there's plenty of time."

"How's the chest?"

"It's got better, sir. Especially now they've moved the servants' hall to the south side of the house—much drier it is. I've nothing to complain about."

"Where does the bell from this room ring now?"

"In the servants' hall," Denham answered, looking rather surprised at the question.

"But where used it to ring?"

"In the butler's pantry."

"Thank you, Denham," the Claimant said. Then he turned in triumph to face us. He now looked far younger, and he was breathing quickly. He reminded me of Jamie as a boy when he had won a race at school. "Now do you believe me?" he asked us.

I looked at the pair of them. Maude's face was white, and her hands were writhing nervously. Edmond was glaring at Denham accusingly as if he were now the impostor. Maude was the quickest to recover from her enemy's first success.

"Denham," she said in a cool, high-pitched voice, "we think that Lady Steede may be returning here shortly. When she comes, will you please be certain to announce her. And under no circumstances say anything about our unexpected visitor—not a word. We want to break the news to her gently."

"I understand, milady," Denham said. Then he turned, and he was moving towards the door when Edmond spoke. "Denham, you're quite a friend of Blaker's, aren't you?" he asked. "So you knew there was a stranger staying at the Bear?"

"Yes, sir."

"And you knew that he had come from Australia?" Edmond was playing his role of a Queen's Counsel once again.

"No, sir, because I haven't been down there for a day or so," Denham answered. "But I'd heard there was a stranger staying."

"However, you do go quite often to the Bear," Edmond persisted. "So I suppose you told Blaker that the servants' hall had been moved to the room facing the orangery?"

"Yes, sir, I think I did."

"And I expect Blaker has come over here to visit you from time to time, hasn't he? In the days when the bell still rang in the butler's pantry?"

"Yes, sir."

"I thought as much," Edmond said as he looked at us and smiled with satisfaction.

Denham moved away slowly towards the door. Then he hesitated and stopped. "Excuse me," he said, turning round to the Claimant, "but what's the reason for all these questions? Is there something wrong, sir?"

"Yes," the Claimant answered. "Something very wrong."

"Anything I can do to help, sir?"

"Nothing at present. But you may be able to help me a great deal later. I'm grateful to you."

"Denham," Maude said in a quiet voice of authority, "you may go."

As Denham looked at her, I saw a flash of contempt in his face. But an instant later his expression was as deferential as usual, and it was the note of deference in his voice which made the implication of his words so definite. "Excuse me," he said, "but from now on I shall be taking my orders from Sir James."

Maude flinched and put up a hand to cover her mouth. Edmond's heavy face was scowling. I decided I must intervene.

"Denham," I said, "I think it only fair to tell you we're not yet satisfied that this gentleman is indeed the James Steede we all knew."

"You, Denham, certainly failed to recognise him," Edmond announced, trying to exude conviction into his tone of voice.

"I'm sorry, sir, but that's not true," Denham answered. "I did recognise him."

"Not until he'd prompted your memory," I pointed out.

"But you must know him, sir," Denham protested.

"I wish I could say I did," I answered. "I'm not certain."

"But I don't understand, sir," Denham began and then stopped. He was staring in the direction of the French windows which were half open. We turned in silence, and through the windows we saw Charlotte walking across the lawn. She looked quite small and frail with the park-land spreading across the whole horizon behind her, and in the bright sunlight her bonnet and cape looked jet black. The Claimant had also turned and seen her. He now stood tensely. But it was the expression of his face which surprised me. For if he were an impostor, I expected him to betray nervousness, even fear; and if he were her son, I expected him to display excitement and affection, even love. But I can only describe the expression of his uplifted face as being openly defiant.

Steadily, with her quick, light steps, Charlotte approached and pushed open the window and moved into the silent room. No one spoke, and she stared at us in astonishment. Then she saw the newcomer, and she stood still. The Claimant was standing facing the windows so that the light fell directly onto his head, which was raised in defiance. Charlotte looked at him, then moved a few steps closer to him and stopped again, staring at him with her intense, dark eyes. But he did not move, nor did his expression alter as she gazed at him. Then Charlotte swayed slightly and gave a little cry. I was afraid she would faint. But in an instant she had controlled herself, and her head was erect and her shoulders were stiff.

"Jamie," she said to him in a whisper so low we could hardly hear it. "My Jamie—you've come back to me."

Then, at last, the Claimant moved. Slowly he lowered his head and walked across the room and took her hands.

"Please forgive me," he said.

But I'm not sure if Charlotte heard his words. Certainly she did not appear to listen. She was examining his face and his clothes, now glancing down at his hands, now fixing her attention on his forehead and hair or the collar of his coat. It was as if she were more interested in his physical presence than in his attitude or speech. And for a while the two of them remained in silence, facing each other. Then Charlotte raised her hand and touched his cheek.

"I knew you were alive," she said. "I knew you'd come back." Suddenly she turned to the three of us. "I told you, didn't I?" she proclaimed. "I told you." Her large eyes were glittering, her lips were parted. She was in a kind of wild ecstasy.

Knowing her stubbornness, I realised that if she persisted in her belief that the Claimant was Jamie, nothing would dissuade her from it in the days to come. "Charlotte," I said gently, "you've only just seen this man. Oughtn't you to put him a few questions? Oughtn't you to make absolutely sure before coming to any definite decision?"

"Are you suggesting I don't know my own son?" Charlotte asked.

"I'm suggesting you shouldn't be carried away by a sudden shock which may only have been caused by a surprising resemblance," I said.

"Do you mean to tell me that you, Ned, of all people, don't recognise him?" she asked.

I tried to explain that even though Denham, who was, of course, still in the room, had eventually recognised the man as Jamie, I could not yet state in honesty that I was wholly convinced. I found it embarrassing to have to make this statement in the Claimant's presence, but there was no hostility in his attitude towards me. In fact, while I spoke he looked at me with an expression of sympathy and understanding. And this confused me still more, because if he were an impostor, surely he would have every reason to dislike me, and if he were Jamie Steede, surely he would be annoyed—to say the least—that an old family friend should refuse to recognise him?

Edmond lifted a flabby hand when I had finished my explanation. "As you're aware, I knew your son well," he said to Charlotte. "Both Maude and I are convinced he's an impostor."

"Maude was only a child when Jamie went abroad," Charlotte answered. "She can only have met him once or twice. And you both have good reason to believe he's an impostor. That will be obvious to everyone."

"Has Colonel Savage any reason not to recognise him?" Maude asked.

"Colonel Savage has not said he doesn't recognise him," Charlotte answered. "He's said that as yet he is not wholly convinced.

It seems that Denham, however, is convinced. Is that correct, Denham?"

"Yes, milady," he replied. "Very convinced."

"Then if the Colonel still persists in his ridiculous uncertainty, that makes two of us who believe in him, and two who don't—for reasons of their own," Charlotte said, her eyes still glittering in a kind of triumph. "But allow me to tell you this. In a Court of Law, it will be my word which will count. It will be my evidence as his mother which they will believe. And I call you to witness—all four of you—I call you to witness that I recognised my son at the very moment I first saw him."

———————

The prospect of a lawsuit is unpleasant. But if Maude and Edmond refuse to accept the Claimant as James Steede, I don't see how it can be avoided, for nothing will now alter Charlotte's mind—or Denham's for that matter. And I am in the odd position of a witness who may be called by either side, because if I am to remain honest, I must—until some new evidence convinces me one way or the other—persist in what Charlotte calls my "ridiculous uncertainty."

According to Edmond, it will be the Claimant who will have to bring an action against the present baronet—young Richard—who, of course, being legally an infant, will be represented by his mother and by Edmond, his guardian and a trustee of the estate.

The Court will certainly have to examine the present events in the light of the past, and I fear that in the course of examining the recent past of the Steede family, many things will be uncovered which should have remained discreetly buried. . . .

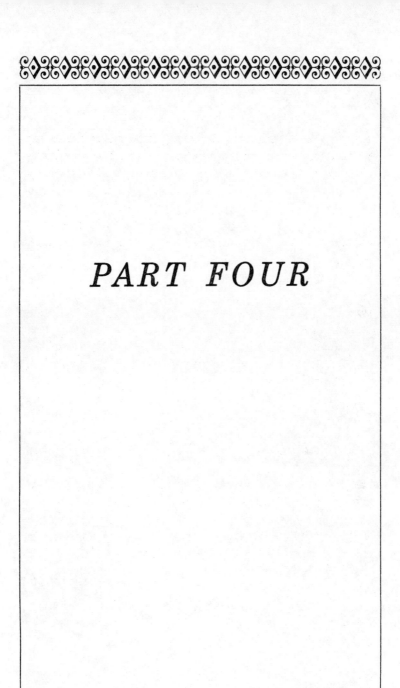

PART FOUR

I HAVE an instinct which tells me if my firm should handle a case or not; and over the years I have discovered I am seldom wrong. Therefore I trust my instinct—even when poor Cradwell, who is really more my figure-head than my partner, scrapes his bony fingers nervously through those thick white locks of his which impress clients so pleasantly and warns me I'm mistaken.

When an agent of the Dowager Lady Steede approached our firm, early in June, 1862, my first thought was that things must be going very badly for the Claimant—as the press had decided to call him. I'd already heard that Anderson and Strutt had refused to act for him any longer because they didn't think he stood a good enough chance of winning, and they were afraid of him going bankrupt. It was obvious to them that the Claimant himself hadn't a penny; his case was being financed by the Dowager Lady Steede, who was a woman of means with a house in Belgrave Square and an annuity left her by her lucky father, beneath whose dilapidated estate in Derby rich seams of coal had been found in abundance. But wealthy ladies are apt to be capricious, and if the Dowager abandoned the Claimant he would be finished within twenty-four hours, for I was certain that it was only her widely known conviction that the Claimant was her son which had persuaded one or two of James Steede's old friends at Eton and Cambridge to recognise him. The rest of them had pronounced the Claimant an impostor after they had met him and talked with him for a while, and their evidence against him would be most useful to the defendants when the case came to Court. So Anderson and Strutt had given up.

But there is a wide range of solicitors between Anderson and Strutt and the firm of Tuke and Cradwell, so I presumed it was because she had been politely turned down by a dozen other firms that the Dowager's agent had approached me—unless, for some reason, the Dowager had decided that the slightly unorthodox methods my firm sometimes uses might be needed. However, my instinct told me there was something strange about the case in general, and something rather interesting about it so far as I was concerned in particular. So I told the agent that my firm would be pleased to act for the Claimant, and a few days later the Dowager consented to visit our office in Chancery Lane. My clerk met her at the door, introduced Cradwell to her as they passed the front office—he bowed his white head to her as if she were royalty—and led her along the corridor to my office at the far end, where all the important business is done. The Dowager is a small, dignified woman of spirit and unusual determination, with large eyes from which gleams a character which is at once imperious and passionate and abnormally self-willed—a character utterly determined to have its own way regardless of others, and regardless of the law, I decided, as she began to talk. But I soon found out that her conviction the Claimant was her son was perfectly sincere. Indeed, it had become an obsession with her to such an extent she had broken with one of her oldest friends, Colonel Savage, merely because he refused to accept the Claimant as the rightful baronet, and I soon realised she would not be interested in any of my unorthodox methods because she was convinced that her son 'Sir James', as she persistently called him, would win as soon as the case came to Court.

Meanwhile, my instinct was stirring with the certainty that in this case lay the prospect of a large sum to be obtained somehow. (When I retire to the small but comfortable house near Brighton which I intend to purchase, and when after dinner I unlock the safe in which my private documents will be kept, and I read my account of this case, I expect I will be shocked at my avaricious-

ness and appalled by my behaviour, for by them I will be a changed
man. Few things can be more conducive to morality than a small
estate in the country and a solid income paid regularly by a rep-
utable bank.) But my instinct now leaped with anticipation, so
I listened in patience while the Dowager rehearsed the case, re-
peating each detail with a pathetic intensity as if the loss of one
small anecdote regarding the Claimant's behaviour might lose him
his inheritance. I offered our sympathy when, later, after my
gentle demeanour had won her confidence, she began to complain
of the amount of money her son was now spending at gambling
clubs and theatres in London. I sighed in unison with her when
she deplored his habit of playing billiards and drinking brandy
all afternoon. I condoled with her when she complained of his
impatience with the slow procedure of the law, and I examined
the portraits and daguerreotypes she brought me. The resemblance between James Steede, aged twenty, and the Claimant,
aged presumably thirty-two, was very remarkable. Certainly they
both seemed to exude the same kind of rather sly charm. But
whereas the expression of young James in the daguerreotype was
reticent, almost furtive, the Claimant appeared more genial and
confident; he had changed from a willowy youth to a sturdy,
handsome young man.

I now listened patiently to the Dowager as she described the
perfidy of Anderson and Strutt, and finally, weary from exerting
so much sympathy, I agreed to go round to her house the following day to meet 'Sir James'.

The door of the impressive-looking house on the west side of
the square was opened by a man whom I recognized from the
Dowager's description as being Denham, the butler, who had left
Steede to come with her to London. He was, so the Dowager
said, devoted to her son. He had known James Steede before he
left England, and he was an important witness, so I spent a few
minutes talking to him. It was interesting to discover that the
Dowager's account of her recognition of her son had been com-

pletely accurate. I examined Denham with some care, for I believed it is important to find out the weaknesses of people one has to deal with. One never knows when it may not be useful. The tinge of Denham's face suggested he was fond of drink, and his fleshy lips suggested he was quite sensual. I had no difficulty in persuading him to accept a little present so he could indulge himself on his evening out. By the time he led me up the wide flight of stairs and showed me into the drawing-room, I had gained an ally.

As I came into the long room, overlooking the square, the Dowager rose from the high-backed chair in which she had been sitting beside, a table set for tea, and moved to greet me.

"I'm so glad you managed to come, Mr Tuke," she said. "I want to introduce you to my son, Sir James Steede."

Across the room wandered an attractive young man in his early thirties who was expensively if carelessly dressed and who gave me a smile of such innocence and charm that I was immediately suspicious. Though slim and wiry, I had the impression he was stronger than his slenderness suggested. There was nothing awkward about him, but one felt immediately he would be happier crossing wide plains than a drawing-room in Belgravia.

"How do you do," he said. "I'm most glad to meet you."

His greeting was warm, but I could see from a slight glint in his very light blue eyes that he hadn't taken to me. I'm very sensitive about people's reactions to me. In my field you have to be.

"Now, Mr Tuke," the Dowager said after I had sat down, "I want you to explain to my son the nature of the ordeal that lies before us."

I gave him a polite smile. "Well, Sir James," I began tactfully, "the position is briefly this." "The opening move in the legal battle to establish your identity and thereby your claim to the Steede estates was an application to the Court of Chancery to direct an issue for trial by jury. That application had to be supported by an affidavit stating shortly the facts on which you intend to rely."

"But we've done all that ages ago," the Claimant said impatiently.

I looked at him sternly and reprovingly. I may be a little below average height, my hair may be thin and my appearance without distinction, but my look of stern reproof is impressive. I know—from practising it in front of a mirror. "I'm merely trying to put things in their proper order," I explained. "The next stage," I continued, "was that the solicitors acting upon the behalf of your brother Arthur's widow then gave notice they intended to cross-examine on the affidavit."

"And so the wretched thing has dragged on and on," said the Claimant. "We started in March, and it's now June already."

"I sympathise with your impatience," I was saying, when the doors at the end of the room were pushed gently open and a young maid came in carrying a tea-pot and a kettle on a tray. She was about seventeen, very slim with a full mouth and a delicate face. Her expression was, I am certain, deliberately demure, for her eyes examined me so shrewdly I felt sure she had already had some experience of men. Neatly, with precise gestures, she put down the tea-pot and placed the silver kettle above the spirit-lamp which she lighted with a match from a little box in her apron pocket. As she turned to go I was quite certain I saw her glance slyly towards the Claimant who had been watching her covertly since she entered the room.

"The Court has instructed a very able barrister by the name of Hesketh," I continued after the door had closed behind her. "He will conduct the preliminary examination, which will take place at the Law Institute on the twenty-seventh of next month."

"Well, at least that's something definite," the Claimant said.

I allowed my stern look to slide into a more friendly expression. "When Lady Steede did me the honour of coming to see me," I told him, "I pointed out I considered it essential you should be represented at this examination by the most able Counsel we could brief. I'm now delighted to be able to inform you we've managed to secure the services of Sir George Learoyd. You've probably heard of him. He's the man who appeared in the Crofter forgery case."

"You've booked Learoyd as my Counsel?" the Claimant asked. I could see that he was impressed.

"He's accepted the brief," I answered. "And I've persuaded him to come round here this afternoon, because he wishes to make your acquaintance."

"But he's got plenty of time for that," the Claimant said.

"He wishes to prepare you for the type of question you'll be asked before a Special Examiner," I explained, taking out my watch, for I had timed Learoyd's arrival carefully. "In fact, I expect him at any moment."

The Claimant scowled. "Why can't I be consulted first about this kind of thing?" he asked with a sudden surge of annoyance. "I'm tired of having people sprung on me."

"Don't be upset, Jamie," the Dowager said. "We're lucky to get Sir George Learoyd, and you know it."

"Lucky" was not the word I would have used—in view of the fee I had been empowered to offer the man.

The Claimant laughed at his irritation. He gave me his wonderfully innocent smile in apology. "You can't imagine how tired I am of answering questions," he explained. "I even find myself being cross-examined in my sleep. 'How many toes have you got? Are you sure you haven't got ten and a half? Are you certain you didn't sprout an extra toe during your first year at Cambridge?' On and on it goes, and it drives me mad."

"I appreciate your vexations," I replied. "But I must ask you in your turn to appreciate that as your legal adviser I'm afraid I shall be bound to add to the number of questions which have already been put to you."

"Of course I understand," the Claimant said. "Obviously I'll try hard to help you."

I then began to ask him a few preliminary questions which were so designed that he would find no difficulty in answering them— even if he were not James Steede. Thus I asked him on what date and on board what ship he had left Australia to return to

England. I asked him at what port he had landed and how long it had taken him to disembark and to reach Steede. And all the time I was questioning him, I was trying to decide whether he was a fake or not. But I could not decide, and I was still uncertain and annoyed with myself that for once my instinct seemed to have failed me, when the pretty little maid opened the door to announce Sir George Learoyd.

Learoyd is a large man of such impressive bulk that the adjective 'fat' is inappropriate. Learoyd is massive, with his huge head, thick shoulders, and ponderous limbs. And it is, I'm sure, his solid weight which has helped to win him his reputation as a Queen's Counsel. It may well be that I notice it more because I am rather small in build. However, the fact remains that people generally are more impressed by the deep, sonorous tones emerging from the vast cavern of a huge man's paunch than they are by the reed-like tones of a small person. Admittedly the resounding bass voice loses its effect once one has grown used to it over the years. This is the reason why in his conduct of a case Learoyd has more influence over the jury than the judge. However, our case when it came to Court depended on winning over the jury, so in view of the Claimant's doubtful position I had been wise in persuading the Dowager to offer an extremely large fee to secure Learoyd's services.

"Since I am pressed for time," Learoyd said after we had settled down, "will you please forgive me if I waive formalities and begin by asking you and your son a few questions?"

"Please do," the Dowager answered.

"I must tell you that this special examination at the Law Institute is bound to be reported by every newspaper," he began. "Therefore it's essential we should be well prepared. It's essential we should acquit ourselves with dignity. So I come to my first question. I gather, Lady Steede, that you recognised your son the instant you saw him?"

The Dowager nodded.

I noticed the slight quiver of Learoyd's jowls as he assumed his well-known benign and reassuring expression. "You must realise that in the questions I put to you I'm thinking not only of the special examination but also of the civil trial to follow. Now, whilst your instantaneous recognition will undoubtedly carry great weight with the jury, I'd like to be able to prove you were convinced he was your son—not only instinctively, but also, subsequently, for a number of important reasons. For instance, was there any particular or unusual physical traits which made you certain he must, indeed, be your son?"

The Dowager screwed up her lips in thought. "None that I can think of," she answered.

"There was no birthmark? No scar left by an operation?"

The Dowager shook her head in silence.

"But surely," Learoyd persisted, "surely few of us grow up without some accident, some fall or cut that leaves a mark?"

Suddenly the Dowager's hands sprang together. "Now I think of it," she said, "Jamie did have an accident, but it was so slight I didn't think it worth mentioning. Just before he went abroad, he had a little mishap and cut himself. He was sharpening a stake to mark out a boundary when the knife slipped. Jamie still has the mark on his left forearm."

I saw the Claimant glance at her quickly, and I was almost sure that her statement had surprised him. For one moment I wondered if he had such a mark.

"Can I see the scar?" Learoyd asked.

In silence the Claimant pulled back the sleeve of his coat and rolled up his cuff. The mark was small but quite clearly defined. Learoyd turned to the Dowager. "Apart from yourself," he said, "is there anyone else who can testify to this accident having occurred?"

"No," the Dowager answered. "Because I bandaged his arm myself, and it was only a few days before he left."

"I presume you remember the accident?" Learoyd asked, turning to the Claimant.

"Of course," he answered.

"I ask because your mother tells me there are gaps in your memory."

The Claimant nodded. "I'm afraid so," he said. "You see, I had this bad head injury in the shipwreck. On board the ship that rescued us I nearly died."

"But you can remember your childhood?"

"Parts of it," the Claimant answered.

"Then with your permission," said Learoyd, rising and lumbering towards him, "I intend with your approval to ask you a series of questions such as will be put to you at the special examination." And without waiting for a word or a nod of consent from the Claimant, Learoyd stuck his fingers into the pockets of his tight waistcoat and began his questions, which I will write down as well as I can remember them.

"You were at Eton, I believe? At what house?"

"Jackson's."

"Where was it situated?"

"Across the road—opposite School Yard."

"What word did you use to describe sweets or fruit or cake?"

"Sock."

Learoyd's cheeks wobbled in approval. "What used you to call masters?"

"Beaks."

"And boys who'd won scholarships to the school?"

"Tugs."

Learoyd's jowls now trembled as he turned towards the Dowager and smiled. "I should perhaps explain that I too was at Eton," he said with a kind of smug simper. "Hence my special knowledge. But I must have been there at least twenty years before your son. And I was a tug, not an oppidan."

"I'm afraid I was never a good scholar," the Claimant explained.

"However, you were taught Latin and Greek?"

"Yes."

"Can you remember any Latin?"

"Very little, I'm afraid."

"But you would know the meaning of the word 'canis'?"

"Yes. It means a dog."

"And if I said '*in finem perseverans*'?"

I saw the Claimant hesitate. "Jamie is hardly likely to forget his family motto," said the Dowager. But Learoyd silenced her with a firm gesture which he softened by a smile. "It means?" he asked.

"Persevering to the end," the Claimant answered.

"And '*pons asinorum*'?"

Once again he hesitated. For a moment there was silence. I was watching the man's face carefully, and I now saw beneath his casual expression a glimpse of such frustration I decided I had better come to his help. "I find my own Latin is a bit rusty after all these years," I said. "But I expect you've heard of the Asses' Bridge?"

"Of course!" the Claimant said. "Do you know I'd absolutely forgotten!"

"Can you remember the names of the Latin writers whose words you studied?"

"Caesar, Virgil, Horace—who else?"

"And the names of some Greek authors?" Learoyd continued.

"I was rotten at Greek," the Claimant replied. "I never got as far as reading anyone."

"But you learned the alphabet?"

"Heavens, yes!" he answered. "Alpha, beta, gamma, delta—and so on. At least I can remember that!"

"Then you could tell me—let's say the seventh letter?"

"I could tell you any of the letters," the Claimant replied. "But quite honestly I can't see the point of these questions."

Learoyd spread out his hands as if he were carrying a large dish. "Let me explain," he said. "I gather that Elliott and Baxter—the 'family solicitors', as they like to call themselves—intend to argue that you are an adventurer from Australia, a common fraud in fact. But if I can prove—as I'm now sure I can—that you were indeed at Eton, I shall destroy their case utterly. So I'll proceed with the type of question which will be put to you. What did we call a 'term' at Eton?"

"A half."

"And the half-term holiday?"

"Long leave."

"What were your house colours?"

"Cerise and black stripes."

"What sports did you play that were special to the school?"

"The Wall Game and the Field Game," the Claimant answered. He was now speaking slowly and it seemed to me rather tentatively, like a man advancing across a pond which is only partly covered with ice.

"And another game?" Learoyd asked.

"Would 'fives' count?"

"What was the origin of 'fives'?"

"Boys used to play it between the buttresses of school chapel."

"Where used you to go and bathe in the summer half?"

"Cuckoo Weir," the Claimant answered without any hesitation.

Evidently this answer—like the others—was correct, for Learoyd's cheeks again wobbled in approval, and he folded his hands across his stomach. "Thank you," he said with a satisfied smile. "I think that is enough. If your answers about Cambridge are equally convincing—and I'm sure they will be—I'm confident we shall come out of the special examination with credit. And in the civil trial, I'm sure we shall get the jury on our side from the very start and keep them with us to the very end," he concluded. Then he turned away from the Claimant towards the Dowager. "Lady Steede," he said, "before I came here this afternoon I had been quite impressed by the papers and arguments which Mr Tuke laid before me. I had been persuaded to believe your son was genuine. I am now convinced of it. And nothing has impressed me more than the candour with which he admits he has forgotten some incident or fact in the past."

As Learoyd moved slowly towards the door I felt sure he saw himself as a famous actor who had just delivered an important speech, but in fact he reminded me of a well-trained performing bear as he turned and bowed to his clients. Then he gave me a brief nod. "Mr Tuke," he said, "I shall hope to see you in the morning," and he lumbered awkwardly from the room.

"You see, Jamie!" said the Dowager. "It wasn't such an ordeal after all."

The Claimant turned to me. "Does that heavy manner of his go down in Court?" he asked.

"Don't be so critical, Jamie," the Dowager said.

"Sir George Learoyd," I told him, "is considered to have a greater prowess in dealing with a jury than any other Counsel alive today."

Then I crossed the room and moved towards the Dowager. "Will you think me very rude if I suggest that perhaps I should be allowed a few words with your son alone?" I asked her gently. "I went through the papers earlier this afternoon, and there are one or two intimate matters I'd like to discuss with him," I explained.

The Dowager's head stiffened. "I can assure you that my son keeps nothing from me," she said.

I smiled to hide my annoyance. It was essential for me to be left alone with the young man. But suddenly the Claimant spoke, "All the same," he said to her, "Mr Tuke may have matters it would embarrass him to discuss in front of you."

"Very well," the Dowager said, forcing herself to smile at us both pleasantly as she rose and moved towards the door at the other end of the room. "If I'm needed I'll be in my sitting-room."

After the door had closed behind her there was silence. I waited for the Claimant to speak because I hoped that what he would say would reveal his motive for his willingness to be alone with me. I occupied myself by examining the room. It was furnished in the fastitious style which was in fashion at the beginning of the century. Some of the chairs and settees were superbly elegant. They would, I decided, look very well in the house I intended to buy when I retired. Meanwhile the Claimant was gazing down at the trees in the square outside.

"I find this room stifling hot, don't you?" he asked with a friendly grin. "Let's go down to the billiard-room and have a drink."

The billiard-room, which was on the ground floor at the back of the house, was bleak and a little damp, but the Claimant seemed to become more cheerful as soon as we came into the place. He bustled around with matches lighting the lamps, because it was already dusk.

"Would you like a brandy?" he asked, striding across to the sideboard.

"No, thank you," I said, for I never touch spirits. "But please don't let me stop you."

"You won't," he answered, smiling at me as he poured himself half a glass of brandy from the decanter and put in a little soda.

"You must need a drink after your gruelling test," I said.

"It wasn't too bad," he answered.

"I was almost certain that Learoyd would ask you about Cambridge," I said. "I thought he'd question you about some little episode such as when you broke your wrist climbing into College with young Derek Ritchey."

"There was quite a row about that, wasn't there," the Claimant replied, smiling as if amused at the memory.

"Yes," I said, and I was also smiling because I knew, now that I'd hooked him. "But I thought you answered Learoyd's questions pretty accurately—considering your memory's so bad," I continued. "In fact, I'd mark you beta plus."

"Thank you," he answered, taking a gulp of his drink.

"Of course, you knew that the fifth letter of the Greek alphabet was iota, didn't you?" I asked gently.

The Claimant smiled. "Didn't I say so?"

"No," I replied, "you didn't."

"But naturally, I knew it," he said. "Iota, of course."

I had begun to walk up and down the room because I was afraid of catching a chill. The weather was unusually cold for June. "Of course," I repeated. "And considering all things I'd say you did extremely well." I paused. Then I turned round and stared at him. "But if you want to be successful," I said, speaking very slowly and deliberately, "you've got to learn to do far better."

He looked at me steadily. "I don't understand," he answered.

"I think you do," I said. "I'm telling you—as almost every school-boy knows—that iota is the ninth letter of the Greek alphabet, not the fifth. I'm telling you that James Steede never broke his wrist climbing into College and never had a friend called Derek Ritchey—because I myself invented both that accident and the name one minute ago. I'm telling you that you're a complete im-postor."

For a moment he gazed at me in silence. Then he took a large gulp of his drink. "Get out, you bastard," he said.

"I'll leave if you want me to," I answered. "I can take a cab straight to Scotland Yard." I smiled at him pleasantly. "But why be so violent? I could help you—if you'd only give me the chance. You'd make a great mistake if you turned me out—because you need me. You only convinced that cunning old hack Learoyd be-cause he wanted to be convinced. So you really would do better to listen to me."

Once again there was silence. But I knew he was uncertain what he should do, for his attitude was less menacing. "Now what nonsense are you talking?" he asked. Then he poured more brandy into his glass and walked across to the mantelpiece and stood motionless, staring down at the empty grate.

"Learoyd wanted to believe you," I explained. "Why? Because Lady Steede had told me to offer him an extremely large fee. And you did convince Learoyd—I admit it. But when you've got a Counsel cross-examining you who's determined to catch you out, then it will be very different. I'm not an expert cross-examiner, but I tripped you within two minutes. Iota and Derek Ritchey indeed!"

"My memory's gone," the Claimant said quietly. "I've told you that already. So can't you see I'm bound to pretend to know things that in fact I don't?"

"You'll need coaching," I told him. "You'll need coaching if you're even to get over the first hurdle of the special examina-tion."

His head was still lowered as he gazed at the grate. "I remember some things," he said. "And then there's a blank. A doctor told me it was because of the accident at the time of the shipwreck."

"I could help you so easily," I murmured.

Slowly he raised his head and turned towards me. "What would you get out of it?" he asked.

I sighed with pleasure. "Now you're being reasonable," I said. "I'm so glad. I think we should get on well together, and we'll be a good team. You've got the poise and the bravado, and I've got the brains. And what will I get out of it? Well, we can go into that later, but I'm not avaricious. My fees may be a little high—but by then of course you'll be in a position to pay them."

The Claimant drank his brandy in silence, glancing at me now and then over the top of the glass.

"There's one question I must ask you," I said. "Is Sir James Steede alive?"

"I've told you," he answered, "I am James Steede."

Obviously he was not willing to answer that question. "Then at least tell me this," I continued. "How do you come to know so much about him?"

"I am James Steede," he answered. "But my mind's gone. How often have I got to say it?"

"Was it just luck that you looked so like him?" I asked.

"If you don't believe me, you can go," he said with a spurt of irritation. "I want no more questions."

"But you're willing to be coached by me?" I asked.

"Yes," he answered. "If you can fill in the gaps in my memory."

I decided to make another effort to break down his pretence. "You know the old saying—one should always tell the truth to one's solicitor. It's very sound," I said. "So why not admit you're a fraud?"

"Because I'm not," he answered. "I'm the rightful heir to the baronetcy and to the Steede estates."

"If that's how you want to play it," I began—but he interrupted me. "I'm not an impostor," he said. "You've got to believe me." His eyes were gleaming with such clear sincerity that for a moment I wondered if he might not after all be genuine. Then I recalled how glibly he had pretended to remember climbing into

College with his friend Derek Ritchey. He was evidently a more intelligent actor than I had supposed. For he was wise not to reveal himself to me as an impostor. It was clever of him to persist in his rôle of the true heir with an impaired memory. A complete confession might have tempted a person less adroit than myself to the mistake of open blackmail.

"Very well," I said, "you're James Steede. But now tell me this quite honestly. How much can you remember of your childhood?"

"Most of it," he answered. "I can remember whole stretches. It's when I get to my days at school that my mind goes blank."

"Do you know any Latin at all?"

"A little. But I can't remember a word of Greek."

"Well, you've got to know at least a little Greek," I said. "So that's where my coaching will begin. You can come to my office every afternoon. If Lady Steede asks any questions, you can tell her we're working together on the case. And every afternoon now until the special examination you'll be getting some useful education, which will be far better for you than playing billiards and drinking brandy."

Suddenly the Claimant smiled. "But I'll still drink brandy," he said.

———

On my way to the office the following morning I bought a Greek primer.

My pupil—James, as I now tactfully called him—was far more patient than I had expected, and we made good progress as the weeks passed by. When he became restive I would talk to him about the case and train him how to answer the questions that might be put to him. Then we would return to the primer. The smell of brandy will now always remind me of Greek verbs.

The special examination—our first test—took place on the twenty-seventh of July as arranged. The Law Institute in Chancery Lane was packed, and the crowds outside, attracted by the publicity the case had received, were so thick that it was difficult to get into the building. The Claimant looked perfectly calm as he walked into the hall with the Dowager on his arm—and indeed I was calm myself, for I was fairly certain I had forewarned James of every single awkward question he could possibly be asked. The Dowager had offered herself for cross-examination, but this our opponents did not desire. The 'family faction', as they call themselves, had given notice that they wished to cross-examine on the Claimant's affidavit. Hesketh, an able but rather dull barrister, had been appointed, as I have already said, to conduct the examination. The family had briefed Sir Henry Scott, a sound, clever little man, sleek and shining as an otter, to cross-examine the Claimant.

Scott began by asking my client about the various stages of his life from the moment he went on board the *Clara*, and as the hours passed by, and Scott delved carefully and methodically into each event, one after the other—the shipwreck, the lowering of the boats, the rescue, and the arrival at Melbourne, I could see that James's confident demeanour was making an impression on the crowded hall. The second day was spent by Scott in taking the Claimant through the different stages of his life in Australia —his offer of employment as a horse-breaker, his journey from Melbourne to Albury, his apprenticeship and his decision to set up as a horse-breaker on his own. The morning of the third day was occupied with questions about events leading to the Claimant's return to England and his arrival at Steede. In the afternoon, George Learoyd was all ready to re-examine with his usual skill—when Henry Scott suddenly switched his questions back to the period before James Steede's departure from England.

It was at this moment that Scott managed to introduce the question of a sealed letter which James Steede was said to have left behind with the family solicitors before he left the country. This was the first I had heard about a sealed letter, and I glanced anxiously towards James. However, his manner was as tranquil as ever.

"Yes," he replied in answer to Scott's question, "before I left England I remember that I made no Will. But I do remember writing a letter which I gave to Elliott, the family solicitor, and which we then sealed."

"Then you can remember its contents?" Scott asked him.

"Yes," James answered. "I can."

"Then will you tell us in your own words the nature of its contents?" Scott asked.

James was silent. I now glanced at Learoyd. He was looking so resolutely placid I was sure he must be worried.

"What was the nature of its contents?" Scott repeated.

James turned towards Hesketh, the examiner. "Must I answer that question?" he asked.

"Yes," Hesketh replied.

Once again James was silent. Every face in the crowded room was turned towards him.

"The contents of the letter were concerned with another person," James said slowly.

"Can you give us the name of the other person?" Scott asked.

"Yes," James answered and was silent again.

"What was the person's name?" Scott asked.

There was a long pause.

"The person's name?" Scott repeated.

"I decline to give you the name," James replied. "I decline to answer any further questions about the sealed letter. And I can tell you why. The contents of that letter were entirely private. I can't reveal what the letter said because it concerned a lady's honour."

If, as I suspected, James had no idea at all what was in the letter his answer was wonderfully adroit, for it effectively prevented Scott from pressing the matter. The danger was that the family solicitors would produce the letter and it would contain not a word concerned with any lady's honour. However, for some reason, Scott dropped the whole question of the sealed letter as suddenly as he had introduced it; and it was not very difficult for Learoyd to gloss over James's refusal to reveal the letter's contents when he came to re-examine. At the end of the proceedings

James left the hall with the Dowager on his arm. He moved easily and gracefully; he looked as if the Steede estates already belonged to him.

———

"What was in that sealed letter?" I asked James as soon as we had returned to Belgrave Square and the Dowager had gone up to her bedroom to rest, and we were alone together.

James crossed to the decanter which Denham had brought into the drawing-room. "I don't know, I tell you," he answered.

I watched him as he poured himself a brandy. I was for once very certain he was lying. "You've found out about everything else," I said. "You must know what was in the letter." James scowled down at his drink and was silent. "Were you just bluffing when you said it concerned a lady's honour?" I asked.

"Not entirely," James said.

"What do you mean by that?" I asked. He was beginning to make me nervous. It annoyed me that I had never managed to persuade him to admit he was an impostor.

James hesitated. "Before I went abroad," he said slowly, "before I left England, there was a girl I was in love with. She was sixteen years old. I was very much in love. I wanted to marry her. But my mother—my mother was insanely jealous of her. She went to see the girl's parents. She persuaded them to forbid the marriage." James paused and took a gulp of his drink. "I know I left behind a sealed letter," he continued. "That I'm certain about. But then my mind goes blank. The letter must have been concerned with the girl. That's why I spoke about a lady's honour."

"Of course you found out the girl's name?" I asked. "Or shall I put it differently?" I added, because James was now glowering at me. "Have you managed to remember the girl's name?"

"I don't intend to talk about it," James answered.

"Then I hope you won't mind if I do," I said. "The girl was almost certainly the daughter of a family who had bought a house not far from Steede. Her name was Margaret Anstey. From various correspondence I've read it certainly looks as if she and James Steede were secretly engaged."

"Is she alive?" James asked.

"I think so," I answered. "I believe she lives with an aunt in Devon."

James frowned. "I wonder why they didn't produce her at the examination?" he asked.

"I'd like to know why," I said. "And I'd like to know the answer to another question. Perhaps you can help me. It concerns one of James Steede's old school-friends at Eton. His name is John Burdock. You met him last week, I gather. He came to this house, and you took him downstairs to the billiard-room, or so Denham tells me. How did you manage to persuade him you were James Steede, and in less than twenty minutes?"

"It wasn't difficult," James answered. "As soon as I began talking about our days at school together he became absolutely convinced I was genuine."

Suddenly James smiled, as if he had just remembered something that had pleased him, and once again I felt uneasy.

———

I had noticed that Learoyd had stayed behind in the hall after the examination. I suspected he intended to make some inquiries on his own. So I wasn't surprised when he joined us in the drawing-room twenty minutes later. His heavy cheeks were quivering with satisfaction.

"I must confess," he said, smiling paternally at James, "that at the conclusion of the examination this afternoon I looked forward to the civil trial with slight apprehension. I was perturbed by your stubborn refusal to reveal the contents of the sealed letter. I may as well tell you it's generally considered that your reticence has been damaging to your cause. As a result we're bound to get bad publicity. However, I can now understand the reason for your reticence, and I can only say I'm deeply impressed."

Learoyd paused and waited for James to speak. But James said nothing. He stood motionless, gazing down at the glass in his hand.

"Even gallantry can be carried too far," Learoyd continued. "I dreaded the task of having to persuade you to reveal the lady's name. Fortunately I've been relieved of the duty, because the lady has come forward herself."

James put down his glass. "Was she there today?" he asked.

"Yes," Learoyd answered. "She was in the hall."

"Then she recognised me?"

"Not at first," Learoyd replied. "She was at the back of the room and thickly veiled so as not to be seen by the family. However, you passed quite close to her as you left the room. When she saw you for the first time at close range, she was convinced. So she approached me and told me who she was. She also told me how impressed she'd been by your discretion."

"How is she?" James asked in a dull, expressionless voice.

"Flourishing, I'm glad to say," Learoyd answered. "I may add that she speaks most highly of you. Her only reproach is you didn't communicate with her the instant you returned."

James was silent. I wondered why he looked so sullen. I had expected him to be delighted by the news of the woman's recognition. Learoyd was obviously puzzled by his lack of enthusiasm. "I expect James was unwilling to stir up old memories," I said, to explain his odd silence.

"Margaret Anstey is an extremely brave woman," Learoyd continued. "Her recognition in due course will change our whole position."

"But didn't you say she'd already recognised me?" James asked.

"As you passed her in a crowd—yes," Learoyd answered. "But I want her to recognise you as she stands close, looking at you as I'm looking at you now. I want her to hear you speak and watch you move. And then—in our presence—I want her to declare you're indeed the James Steede she knew so well."

I thought quickly. There was the danger that when she saw him and could examine his appearance at leisure she would change her opinion and declare he was an impostor. But it was too late now to avoid the risk. "When do you propose this meeting should take place?" I asked.

"Some time this afternoon," Learoyd answered. "Before she goes back to Exeter."

"You've asked her to come round here?" James asked.

"I have," Learoyd answered, a little surprised by the tone of James's voice.

"Without even asking me?" James continued.

"I am in charge of this case," Learoyd replied sharply.

I decided I must move quickly to prevent a row between them. "After all, Margaret Anstey did recognise you," I reminded James. "She's on your side, remember."

James put down his glass. "I'm sick of being treated like a child. I insist on being consulted first before people are flung at my head. I'm tired of it, and I shall refuse to see her."

"I must tell you that next to your mother," Learoyd said, "I consider Margaret Anstey is our most important witness."

"I don't care," James answered. "I still won't see her."

"I must confess I can't understand why," Learoyd said, frowning.

"No one ever wants to be reminded of an affair that's over," I murmured blandly. "But there's no need to go back too deeply into the past. I'm sure that apart from this meeting there'll be no need for a second one."

Learoyd turned coldly to James. "That will be entirely for the two of you to decide."

"The important thing from our point of view is the evidence of her recognition," I explained to James. "There's no reason for you to see her alone, if you'd rather not."

James picked up his glass and walked across to the side-table. "Very well," he said. "One short meeting with the two of you as witnesses."

Learoyd nodded as he lowered himself into an armchair. "You don't seem to realise," he said to James, "that at the trial there will be far more witnesses against us than on our side. We must admit the unpleasant fact that for one reason or another almost all your schoolfriends at Eton and your friends at Trinity are going to state they're convinced you're not James Steede. So Margaret Anstey's evidence is essential to us. So is the evidence of another person who knew you well as a child—Colonel Savage."

"But I thought he was still uncertain?" James said.

"He was at the back of the hall this morning," Learoyd answered. "He approached me after the examination was over to tell me that at last he's convinced. I gather it was your obvious reluctance to reveal the contents of the letter which impressed him the most. Of course, I told him in confidence about Miss Anstey's recognition."

"Does my mother know?" James asked. "She'll be so pleased he's come over to our side."

"I think the Colonel sent her a note this afternoon," Learoyd answered.

"But now that we've got Colonel Savage on our side. . . ." James began. I had already planned my answer, when Denham opened the door and announced the arrival of Margaret Anstey.

An instant later a small woman in a green dress, with a small green hat from which there fell a white veil, walked into the room. No one spoke, because each of us was waiting for the other to speak. In silence the woman waited until the door had closed behind Denham. Then she advanced towards James. Slowly she lifted her veil and stared at him fixedly. Her age, I reckoned, must be twenty-eight, but with her smooth unlined face she looked far younger, and there was something rather girlish about the way she moved, as if her amazingly young appearance had influenced her behaviour. But then I noticed that her waist, though it appeared to be tightly corseted, was quite thick, and there was nothing young about her eyes, which had an oddly intense expression I found disturbing. Suddenly she stretched out her arms.

"Jamie," she said, "I'm so happy to see you again."

James blushed as he took her outstretched hands. "You shouldn't have come here," he muttered.

"Don't you see, I *had* to come!" she cried. "When I was told your case was in danger because of this morning, I knew I must come."

"We're very grateful," I said, and I introduced myself to her, and she muttered some conventional phrase of greeting. But I don't think she took much notice of me, for her eyes with their hectic expression seldom moved away from James.

Learoyd now came up to her. He stood with his thumbs stuck into his waistcoat, gazing down at her. "As Sir James Steede's Counsel," he began impressively, "will you forgive me if I ask you a direct question?"

The young woman turned unwillingly away from James. "Please do," she said with a coy jerk of her head.

"Now you have met him face to face," Learoyd asked, "have you any doubt as to my client's identity?"

"None," she answered. "None. I was fairly sure when I saw him at the back of that terrible hall. But now I'm certain."

"And another question," Learoyd continued. "Do you know the contents of the sealed letter which my client left behind with the family solicitors?"

"I do," she replied.

"Did he show it you before he left?"

"Yes," she answered. Then she swung round towards James. "You can remember, can't you?" she asked.

James turned away from her intense gaze. "It's all past," he said. "Please let it be. If you speak about it, you can only do yourself harm."

"But it's important—all of it, don't you see?" she cried, shaking her head in a kind of ghastly eagerness. Then she turned back to Learoyd and to me. "I can remember the afternoon so well," she said. "We were down in the wood beyond the orchard, and Jamie told me he was leaving for London that night. I can see him even now. The sun was glowing through the trees, I remember. I can remember the expression of his face as he took the letter out of his pocket. 'I want you to read this', he said to me, 'because it concerns you'."

She paused. The room was so quiet I heard the sound of the handle turning before the door opened, and the Dowager walked in. Immediately she saw the young woman she stiffened.

"Good afternoon, Margaret," she said. "What are you doing here?"

"Miss Anstey came at my request," Learoyd explained quickly.

"Certainly it's improbable she came at my son's request," the Dowager answered. "Since his return he's never even mentioned her name."

The young woman's head shook nervously. "He'd never mention my name to you," she said.

James moved towards the Dowager. "Please realise she's only come here to help us," he said, and I noticed yet again that for some reason he couldn't make himself say the name Margaret Anstey.

"We can do without her help," the Dowager replied.

"Very well then," the young woman said in a strained, high-pitched voice. "Very well then." And, with her cheeks flaming, she moved towards the door.

I must confess I made no move to stop her, because I was convinced by James's odd behaviour that he knew something which made him determined not to let her be encouraged. However, Learoyd had no intention of losing her.

"Wait," he said to her in his deep, resonant voice. Then, when he saw she had paused, he turned ponderously towards the Dowager. "Do you wish me to continue with this case, madam?" he asked.

"Of course I do," she answered.

"Then I must beg you to treat Miss Anstey with respect," he said, staring at her severely. "Otherwise I warn you I shall drop the brief."

One thing I now realised was certain. When he stayed behind in the hall of the Law Institute, Learoyd must have heard rumours which made him believe there was a chance of losing the case, for if he had been at all certain of winning, he would never have threatened to leave us.

"Then I shall be silent," the Dowager replied, sitting down in her high-backed chair.

Learoyd gave her a small nod and turned back to the young woman. "I'd be grateful if you'd let me resume my questions."

"If you wish," she answered, bowing her head.

"You were telling us that James Steede showed you the letter which he subsequently sealed," Learoyd said. "Can you remember the contents of the letter."

"Yes," she answered. "It was only a few lines long. It was a kind of bequest to me in the event of his death."

The Dowager leaned towards me. "I find that a little hard to believe," she said to me in a whisper. But it was loud enough to be heard.

"You never saw the letter," the young woman said, swinging round at her like an angry schoolgirl. "Elliott, your family solicitor, destroyed it."

I now understood why they had been unable to confront us with the letter at the examination earlier in the day. "Excuse me, Miss Anstey," I said gently. "But may I ask you a question? You've just told us the letter was in the nature of a bequest in the event of James's death. But James was in fact presumed dead. So the bequest must have become effective."

"No, because there was another clause," she answered. "The bequest depended on another event taking place."

"Can you tell us the nature of the other event?" Learoyd asked.

"No," James cried out suddenly. "Don't tell them. It was a secret between us. Please let's keep it."

"I think you should realise our position," Learoyd said, frowning at him with displeasure. "I believe that if Miss Anstey doesn't reveal the contents of the letter in full we shall probably lose the case."

"Then we must lose it," James answered.

The young woman shook her head at him. "No, Jamie, you won't stop me. I'm no longer a young girl, remember. If they think it can help your case, I can give them the very words of the letter."

"How can you remember the words after all these years?" the Dowager asked her.

"Because Jamie gave me a copy of the letter," she answered with a little shiver of triumph. "And I didn't destroy my copy. I kept it—even when the event didn't take place—because they were the last words I had in his own writing. I still have the letter."

"Have you got it with you?" Learoyd asked.

The young woman nodded. She fumbled eagerly in her handbag and produced a folded piece of thick note-paper. Suddenly James turned to me. "Tell her there's no need for it," he said in desperation. "Tell her we can win without it."

"I wish I could," I answered tactfully. But even while I spoke, she had unfolded the letter and had raised her head in readiness for the moment which, when she returned that night to her aunt's house in Exeter, she would recall to herself over and over again. I think I can now easily guess the reason why she was so determined to sacrifice herself.

"Shall I read it to you?" she asked Learoyd.

"Please," he answered, with a wave of his large hand.

"'I, James Edward Steede'," she read out slowly, "'do hereby request my executors in the event of my death and in the event of Margaret Anstey becoming with child to give her the house at Ruston and one thousand pounds a year and to make suitable provision for our child'."

For a few moments there was silence. I glanced at James. His face was dark; he was scowling down at the fireplace.

"I have only one more question to put to you," Learoyd said to her quietly. "Are you willing to go into the witness box and to allow that letter to be produced in Court—realising the harm it may do your reputation?"

"The letter I've just read shows that Jamie and I were lovers," she answered. "But I must tell you that he wanted to marry me. However, I was only sixteen, and my parents refused their consent because their minds had been poisoned against him. That's why Jamie went abroad. But I promised I'd wait for him, and I have waited." As she gazed round at us I suddenly realised it was quite probable that during the long drab evenings in her aunt's house in Exeter this had been her dream. This might well be the moment she had worked out in her imagination to atone for the desolate days she had spent during the last twelve years. "Put me in the witness box," she now cried out in a tremulous voice. "Produce that letter in Court. Let it be quoted in every newspaper. There's nothing in it I'm ashamed about. I didn't bear a child. But I now wish I had. I wish I'd been able to go to Ruston to live quietly, waiting for Jamie to return." Suddenly she lowered her head. "Because I loved him," she said.

For a moment her lower lip began to tremble. Then she controlled herself and raised her head and moved, without faltering, across the room. Learoyd opened the door for her. As she went out, Learoyd allowed himself a smirk of triumph. Then he bowed to us in farewell, and escorted her down the stairs. I closed the door behind them.

For a while none of us spoke. The Dowager's hard, clear voice broke the silence. "What a lot of hysterical nonsense!" she exclaimed. "Don't let her trap you, Jamie. She tried once before. Now she's trying a second time. Don't get entangled all over again."

James was standing with his back turned to us. His fists were clenched at his side. He did not answer. By now I was certain that Margaret Anstey was a remarkable asset to our side, so I felt I should try to change the Dowager's attitude towards her.

"A dozen years is quite a time," I said. "Don't you think perhaps now you could bring yourself to soften your attitude?"

"She was a little schemer at sixteen," the Dowager replied. "She hasn't changed."

"Yet apparently she's prepared to ruin her reputation for your son's sake," I pointed out.

"Can't you see why?" the Dowager asked. "If she goes into the witness box and throws away her reputation for his sake, you know as well as I do there's not a single person in the county who'd speak to Jamie again if he didn't marry her."

In my own defence I must put it on record that I did not know as well as the Dowager did that "not a single person in the county" would ever speak to James again if he didn't marry the woman. I have never visited Nottinghamshire. Were I to do so, I doubt if I should be introduced into the society the Dowager and the Steedes lived in. I was vexed with myself for my slight blunder, and this accounted for the lack of tact of my next remark.

"Your son's no longer a boy," I said. "You must allow him to decide such matters for himself."

The Dowager glared at me. "How can you say such a thing?" she asked. "Since he grew up, I've never interfered with his decisions. I've always allowed him to decide for himself. When he wanted to go abroad, did I stop him? No, I let him go—even though I knew I'd miss him bitterly."

Slowly the Dowager raised herself from her chair and moved towards the door. "I'm an old woman," she said. "I've had an exhausting day. I come into my own drawing-room in my house, and no one is the slightest degree sympathetic to me. Well, I've had enough. I won't stand any more. I'm going upstairs, and I don't want to see anybody."

James and I were silent for a while after she had left. I was afraid to speak, for it seemed to me that my usual deftness and tact in handling matters had suddenly deserted me. James walked across to the side-table and poured himself a drink.

"Is it true what she says—I mean about marrying?" he asked.

I managed to smile. "I don't think so."

"Then why did she say it?"

"Let's put it this way," I said. "When Margaret Anstey goes into the witness box and that letter is produced, you can easily imagine what a fuss the newspapers will make out of it. There's bound to be a scandal. That's all she's worried about."

"I see," James said. Then he gulped down his drink. "Do you mind if we go downstairs?" he asked. "I can't bear this room. It's like a bloody museum."

The billiard-room looked as bleak as ever in the fading light of the afternoon, but at least it had been aired, so it was less damp. The table's baize cover had been removed, and as soon as we came in James took down a cue from the rack and began knocking three balls around. I was glad to see James begin to look less tense as he played in silence. At that moment, I must confess, as I sat on the leather sofa at the far end of the room and watched him play, I felt quite benevolent towards him. He had been a good pupil, and we were now certain to win.

"Well, James," I said, "you can now be sure of being at Steede in time for Christmas, with a turkey from your own estate. Perhaps you'll ask me to stay in the spring. I'm very partial to daffodils."

James did not answer. He seemed absorbed in his game.

"Why were you so worried by the prospect of Margaret Anstey appearing?" I asked him. "I think she'll be a perfect witness. She's firmly on your side. She'll cause a sensation in Court. Nothing wins the sympathy of a jury more surely than a thoroughly sentimental love affair."

James crouched down to make his next shot. "We're not going to use it," he said. "We're not going to have that letter produced in Court."

"But why not, for heaven's sake?"

"Because I'm not going to marry her," he answered.

I laughed. "But you don't have to marry her. You can get secretly engaged to her—just to keep her happy. Then, when we've won the case, you can break it off."

James shook his head. He was beginning to make me feel nervous again. "Why not?" I asked.

"Because I'm sorry for her," he answered.

I gaped at him. "You're not serious!"

James put down his billiard cue. "Look at it from her point of view. At sixteen she's seduced by a young man. She's in love with him, but her parents won't let her marry. So the young man goes abroad, and she waits for twelve years. Then he comes back to England, and he gets engaged to her secretly. So for his sake she goes into the witness box, and a letter's read out admitting she's been seduced by him. Her name is plastered on the front page of every newspaper. In the dull, strait-laced society she lives in, she's finished. No one will marry her now. Most people won't even talk to her. And then the man drops her. He just breaks off the engagement." James clicked his fingers. Then he made a grimace of distaste. "No," he said. "It won't do."

I knew then that I must now attack—even if I alienated him for good. "Isn't it rather late in the day for you to get soft?" I asked. "Before you started out on your career as an impostor, you ought to have considered the consequences if you were going to get sentimental about them." I got up from the sofa and went over to him. "What about poor little Richard Steede? Such a pretty child, I'm told. You're defrauding him of his title and wealth. And what about Arthur Steede's widow? You're taking her house and all those estates from her. And then—what about the dear Dowager? Taking advantage of an old woman's doting love for her son! That's not quite correct, is it?"

His face looked very dark in the fading light. "Why shouldn't a woman be devoted to her son?" he inquired.

"To her son, yes. But it's wrong she should be devoted to you. However, I can see you're not concerned by that particular aspect. So it looks as if it's only poor Margaret Anstey you're worried about. Then why don't you marry her?"

"Are you mad?" he asked.

"Remember you'll have enough money to keep a whole string of mistresses on the side," I continued. "Get a child by her, and that'll keep her quiet. She won't miss you so much after that."

"I might want to marry someone else," he said.

"Nonsense. I watched you at that reception the Dowager so kindly invited me to, and there wasn't a single girl you looked at. I was quite disappointed in you."

"They weren't my type."

"You can't expect to get Steede without having to make a few sacrifices," I pointed out.

"Why should I make sacrifices?" he asked. "I want Steede on my own terms or not at all."

His attitude irritated me exceedingly. "I don't think you quite realise your position," I said to him. "Or you wouldn't make such a silly remark. Really, your behaviour this afternoon has distressed me. You don't seem to appreciate that it was you who started this action we're all now engaged in. And you can't stop it. You can't turn back now. You can only go forward, and get as much out of it as you can."

James turned away from me and crossed over to the sideboard to get himself a drink. "I can promise you this," he said. "If I'd known how it would turn out, I'd never have begun it. I was all right back in Australia. But this life is stifling me. I'm fed up with being pestered by journalists and lawyers. I'm tired of having to behave like a stuck-up dummy. I'm bored with all the parties she makes me go to." He took a long gulp of his drink and wiped his lips with the back of his hand. "I'm sick of the whole business of pretence," he cried out suddenly. "I want to be myself, can't you see?"

Nothing calms me more than another person's display of emotion. The warmer he grows, the cooler I become. So I now gazed at James quite dispassionately. "You say you want to be yourself. But do you really know," I asked, "who 'yourself' is? I don't. When we first met I thought you were an adventurer—a hard, calculating, rather malicious character, ready to do almost anything to get what you wanted. Now, I'm beginning to wonder if you're anything more than a sentimental rogue who has bitten off more than he can chew."

"I don't care what you think," James answered.

As he spoke, the attractive little maid, whose name I had by now discovered was Rose, came in and smiled at us both with her usual demure but experienced expression. Then she took a taper from a vase on the mantelpiece, lit it with a match from the little box she carried in her apron, and began to light the gas-mantles round the gloomy room. I had now said to my client all I wished to say for the moment, and I was feeling very tired. I moved to the door.

"I expect you'll feel quite differently tomorrow," I said as I turned to go.

"I suppose so," he answered. "Good evening to you."

I closed the door behind me. It was the end of an exhausting afternoon. But as I walked along the passage which led to the hall I knew there was another slight worry as yet only lurking in the back of my mind. Then it came swimming into my consciousness like an odd goldfish. Was James having an affair on the side with Rose? The girl was certainly very attractive, with her slim little body and pert face. There was a definite charm about her large eyes and tilted nose and full lips, and once again I had seen a look of understanding flicker between them. Suddenly I had an instinct to go back and listen at the door. But I was already late for an appointment at my office, and there was always the chance that someone would catch me eavesdropping. So I moved on down the corridor.

I regret now that I didn't listen, because if I'd discovered what was going on between the two of them, I would certainly have found a way of stopping it promptly, for we had enough difficulties littered around the place already. However, I dismissed my instinct, and I continued on my way towards the hall. And, of course, I was wrong to do so. Fifty years of life have taught me that we should always trust our baser instincts. That's why we were endowed with them.

But as I drove back to my office that evening I forgot about Rose as I recalled the various events of the day. In his final outburst in the dark billiard-room, my client had come very near to confessing he was an impostor. But if he were an impostor, how did he come to know so much, and who was he?

It was all most unusual. I had now been working on the case for nearly two months, and still I did not know for certain who my client was. However, I had one consoling thought. My fees and expenses were being paid with a pleasing regularity. So what more—at this stage—could I ask?

PART FIVE

I WAS BORN in a back street of Lambeth, across the river in South London, in March, 1830. So I'm half a year younger than Jimmy —though I believe I look older. (How anyone can drink as much as Jimmy does and look so young, I don't know.) My father was a butcher by trade, and my mother kept house for him and looked after me, when I was a kid. I was the only child. I don't know much about my grandparents. My father's people, the Ashbys, had been ships' butchers and had then retired to Essex somewhere. My mother's parents were both dead by the time I was born. They had run a pub at one time, and my mother had been a barmaid.

When I was twelve, I was taken away from school and made to work for my father in his butcher's shop. I hated the work, and I loathed the stench of meat. But I had plenty of friends of my own age, so life wasn't too bad.

When I was fourteen I had my first girl. She was sixteen years old, with long soft legs, I remember, and her skin seemed to burn me when I had her. Jennie, her name was, and at the time I was quite struck with her—even though I knew that at least three other boys in the street had been with her.

Though I went with Jennie quite often, I'd never given her a present, so I'd made up my mind to give her something really pretty for her seventeenth birthday. I'd seen a garnet brooch in the pawnbroker's shop on the corner which I was sure she'd like. The trouble was it would cost seven shillings. (The old man had marked it at nine shillings, but from various talks with him I knew he'd go down to seven.) My father didn't pay me a proper wage. He just gave me pocket-money, and at the time I'd only got two shillings in the world. But I was determined to buy that brooch. So I tried to get an advance from my father. But it was useless, and I didn't like to ask my mother because she was very touchy about money. My mother used to keep the house looking perfect. She always dressed well, and she always saw to it that I had good clothes to wear. But I knew she had to make a tremendous effort to pretend we were quite well off—when in fact my father's business wasn't doing well. People weren't going to his shop, because they said the quality of the meat had gone off and that my father was always charging them too much to keep himself in booze. My mother now in secret had begun to take in old lace to mend in order to bring in some extra money. I knew the long hours tired her because at that time I'd begun to notice she wasn't young any more. Up to then, I'd always thought I had the youngest mother in the street—and the prettiest and most lady-like. But she now looked worn and ill.

So I didn't want to ask my mother for a loan, because she was so kind-hearted where I was concerned that I knew she'd give it to me.

Three days before Jennie's birthday my father went out of the shop for a moment, leaving the till open. There was over two pounds in silver in it. The temptation was too much. I nicked five bob, hoping he wouldn't notice—because when he was drunk, he'd just grab a handful of silver from the till and make for the pub. So I bought the brooch, and when I gave it to Jennie on her birthday I'd never seen her look so happy. Of course she had to go and show it to all her friends in the street. But when the excitement was over I got her to come with me to our favourite place, which was the back yard of an empty little house that used to be a pie-shop. There were some trees in the yard, and it was so dark you couldn't be seen. Jennie, that night, was better than she'd ever been, and I was all keyed-up too from the general excitement. She was wilder and more loving than I'd thought possible. It was wonderful, but it was painful somehow. At one moment I thought I was going to die, it was so marvellous. We'd stop for a while and lie there panting in each other's arms, and then we just couldn't keep ourselves from starting all over again. Though it was late, and I knew I'd get into trouble, I just didn't care.

When I came into our house, my father was waiting for me in the kitchen. His watery eyes stared at me. I could see he was drunk. He got up from the table and lurched towards me.

"Five shillings was missing from the till this week," he said. "You paid seven shillings for the brooch you gave that little slut round the corner. Where did you get the money from?"

"I'd saved up for it," I answered.

Slowly he began to undo his belt. "I'll tell you where you got the money from," he said. "You stole it. You stole it from my till. You stole money from me so you could have that slut."

He seized my by the neck and tore off my shirt.

"You fornicating rotten little thief," he said. Then he took off his belt and threw me across a chair, and he began strapping me. He was a huge man, thickly built and with powerful arms. He was drunk, so I don't suppose he knew how hard he was lamming into me. I don't expect he was even aware he was using the end with the buckle, but I could feel it tearing away my skin. After a while—I couldn't help it—I began to scream. But still he didn't stop. Suddenly the kitchen door was flung open. At that instant he paused. I looked up. It was my mother. I can remember that her hair was all untidy, and she was wearing a pale blue nightdress. But it was the expression of her face I can recall best. I can recall it because as I saw her look towards my father, I realised for the first time that she hated him. Until then, I'd thought they got along together as well as most other people seemed to. Sometimes she would be upset when he came in drunk—though he never hit here. Sometimes they'd quarrel a bit, but somehow he always seemed to show respect for her. But now I suddenly understood they must have kept up the pretence for my benefit. For now I could see my mother's eyes were glaring at him with hatred.

Then she walked across the room and took the belt from his hands.

"Leave my son alone," she said. "If you try to take it out on him, I'll see the whole street knows."

"He stole from the till," my father said. "He stole five shillings from the till."

"And whose money was it to begin with?" my mother asked. "Would you tell him *that*?"

My father lumbered towards the door which led out into the street. "Your son's a thief," he said. "He stole the money to buy the favours of that slut he's been going with."

"Look at the boy's back," my mother answered. "Look at it and remember—because I'm never going to let you forget this day so long as you live."

My father opened the door. "You're rotten, the pair of you," he said. Then he stumbled out into the street.

After my mother had dressed my back, she took out a bottle of port from the back of the cupboard, poured out two glasses, and sat down at the kitchen table opposite me.

"Did you steal the money, Ben?" she asked.

"I took five bob," I answered. "I would have paid it in again bit by bit."

"Have you been going with Jennie Howlett?" she asked.

I felt myself blushing. "Yes," I answered. "I have been."

My mother sighed. "Are you man enough already? It seems only yesterday you were a child. Well, there it is. You've been punished too much already, so I'll say no more—except to warn you not to get mixed up with a girl like that again. I know her type. If it took her fancy, when you were a bit older, she'd say she was going to have a baby so you'd have to marry her."

"I wouldn't mind," I said.

My mother smiled. "You would when you found she was still carrying on with all her old friends," she answered. Then she leaned forward across the table. "You've always been fond of ships, haven't you?" she said. "Ever since you were a boy."

"Yes," I answered, rather surprised by her remark. "Why?"

"You don't like working in the shop, do you?"

I grinned at her. "I hate it," I answered.

"Then how would you like to go to sea?" my mother asked.

I jumped up from my chair, then remembered my back. "I'd love it," I answered.

"Then I'll get you apprenticed," my mother said, "because I think it's time you left home." She took a sip of port. "But now there's something else I want to tell you," she went on. "It's a secret only your dad and me and one other person know the truth about. . . ."

I can see her so clearly, leaning across the table in her blue night-dress, with her hair all wispy, holding her glass of port as she always held a glass, with her little finger curling out separate from the rest. I can see the nervous yet determined expression in her faded eyes.

I can understand now, of course, why she told me the story in high-flown romantic terms. Perhaps, without her knowing it, that was the only way she could cover up what was in fact a squalid, ugly business. Probably by now she had come to see it as a kind of beautiful romance which began in style but ended up all wrong. So I was told of the plush bar she used to work in the other side of Lambeth when she was fifteen, and the red dress she used to wear with white trimmings, and the handsome, sallow-faced, tall man who came into the bar one night and was obviously a gentleman—even though the clothes he was wearing were quite plain. It was a question of love at first sight, my mother said. But before her new friend took her away in his carriage he explained he couldn't marry her, for his wife would refuse to leave him. However, he insisted on making my mother a large allowance every week and rented the finest set of rooms they could find in the most expensive lodging-house in Bermondsey. Presents arrived from this handsome, rich man almost daily. I accepted every detail of her story at that stage—because it all seemed so unreal, I suppose. But gradually, as my mother continued with her tale, her voice seemed to lose some of its romantic intensity. The glow of recollection left her face. Yet she still managed to cover the affair with a semblance of decency.

I now learned that after nearly a year of this lavish existence, my mother discovered she was pregnant. So she told her generous friend, expecting him to be delighted. And indeed he was pleased in a way, but my mother could see there was something disturbing him that evening. At last she contrived to wheedle it out of him. His worry was that he had been entrusted by the Government with an important secret mission to India. He must leave in a week's time. There was danger involved. He might never return. So in view of that sad prospect, he insisted on making my mother a farewell present—sufficient for her to buy a shop and set up in business. Earlier that very night, her lover said, he had begged his wife to agree to a definite separation. But his wife had refused firmly once and for all—for the sake of their own child. Therefore, as he could never marry my mother, perhaps—he suggested—my mother might contemplate marriage with some other man. Someone of her own age, perhaps, so her child should have a father. The following day her heart-stricken, disconsolate lover arrived with exactly enough money to purchase a property which a friend of his had happened to see was for sale in Lambeth. Conveniently enough, it consisted of a shop with a freehold house beside it. A week later her gallant lover left for India.

"What could I do?" my mother asked, staring down at the glass in her hand. "I wanted my child to have a father. I knew John Ashby fancied me because, when I'd been working in the pub, he used to come round almost every night. I didn't know then that for all his swagger he was no man at all, and I wasn't to know he'd end up a drunkard."

My mother put down her glass. "John Ashby married me," she said. "Six months later you were born. But John Ashby isn't your father. Your father is Sir William Steede, a baronet with an estate near Nottingham."

I was silent. For a while I couldn't think of anything to say. I couldn't look at her. When a boy is fourteen he's apt to think his parents should behave like saints—even though he knows he doesn't behave well himself. I had always admired my mother in every way. So I was shocked and disgusted by the thought of someone using her like a prostitute. I felt humiliated. I couldn't understand how my mother could not only appear to accept what had happened but could even seem proud, in some way, of the relationship. I felt somehow I had been cheated. By all rights I should have been thoroughly aggrieved—there was no doubt about it. But I was surprised and rather dismayed to find that above all my other emotions I was excited and extremely curious.

"Where is my father now?" I asked. "Is he still alive?"

"He's back in India," my mother answered. "He's on one of his travels. It may be secret again, for all I know."

"Do you mean you've never seen him since?"

Again my mother sighed. "When he returned to England he sent a message to me saying he daren't come and see me."

"Why not?"

Though there was no one who could be listening, my mother dropped her voice to a whisper. "Because Lady Steede was having him followed by detectives," she answered. Then she got up from the table. "We're both tired out," she said. "I'll tell you more tomorrow, when we're alone together—though there's not really much more to tell." Then she tried to smile. "But at least one good thing has come out of tonight. At least we've made a decision. We've definitely made up our minds that you'll go to sea, haven't we?"

"Yes," I answered. "We've made up our minds."

Three weeks later, I was apprenticed to Captain Broome of the ship *Viking*, a brig of about four hundred tons, bound for Vera Cruz. Only a few hours before we sailed, I heard of my mother's death.

My duties on board were quite simple. I waited at table in the saloon, and I did the general work of a cabin-boy. At first I was confused by the lay-out of the vessel, and I was dismayed when a stiff breeze sprang up and the ship began to heave with the swell.

The life was rough. But I didn't mind—I was so glad to be away from the reek of meat.

I messed with the crew forward. My berth was in the fo'c's'le. I worked hard, and as the days passed by I began to settle down. Soon I became quite friendly with the second mate and his young friend George, who was a deck-hand. The second mate, Russell, was a spry, slim little man of thirty with large eyes and thickly curling fair hair. A second mate is really neither officer nor man: he works with the crew. So Russell was on the same watch as young George, and they always seemed to be together. George was a plump, gentle-faced boy of sixteen. He was quiet, almost furtive, and he had a pleasant, rather girlish smile. He looked soft, but he was surprisingly strong in the arm, and he drank as much grog as his friend Russell did. George appeared to dote on Russell. He almost fawned on him.

At first I hadn't liked Russell. I felt awkward with him because when I was alone with him on deck he'd keep staring at me. But he was always kind to me, and he helped me to find my way around. However, there was one thing I didn't like about him— he enjoyed being mysterious. He used to have secret little jokes with George which I couldn't understand. I felt sometimes Russell was teasing me. When he'd see me come out of Captain Broome's cabin after I'd finish cleaning in there, Russell would come up to me. He'd take hold of my chin in his hand and stare at me.

"Has the Captain offered you a glass of grog yet?" he'd ask. And when I'd shake my head, he'd smile. "Well, it's early days yet," he'd say. "But I'll be surprised if he doesn't—a lad like you. And if he does offer you a glass, my advice to you is to drink it. Drink every drop of it."

One afternoon Captain Broome sent for me. When I went into his cabin he was lying on his bunk. He was a tall, stout man of about fifty with a heavy red face which always seemed to be scowling. He had a small beard and a thick moustache beneath a nose which seemed to spread all over his features. His eyes were small but keen, and now they seemed to pierce me as he looked at me.

"Close the door," he said. Then he stared at me for a while. "How old are you, Ben?"

"Fourteen," I answered.

"Fourteen, *sir*," he said, glowering at me.

"Fourteen, sir," I repeated. "Nearly fifteen."

"And you come from Lambeth? Is that correct?"

"Yes, sir."

The Captain took a gulp of grog from the glass beside him. "Have you been with a girl yet?"

I didn't answer, but I could feel myself blushing.

"I asked if you'd been with a girl yet?"

"Yes, sir," I answered.

The Captain laughed quietly. "Good for you. Now then, I want us to be friends on this voyage. So pour yourself a glass of grog, Ben, and we'll have a drink together."

I'd had a few sips of grog and I didn't fancy it much, so I poured myself out a small measure.

"Fill the glass right up," the Captain said. "Right up, do you hear me?"

He watched carefully to make sure I poured myself a full glass. Then he gave a short laugh. "Now let's see you drink it down," he said. "Drink it down, I tell you."

I began to drink, and then choked.

"Drink it all down," he repeated.

I made another effort and choked again. "I can't, sir. Not all of it, or I think I'll be sick."

The Captain watched me in silence for a moment. "All right. Now come over here," he said after a pause. "Come over here and stand by the bunk."

I moved cautiously towards him. I'd begun to guess what it might all be about.

"Come closer," he said.

I took another step towards him. Suddenly he seized hold of

me and pulled me down on to the bunk beside him, and his hands started snatching at my clothes. I could smell the stench of his breath and the sweat of his body. For an instant I was stunned by the violence of my disgust at what he was trying to do. Then I gave a kind of leap. I wrenched myself away from him and made for the door.

"Come back," he cried. "Come back here!"

But I rushed out of the door and closed it quickly behind me. Suddenly I leaned over the side and was sick.

When I got into the fo'c's'le, Russell was there. Immediately he noticed my torn shirt. He walked across to me, took my chin in his hand, and gazed at me. Then he leaned forward and sniffed. I suppose he was smelling my breath.

"Did you drink the whole glass?" he asked.

I shook my head. Russell looked into my eyes intently for a while. Then he sighed and made a clucking noise with his tongue.

"You should have drunk the whole glass," he said. "You'll regret you didn't take my advice. But remember—it's never too late."

A few days later I was in the saloon. I'd done a bit of cleaning but the ship was rolling heavily and I felt tired because I'd stayed up late the previous night playing crib with Russell and George. I sat down on the bunk by the table, and I must have dozed off. I was awakened by a cuff on the head. I looked up. The Captain was standing over me. He was holding a length of rope in his hand.

"I'll teach you to sleep, when you should be doing your work," he said. Then he started lashing me. He never spoke again, but I could hear his heavy breathing between each lash. When he'd finished, he turned away quickly and walked out. I limped over to the fo'c's'le. Russell was drinking grog with George. Both of them were fairly drunk, but there was nothing surprising in that. Ships carried huge casks of spirits in those days—I dare say they still do—and I'd heard that drunkenness in masters, officers, and men was a frequent cause of ships being wrecked. The officers when drunk would give the wrong orders; the men when drunk would fall asleep on look-out or at the helm.

As I limped in, Russell glanced up at me. "No grog this time?" he asked. He shook his head at me in exaggerated reproach. "Take my advice—drink every drop of it when you next get the chance." Then he turned to his young friend and ruffled his hair. "George did in his time. Didn't you, Georgie?" he laughed.

George simpered and wriggled his shoulders. "I'll say I did," he answered, smiling up at Russell and leaning his head against him.

The following day I was sent for by the Captain soon after sundown. The ship was rolling gently in a mild swell. Already the air was growing warmer as we moved slowly south. As I came in I noticed the portholes of the cabin were closed and the little curtains drawn. The Captain was sitting in a chair by his seachest. The brass lamp shone down on his bunk. Lying on the bunk was a long white whip with a silver handle. I'd never seen anything like it before. I couldn't stop looking at it. The whip, where the handle began, was as thick as a man's thumb, but it slowly tapered down until the end of it was as thin as the tip of a pencil. There was something horrible about its stained whiteness and slight curve. It seemed to speak of evil, and torn flesh.

"Close the door," the Captain said. Then once again he stared at me, examining me very carefully. "You know I like this ship to be kept clean and polished?" he asked me after a pause. I nodded. "So now look at the lamp above your head," he said. "The glass hasn't been cleaned, and the brass hasn't been polished for a week. That's your job, isn't it?" Again he paused. His gaze was now moving up and down me, from my feet to my head. Then he glanced towards the long white whip. "I don't want to have to punish you," he said. "So I think we should have a little talk. But first let's have a glass of grog. Pour out two glasses, Ben. Two full glasses. . . . That's right."

He took one of the glasses from my hand, watching me closely. "Now then," he said. "Let me see you drink the whole of your glass down this time. . . . That's right, Ben. . . . That's right."

I put up with it because I obviously had to. But each time it sickened me. And when he saw how much I detested it all, he went still further. It was as if he were determined to break me down so I'd fawn on him, like George now fawned on Russell. But I wasn't going to be broken down like that. He could abuse my body, but he wasn't going to break my spirit. So I put up with it. I even put up with the sly remarks and jokes which were now made by Russell and George and the rest of them. But I counted each day that brought us closer to Vera Cruz. For I'd made a plan.

I was on deck at noon when at last we sighted land. Vaguely we could see a low-lying stretch of sand-dunes on the horizon. Then we could make out the outlines of a fort. Presently some houses and one or two churches came into view. Soon we could see the pilot boat sailing towards us.

That evening the Captain entertained the harbour-master and the ship's agent on board, and they went ashore to dine. The Captain was very drunk when he came back and sent for me. When it was over, he fell asleep. I moved fast. I didn't hesitate, because I'd already planned exactly what I would do. Quickly I took the money from the pockets of his jacket. Without making a sound, I picked up his silver watch and chain which were lying on his sea-chest and slipped them into my trouser pocket. Then I crept out of the cabin, closing the door gently behind me.

Ten minutes later I was on shore.

The wharf was almost deserted. Some carrion birds, black and hideous, were hovering over the carcass of a dead dog. Hurriedly I walked towards the main square where lights were still burning. But I knew I mustn't stay in the centre of the town in case the Captain woke up and discovered the theft, so when I reached the huge white church in the empty square I turned to the left up a side street. Presently I came to a small inn from which a light was shining. I could hear voices and the sound of a guitar. I pushed open the door and walked inside. The room was crowded with Mexicans and Indians, but through the dense smoke I could see two or three sailors who were drinking with girls. I went up to the bar counter. I couldn't speak any Spanish, but I knew that *vino* meant wine.

"Vino, please," I said to the Mexican behind the bar. As I spoke a small man approached me. He moved shyly and delicately. He was a half-caste. He had a round, yellow face and a wispy black moustache which drooped over his thick lips.

"I haven't seen you before," he said, and he spoke as delicately as he moved. "Are you off a ship?"

"Yes," I replied. For some reason he now reminded me of the carrion birds I had seen fluttering on the wharf. Perhaps it was because of his quick gestures and his hands, which looked like claws.

"Then you may wish to change some money," he suggested gently, with a smile.

When I nodded, the half-caste smiled again. Some of his teeth had been rotted to black and others were missing. "Have you any gold coins or only silver?"

While he spoke, the barman pushed a glass of red wine across the counter to me. The half-caste seized the glass, sniffed it, then said something to the barman quickly in Spanish and pushed the glass away.

"That wine was no good," he explained to me. "I tell the man to bring us a bottle of the best wine, and you will be my guest. For you are now in Mexico. I am Mexican. Mexico is my country. So you must be my guest."

An hour later, we were drinking brandy; I was getting very drunk. I peered across the table at the half-caste, who had murmured something I couldn't catch.

"I say that after all those weeks at sea, a strong young boy like you may perhaps need a girl," the half-caste mestizo said, still smiling at me with his thick lips and rotting teeth.

I thought of lying with Jennie in the back garden behind the old pie-shop. Suddenly in my drunken haze I realised I did need a girl. The mestizo was right. I needed a girl to wipe away the humiliations of the past few weeks. I nodded my head. The man's smile grew wider. He slid some coins across the counter to the barman. Then he moved delicately closer to me. "I can find you just what you want," he whispered. "Follow me. I can take you to a house where there are girls of your own age, younger even."

The brothel to which he took me was a two-storeyed little house with a wooden balcony on the outskirts of the town. We sat on greasy upholstered chairs in a whitewashed room, and we drank more brandy. Presently a stout woman appeared from a back room followed by four young Indian girls. They were all dressed in low-cut white dresses with white bows in the plaits of their shining black hair. While the woman jabbered away in Spanish to the half-caste, I looked at the four girls. One of them who was younger than the rest, thirteen perhaps, caught my eye because she was gazing at me intently as if she wanted to convey to me some message. She was very slim. Her breasts were only beginning to form. The mestizo stopped his conversation with the stout woman and turned to me.

"Which one have you chosen?" he asked.

When I pointed to the slim little girl, he nodded in approval. "You have chosen well," he said. "I know her, and she is quite new and she is very good. Her skin is soft like silk. You can spend the whole night with her if you wish."

I hesitated. I was so drunk that it was probably best to stay the night there. They'd never find me so far from the centre of town.

"How much do I pay?" I asked.

"Show me the money I changed for you," the man ordered.

I held out some of the coins. He took two of them and gave them to the stout woman. "That will be enough," he said. "Now I will say good-night to you. Be careful of the rest of your pay which you haven't yet changed."

Without thinking, I put my hand to the breast pocket of my

jacket, and the half-caste smiled. "You are a rich man," he said. "Be careful of your wealth. I will see you in the morning. Enjoy yourself well with the girl. Goodnight."

He turned and left the room. When the front door had closed behind him I glanced towards the stout woman, who smiled. Then she pointed to the staircase. The girl gave me a nervous nod, and then walked ahead of me. I followed her up the rickety stairs and along a short corridor which led to a small room in which a lamp was burning.

When the girl had closed the door, I put my arms around her. For an instant she let me kiss her. Then suddenly she turned away her head and began whispering to me urgently in a language which I supposed was Spanish. In my drunkenness I imagined she wanted some more money, so I gave her a large silver coin. When she slipped it away in her dress I thought I had guessed rightly the reason for her whispers. I began to take off my clothes. But she shook her head violently. She seized hold of my hand and dragged me across to the window which was open, and pointed downwards. I looked out. In the faint moonlight I could see there was a drop of about twenty feet into a small back yard overgrown with weeds. Almost frantically now, the girl pointed downwards. Obviously she wanted me to jump down. But I was too stupid with drink to understand her message. I only knew I wanted her so badly I couldn't wait any longer. I grabbed hold of her and pulled her down onto the bed.

Suddenly the door was flung open. I looked up. A burly-looking Mexican strode into the room. Following him was the half-caste. As I stared at them in bewilderment, the big Mexican rushed at me, and the girl screamed. Then, at last, I understood.

I was young, but I was strong for my age. I fought back. I managed to hold off the Mexican's attack while I backed towards the window. Then I saw the half-caste draw a knife. At that instant the Mexican caught me a blow in the forehead. I can remember struggling in their grasp as their hands tore at me and the girl screamed still louder. Then I remember nothing more.

When I opened my eyes in a daze of pain, I was lying almost

naked on a beach. Half a dozen ragged Indians were standing around me, staring down at me. I was all sticky with blood. I tried to move, and I felt a stab of pain. Vaguely I can remember a voice saying "*médico*," and I can remember their dark stolid faces as they stooped down to lift me. Then I lost consciousness again.

Next time, when I opened my eyes, I was in a small white-washed room. A woman was standing at the foot of my bed, and a man was beside me, bending over me, adjusting a bandage round my chest. I was still dazed, so I stared at them in silence. The man fastened the bandage and stood up.

"Is he all right, do you think?" the woman asked. I was surprised she spoke English. I wondered if I'd heard rightly or if I was dreaming.

The man gave a short laugh. When he answered her, I noticed he spoke English with a foreign accent.

"He will live," the man said.

The man was a Spanish *médico*. Dr Armando Pineda was about forty-five years old, slim and alert, with a pallid face, a pointed beard and worn, rather yellow eyes which seemed to bulge out from behind his gold-rimmed spectacles. His manner was always exaggeratedly meek and humble as if he were apologising for the arrogant expression of his face. He had, I discovered, private means, but he ran a little hospital in the centre of the town for the poor of the district.

The woman who had been standing at the foot of my bed was Ellen, his wife, who was English. She had met him many years previously when he had been a prosperous young doctor in Madrid. I never found out how old Ellen was. She might have been forty, because there were streaks of grey in her mouse-coloured hair. Her pale complexion was very fair and so delicate that her skin turned bright pink in the sun, and her nose was always peeling. Though she was fragile-looking, the long hours she worked at the hospital never seemed to tire her. When she came back to the house where they lived by the sea, a mile out of the town,

Ellen always seemed jaunty. But once, when I came into the room quietly and she wasn't expecting me, I found her crying.

It was to Dr Pineda's house by the sea that the Indians had carried me. It was the doctor and his wife who nursed me back to health. At first, I was just another of the 'poor' whom it was their mission in life to look after. But gradually, as the days passed by, they became quite fond of me. Certainly I became devoted to them, for they were kind, gentle, understanding people who honestly dedicated themselves to the good of others.

One of the reasons they became fond of me so quickly may have been that they were childless. By the time I was strong enough to leave, they had more or less adopted me.

Once Ellen and Dr Pineda had decided to "take on the responsibility" of looking after me, as he put it, they went about their task with enthusiasm. Ellen gave up going to the hospital in the mornings so she could stay home to educate me. Patiently and gently she gave me lessons in writing and grammar, and she taught me Spanish, which she spoke fluently. In the evenings, when the doctor came back from the hospital, he would give me "general instruction," as he called it. Dr Pineda would sit in his little study alone with me, talking about subjects which ranged from religion and philosophy to astronomy and physics. The afternoons were my own. I could go swimming or I could ride one of the horses they had in their stables. From a state of misery, my life had now, at the age of fifteen, become almost perfect.

I say "almost" because now I was well again I'd begun to long for a girl. Unfortunately the few girls I ever met with Ellen or the doctor were so carefully guarded they were not even allowed out into the streets alone. A relation or a maid always had to be with them. At nights, now, I'd lie in bed in my neatly-furnished whitewashed room at the back of the house and I'd think of the little Indian girl with her unformed breasts and her skin like silk. I began to think about visiting a brothel. This time, I told myself, I wouldn't be drunk. I'd only have just enough money on me, saved up from the weekly pocket-money Ellen gave me. I wouldn't look like a sailor; I'd be dressed more like a Mexican, and I'd be able to speak in Spanish. Moreover, I'd go to the place in daylight. On one of my rides I'd seen a house on the edge of the town which I was fairly sure was a brothel, for I'd seen two girls at the upper windows who'd beckoned to me and laughed when I rode on. I could remember the house because its decrepit balcony was painted a dark blue and the front was a faded pink.

One afternoon when Ellen had left for the hospital I walked towards town. I found the faded pink house and I knocked firmly at the door. For a time nothing happened. Then a grill in the door was slid open, and a pair of dark eyes with a wisp of grey hair dangling between them examined me. After a pause I could hear bolts being pulled back, and the door was half opened by an old woman in a black dress with beads sewn all around the collar. She looked cautiously up and down the street to make sure I was alone. Then she let me in. She closed the door behind me.

"*Qué quieres?*" she asked.

I smiled at her. "*Una muchacha,*" I answered.

The old woman gave a short cackle. "*Una muchacha,*" she repeated, imitating my accent. Then she said in Spanish, "How much will you pay?"

I produced the coins from my pocket, and she peered at them carefully.

"*Nada más?*" she asked. "Nothing more?"

"No more," I said. In fact, I'd got some more money, which I intended to give to the girl herself.

"Only Conchita's in," the woman said. "The others are in town."

"Then let me see Conchita," I answered.

The woman nodded and bolted the door. Then she pointed to an armchair in the corner of the dimly lit room. I sat down, and the woman shuffled away along a corridor which led to the back of the house. Presently she came back. She was followed by a tall Mexican girl of about eighteen who was wearing a red silk wrap. The girl's hair was undone. Her dark eyes were still heavy with sleep. Obviously she'd just been woken from her siesta. Her face looked petulant and sulky, but my gaze was fixed on her slender body. Beneath the thin wrap I could see the outline of her breasts and her long slim thighs. The sudden intensity of my desire almost choked me. I couldn't speak. I nodded my head. The old woman looked towards the girl, who turned indolently and moved back along the corridor. I followed her into a small, fetid room with a window which looked out onto a shady courtyard. The shutters were half open, and I closed them. Then I came back to the girl. I took off her wrap. Her body was tawny and gleaming. I ran my hands over her warm skin. She watched me with her impassive dark eyes. As I stripped off my clothes she glanced at me for an instant quite indifferently, then languidly she crossed over to the bed and stretched herself out on it, waiting for me. Only when I had thrust deep into her did she show any sign of awareness. Then she gave a little sigh. Soon her fingers began to slide up and down my back, and presently they were moving faster with each thrust, until finally she clutched my neck in the frenzy of her wild fulfilment.

Whenever I had enough money I would visit the faded pink house, and I always took Conchita because it excited me to pierce through the languor of her indifference and to watch her panting while she reached her last spasms of ecstasy.

Six weeks later, when I went into the doctor's study for my evening lessons, I noticed he looked even more tired than usual. His large protuberant eyes blinked at me wearily from behind his gold-rimmed spectacles.

"Vera Cruz is really a small town," he said to me after pretending to search for some papers. "A small town," he repeated, in his calm, precise voice with its faint accent. "So rumour spreads fast in it. Now, I don't want you to think I'm in any way angered with you, Ben, because I'm not. Not at all so. But I've learned for certain you have been visiting a *burdel* in town—or rather on the edge of town. Now, I must tell you this is wrong. It is morally wrong, and it is dangerous for your health, for at least a quarter of the poor girls working in those places are diseased. Lastly, it harms your reputation and, since you are living with us, it harms Ellen's reputation and to a lesser extent mine."

The doctor took off his glasses, examined them sadly, and began to polish them. His eyes looked oddly naked. "So I must ask you to promise me that so long as you live with us in this house, you will never visit a *burdel* again."

I made the promise, and because I was fond of them both I kept it.

The summer was unusually hot. In Vera Cruz there was a serious outbreak of yellow fever—the dreaded *vómito*. The disease spread rapidly. Soon nearly a hundred people were dying every week, and the doctor insisted that Ellen and I should leave.

He was so concerned about us that he wanted us to go to his hacienda near Taxco, the other side of Mexico City. But Ellen refused to be so far away from him. The doctor therefore arranged for us to ride up to Jalapa in the mountains, fifty miles inland.

Three weeks later, in Jalapa, a tear-stained servant from the house in Vera Cruz brought us the news that the doctor was dead from the fever.

Abruptly our whole lives were changed. The little hospital could not be run without a doctor, and there was no one available to replace Dr Pineda. So Ellen closed the whole place.

In those days Ellen seemed quite stunned. She was often vague and absent-minded. She moved with a strange slowness as if she were walking in her sleep. There was no longer any reason for us to remain in the disease-infected town. Ellen sold the house by the sea, and we moved up to the hacienda south of Taxco, which now belonged to her.

The view of the hacienda which I shall always remember was to be seen when riding southwards from Taxco, with its steep terraces of narrow cobbled streets, and small whitewashed houses, your horse picking its way carefully along a narrow rutted lane, strewn with boulders. On either side of you were dun-coloured mountains. The small patches of grass on their slopes were scorched brown by the fiercely burning sun. All around you, the land was parched, and the scanty blades of grass were withered. Then, as the lane turned a corner into the valley, spread out before you was a blaze of jacaranda, a shining cloud of purple-blue flowers rising with a startling suddenness from the dusty ground. Beyond this vivid blue haze could be seen the grey stone walls and the red-tiled roofs of the sprawling old farm-house, which was my home for over a year.

At sixteen I never for an instant worried about the future. I revelled in my enjoyment of the present. Each day seemed too short for me. I now only had two hours of lessons with Ellen in the morning. The rest of the day I spent on horseback, riding around the property which we were now trying to get into a state of repair after it had been neglected for so long. Walls needed rebuilding, gates renewing, fences had to be put in order, the cowshed roofs repainted, the ground replanted. My day was full. In the evening after supper on a clear night I would sometimes ride into Taxco to search for a girl. For a long while I was unlucky. The prostitutes in the local brothel seemed unattractive, so I was never tempted to break my promise; the girls I met in the narrow cobbled streets were timid or unwilling. It was only a few weeks before my seventeenth birthday that I met Orinava, who was an Indian girl of eighteen.

Orinava lived in a little side street behind the church of Santa Prisca with an old woman who she said was her aunt, but who might well have been a servant, for her room was at the very back of the house, and at a glance from Orinava the old woman, her face half hidden by her black *rebozo*, would retire there, mumbling to herself. As soon as the door had closed behind her, Orinava would stand looking at me, her dark eyes gleaming, her nostrils a little dilated, as if she could smell the fierce excitement rising in me as well as watch the visible signs of it. Then, without a word, she would move up the staircase to her room above. When she had closed the door she would very deliberately take off my clothes, piece by piece, until I was naked. Then she would throw off her dress and kneel down before me, as if I were a god, pressing her lips against my taut flesh while I stroked the tresses of her jet-black hair. Next, as if she were taking part in some native ritual, she would clasp my ankles with her two hands and slide her hands up my legs until they reached my thighs, which she would hold in silence, while her lips caressed my skin. Then, as if she could sense the very instant when I was finding the strain almost unendurable, she would fling herself on to the bed, and her strong dark arms would drag me down on to her. As I entered her, she would begin to tremble, and she would writhe with her whole body, coiling and uncoiling herself like a smooth, brown snake.

Sometimes I would try to find out if Orinava went with other boys in the village. But she would shake her head. "You are my one man," she would say. "So long as you are here to love me, there will be no one else, I promise."

Once I had found Orinava, I began to go into the village more often. Though I would always wait till Ellen had gone to bed before I crept down to the stables below the farm-house to get my horse, during those weeks before my birthday I think Ellen must have known I was visiting Taxco, for sometimes I would see the lamp burning in her bedroom on the first floor when I came back late.

From the gossip of the Indian girls who worked as servants in the house, I gathered that Galdina, the old Indian cook, who had lived at the hacienda since she was a small girl, had planned with Ellen a special dinner for my seventeenth birthday. There were to be five courses and two bottles of wine. I realised therefore that I would not be able to get away to Taxco that evening until well after eleven. So I told Orinava not to expect me until after midnight.

As a birthday present Ellen gave me the gold watch which had belonged to her husband. "Armando would have wanted you to have it," she said. As she spoke I could see the tears in her eyes. But she smiled at me brightly. "Now then, since it's your birthday, what about a glass of sherry before dinner?" she asked.

I looked at the new watch I'd been given. The time was only half past six. Dinner was at seven. Suddenly I was shocked to find I dreaded the prospect of a long evening alone with Ellen. Ever since her husband's death she had grown strangely nervous. At times she would move jerkily as if her slender arms and legs were attached to invisible wires. The grey streaks were more noticeable in her mouse-coloured hair. Her expression was strained. But she always made an effort to be cheerful, and I was grateful to her for all her kindness and affection. So I was now ashamed of my disloyalty, and as we drank our sherry I tried hard to look as if I was enjoying myself.

Over dinner, we talked about the farm and the peons working on it, and the new silver mine which had just started at the foot of the valley. Ellen seemed, for once, to be genuinely happy. She drank her share of the first bottle of wine. By the time we had finished the second, her face was flushed and her faded eyes were shining. I noticed that as usual the skin of her nose was peeling, but for once she had tried to disguise it with powder.

"Shall we go into the living-room for coffee?" she asked, rising from the table, her cheeks glowing. "Since it's such an important occasion, I thought for a special treat we might open a bottle of brandy."

As she walked through the door, I glanced at my watch. To my dismay I saw the time was only a quarter to nine. One of the Indian girls brought in the coffee. While Ellen went to unlock the cupboard to get the brandy, I went into the kitchen and kissed old Galdina on both cheeks and thanked her for the splendid dinner. When I came back into the living-room, I saw to my surprise that Ellen had filled two large glasses almost to the brim.

"Now," Ellen said, "I shall drink a toast." She raised her glass. "Here's to Ben Ashby's seventeenth birthday!" she cried, and she took a long gulp of her drink.

I raised my glass. "Here's to the kindest person I've ever known."

Ellen gave me a bright smile. "I've suddenly thought of something," she announced. "You're now a grown-up young man of seventeen. The time's not yet nine o'clock. You don't want to spend the whole evening at home. Besides, I'm feeling tired. As soon as I've had a little talk with Galdina about meals for tomorrow, I expect I'll be going to bed. So, if you feel like it, and provided you promise me not to get into any mischief, why don't you go down to the village for an hour or two?"

I stared at her in surprise. "Do you mean go now?" I asked.

"Why not?" Ellen asked brightly. "After all, it's your birthday."

I was slightly worried for some reason. Perhaps it was because I felt guilty at leaving her so soon after the elaborate dinner she'd arranged for me. "Are you sure you wouldn't rather I stayed?"

Ellen smiled at me. "I'm feeling quite tipsy from all those glasses of wine," she said. "I'll be going upstairs presently. So come here and kiss me goodnight. Then you can go for a ride to the village. It's a full moon, and it's a Saint's day too. So there'll be plenty of people about."

I kissed Ellen on the forehead. "Goodnight," I said. "Thank you for the birthday present, and thank you for a lovely evening." Then I turned quickly and left the room, because for some reason through my haze of drink I suddenly felt very unhappy.

"Goodnight, my dear," she called out after me.

I reached Taxco before ten. As usual, I left my horse in the charge of the wizened-face Indian I knew in the plaza by Santa Prisca. Then I walked down the tiny, dark cobbled side street to Orinava's house. I knocked softly on the shutters. After a pause, the door was opened by the old woman who pointed up the alley towards the plaza which was lit with lanterns for the fiesta.

"*Orinava está fuera,*" she said. "*No está aquí.*"

But I could see a light in Orinava's room. I was suddenly suspicious. I brushed the old woman aside and walked into the house. I ran quietly up the stairs. Then I threw open the door. Orinava was lying face downward on the bed, and straddling her was a man with thick shoulders and hair all over his pale, bloated body. As he turned, I recognised him. He was the Mexican manager of the new silver mine in the valley.

"Get out," he said.

Orinava gave a little gasp as she lifted her head and saw me. Then she lowered her head on to the pillow.

"Tell him to go," the man said to her.

Orinava shrugged her shoulders and was silent. The man stretched out his hairy arm to the holster in the belt which was lying on the table by the bed. "Tell him to go," the man repeated. "Tell him I'm your man."

Orinava lifted her head. "You must go," she said. "I have now found my man." Then she twisted round her face and kissed him.

For an instant I stared with loathing and disgust at the obese, hairy body she was embracing. Then I swung away from them and ran down the stairs and rushed out into the street. The blood was surging round in my head, swirling with rage and humiliation. The cantina was open in the square. I walked into it and drank three tequilas in quick succession. I couldn't bear to think that even as I stood there at the bar, his gross body was abusing her. Had she knelt to him, I wondered, as she had knelt before me? I drank several more tequilas. I was now very drunk. Even with the old Indian's help I could only just climb onto the saddle. I gave him some money and rode off, clinging on to the pommel of the saddle, knowing my horse would find his way home.

In the stables, I unsaddled my horse and walked up towards the house. The ride home through the cool night air had cleared my head a little, but I was rather unsteady on my feet. As I walked along the cobbled path, I was vaguely aware that the night was heavy with the fragrance of the huge trees of frangipani which grew around the house. To my surprise I saw the lamps were still alight in the living-room. The shutters had not been closed. When I reached the terrace I looked in. Ellen was standing by the table, with her back to the window. In her long black dress she looked as slim as a girl. Then I noticed there was a glass of brandy in her hand. As I watched, she finished the drink and leaned over to the table where the bottle was standing and poured herself another. At that moment I remembered I had only been away a short time. Ellen would not be expecting me back till after midnight. Suddenly, with an odd flash of instinct, I understood the reason for her strangely nervous ways and quaint mannerisms since the doctor's death. I moved quietly along the terrace until I reached the front door. I knocked gently once or twice because I knew she wouldn't want me to find her drinking. Then I walked into the house. "I'm back," I called out.

"Well!" Ellen cried, as I entered the living-room. "You're certainly back early."

"It wasn't much fun in the village," I answered. Then I tried to laugh. "Besides, I didn't like the idea of leaving you alone on my birthday."

Ellen smiled at me brightly. Her face was flushed, her eyes were wide and gleaming, and her hair was all untidy, which made her look quite young. "Anyhow, welcome home, Ben," she said. "Welcome home."

I noticed her glass had vanished. The bottle of brandy now stood on a table in the far corner. I looked at my watch. "It's still not midnight," I said. "So it's still my birthday. So please can we have a last drink together?"

Ellen smiled at me. "If you insist," she answered. "You can help us both to one last drink. You'll find the bottle in the corner. The glasses are in the cupboard."

At that stage, I still hadn't made up my mind. But as I handed Ellen the glass, I saw her dress was unbuttoned at the neck. I could see the wonderfully soft skin of her throat running down to the cleft between her breasts. As soon as Ellen noticed the direction of my gaze she flushed. I could see the waves of redness coursing over her. Quickly she put down her glass and fastened her dress. For some reason it was her gesture of modesty which awakened my desire.

I raised my glass. "I'm going to drink a toast," I said. "I drink to a very sweet person and a very charming one."

Ellen laughed uncertainly. She raised her glass. "I drink to a very sweet and charming young man," she replied.

"Then let's see you drink," I said. "You're only sipping at it."

Ellen laughed again. All the lines had left her face. She was certainly as slim as a girl, and in the lamp-light she looked quite young. "Do you want to make me drunk?" she asked.

As she spoke, I had a sudden vision of her slim body, lying stretched out on her bed, and I could see myself, naked, moving over to her. The surge of desire I now felt was so strong that I turned away from her, because I knew it must show.

"Yes," I answered. "I'd like you to get drunk for once."

"I'm sure it wouldn't be a pleasant sight," Ellen laughed. "Why, already you've moved away from me! So I'd better be careful."

"Finish your drink—please."

"Then turn round and look at me," Ellen said.

"When you've finished your drink. Not until then."

For a moment there was silence. A few grey moths were fluttering around the lamp on the table.

"Have you finished?"

"Yes," Ellen answered in an odd voice. "I have."

Slowly, deliberately, I turned round and faced her. She was standing with her arm on the back of a chair. Her wrist was trembling. Yet the set of her features which before had been taut was now loose. As her eyes met my gaze, she drew in her breath. Then I saw her glance downwards at me, and she gave a little sigh. I was about to move across to her when she raised her head. "Well," she said—and I could hear the effort she made to force her voice to sound casual. "Well, I think I've had enough to drink for this evening, so I shall say goodnight to you." Her eyes now seemed to be pleading with me, beseeching me to accept her remark as her true intention. But she did not move. She remained with her arm resting on the chair. Her wrist was now trembling as frantically as the wings of the moths round the lamp. For a while I stared at her.

Then I moved towards her. I put a hand on her shoulder, while my other hand began to unbutton the top of her dress. Her whole body now was shaking as if with a fever.

"No, Ben," she whispered. "Please. You mustn't!"

Then I kissed her lips while my hand slid inside her dress, and suddenly I felt her arms clasping me.

Presently I took her upstairs to her room. I undressed her and laid her down on the bed. Then I took off my clothes until I was naked as I had been in my vision. Slowly I crossed over to the bed and stood beside her, gazing down at her. Then I lowered myself onto the bed. I took her in my arms, and soon we were joined, and at last my desire was released in a long surge which mingled with her spasms and little moans of anguish. "Oh, my darling," she cried out in her moment of ecstasy. "Please, now. Now, my darling. Now."

When I woke up in my bedroom I was at first only conscious of the painful throbs of my headache and of the shrilling of the cicadas outside. The shrilling would fix onto a single high-pitched note which seemed to drill piercingly into my ears. Then, with a lurch of remorse, I remembered. As I dressed I was filled with a sensation of guilt mixed with dread. I knew I'd committed no terrible crime, but what I'd done was just as irrevocable. I felt weak from my apprehension as I went downstairs. I could see no one about. I walked into the dining-room. There was an envelope on the table addressed to me in Ellen's writing. I ripped it open. I can remember the exact words of the letter even now.

"Dear Ben,
I've gone to Mexico City to stay with some friends for a while, because I can't face seeing you. I know I'm equally to blame. But the fact remains we both of us betrayed the memory of a fine man who loved us. When you think it over, I'm sure you'll understand why we never meet again. You're strong enough now to make your own way in the world.
Before we left for Jalapa in the epidemic, Armando

gave me some money. This included three hundred dollars which he wanted you to have in the event of his death. I've put it for you in the top right-hand drawer of my writing-desk. The key to it is under the inkstand. The horse is yours, of course, and the saddle as well.

Good luck to you, Ben, my dear,
Ellen."

I left the hacienda that afternoon. It was a day of bright sunshine, I remember, without a cloud in the sky. I suppose I ought to have been feeling wretched. Certainly I felt very sad about Ellen, and I regretted what I'd done. But when I considered my position I felt less unhappy. I was seventeen; I had three hundred dollars in my pocket and a strong horse beneath me; I spoke quite good Spanish, and I wasn't afraid of work. I was confident about the future.

For a year or two I wandered. At various times and places I was cook, farm-hand, clerk, storekeeper, and barman. It was in Mexico City that the event occurred which led indirectly to my journey to Australia.

One evening I was having a drink at a café in the Zocalo. Sitting at the table next to me was a large, flabby man with grey hair and a grey, carefully trimmed beard and large, plump fingers which I noticed because there were several rings on them. He was wearing a dark-blue velvet coat, a floppy necktie, and black and white sponge-bag check trousers from which his paunch bulged out obscenely. Though he spoke to the waiter in Spanish, I was certain the man was English. I glanced at his companion, who was a young Mexican boy of about seventeen, with a smooth oval face and over-large, over-expressive eyes which were now fixed admiringly on the florid, bulky man. The boy's ardent expression reminded me of young George when he would fawn on Russell. Suddenly as I watched the two of them, the man turned and saw me. For a moment he looked at me in surprise. Then he waved his hand. As he rose heavily to his feet, and lumbered towards me, I saw he was drunk.

"Hallo!" he cried. When he spoke I knew he was certainly English. "Hallo, Jimmy! I thought you'd gone to Acapulco."

I smiled and shook my head. "My name's not Jimmy," I said.

The Englishman stared at me. Then he laughed. "Sorry," he said. "For a moment I thought you were James Smith—or Jimmy, as he prefers to be called. But I *can* see you're not. You're heavier than he is. There's an amazing likeness, though. You haven't by any chance a brother called Jimmy Smith?" The man laughed again. "Or perhaps I should put my question differently," he said. "You haven't by any chance got a brother *calling himself Jimmy Smith*—because I'm quite sure that in fact the young man's name was no more Smith than mine's Queen Victoria."

At that instant my mind began to work. James or Jimmy, he'd said, and there was an "amazing likeness." Now, I suddenly remembered the paragraph I'd seen some months previously in an English newspaper which announced 'it was believed' that James Steede, 'son of Sir William Steede, Bart.', had left for Mexico. I recalled the announcement because naturally I was interested in Sir William Steede. After all, I was his son too—though only a bastard one. So, of course, James was obviously my half-brother.

Suddenly I realised this could well be the explanation for my "amazing likeness" to someone *calling himself Jimmy Smith*.

I nodded my head. "All right," I said, smiling at him. "I confess it. I am Jimmy's brother. My name's Ben Smith." And I gave him a wink.

The man peered at me suspiciously through his watery eyes and was silent.

"When did Jimmy leave for Acapulco?" I asked.

The man hesitated. I noticed he was swaying slightly. "A month or two ago," he answered. "But you're not his brother, and I'll tell you why. Jimmy's accent was put on—I'm sure of it. Yours isn't."

I remembered Ellen's lessons in diction. "Are you sure?" I asked, speaking very correctly.

The man did not answer. But his bleary eyes examined me for a while.

"No, I'm not sure," he said after a pause. "But you're certainly a very attractive young man. However, I don't suppose you and Jimmy share the same particular tastes?"

For a moment I gaped at him. The man shook his head in disapproval. "No," he said. "Somehow I didn't think you did. Never mind." He paused. "One can't have everything," he added. Then he turned slowly away from me and swayed back to his table where his young companion sat waiting for him patiently.

I was fed up with the drunken life I'd been leading in Mexico City. I was intrigued with the prospect of meeting my half-brother—if my guess was right and Jimmy Smith was James Steede. I liked the idea of living beside the sea again. I'd always longed to see the Pacific. So a few days later I left for Acapulco.

I arrived in Acapulco in the middle of May—only to discover, after a while, that Jimmy Smith had sailed to the port of Lima, on board the *Clara*, three weeks previously.

Four days later the rumour about the *Clara* was officially confirmed. There was some wreckage—but not a single survivor.

By then I'd taken a fancy to Acapulco. I enjoyed the lazy sun-drenched life. I liked walking round the vast sweep of the harbour, gazing at the ships lying at anchor in the smooth stretch of shining water. I was amused by the cantinas where the people sang and drank coffee laced with rum or brandy. The balmy, soft air from the ocean seemed to lull me into a delicious torpor of idleness, and I'd met a little mestizo girl who moved into my room in the shabby old hostel where I was living. I decided to stay in Acapulco for a while.

But I needed to make enough money to pay my bill at the hotel. So I found myself a part-time job, working as barman in a sailors' bar down by the harbour.

A few weeks later, I was talking at the bar with an American sailor who had arrived in a schooner from Melbourne three months previously. He was a tall, big-boned man with a solemn, long-jawed face which made him look taciturn. But, to my surprise, after a few drinks he became almost garrulous. Presently he began talking about life in Australia. Then it was that he mentioned the gold-rush.

"People are making their way to the gold fields they've found out there from all parts of the world," he said. "People are spending their last bean to get a passage. Ships are being hijacked and turned round in mid-voyage so the crew can get there." Then he lowered his voice. "Take the ship *Clara* that disappeared some weeks ago," he said. "They found wreckage, it seems. They found rafts, and her long-boat was drifting and derelict. But I don't believe it." He rubbed his nose with his thick finger. "What cargo was the *Clara* carrying? I'll tell you. Phosphates, lentils, and coffee-beans. Who in their senses would take coffee-beans to Lima? All right, maybe the coffee was for a port further on. But I doubt it, and for a very good reason. Why did Captain Leigh order a dozen spare rafts a fortnight before the ship sailed? A dozen, mark you—I only found out about it because I happened to go to the chandler's soon afterwards. A dozen rafts."

The American finished his drink. He pushed his glass across the counter for me to refill it.

"A dozen rafts," he repeated. "Each with the *Clara's* name painted on it." The American grinned. "You might be tempted to think someone was keen that if the *Clara* was wrecked, everyone would know about it," he said. "And I'm pretty sure you'd be correct—except that the *Clara* wasn't wrecked. They lowered the long-boat, and they dropped the rafts to make people think she'd been wrecked. It was all a put-up job, I'm sure of it. I don't mind betting you that at this very instant the *Clara* is sailing hard for Melbourne."

By this time I was oddly certain that Jimmy Smith *was* my half-brother. When I had reached Acapulco and found that he had died in a shipwreck I'd suddenly realised how badly I'd wanted

to meet him. It wasn't only because I'd never had any brothers
or sisters. It was more than that. I was curious to see what kind of
a person my aristocratic half-brother would turn out to be. Yet it
went deeper than that even. People sometimes talk about "meeting their destiny," and I think that using the phrase is the only
way I can explain what I felt. I believed it was my destiny to meet
James Steede. I was certain, now, that I'd never rest until I'd
tracked him down.

I'd gone all the way to Acapulco to meet him. Why shouldn't I
go to Australia to find him—when I could get there for nothing?

In June I shipped as a deck-hand in a brig sailing to Sydney.

I arrived in the middle of the Australian winter. Heavy rain
clouds hung low over Sydney as we sailed in between the heads.
But a mild drizzle could not diminish the great sweep of the harbour with its green coves and lovely headlands.

Sydney itself very much resembles an English seaport town.
There is the same jostling throng of cabs and carts and omni-
buses and private carriages—though I don't know why I should
have expected it to be any different. Yet I was surprised to see
that the cab-drivers, 'bus-conductors, butcher-boys, and bakers all
looked as they did in London—even the policemen looked the
same from their hats to their truncheons. The men I saw walking
along the street wore coats of tweed or black cloth, light-coloured
waistcoats and the usual black chimney-pot hats. The women
were a little more informally dressed than in England, wearing
very light materials—generally the brightest colours of muslin. To
find something typically Australian I had to go to the Natural
History Museum in Hunter Street where in the window I could
see stuffed specimens of kangaroos, opossums, bandecoots, and
dingoes.

But after I'd settled down in a little room in some cheap lodgings I began to observe the differences rather than similarities.
The Australians seemed very slightly taller than people you'd see
in London. They were larger and looked healthier, leaner and

tougher, and they seemed far more easy-going and carefree. Even their speech was indolent. They were capable of prodigious bouts of energy and hard work. Yet deep down there was a strange laziness in their character. They lived for the present, and they enjoyed their pleasures heartily, without any shame. They took it for granted that life should be enjoyable, just as they took for granted the wonders of their scenery and the beauty of their children.

I found a part-time job as a waiter. In my spare moments I wandered round the town in search of any scrap of news I could glean which would help me to find Jimmy Smith. I didn't go to the gold-diggings, because the little I knew about my half-brother made it hard to imagine him wielding a pick-axe or cradling ore in some forlorn creek. Besides, why should a man who owned Steede Hall with rentals of thousands of pounds a year want to toil in the gold fields? For my half-brother now owned Steede. A few weeks after I'd arrived in Australia, I'd seen an announcement, in an old London magazine I'd found in my lodgings, that Sir Willian Steede was dead. The title had passed to Arthur Steede, James's younger brother, since James had been presumed dead after the shipwreck of the *Clara*. I felt certain James Steede had reasons of his own for living abroad in Mexico and Australia under an assumed name—reasons other than a desire to make a fortune.

As I went about the town in my spare time, I soon made friends. The Australians were the friendliest people I had ever known—though there was some cruelty mixed up in their kindness. Almost every night I'd visit a new bar, because I had an idea it would be in a bar I'd find the information which would lead me to my half-brother. I might even meet him one night. For I was fairly sure Jimmy would frequent bars. When my mother had warned me —amongst other things—of the wickedness of drink, she had told me the Steedes had been heavy drinkers for many generations, so a taste for drink was in my blood. Jimmy would have inherited the same weakness. But there were about five hundred public houses in Sydney—many of them as huge and garish as the gin palaces of

London—so I realised that even if James were living in the town I might never meet him.

Soon I became so absorbed by life in this new world and so fascinated by the new friends I was making that I began to forget about my quest for Jimmy Smith.

One evening I was drinking at a table with three young Australians and their girls in the largest of the gin palaces. I was laughing because they'd christened the girls, who were recent immigrants, by the name of the ship in which they'd arrived, so that one, for instance, was called Susan Endeavour and another was called Matilda Agamemnon. As I laughed, a tall, well-made, pleasant-looking young man, who had just come into the saloon, caught sight of me and walked straight towards me.

"Hullo, Jimmy," he said.

The moment had come at last, and this time I was prepared. "Hullo," I answered, getting up and smiling at the man. "What will you drink?" My voice sounded friendly and calm.

"A Spider," he said.

I'd no idea what a Spider was, but I walked with the young man to the bar and ordered two of them, and I discovered that a Spider was a drink made of lemonade and brandy.

"How's life?" the young man asked cheerfully. "I see you've managed to keep out of the jail so far."

"I've been lucky," I answered, laughing.

"You've certainly put on a little weight at last," he said.

The man was a friendly, exuberant, unsuspicious person. He was already a little drunk, and with each drink he became less reticent. By the time we had finished our first drink, I had found out without any difficulty that his name was Harry Denkin. By the time we had drunk three Spiders each, I had discovered that my half-brother, for whom he mistook me, lived in a shanty house on a small homestead, a short distance outside the little township of Berrima, eighty-five miles from Sydney. Jimmy Smith had a large paddock, and he broke in horses for a living.

"What are you doing in Sydney?" Harry Denkin asked me later in the evening. "Why aren't you in Berrima?"

"I thought I'd come here for a bit of a break," I answered, giving him a wink and looking towards Susan and Matilda. But Harry missed the implications of my glance.

"Where are you living?" he asked.

"In lodgings just off George Street," I answered.

Young Harry stared down at his glass and was silent. His face was suddenly stiff and dark with embarrassment. "Look," he said after a pause. "I've got a bed for the night, so I shan't be going back with you." He took a gulp of his drink. Then he looked up at me. His expression was a mixture of apology and defiance. "If you want to know, I'm living with a girl," he muttered.

Then I knew my guess about James Steede had almost certainly been correct.

"Good for you," I said with a grin. "Now what about another Spider? It's my shout."

Two days later I took the coach to Berrima—which I discovered was the aborigine name for a black swan.

Convict labour had made a road of sorts to Berrima nearly twenty years previously. But the going was so rough that it took the coach a whole day to drive thirty miles. The road the whole way was littered with broken-down vehicles of every description —from gigs and spring-carts to the heavy bullock-driven drays —all stuck fast or buried in the mud. The wild, broken country through which the road passed favoured bush-rangers, so a detachment consisting of a sergeant and three troopers was stationed at various townships on the route.

In the afternoon of the third day we arrived at Berrima township.

Berrima was a prosperous-looking settlement not unlike a small country town in Kent, with its imposing stone Court House, and trim little whitewashed houses, and grey stone church and grim-looking gaol. The coach stopped on the green outside the Surveyor-General Inn. While I drank a glass of beer in the warm, cheerful parlour I discovered how to get to Jimmy Smith's homestead, which overlooked the Wingecarribee river.

As I approached the homestead, I felt suddenly nervous. I was conscious of my heart beating, and I was sweating. At last I was approaching the end of my long search. Within a few minutes I would meet my half-brother. I had only a vague idea what he would be like. I couldn't tell what reception I would get from him.

I could see a man in the homestead's upper paddock. The man was busy fixing a rail between the posts, so at first he didn't notice me. The first thing I observed about him was the light colour of his hair—the very same pale straw colour as mine. Then I saw he was about the same age as I was. Next, as he turned towards me, I immediately saw the likeness between the two of us. It was so startling I nearly gasped in surprise. With his light-blue eyes, straight short nose, and his mouth which lifted a little at the corners, Jimmy might have been my twin. The resemblance was astonishing. I was staring at my own image. Perhaps I was a little more strongly built. Apart from that, I was almost a model of him. As I looked at him, I saw that he was staring back at me with an expression close to fear in his eyes. I could guess the reason. I was prepared for the shock of meeting someone who could have been my double. He, of course, wasn't. So I gave him a smile to show I'd come as a friend.

"You're Jimmy Smith," I said.

He was silent for a moment. Then he swallowed, as if his mouth was dry. "Who are you?" he asked. "What's your name, for heaven's sake?"

The likeness was extraordinary. Even the sound of his voice seemed the same. When I gazed at him, it was like looking in the mirror and seeing a slightly altered image of myself—an altered image, for I now saw that his features were softer than mine; his shoulders were a little narrower, and his waist a trifle slimmer.

Suddenly it occurred to me how odd the situation was. He was the rightful baronet and the heir to all the Steede estates, and he was obviously nervous. I was the bastard son, almost without a penny left in the world, and I was perfectly confident.

"Who are you?" he repeated.

"My name's Ben Ashby," I answered.

"Where do you come from?" he asked.

"London," I answered. "From Lambeth."

He glanced down the road I'd come along, but there was no one in sight. "How did you know my name?" he asked. "What brought you here?"

His face was screwed up in perplexity. Again I smiled at him. "When you've done staring at me, can't you guess?"

Then for the first time he smiled. "I can guess one reason," he said. "But I'd still like you to tell me."

However, I wasn't going to give in to him right away. Besides, I found to my surprise I rather enjoyed seeing him bewildered.

"What made you decide to call yourself Smith rather than Jones?" I asked. "Because the name began with the letter 'S'—like Steede?"

He flinched as if I had struck him. His hands were shaking. Again he swallowed nervously. Then he frowned. "Is your real name Ashby?" he asked. "Ben Ashby?"

"Yes," I answered. "It is. I've even got papers to prove it."

"Do your parents really live in Lambeth?" he asked.

"My mother lived in Lambeth," I said. "But she died some years ago."

"And your father?" he asked.

"My so-called father's still alive as far as I know," I answered. "As far as I'm aware, he still runs a butcher's shop in Lambeth." Then I gazed at him steadily. "But my real father," I said, "was Sir William Steede. And he's dead—as I expect you know. He died in July, so by law you should have inherited the title. But you were presumed dead after the wreck of the *Clara*. So the title passed to your younger brother, Arthur."

He stared at me in silence. Then, once again, he glanced down the road. "Let's go up to the house," he said. "I have an idea we'd both feel better for a drink."

The light was fading as we approached the two-storeyed little shanty house which was surrounded by a verandah on all sides. As we came in, I could see that the room to the left was the one which was used to eat in. The small room we entered to the right, with its pleasant furniture and chintz curtains, was evidently the living-room. Jimmy pulled forward a comfortable chair for me and crossed to the side-table. Quickly he poured out two brandies and soda. As he turned to hand me my glass I noticed he glanced out of the window. Then he took a long gulp of his drink. He was frowning again. "I can believe we had the same father," he said after a pause. "I can believe you're my half-brother. I've only to look at you and then look at a mirror to have proof. But who, then, was your mother?"

"My mother was a barmaid when your father first met her," I answered. "She was working in a saloon in Lambeth. She was fifteen years old and very pretty, from all accounts. Your father took a fancy to her. So he installed her as his mistress in lodgings in Bermondsey."

I'd thought I had long ago got over the shame and disgust I felt about the whole episode. But as I spoke, bitterness came sweeping back over me from the past. "My mother was his mistress for quite a while. Then she became pregnant. But unfortunately your father had to leave England then—for India."

Jimmy stared at me in silence for a while. "I'm sorry," he said. "From what you say, I'm afraid it seems he treated her badly."

"Oh no," I said—and I couldn't keep the sarcasm away from my voice. "On the contrary. He behaved like a perfect gentleman. He bought her a freehold house in Lambeth with a shop attached to it. So my mother became a lady of property in the circles she moved in. She was in a position to marry almost anyone she pleased—even though she was expecting a child. She married the youngest son of a butcher who'd always been keen on her. His name was John Ashby, and he was able to set up in business as a butcher in her shop."

"Another question," Jimmy said. "Why did you come to Berrima? Was it only to see me?"

"It was," I answered.

"How did you find out I was here?"

Briefly I told him of the chain of events, ending with my meeting with Harry Denkin in Sydney.

"Did Harry tell you he'd stayed here?" Jimmy asked.

"No," I answered smoothly. "I don't think he mentioned it."

"I just wondered," Jimmy said, taking another gulp of his drink. Once again he glanced nervously out of the window. I wondered who it was he was expecting to appear.

"One more question," Jimmy said. "Why have you come here to see me?"

Odd as it seems, up to that moment I'd never tried to put my reason for searching him out into precise words.

"Curiosity mainly, I suppose," I answered. "Besides, I've never had any brothers or sisters. My mother and her husband had no children, so I was the only child in the house. It sounds rather stupid—but I thought I'd rather like to find a brother."

Jimmy's head jerked back. "A brother!" he cried out. "You'd want me for a brother?"

"Why not?" I asked. "You obviously are my brother."

"You didn't come here for money?"

I smiled at him. "If there's any money around," I said, "I'd be glad of a loan—though that wasn't my point in coming here."

The light was growing dark. Jimmy struck a match and lit one of the lamps. He stared at me in surprise, almost in alarm. "Do you mean you want to *stay* here?"

"Is there any reason why I shouldn't?"

Jimmy did not answer. "I don't mind calling myself Ben Smith, if that makes things any easier for you," I continued—and the more I thought about it, the more the prospect of staying in Berrima pleased me. "I like an open-air life. I hate being cooped up in a town. I like riding, and I'm fond of horses."

Jimmy was standing by the window, gazing out along the road. For a few moments he was silent. "If you stay here," he said slowly, "can I really trust you to be Ben Smith, my brother? Can I trust you to stick to the part? Can I trust you not to tell anyone —and I mean anyone—who I really am?"

His face looked so strained, and his manner was so intense that I felt I must do something to calm him. I smiled at him. Then I crossed the room. I stretched out my hand and put it on his shoulder. It was all I could think of to do.

"Yes, you can trust me," I answered.

As I touched his shoulder, Jimmy stared into my eyes. Then he sighed, and suddenly he smiled at me. "You may not like it here," he said. "You may not get on with my partner. But certainly I'd be pleased if you stayed."

"Then let's try it out and see," I answered.

"Very well," Jimmy said. "Now tell me this. We must get things right. Will you be my older or my younger brother?" He laughed. I felt that at last he was growing more at ease with me. "We must make up our minds on that point."

"In fact, I'm half a year younger than you are," I answered. "But I definitely look older." I grinned at him. "Probably because I've had a harder life," I said. "Anyhow, I'll be your older brother."

"Right," Jimmy said. He took my glass and his own and went over to the side-table to pour us out more drinks. I noticed his hands quivered.

"Let's take our drinks onto the verandah," he said, when he handed me my glass. "It's stuffy in here. And there's lots more to get straight."

As we walked out on to the verandah, I saw a slim man with a slight stoop walking up the road towards us.

I was set against Clint from the start because of his proprietorial attitude towards Jimmy.

That evening, when he saw there was someone standing at the corner of the verandah talking to Jimmy, he raised his head a little, and his slouch seemed more noticeable as he sauntered forward to join us. When he spoke, I realised he had been drinking heavily.

"Good evening," Clint said. "It's great to see a guest here for a change." Then, as he came closer, he saw my face in the light of the lamp which was burning in the room inside. For an instant he stiffened. He now eyed me with the tense suspicion of an animal suddenly confronted by an unknown presence which might prove dangerous. But he recovered from his alarm with a surprising rapidity. He forced himself to smile.

"Am I drunk, Jimmy?" Clint demanded with a chuckle. "Or do I now see two of you?"

Jimmy laughed, but I was aware of his intense uneasiness. Suddenly he stretched wide his arm in an exaggerated gesture. "My dear Clint," he said, "allow me to introduce to you my long-lost brother, Ben."

Clint's large eyes were fixed on me. "If you didn't look the image of my partner, I'd think Jimmy was lying," he said after a pause. "He's never even mentioned that he had a brother. But I've only to take a good look at you to see that it's true. Where have you been all these years?"

"I've been a sailor," I answered, smiling at him.

Clint glanced towards Jimmy as if for confirmation, then turned back to me. I now noticed his skin. It was so dark and smooth I wondered if he had native blood in him.

"So I suppose your name's Smith too?" Clint asked.

"That's right," I answered. "Ben Smith."

For a while Clint gazed at me without speaking. I had a curious feeling he was making some kind of assessment of me. "Are you staying here for long?" he asked.

"I hope so," I replied.

"I thought we might clear out the shed behind the kitchen," Jimmy said. "We could turn it into a room for Ben."

Clint looked straight at Jimmy. "Are you sure you wouldn't rather he shared your room?"

Jimmy stared back at him steadily. "I'm sure Ben would prefer a room of his own."

For a moment there was silence. I could feel the strange force of the tension between the two of them. Clint was leaning against one of the wrought-iron supports of the verandah's roof. He seemed perfectly at ease, yet I was aware he was exerting himself in an invisible but fierce effort to overcome some odd, and equally invisible, resistance on Jimmy's part. And I felt Jimmy was using all his energy to ward off the power of Clint's dark gleaming eyes. The struggle between them only lasted a few seconds, but during it I had an impression that each of them was summoning up reserves of strength. Each of them was seeking to explore points of weakness derived from their past relationship. Clint broke the silence.

"Great," he said. "We'll clear the shed for Ben. But first let's have a drink to celebrate his arrival."

That night it was agreed I should be employed by them as a hand in the paddocks, and I should gradually learn the business of breaking in horses.

Hopefully, I had believed the tension between Jimmy and his friend Clint would have been dispelled by the morning. But I soon learned that their antagonism was a permanent part of their relationship. Clint sought constantly to dominate Jimmy and to humiliate him; Jimmy struggled constantly to rid himself of the influence of Clint's power over him. One of his ways of escape lay in drink.

I was amazed how heavily Jimmy drank. He was seldom completely sober, but his drinking never seemed to interfere with his work. As soon as I saw Jimmy in the breaking yard with a colt I knew he had a natural gift with horses. The colt seemed to sense immediately he was a presence not to be feared, and soon it was nuzzling him as he stroked its neck.

"Never pat a horse," Jimmy told me. "It makes him tense. Always stroke him."

I enjoyed my lessons with Jimmy. But I dreaded the hours I had to spend down in the paddock with Clint, for Clint's methods of breaking in a horse, though quick and apparently effective, were unpleasant to watch. The horse would have been confined to the paddock for three days. Clint would then walk into the paddock carrying a hat full of water, and the horse would come up to him. A second later Clint would have a lasso round the animal's neck, and he'd be half choking it. The breaking in had begun. His method ended a day or so later when he would spur the poor exhausted brute round the paddock.

There were few secrets of Clint's friendship with Jimmy I didn't know about after a few weeks, because the shed where I slept was immediately below Jimmy's bedroom, and I could hear them talking when Clint left his room to join Jimmy late at night. I had a feeling Clint was aware I knew about the relationship.

One evening Jimmy got more drunk than usual and staggered upstairs to bed quite early. Clint did not move from his chair by the log fire in the living-room.

"Have you found yourself a girl down in Berrima yet?" Clint asked, a few minutes after Jimmy had gone.

"Not yet, I've been round most of the pubs, but there don't seem to be all that many girls about."

Clint settled himself comfortably in his armchair. "There aren't many," he agreed. "And there's quite a keen competition for the few there are. But with your looks I'd reckon the girls would run after you. There aren't many men as attractive as you to be found around Berrima. Jimmy and I are really your only rivals. But neither of us will stand in your way. I've already got a girl of my own I visit when it takes my fancy, and Jimmy's not interested in girls, as I'm sure you know."

I was silent. I watched the flames flickering up the chimney.

"You'll probably find a girl in time," Clint said. "In the meanwhile, why don't you follow your brother's example?"

I turned and looked at him. As I stared, he withdrew his hands from the pockets of his tight trousers, and stretched out his legs so that I could not avoid seeing his exact shape.

"You've been a sailor," Clint said softly. "So you must have gone in for side-kicks in your time." He smiled at me. "Jimmy sleeps very soundly when he's drunk too much," he added.

I got up from my chair. I spoke casually as if I had not understood I was being offered a direct invitation. "I think I'll go down into Berrima and wander round a pub or two," I said. "I might be lucky and find the very girl I want."

Clint's smile remained fixed on his face, but it now looked incongruous, like a false moustache. He waved his hand gracefully to me as I moved to the door.

"Have a good time," he said.

———

From that moment Clint deliberately ignored me—except when I came down to the lower paddock, when he would sometimes give me flashy displays of horsemanship. He was certainly an astonishingly skillful rider. The more wildly the horse bucked or capered, the more savagely Clint appeared to exult in his final mastery.

Meanwhile Jimmy appeared to grow quieter and to become more sodden every week. By now he had reached a state where he was never quite sober.

The final row took place some three months after I had arrived in Berrima.

At noon that day, when we broke off work for lunch, I noticed that Clint for some reason was drinking brandy and not beer, which he usually had at mid-day. As he rose from the table and crossed to the sideboard to help himself to another brandy he happened to notice that Jimmy glanced at him. I could see Jimmy's look had only been a glance of surprise. But Clint took it as a gesture of disapproval.

"Are you the only one who's allowed to drink round here?" he asked.

"I don't know what you're talking about," Jimmy said. "We all drink as much as we want, and you know it."

"So long as that's agreed," Clint said. Then he lifted the bottle, poured himself half a glass of neat brandy and gulped it down. "It helps to keep out the cold," he chuckled, pouring himself another glass. "It's a cold bleak day, and I feel cold and bleak all over. So I'll get some warmth from brandy—if I can't get it from any other quarter."

"Finish the bottle," Jimmy said. "Why not? There's plenty more."

"I'll think about it," Clint answered. He picked up the bottle and left the room.

After lunch I cleared the table and washed up. I laid the fire in the living-room so that it was ready for the evening. Then I walked to the upper paddock to watch Jimmy at work. His method took a fortnight in all. He was now working with the horses he'd got in the paddock at the stage of the second day. In the breaking-yard was a grey colt, with one eye covered by a blindfold.

"Now then," Jimmy said to me, "I want to get him used to being hobbled. Now watch."

Placing the back of his hand on the wind-pipe, Jimmy slowly but hesitantly ran his hand down the colt's neck to his shoulder. Then he placed the back of his hand against the colt's near-side leg. The colt shifted restlessly but presently stood still.

"When he stands still and gets used to it," Jimmy explained, "you run your hand down the inside of his other leg. When he's got used to that, you take a set of front hobbles and buckle them carefully on. He won't move with the blindfold on him. Then you take off the blindfold, and step back a little behind him, being careful not to scare him. Let him move to feel the hobbles. The next step is to put on a girth. So you put back the blindfold and handle the colt all over his body and under his brisket—his chest. Then you slide the girth on. You let him feel it a couple of times. Then you buckle the girth up firmly, but not too tight. You take off the hobbles. You remove the blindfold, and you let the horse feel the girth."

All the time he'd been talking, I had watched Jimmy with fascination, for it seemed almost magical the way the colt responded to his treatment. Jimmy grinned at me. "Now then," he said. "Let's see you go through all that yourself before we get to the next step."

An hour later Jimmy's lesson for the day was finished. "Now

I'll go through the same thing with the other nine horses that are mustered out there," he explained. "Tomorrow I'll be teaching them to back—which you've already seen. But why don't you go down to the lower paddock and watch Clint for a while?"

I shook my head.

"Why not?" Jimmy asked.

"Because I don't like the way he goes about it," I answered. "I've told you so once before."

Jimmy hesitated. "Go just for a short while," he said. "Clint gets jealous if you only learn from me. He takes it as a criticism of himself." Jimmy smiled at me. "Please go, Ben," he said.

"All right," I answered. "But I won't be able to stay long anyhow. I've a fence to repair in the back yard."

As I walked down through the woods to the lower paddock I suddenly heard a strange sound that was almost a shriek. It was a horse screaming in terror. I shuddered. For an instant there was silence, then I heard Clint's drunken voice. "I'll teach you to kick me," he shouted. "I'll teach you." Then I heard the crack of a whip and another horrible scream—part neigh, part whinny.

As I came out into the clearing, I saw a horse lying on the ground, its front and back legs hobbled. Clint was standing over the horse, a black stallion. His right hand wielded the whip, while his left hand clasped his thigh, and his face was twisted with pain. I noticed he hadn't been too careful where the whip fell, for the horse was bleeding.

"Stop it," I said. "That's enough."

Clint gave a grunt of contempt. He raised the whip again. It fell once more, and the horse screamed. I climbed over the paddock railings. When I got close to Clint I saw his eyes were wild, staring vacantly. At that moment I really believed Clint was near to madness. He was breathing heavily. His black hair had fallen over his forehead. His whole body seemed to be shaking with odd convulsions.

"Stop it," I said. "You'll kill the poor brute."

Clint gave another grunt. "Who cares?" he asked. "The bastard belongs to us anyhow. There's more where he came from."

As he spoke, Clint lifted the whip and brought it down. This time I could see the slash had been deliberately aimed. The stallion shrieked. I couldn't bear it any longer. I walked up to Clint. "Stop it!" I shouted.

Clint turned and grinned at me. "Try and make me," he said. He raised the whip once more. I sprang at him. But as I moved, he swerved round quickly and brought the lash of the whip down onto me. The full length of the lash caught my chest and back. For a moment I was dazed by the pain. Then I leaped at him. Once again he tried to use the whip, but I was sober, I could move faster than he could, and I was too quick for him. I seized the whip with my left hand and hit him as hard as I could with my right. He was drunk, and he fell heavily. I watched him as he picked himself up from the mud. I was still holding the whip. As he glared at me, I was afraid of him for the first time, for his bruised face was perfectly calm, yet from his eyes there gleamed a hatred which was frightening, because it was unreasoning, wholly insane.

"Right," he said, hissing out the word between his bloodstained lips. "I've been waiting for something like this to happen. Now we'll see who wins. Now we'll see." Then he limped to the breaking-yard gate, opened it, and moved off along the path which led to the house.

I went over to the horse and unhobbled him. The bleeding was growing less. I let him out of the breaking-yard into the paddock and brought him some feed and some water in case Clint had been keeping him on short rations. Then I walked up to the house.

Clint was alone in the living-room. He was sitting in the arm-chair beside the fire with a bottle on the table beside him. He glanced up as I came in, then turned his head away and stared down at the flames. My fist had landed on the corner of his mouth, cutting his lip and bruising his cheek. Suddenly as I stood looking at him I noticed how small the room was, and I wondered how the three of us had managed to live in it for so long. A moment later Jimmy came in. As usual he glanced first at Clint. Immediately he saw the purple bruise and cut lip he knew the reason for it. He crossed to the side-table to help himself to a drink. Then Clint raised his head.

"Before you begin on the grog," Clint said, "there's something I've got to say to you."

"Yes?" Jimmy answered. "I'm listening."

"You've got to make up your mind very carefully."

"Make up my mind about what?" Jimmy asked.

"You've got to make a decision," Clint announced. "It's quite simple. Either your brother leaves Berrima—or I do."

Jimmy swallowed some of his drink. "If I were you," he said to Clint, "I wouldn't try to force me to make that decision."

His voice was quiet but there was an unusual tone in it—which made Clint stare at him. From the little thicket at the end of the back yard, a kookaburra began its weird call, screeching it would seem endlessly, until the call finished with a sly, derisive chuckle. Then there was silence. Jimmy finished his drink and helped himself to another.

"So that's how it is between the two of you," Clint said. "I should have guessed."

"You're mistaken," Jimmy said.

"Or perhaps that's how you hope it'll be?" Clint asked. "Am I right?"

Jimmy was silent. Slowly Clint got up from his chair and went over to him. "Well, if that's how the ground lies," he said, "I've only one question to ask. How much is my share of our partnership worth to you?"

"I'm not asking you to go, Clint," Jimmy said.

Clint took a step closer to him, leaning forward a little, as if in some way he believed his physical closeness to Jimmy could increase his influence over him. "I've made my terms clear," he said. "I won't stay unless you turn your brother out of the house. And since you seem to want the bastard more than you want me, I'm asking you, Jimmy—how much is my share of the business worth to you?"

Again Jimmy was silent. He stood very still, gazing down at his glass. Then he sighed and looked up at Clint. "If you want to go," he said, "you can take the whole lot. You can take all the money there is in the case in my bedroom. You know where I keep the key."

"Do you mean that?" Clint asked.

Jimmy nodded. "I've got the house and the stock as security. I can raise money to carry on."

"I mean—are you willing to see me go? Do you really want to let it happen?"

"It's you who's forcing the decision," Jimmy answered.

"Hadn't you first better find out if your brother wants to stay on here all alone with a drunkard?"

Jimmy swung round towards me. "I'm sorry, Ben," he said. "I'm afraid I took it for granted you wanted to stay on. I should have asked you." He took a swallow from his glass. "Do you think you could bear to stay on here alone with me?" he asked.

"Yes," I said. "I'll stay on."

Clint put out his left arm and leaned on the back of a chair. Then he stretched himself. The movement seemed quite casual. But it had the effect of revealing the outlines of his whole body.

"Jimmy," he said quietly, and Jimmy turned away from me and looked towards him. Then, as Clint stared at him fixedly, I was aware he was making his last effort, exuding all the powers in his possession in an attempt, by the strange, indefinable force of his will, to reach a peak of strength in his influence over Jimmy so he could dominate him once and for all time. In the silence I could hear the clock ticking on the mantelpiece. A large fly was buzzing round the room. It was growing dark.

"I'm giving you a last chance, Jimmy," Clint said.

Jimmy stared back at him steadily. "The key to the case is in the chest, if you remember."

Clint smiled as if suddenly he had recalled a joke. Then his face became hard, and his look was again intent. "You're sure you know what you're doing? You won't come crying after me—saying you were drunk and didn't know what you were about?"

"I'm not drunk yet," Jimmy said.

Clint stared at him a moment longer. Then with a shrug he

moved towards the door and opened it. At the door, he turned. It won't take me long to pack my things"—and swiftly he left the room.

Jimmy took his glass and went to sit down by the fire. Now that Clint was no longer in the room he made no attempt to hide his exhaustion. He sat in silence. I could think of nothing to say. Presently I got up from my chair and lit the two lamps. From upstairs we could hear quick footsteps as Clint moved around his room. Suddenly Jimmy looked up at me with his stricken face.

"Promise you won't turn against me," he said in a whisper. "Promise me you won't leave me."

"I promise," I replied.

Clint drove away in a light cart that evening with his belongings. He harnessed the cart in the back yard. Jimmy remained in the living-room, crouched over the fire with his drink. So he did not see Clint leave.

That night, Jimmy and I got very drunk. It was then he made me tell him the full story of my life—which he's since made me write down.

Later, towards midnight, we went out onto the verandah for a breath of air. It was a cold moonlit night. The stars seemed so close you could pick them out of the sky. Suddenly Jimmy rushed to the edge of the verandah and began to retch. When he turned back to me, I saw his face was very white. For a moment he swayed, and I thought he would fall. Then he took out a handkerchief and wiped his lips. As he put the handkerchief back into his pocket I noticed it was stained a strange dark colour. I looked closer.

"That's blood," I said.

Jimmy smiled. "Nonsense," he answered.

"Give me that handkerchief. Please, Jimmy. It's stupid for us to lie to each other. Please give it me."

Jimmy threw me the handkerchief. I held it up to the light from the lamps in the living-room. It was sodden with blood.

"It's only a little," Jimmy said. "I've known it worse."

"How long has this been going on?"

"Since Christmas," Jimmy answered.

"Have you seen the doctor?"

"What's the point? What could he do?"

"Give you some medicine. Send you to the hospital in Sydney if it's really serious."

Jimmy laughed. "Poor Dr Turner can't even cure his own horse of croup."

"Give him a chance, Jimmy," I said. "Give him a chance."

The next morning I brought Jimmy some tea and damper, and I told him he must stay in bed. Then I rode across to Dr Turner's homestead which was on the far side of Berrima. I found the doctor mending the roof of a barn. He was so absorbed in the work I had some difficulty in persuading him to leave it. However, at last I persuaded him—by promising we'd break in one of his horses for nothing. Dr Turner was a round-faced, squat man with short grey hair and a purple complexion. The children in Berrima called him Dr Turnip.

While he examined Jimmy, I began moving my things from the shed behind the kitchen into Clint's room. Presently Dr Turner called me into the living-room.

"You're this man's brother," he said to me. "So I want you to hear what I've just told him upstairs. It's a plain statement of fact, and I've no doubt I'm right in my prognostication. If your brother doesn't stop drinking, he'll be dead within a few years."

"Well, that's my death-warrant," Jimmy said when I went up to his room after Dr Turner had gone.

"Nonsense," I answered. "You can stop drinking if you want to. You know you can."

"I wonder," Jimmy said.

"Why do you have to drink so much?"

Jimmy was silent for a while. "I suppose it started when I was eighteen, at Cambridge. Yes, that's when it really began. And now—well, somehow I don't seem able to stop any more."

"You're going to have to, I'm afraid. Can I get you anything before I go down to the paddock?"

Jimmy smiled and shook his head. "Thank heaven you're here, Ben," he said.

That evening as I sat beside his bed and he sipped the milk Dr Turner had ordered him to drink, Jimmy went through the story of his life from beginning to end.

"I want to get it off my chest while I'm sober," he said. "The facts somehow seem to get distorted when I'm drunk."

He told me of the events very quietly, without any attempt to show himself in a good light. I could see that throughout he was trying to be completely honest. From time to time he would glance up at me. I think he was relieved when he saw I wasn't shocked.

"I'm a pretty hopeless person really," he said in conclusion. "I'd never have brought myself to break with Clint if you hadn't turned up."

I smiled. "But I *have* turned up. And now you've got to stop drinking—altogether."

Jimmy stretched out his hand and touched my wrist. Then he withdrew his hand quickly and grinned at me.

"All right," he said. "I'll try."

Until yesterday, I've been giving what I've written down each night to Jimmy the next day for him to read. But I've started writing this in a new notebook, and I shan't give him one. I shall tell him I've finished my homework—because this notebook will be written wholly for my own benefit. It *must* be. For I want to get things straight in my own mind. I've got an important decision to make—important for me, I mean. . . .

Jimmy was back at work after a few weeks.

He had taught me his training method so well that I was able to take Clint's place in the lower paddock. As the months passed by, and I became more expert at the work, I began to enjoy it. And I enjoyed the life I was leading. I liked the wide, open, rolling countryside of Berrima; I liked the little shanty house we lived in; I was happy drifting round the pubs of an evening; and I'd found a lanky seventeen-year-old Australian girl called Gwen who had appeared from Sydney and went with any man for ten shillings. Gwen seemed to have a special liking for me—because she'd leave anyone she was with as soon as I came into the Surveyor-General Inn, where she was usually to be found. So I was contented. Jimmy was a perfect companion. He was considerate and patient with me. He knew I liked listening to him talk about his life in England and the little world in Nottinghamshire to which I might have belonged if my mother had been a wife rather than a mistress. Yet he knew when to be silent, and he could tell when I felt like being on my own. As the pleasant months passed by, I became very fond of my half-brother. . . .

———

For nearly three years Jimmy gave up drink. During that period I stopped having even a beer, for if I drank when I was with him, I'd see his eyes fixed on my glass. Sometimes he was quiet and sullen, and I was afraid he was still missing Clint. But this moodiness seemed to pass, and it pleased me whenever I came into the living-room in the evening and found he was more his old self again. Then I began to suspect the reason for his renewed cheerfulness. But Jimmy now drank so stealthily that it was quite a while before I was certain.

When I found out, I was about to accuse Jimmy of his deceit. But I hesitated. Then it occurred to me it might be wiser if I pretended not to know. If Jimmy could drink only in secret he would certainly drink less than he used to. So I said nothing, and the years passed by.

———

I was in the pub, waiting for Gwen to appear. I was glancing through the pages of an English newspaper, which someone had brought from Sydney, when I came across a short paragraph announcing the death of Sir Arthur Steede, Jimmy's brother. The title had passed to his son, who was still an infant.

I knew Jimmy had never been particularly fond of his brother Arthur, so when I returned a few hours later and found Jimmy in the living-room I told him the news straight out.

"Poor Arthur," Jimmy said. "I never cared for him much, though I suppose I should have done. *There* was an odd person, to be sure. I'm sorry he's dead. How old is the child?"

"Only two. He's called Richard," I answered.

"Poor little brat. I pity him. What a ghastly life he's got ahead of him. Perhaps they'll pack him off to Brierly Lodge at the age of nine. They're sure to send him to Eton and then to Cambridge. Poor little devil."

As he spoke, I noticed that his voice was slurred. Suddenly Jimmy moved towards me and began to sniff.

"You've been with that prostitute again," he said. "The reek of her scent is still on you. You've been with that lanky, rotten girl, Gwen—or whatever her name is."

"I have indeed," I answered, "and you've been drinking."

"Right," Jimmy said. "I've been drinking, and now I intend to have another drink." Quickly he crossed to the cupboard, seized a bottle and poured himself half a glass of brandy. He drank it down. "Can't you see she's disgusting?" he asked, anger suddenly flashing out at me.

"Listen," I said. "Let's understand this once and for all. I shall go to bed with any girl I like—when I like."

"Why do you have to prove to yourself that you're a man?"

"I don't have to," I answered. "I go with Gwen because I enjoy it."

"She's a whore," Jimmy said.

"I suppose that's what people called my mother at one stage," I answered. "But your father didn't seem to have any objection."

The next day Jimmy was as kind and friendly to me as usual. That evening when I went into the living-room I found him sitting in the armchair by the fire with a glass of brandy in his hand.

"Jimmy," I said gently, "you've got to stop drinking. You know you must."

He shook his head. "I can't. When I'm without drink I feel somehow I'm living in the shade, almost in darkness. It's cold there and dark and very lonely. I can't bear it any longer. But I promise you I'll be sensible. I'll limit myself to two glasses a night. I reckon that should be enough to keep away the black fog."

The two glasses a night soon became three or four, and there seemed nothing I could do to stop him. Drink had now begun to affect his mind. He would become intensely suspicious at times—perhaps because he had been hurt and deceived so often that he could no longer trust anyone.

Once, when I had sold a horse for ninety pounds, Jimmy for some reason became convinced I had sold it for more. His suspicion was as hard to bear as his pathetic apologies when he discovered he was wrong. His moods could swing rapidly, from depression to wild elation. In depression, he would be secretive and withdrawn. In elation, he would sometimes indulge in fantastic day-dreams which he would enjoy telling me because I was almost always involved in them. But his attitude towards me was uncertain. Most of the time I lived with a friend and brother who was fond of me. On occasions, I would find myself confronted by a hostile stranger.

Jimmy's fantasies were set in various places, and I appeared in them at various ages.

In one fantasy, I remember—as he told it me—I was twelve years old; I had come to Steede Hall as pantry-boy in the days when old Lucas was the butler, and thirteen-year-old Jimmy and I would go out riding together. We would ride through the park, past the Dower House, through the village and out onto the Trent hills. Then we would gallop. But my horse would shy, and

I would be thrown. Jimmy would kneel beside me and discover I was unhurt. But I would observe how worried he was, and this would be the beginning of our friendship. In another fantasy, Jimmy met me in Lambeth when I was fourteen—a few days before I sailed for Vera Cruz—and we ran away to Scotland together and found work on a farm. In his third fantasy, Jimmy would be sitting on the balcony of his hotel in Acapulco and he'd see me strolling past in the street below—he would see me, not Clint. And we would sail to Australia together.

"It wouldn't have been too late if I'd met you then," Jimmy would say. "I still wasn't involved. I could even have taken you back to Steede and told them you were my half-brother."

"Why can't you tell them now?" I once asked.

"Because it's too late. I've gone too far down the road. Besides, I couldn't face their looks of disapproval and their hypocrisy. And it all means so little to me now." Jimmy stared down at his glass. "Would you like to go back to England?"

"If I could live with you at Steede Hall? Yes," I answered. "I suppose I would."

"Perhaps you might enjoy it," Jimmy said. "But I'm afraid, Ben, that's one of the things I'm not willing to do for you—because I hate the lot of them."

"Do you still hate your mother? After all these years?"

Jimmy crashed down his glass on the table. His eyes were glittering. "Wouldn't you?" he cried. "Wouldn't you hate her—after she'd told the girl you loved that you were rotten with syphilis?"

"I know it was a terrible thing to have done," I answered. "It was—hideous. But I'm not sure. I expect after a time I'd forgive."

"Well, I don't forgive," Jimmy said. "Ever."

But though Jimmy might protest that he loathed his mother, I noticed as the months went by that after a few drinks his thoughts began to turn more frequently to Steede. Sometimes his mind drifted back to the days of his childhood, and he would recall the evening when he had run away from school, and his mother had met him in the drive. It seems she had taken him secretly to his room, brought him his supper, and had sat with him, sheltering him for a while from the world he feared so much.

Jimmy's other fantasy was his favourite. In this one, we both of us left Berrima, and sailed back to England together, arriving in London docks.

"From London we'd catch the train to Nottingham," Jimmy said. "We'd take a cab from Nottingham station, and we'd appear together at Steede. And there we'd find Maude—probably with that smug bastard of a brother of hers. Yes, to be sure—I bet Edmond has moved in to live with her. That would be just like him. Then he could let his own house. So there they'd be at Steede—Maude and Edmond. And then we'd give them something to worry about, wouldn't we? Because there'd be two of us. And you could pretend to be me—just to fool them."

I laughed. "What if they believed *me*? Then what would *you* do?"

"Get you to decline a Latin verb," Jimmy answered.

"How would that help?"

"As you know, I went to a preparatory school and to Eton," he answered. "So at least I can remember a few Latin verbs. But you'd be stumped."

"Why *don't* we go back?" I asked. "Why don't you appear at Steede and claim your inheritance?"

"For many reasons."

"Tell me one of them," I insisted. "Tell me the main one."

"Because too many people know about Jimmy Smith and his friendship with Clint," he answered.

The months passed. I was happy, and I think Jimmy was as happy as he ever could be. Though he was often in pain now, I still couldn't persuade him to stop drinking—not permanently. He'd lay off for a week, but then he'd start again.

Three months ago, when I returned to the homestead after a jaunt with Gwen, I found Jimmy waiting for me in the living-room. He grinned as I came in.

"Have a good time?" he asked.

"Great," I answered.

"Shall we have one last drink before we turn in?" he asked.

I could see he'd had several drinks already, but since he'd stayed up for my return, I didn't like to refuse him a last one.

"Fine," I said.

Jimmy poured out two brandies and handed me a glass. "I must be a prodigious nuisance to live with at times," he said. "But I hope that on the whole you're happy, Ben?"

"Wonderfully happy," I answered. "I had an odd instinct which made me search you out. Thank heaven I found you. But let me ask you the same question. Are *you* happy?"

Jimmy smiled. "Tonight, when I saw you come into this room," he said, "I realised with quite a jolt of surprise I was as happy as I've ever been since I was a child." He raised his glass. "So I drink to you."

He took a few gulps. Then he put down his glass. His face was very white. Without saying anything, he walked out of the room quickly and went to the corner of the verandah. Then he began to retch. I hurried across to him. I could see the dark-coloured blood pouring out of his mouth. As the retching continued, he swayed and I had to hold him from falling. When at last it was over, I helped him up the stairs and put him to bed. Then I walked to the door.

"Where are you going to?" Jimmy asked in a weak voice.

"To try to get Dr Turner."

Jimmy shook his head. "He'll never come at this hour," he said. "Besides, it's finished now. Let him come in the morning. Perhaps he'll be able to give me something for the pain I've had these last few days."

Early the following morning I managed to persuade Dr Turner to make our homestead the first visit on his rounds by suggesting he could watch the progress of a farm horse of his I was breaking in.

When he came down the stairs from Jimmy's room, Dr Turner's scarlet face was grim. "If your brother doesn't stop drinking for

good and all," he said, "I can tell you he'll be dead in three months
—perhaps three weeks."

"Have you told him that?"

"I have indeed," the doctor answered.

"And if he does stop?"

"His liver's diseased," Dr Turner said. "I wouldn't give him
long."

"Have you told him that too?"

"Yes," Dr Turner answered. "I have." Then he saw my look
of surprise. "I've no patience with people who deliberately wreck
the gift of life that God's given them."

Jimmy looked so ill and wretched I couldn't bear to lecture
him when I went up to see him. But that evening, as he sipped
the milk mixed with the powder the doctor had left him to calm
his pain, I made a last and desperate effort.

"You've got so much to get from life if you want it," I told him.
"Just think of it. You could be rich if you wanted to be. I know
you don't want to go back to England. But you don't have to appear at Steede to prove you're the baronet. All you need do is to
go to Sydney and see a lawyer and make a statement. A statement
from you and a photograph would surely be enough to do the
trick . . ."

"But I've told you time and again," Jimmy interrupted. "The
person known as Jimmy Smith can't leave Berrima and appear as
Sir James Steede."

"Why not?" I asked.

"Because there are at least half a dozen people who could blackmail him—and wouldn't hesitate to do so," Jimmy replied. "Besides, I'm quite fond of Jimmy Smith. He's all right, is Jimmy—
when he hasn't had too much to drink. He's not wholly rotten,
is he? And at least he's made his own way out here—without the
influence of money and a title. But I doubt if anyone would have
much to say for Sir James Steede, the prodigal son. So let's forget
about it."

But I wasn't going to give up my effort, for at the back of my mind was the idea that if I could get him to England, he'd be looked after properly. "When you think of the house and the park and all those fine horses you keep talking about, I can't see how you can bear not to go back," I said. "Take the risk of being black-mailed. To hell with it! You'd have the money to pay them off or have them silenced."

Suddenly Jimmy raised himself in the bed and grinned at me. "I've had an idea," he said. "Why don't *you* go back? Out here, even now, we're sometimes mistaken for each other. So why not?"

"First, because I couldn't succeed with it," I answered. "Second, because I don't want to leave you."

"But supposing you weren't leaving me?"

"You mean—supposing you went with me?"

"No, Ben. I mean supposing I were dead." Then he smiled at me gently. "Don't look so dismayed," he said. "I'm serious. Remember what the doctor said this morning. It could be three months or it could be three weeks—because I can't stop drinking. You know that's true. And even if I did, I don't suppose it would make much difference now." He lay back against the pillow and gazed at me. "So when I'm dead," he continued, "when Jimmy Smith of Berrima is dead and buried—why don't you slip back quietly to England? I'm leaving you what I've got out here. When you've sold off everything you won't even have to work your passage. You'll be able to sail back in style." Jimmy nodded his head and smiled at me. "Go back to England," he said. "Take the train to Nottingham. Turn up at Steede and tell them you're their long-lost James—come back to the fold."

I laughed. "I wouldn't last five minutes."

"But you know the hell of a lot about my life from listening to me drooling on about it over my brandy," Jimmy replied. "You could invent a bad head injury to account for the gaps in your memory. I should have to give you lots more information, of course. But we've at least three weeks—supposing old Turner is right. So why not try it, Ben?"

I thought at the time this was just another of his fancies. "All right," I said. "But you're not dead yet—far from it, thank heaven. So let me tidy your bed and make you comfortable for the night. You need a good night's sleep."

"Dear Ben," he said. "I'm so glad you're with me."

———

That night, when Jimmy was sleeping soundly with the help of the pills the doctor had given him, I lay awake in my room next door to him, and I began to think of this new fantasy of his —for me to return to England as Sir James Steede after he was dead. Suddenly I almost gasped aloud. For suddenly I had begun to think of it as a real chance; for what Jimmy had said was true. I *did* already know a great deal about his past life. Certainly I could fake a head injury easily enough. I even had a scar on my scalp from the night they'd attacked me in the brothel in Vera Cruz to show as proof. I knew much more than any outsider could possibly know about Jimmy's life abroad and his life in England. I could learn still more. I looked very much like Jimmy. After he was dead, how could they prove I wasn't Sir James Steede?

Then another thought slid into my mind which it seemed to me would justify our plan. If William Steede had married my mother —if I had been born legitimately, then, on Jimmy's death, I *would* have succeeded to the title. Jimmy's brother Arthur was dead. Why should the estate go to some brat of *his*?

Those were my thoughts. But as I put out the candle, I remembered that Jimmy had produced many wild fantasies before now and had forgotten them in the morning. So I determined not to refer to his new plan. Probably by noon tomorrow he'd very much dislike the idea of an illegitimate bastard like me establishing himself at Steede Hall.

A few evenings later, when I came back from work, I found Jimmy in the living-room. He was drinking milk, but I could see he'd had a brandy or two. I said nothing, for by then I'd learned it was wiser to pretend not to notice.

"If you recall," he said, "I was perfectly sober the evening I came out with my idea for you to appear at Steede. And the more I think about it, the more keen I am on the plan. If you invent a serious head injury to account for any gaps in your memory, they're going to find it very hard to prove you're not an impostor." Jimmy smiled as he sipped his milk. "After all," he said, "in a way you're *not* an impostor. You've a right to Steede. You're a Steede by blood. And it pleases me to think of you established in my place. But I must warn you there's a risk. You're certain to be cross-examined by the cleverest lawyers they can find. They may trip you up. If they do, it'll mean a long jail sentence. Dartmoor isn't as ghastly as the jail down the road, or so I'm told. But it's still a grim place. So it's for you to decide whether you want Steede sufficiently for it to be worth your while."

The words came into my mouth before I'd really worked out my answer. "I've thought it all over," I heard myself saying. "And if the plan still has your blessing, then—if you die before I do— I'm prepared to take the chance. I'll go to Steede to claim our inheritance."

Jimmy gazed at me for a while in silence as if he were trying to picture me in the surroundings of Nottinghamshire. "I'd leave you Steede in my will, but it wouldn't help you," he said. "Because you'd have to prove my identity—which would be difficult after my death. Besides, that isn't what you really want, is it?" Jimmy laughed softly. "Oh, my dear Ben," he said, "what a romantic person you are!"

"Why does wanting Steede make me romantic?"

"But you don't want Steede. That's just it. You don't want the house with its furniture by Kent and Sheraton and its pictures by Van Dyck and Lely. You don't want the gardens and the lake. You don't even really want the hunters in the stables—because you're the least grasping person I've ever met. You want possessions and money far less than most do. So it's not the estate you're after, to be sure."

"What is it then?"

"You want to be Sir James Steede, the seventh baronet. It's the idea of the whole thing that excites you—not the cash."

"All the same, I do want it," I said. "I do want it all. So I've made up my mind to take the risk. That's my decision."

"You mean it?"

"Yes, I do," I answered.

"Right," Jimmy said. "Then this evening we'll begin work—because it means I'll have to go through my childhood with you again month by month. I'll have to tell you every incident you'll be expected to remember from the colour of my nurse's hair to the name of the colonel who taught me to ride my first pony. Then I mustn't forget to tell you about my life out here when I first arrived. I must tell you about Dimmock and his homestead where I lived for a while, learning about horse-breaking. You must tell them about Dimmock, and you must give them his address, because you can let them trace you as far as Albury. If they show Dimmock a photograph of you, he's certain to recognise it. I don't suppose they'll bother to trace beyond that. So you can invent some place where you lived afterwards. But never mention Berrima—for obvious reasons."

Jimmy laughed. "Poor Ben!" he said. "I'm going to make you work harder than you've ever done before. But at least it'll keep you away from the pubs and away from that awful-looking Gwen with her gooseberry-coloured eyes and simpering smile."

"Now and then," I began.

"Twice a week," Jimmy interrupted me, "I shall release you, and you can defile yourself with any girl you fancy. But on all other evenings you must work. The more you work, the less the risk will be. In the evenings I'll coach you. I'll tell you about Steede, and I'll teach you such school-lessons as I can remember. I'll tell you about all my school-friends. There are two of them you can discreetly blackmail into believing you. I can give you various details that will convince them. In the meantime, for practice in writing, as a first exercise, I want you to write out more about your own life. You can spend half an hour doing that each night before you go to sleep. You've got to learn to write like me and talk like me." Jimmy laughed again. "My dear Ben," he said, "I do pity you. But it'll be worth it, I promise you."

In his excitement Jimmy had got up, and he'd begun to pace up and down the little room. He now swung round to face me. His hair had fallen across his forehead, his eyes were shining. I'd never seen him look so elated. "If we both of us work hard," he said, "the plan will succeed." For a moment he stood motionless, staring at me. Then he flung out his arm and raised his head as if in defiance.

"We'll beat them yet," he cried. "We'll beat the bloody lot of them!"

———

That night, after Jimmy had gone to bed, I turned out the lamps and carried the notebook he had given me to my room.

As I passed in front of the spotted looking-glass which hung above my washstand, I paused. I stood for a while staring at my image in the candlelight. But I was no longer examining the features of Ben Ashby. I was staring at the pale, straw-coloured hair and wide-set eyes and rather small straight nose and curving mouth of Sir James Steede, the seventh baronet.

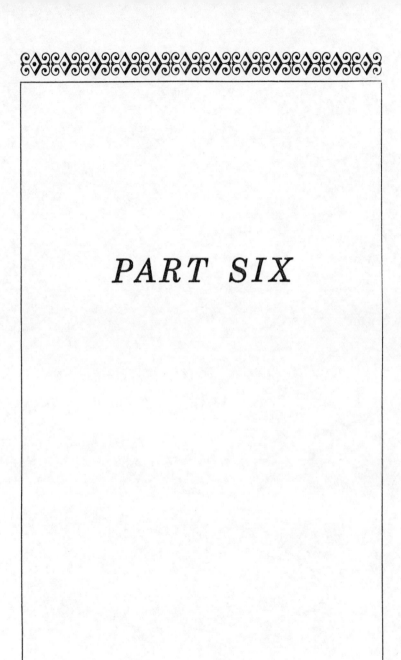

PART SIX

I SUPPOSE that almost every man who has failed in life tries to find some excuse outside himself for his failure. He tells himself he never had a chance because of poverty or bad luck or ill health. But I have to confess that when I started out I had almost every chance—or so it seems to me. I was healthy and well-born; I was heir to a pleasant house and a fine estate; I was reasonably intelligent, and I was fairly well endowed by nature.

What went wrong? When did the rot begin? Was it at Eton, when I chose the easiest path out of unhappiness? Or at Cambridge, when I took to showing-off and drink? Surely not. Surely my decline dates from the day of my mother's visit to Margaret Anstey's parents. For if I had been allowed to marry Margaret, I could—in those days—have made the effort to lead a so-called normal life. I would have had children, I'm sure, and I would have adored them. In Margaret I would have had a loving undemanding companion. I would have led the life of an English country squire. And if I had felt the urge for other pleasures, I could—without occasioning either suspicion or surprise—have left England for a while to visit France or Italy or Greece.

I have just gone to the side-table and helped myself to a brandy —my first tonight. As I poured out the drink, Ben glanced up from the bridle he'd brought in to stitch.

"What are you looking so grim about?" he asked.

"This may be one of my evenings when I begin cursing my mother," I told him.

"Oh heaven," Ben groaned. "Not another. I don't think I could bear it." And he gave me a wink.

I let Ben read the pages I wrote previously. In fact, I wrote them partly for his benefit. But I won't let him read this. Either I shall destroy it or I shall hide it so that Ben will only be able to read it after my death.

But Ben must be very careful to burn all my notes and diaries, because though he's learned to sign my name so well I defy an expert to tell the difference, he can't copy my exact handwriting as yet. Besides, he must destroy all evidence of the true identity of Jimmy Smith—every scrap of it.

Jimmy Smith must die as Jimmy Smith, and he must be buried as Jimmy Smith.

My decline started with my mother's visit to Margaret's parents. But it was accelerated by my liaison with Clint. Most people are mercifully blinkered by their passions so they are unconscious of demeaning themselves. My eyes remain wide open. At the very moment I drink the last drops of humiliation, a part of me is aloof and watching the abasement.

It's quite a time ago since Clint strode out of my life, and now, occasionally, I find it hard to recall the reasons for my passion. I can't comprehend how I could have been so besotted. 'Besotted', of course, is the right word, for I was very seldom sober when Clint was with me. Yet as I stare down at my glass, I can still see him, impudent and lithe, with his soft face and hard muscles, his cheerfulness and his fits of rage and cruelty. I can see the sunshine flickering on the curls at the back of his head. . . .

And then I raise my head from my glass and look at Ben, intent on his stitching. Ben, my friend and my half-brother; Ben, the likeness of all I would have wished to have been. Ben, uncomplicated, unreserved in his emotions, outward-looking, robust, warm-hearted and—I must add to balance the picture—Ben, sentimental and feckless. Ben, with his indestructible quality of innocence.

After Ben had appeared in Berrima, and after Clint had gone, why couldn't I have fought the decline?

The excuse I gave to myself at the time was that Ben had arrived too late. But was that true? Was I already too drink-sodden, too hopeless? Was I already waiting for defeat because by then the part of me which wished for oblivion had triumphed over the weaker part which desired the consciousness of living?

Perhaps the truth is that my break with the society into which I was born was never complete. For the last ten years I have led an existence which would be judged by English society not only to be unconventional and debauched, but criminal and disgusting. Vile or stupid words—a catamite, a Sally-Anne, or a "rotten sodomite" as Michael Fairley called me—would be used to describe my nature. Yet I never allowed myself to face the full implications of my behaviour. I carried hypocrisy to its furthest extent, for I practised it on myself. I pretended I had no feeling of guilt for my behaviour—even while my conscience was throbbing with long stabs of pain. I had tried to destroy my conscience with drink; I only succeeded in dulling it. In my heart I still felt guilty not so much for my unconventional behaviour as for my cowardice in running away from it all. I was at war with myself, and my wounds could never heal. How could I give myself to Ben? The gift was too mutilated.

Perhaps it is because of this conflict inside me that I've never been able to merge myself entirely with another person. Part of me has always been a spectator on the river bank, unable to flow with the current, unable to attain oblivion in ecstasy—only in drink. Happy are they who can join with their lover. Happy are

they who can connect to become not only one flesh but one single
being.

For a while after Clint had left, the scales of my wish for life
or death hung evenly balanced. I realised that Ben confronted
me with the last chance of my life. But I suppose by that time I
was too twisted and suspicious. I was too much afraid of being
let down again; I couldn't face the chance of a last and final failure. So I missed the opportunity those first months offered. Besides, there was always a side of Ben which resented me. There
still is—though it's not as strongly fixed as it used to be when we
first met.

Physically, of course, Ben takes after our father, and he has
inherited the same romantic trait which our father possessed.
But emotionally, Ben takes after his mother. Emotionally he belongs to the working class. So he is split in two. For part of him
admires the extravagance of the aristocracy, while part of him
resents the aristocratic attitude with a profound bitterness.

This resentment came out in a torrent when I was teasing
him about Gwen some time ago.

"Do you still pay that gooseberry-eyed trollop her ten bob?"
I asked facetiously.

"I don't pay her any more," Ben answered with a sudden flash
of anger. "Because we're friends. But I don't expect you'd understand that."

His tone of voice annoyed me. "Why shouldn't I be able to understand it?"

"Because to you she's just a common tart," Ben replied, glaring
at me. "Because you think she's of a class far below you. Because
you'd only condescend to talk to her if she'd got a little body you
could buy for the night—like you bought almost every other girl
you've ever been with, and then chucked them away like a worn
shirt as soon as you got tired of them. Because to you Gwen just
doesn't exist, because she comes from a class which you only think
of as servants or farm-labourers or menials whose only justification

in life—so far as you're concerned—is to sweat their guts out in order to make your sort comfortable."

Ben drained down his drink and stood glowering at me. "Sometimes when I hear you talk about your life back in England," he said, "I wonder if you're even talking about the same place I lived in. While you were 'suffering,' as you put it, at Brierly Lodge with a vast house and a great estate to go back to in the holidays—with ponies to ride and servants to look after you—I was cutting up hunks of reeking meat in a slum street of Lambeth, and my mother was wearing her eyes out in a poky little room mending old lace till past midnight to earn us a few more sixpences. You don't know how most people in the world have to live. You don't know the grind of their lives, and you never will."

A few minutes later, Ben's storm of bitterness had blown away. But while it raged and its waves dashed over me I had seen the shape of the reef that lay beneath the lagoon of our friendship.

But since then I've been careful not to cause another outburst, and I feel that as each year passes the reef is being worn away. For his affection seems to increase as we spend more time together.

One can try to give reasons for love, but they're specious excuses. Another person could possess Ben's qualities—but I wouldn't care for him. So I won't try to find any reasons. I simply know for certain that I love Ben more than I've ever loved anyone. However ill I feel, my heart lifts when I see him. From my lonely bank on the dark side of the river I love him. And I know he is at least fond of me.

The opportunity is still there. But it's almost too late.

In a minute I shall rise to refill my glass, but Ben won't look up from mending the bridle, because he knows that his look of concern only makes me pour out more brandy. . . .

It's too late for me to try to stop drinking at this stage, for I can feel that inside me I'm already rotted with an incurable disease. I'm too far gone. Three weeks or three months—it doesn't very much matter. My concern is to blunt the pain and forget my failure. My concern is to forget that though I'm only thirty years old, I shall probably be dead before I'm thirty-one.

Arthur's widow, Maude, and that white slug Edmond, her brother, won't live at Steede much longer after my death. Nor will Maude's child inherit the estate.

For Ben is now determined to return to England after my death. He will appear at Steede. He will be the prodigal son who has at last come home. Ben has persevered superbly patiently with all his lessons; I'm now confident he'll succeed. "He knows so much about Steede," people will say. "He knows the most intimate details of James's life at home—from his childhood to the day he left England. He knows so much about James's life in Cuba, Mexico, and Australia that he must be James himself. James must have survived the wreck. He was picked up by another ship, as he says." It will never occur to them that James might have survived and lived abroad and have been unwilling ever to come home to claim his wealth and title, for such an idea would—to them—be completely unthinkable.

"What if your mother is still alive when I get back?" Ben has asked me several times, and I'm aware my answer hasn't altogether convinced him. Yet I am certain my reasoning is correct. My mother was fiercely possessive about me. She was never very fond of Arthur, and she disliked Maude; she detested the whole Parker family. When I was presumed dead, my mother must have been distressed, for she must have known she was responsible. But for her final action, I would never have left Steede. However, at least she had another son to inherit the title. My mother could always control Arthur, and I expect she would still have lived in the big house while he was alive. But all must be changed now that Arthur is dead. Edmond has doubtless moved into Steede to be a companion to Maude, and my mother has probably moved out to the Dower House—a rather gloomy building on the far side of the park which she never much liked. Imagine with what joy she would therefore be bound to welcome the return of her elder son. She will *want* to recognise Ben.

Ben now looks the very image of my father when he was thirty. I know, because I can remember the portraits of him as a young man.

As soon as she sees Ben, my mother will be convinced he is her long-lost son.

———

Ben has finished mending the bridle.

"I think I'll just go and stretch my legs for a bit," he said to me. That means he's gone to the nearest pub for a quick drink. I'm glad—so long as he doesn't stay out too long. It's good for him to get away from me for a while.

I think I may have another brandy. I shall pour it out from the bottle which I keep hidden behind the cupboard, so Ben won't be upset when he sees the amount I've drunk while he's been away.

Perhaps I should pour myself out a big one, because I may need it. I'm beginning to have a feeling it may be possibly tonight which will provide the occasion when I must take my last opportunity. It may be.

It may be. For I daren't leave it much longer.

———

Now I've got some drink inside me, let me determine what it is I want.

But even as I try to contemplate it, I know it's impossible to define. Because I want what all of us who are sensitive must long for, with our frantic hearts and aching bodies and poor twisted minds. The fulfilment I want can't be described by words. For love can only be glanced at by words.

So I won't begin by trying to explain to myself what I hope for. I'll begin by admitting what my stupid inbred pride would prevent me from accepting from him.

I don't want pity. I don't want a spasm of drunken lust. Nor do I even want a clasp of affection and tenderness.

When the moment comes, I want no kindness. I want no gratitude . . .

———————

Time is getting short, and I don't even yet know how I should prepare for the moment.

Suddenly, a few minutes ago, as I came back to my chair from helping myself to a drink, I laughed out loud. For I'd suddenly thought of one excuse I couldn't use with Ben. I can't help my plan along by telling him the bed in the room next to mine is damp—as I used to tell my companions. I shan't lie. I shan't make any excuses to make it easier for either of us. When the moment comes, I'll tell the truth. I'll tell him what I've felt from the day I first saw him strolling towards me across the paddock in the waning light.

When the moment comes, perhaps Ben will understand what I feel—even though I can't quite understand it myself. And it's very possible that Ben with his strange quality of innocence *may* understand—because he's less twisted inside himself and less tortuous, so the light of understanding may reach him, since there are fewer corners to deflect it.

Ben in his very innocence may understand, and the final decision will be his. Perhaps his instinct will overcome any need for a deliberate decision.

Perhaps Ben may come into my room. If he does, then I'll know he's understood what I can't even explain to myself. And then all my mistakes and humiliations won't have been quite in vain. My life won't have been all failure. For then, to be sure, I'll know that he'll be with me till I retch the blood out of my throat for the very last time.

PART SEVEN

By NOVEMBER, 1862, the stage was set for the civil trial, and everyone who was involved in it—even an unimportant retired Colonel like myself—was pestered by reporters from the newspapers. But on the whole the national press seemed to be flummoxed by the case. A newspaper these days likes to be able to present a cause to its readers in simple, clear-cut terms. If the Steede Case, as it was called, could have been presented in the terms of Gentile against Jew or Protestent against Catholic, I'm sure the whole nation's interest could have been aroused. But no such divide was possible. At one stage the press had made an effort to introduce a class element, suggesting that a poor adventurer returning from Australia was seeking to establish his rights against the entrenched mass of English society. The Claimant was portrayed as a member of the under-privileged class trying to fight the bastions of privilege. Another newspaper presented the case in political terms. The Claimant, they maintained, was an unorthodox, adventurous liberal—struggling against the powerful ranks of conservative nobility. But the Claimant's cheerful attitude and his genial character didn't fit in with either picture which was contrived for him. He refused to play the part of a plebeian outcast or of a rabid liberal. So the newspapers lost some of their interest in him—though he was surrounded by reporters when he appeared on the first day of the trial, which took place in the small, ill-lit Session Court of Westminster before the Chief Justice of the Common Pleas.

Sir George Learoyd's opening speech, which lasted for a day

and a half, was lucid and held the jury's interest throughout. In clear short sentences he told the story of his client's life from childhood at Steede to his departure from Acapulco and the shipwreck, from his rescue and his arrival in Australia to his appearance at Steede Hall. The next two days were occupied in the reading of affidavits and in the proof of various documents. This included a written testimony by Jamie's best friend at Eton. I can remember the boy well. He was a pleasant-looking lad called Adeney, who was a year older than Jamie was. Major Adeney of Her Majesty's Sixth Dragoon Guards, who was stationed in Bengal and unable to return to England to give evidence in person, had testified that he recognised James Steede's writing and signature. He testified that he was convinced of the Claimant's authenticity from various events to which the Claimant had referred in a long letter he had written him. This was important to our side, because Adeney and John Clive Burdock were the only two people who had been with Jamie at Jackson's House who now claimed he was genuine. All the others who had met the Claimant after his return from Australia were intending to give evidence against him.

On the fifth day it had been expected at the Bar that the Claimant would go into the witness box. But Learoyd decided to call a number of other witnesses first in order to let the Claimant get accustomed to the atmosphere of a Court of Justice.

So I gave evidence, and then Charlotte was called. All who were present during the afternoon—even those in opposition to us—are agreed that she gave her evidence superbly. Her manner was dignified, quiet and restrained. She answered the questions which were put to her with an unexpected deference to Counsel, and I could see that every word she spoke was having a distinct influence on the jurymen. Even Sir Henry Scott's sly cross-examination didn't shake her. He tried, as I thought he might, to show subtly that it was in her own interest to recognise the Claimant as her son. But his effort was demolished by Learoyd in his re-examination.

The following morning Learoyd called John Clive Burdock,

who had been Captain of Games at Jamie's house his first term at Eton. Burdock at the end of a meeting with the Claimant in Charlotte's house in London had announced he would give evidence for our side. He and Denham were two of our most important witnesses. So I was very disappointed by the strangely unconvincing manner in which Burdock gave his evidence. I am still at a loss to account for it.

At first when he got into the witness box, Burdock looked quite impressive. There he stood, a heavy, thick-set, burly man with a red face and a huge beak of a nose, exuding honesty, one felt, from his broad shiny forehead and small, close-set eyes.

"You reside at Caldon, near Malvern, Worcester, and you are now Justice of the Peace and Deputy-Lieutenant for the County of Worcester?" Learoyd asked him.

"I am," Burdock replied with confidence.

"You were at Eton with James Steede?"

"I was."

"How was your interview with the plaintiff arranged?"

"I received a letter from him, saying he wished to see me," Burdock answered.

"Had you known his handwriting as a boy?"

"I had a distinct recollection of it."

"Had you any doubt about the handwriting when you saw that letter?" Learoyd asked.

Burdock flushed. "None," he answered.

"Have you still got that letter?"

Burdock stared down at his red hands which were clasped tightly together. "No," he answered. "I think I must have torn it up. In fact, I am almost sure I did."

"Where did you meet the plaintiff?"

"In a room in Lady Steede's house in Belgrave Square."

"Were you alone with him?"

Burdock stared down at his hands. Suddenly he looked grim. "Yes," he said.

"Did you recognise him?"

Burdock's narrow mouth seemed to tighten. He was silent.

"Did you recognise him?" Learoyd repeated.

"Yes," Burdock mumbled. "I recognised him."

"When you separated at the end of the interview, what conclusion had you arrived at from his appearance and from the conversation you had had?"

Burdock's face was stiff with embarrassment, I noticed that never once did he glance at the Claimant. "I arrived at the conclusion he was Sir James Steede," he answered in a dull, flat voice.

In cross-examination by Scott, this odd lack of conviction became even more obvious.

"Do you remember the colour of James Steede's eyes when he was a boy?" Scott asked him.

Burdock flushed again. "No, I don't," he said. "I'm very bad at the colour of people's eyes."

"I'll try you with the nose," Scott said. "Do you recollect the boy's nose?"

"No," Burdock answered. "I can't say that I do."

"Do you recollect the ears?"

"Nothing particular about them."

"Do you recollect a single feature in the face?"

"Yes," Burdock answered. "The forehead and the mouth."

"He was a very narrow-chested person, wasn't he?"

Burdock hesitated. "Not remarkably so."

"He was very slim as a boy, wasn't he?"

Burdock swallowed. "He was very lean," he replied.

"Do you recollect his shoulders as a boy?" Scott asked.

Burdock's face twitched. It looked almost as if he winced. "No," he said, "I can't say I do."

"At school, you must have had a friendly tussle with him—wouldn't you say he was very slight and weak?"

Burdock scowled at Scott. "I can't say," he answered. "I was two or three years older than he was. I can't remember any tussle."

"You never wrestled with him?"

"Never."

"But you remember that he was slim and thin?"

"Yes."

"And you now recognise the plaintiff as James Steede?"

Burdock unclasped his hands and stared down at them. Then he clasped them together again, for they seemed to be trembling slightly.

"Yes," he muttered. "I do."

The next day Denham was called. The sincerity with which he gave his evidence must have helped to remove the bad impression Burdock had made, for Burdock's obvious confusion and embarrassment had started a rumour to the effect that he had been bribed. Burdock was known to be in debt, and the rumour of bribery spread rapidly around London. There was also an odd suggestion that he had somehow been blackmailed. Whatever the reason, Burdock's strange behaviour had done us a great harm.

On the ninth day, the Claimant himself was called. His examination in chief was conducted by Learoyd. Under his skilful questions, the Claimant, who seemed calm and quite unmoved by the importance of the occasion, gave a connected account of his adventures. The examination lasted two days. But though the Claimant's placid manner must have counted in his favour with the jury, I could see that the jurymen were perplexed by his absent-mindedness which at times seemed to amount almost to indifference.

As soon as Sir Henry Scott, looking more sleek and rotund than ever, got up to cross-examine I had an uneasy feeling that the Claimant was going to have to face a long ordeal. Scott began with questions about Jamie's childhood. The questions were put very gently and softly, and almost each one contained a trap of some kind which only became apparent later. Scott was patient, courteous and deliberately considerate. After the third day of his cross-examination I began to wonder if he did not intend to wear down the Claimant by the mild yet continuous force of his bland, incessant questions.

The Claimant seemed to me to look very much alone as he

stood in the witness box, and the manner in which he would answer the questions put to him seemed most strange. Sometimes
he would answer a really difficult question without any hesitation.
Sometimes he would appear to be defeated by some perfectly
simple question of fact which I was sure he could have answered
if he had wanted to. What now worried me was that his behaviour
looked as if he no longer cared whether he won or lost.

"In your last year at Eton, used you to smoke a pipe in secret?"
Scott asked him on the fourth day of his cross-examination.

"Yes, I did," the Claimant answered after a pause.

"Where?"

"When did I smoke? Whenever I got the chance."

"I asked you *where* you used to smoke," Scott said gently.

"Anywhere I thought I wouldn't get caught."

"Can you recollect any particular place?"

"I don't think so," the Claimant answered.

"Does the name 'Towers' have any special meaning to you?"

"None that I can think of."

"Did you practice archery?"

"Yes."

"In a field?"

"No. In a garden at the back of some shop."

"With a bow and with arrows?"

The Claimant was silent. His mind seemed far away is if he
were in a trance.

"Did you use a bow and arrows?" Scott asked.

"I suppose so," the Claimant answered.

"Was it a long-bow?" Scott asked.

Suddenly the Claimant appeared to shake off his lethargy.
"No," he answered. "It was a cross-bow." And when Scott moved
smoothly to a question about Cambridge, I knew his answer had
been correct.

————

By Wednesday the cross-examination had lasted a week.
Wednesday seems a month ago. In fact, it was only the day before
yesterday.

Charlotte had not attended the trial since the afternoon she gave evidence, for she had caught a bad chill. However, on Tuesday evening she sent a note to my hotel telling me she had recovered and asking me to call at her house on my way to Court on Wednesday so that she could come with me. For her son, she said, would have to leave home to attend Court inconveniently early.

When I pulled open the curtains and looked out of the window of my hotel room on Wednesday morning I saw that London was shrouded in a fog so thick I could not see the lamp-posts on the far side of the street. Almost with each minute, the fog seemed to grow darker. Slowly my cab found its way to Belgrave Square, and I went in to see Charlotte. She was dressed for going out and ready to leave. But I refused to let her venture into the cold yellowish darkness which seemed to be growing thicker each instant.

"I'll call in on my way back to the hotel," I promised her. "I'll give you a full report of the proceedings."

When I arrived, the Claimant, looking pale and oddly listless, was in the witness box. In spite of the fog, the Court was crowded. The Steede Case had become a fashionable topic in London society. The Lord Chief Justice had been plagued by applications for seats by ladies and gentlemen of high standing who dressed for the occasion as if they were attending the theatre. Sitting behind the 'family' solicitors were Maude and Edmond. They stared at me without recognition as I took my seat near to Tuke and his partner Cradwell, who were acting for the Claimant. I had been told that Maude had proclaimed she would never receive me at Steede Hall again after my 'act of treachery' in giving evidence against her side. Behind Maude and Edmond were clustered the local landowners and Jamie's contemporaries at Eton and Cambridge who were present to give evidence against him. Behind them were the newspaper reporters. Though it was cold outside, the Court was unpleasantly warm and airless.

Soon after I arrived, Sir Henry Scott reached the question of the sealed letter. I had already heard from Tuke that the Claimant had been determined in his chivalrous resolve to protect

Margaret Anstey's good name. However, a compromise had been reached. Both Tuke and Learoyd were convinced that our opponents would be unable to confront the Claimant with the sealed letter, since Elliott the family solicitor had destroyed it. Elliott had died some years previously, and we were almost certain that neither his son nor his partner, Baxter, had ever seen the letter. Therefore it had been arranged that the Claimant should state that the second clause in the letter concerned a lady's honour and he would refuse to divulge its nature. "If you insist on producing the letter," his attitude would in effect proclaim, "produce it. Let it be read out in Court, and the reason for my reluctance to reveal the second clause will become apparent." Margaret Anstey would be in Court to give evidence if the plan failed. This compromise had been devised by Tuke. I dislike Tuke. The man sets my teeth on edge each time I look at him. But I must admit he's a shrewd lawyer.

"Before you left England in 1850 and went abroad, I believe you left behind a sealed letter?" Scott now asked.

"Yes," the Claimant answered.

"With whom did you leave the letter?"

"With Elliott, my family's solicitor."

"You've stated in your previous evidence that the letter was not to be opened except in certain events."

"Yes," the Claimant answered. "I did."

"What was the first event?"

"My death."

"And the second?"

Now was the moment for the Claimant to make a brief reply along the lines that Tuke had suggested. But for some reason he hesitated. There was silence. The whole Court seemed to be motionless—as if frozen into immobility by some spell. Tuke was staring down at a document in front of him. His pale face was set stiff like a mask. Learoyd was leaning his huge bulk against the bench in an elaborately casual manner, staring up at the ceiling.

"I'm asking you what was the second event?" Scott said.

"I won't say," the Claimant answered.

A kind of massive sigh arose from the Court.

"You're unable to answer?" Scott asked.

The Claimant was silent for a moment. Then he lifted his shoulders in a shrug. I saw Learoyd glance at him quickly and begin to scribble a note.

"Are we to understand that you're unable to answer?" Scott repeated.

The ageing Lord Chief Justice who had listened to the long cross-examination with an air of intense weariness now leaned forward.

"The witness stated he was *unwilling* to answer," he said quietly, "which is a very different matter."

Scott bowed to him courteously. Then he turned back to the Claimant. "Then are we to understand that you are *unwilling* to answer?" he asked.

The Claimant shrugged his shoulders again. "You can understand just what you please," he said.

I could hear a gasp from the benches behind me. Then faint mutterings spread round the Court. Learoyd turned and handed the note he'd written to Tuke, who read it quickly, then shook his head. When Scott spoke now his manner was no longer courteous and urbane. His voice was cold in its severity.

"I must warn you," he said to the Claimant. "I must warn you that the members of the jury may take your reply in an unfavourable light."

The Claimant made no answer. His expression was so calm that I wondered if he'd heard what Scott had said.

"I must warn you that the members of the jury may infer that the reason you are unwilling to answer the question is because you're unable to do so," Scott continued. Then he flung out his hand and pointed his finger directly at the Claimant. "They may accept my suggestion that the reason you're unable to reveal the full contents of the sealed letter is that you are not James Steede, but a cunning impostor."

"Let them," the Claimant answered, with sudden anger. "Let

them—if they're all that stupid. I've already said it concerned a woman's honour."

"Then you'll be able to tell us the name of the woman," Scott said.

This, surely, was the moment for the Claimant to challenge Scott to produce the letter. But the Claimant hesitated. For a moment it seemed as if he would answer. Then he shook his head and was silent.

"Are we to understand that you're unable—or should I say, are you *unwilling* to give us the name of the woman?"

"Yes," the Claimant answered. "I can't give it to you."

Deliberately, it seemed to me, the Claimant had thrown away his opportunity. I could bear no more. I got up and left the Court.

Outside, the streets of Westminster were wrapped in dense fog. The street lamps had ben lit and cast small circles of light in the prevailing blackness which seemed to muffle all sound. I found an eating house, and I had lunch. But I had little appetite, though I drank some wine. Then I went out again into the fog. My eyes were smarting and my throat was aching by the time I found a cab to take me to Belgrave Square.

Even though I had no good news to bring, I was glad to reach the warmth of Charlotte's drawing-room. A large fire was glowing in the wide grate, and all the gas lamps had been lit. Charlotte was sitting by the fireside. A stack of newspapers and magazines lay on the table beside her. Rose, her young maid, was standing opposite to her. The girl's face seemed oddly red in the firelight. I noticed she was breathing heavily.

"Ned, I'm so glad to see you!" Charlotte cried as I came in. Then she turned back to the girl. "Rose," she said coldly. "You can go now."

Rose jerked back her head. "Thanks," she answered, "I will" —and she walked quickly out of the room.

Charlotte sighed, then smiled at me. "What is the news?" she asked.

"None too good," I answered, for Charlotte would certainly

read the papers that evening, and it was better she should be fore-warned that the case now seemed to be going against us.

"Scott's a clever advocate," I told her in conclusion. "As for Jamie, I can't imagine what's happened to him. He seems in a kind of trance."

"He will hold his ground," Charlotte said.

"I hope so," I answered doubtfully.

"Learoyd's chance will come when he re-examines." Evidently Charlotte was determined to be optimistic that afternoon, and I had done my duty in trying to warn her that our case was in danger. I decided to make an attempt to change the conversation. "What's wrong with that girl of yours—Rose?" I asked. "Why is she so upset?"

Charlotte gazed at me calmly. "I'll tell you why the girl's upset. A few minutes before you came in, I decided for various reasons to let her know I was aware of what had been going on between Jamie and her these last six months."

I gaped at Charlotte in silence.

"I told the girl I wasn't angry with her," Charlotte continued. "I explained that if I'd objected, I'd have dismissed her long ago. The girl confessed about the affair, of course."

I stared at Charlotte in amazement. "You knew," I said, "and you did nothing about it?"

"Why should I? Surely you can see I preferred it to Jamie making his name notorious in every low place of entertainment in town?"

For once Charlotte had shocked me. "You mean, you thought he was safer at home?" I asked.

"If you like to put it that way—yes. But I may well be proved wrong. It appears that Jamie's quite taken with the girl. I thought he'd get over his infatuation. So I said nothing—even when I gathered from an unpaid bill which was sent to me that he'd been stupid enough to give her a diamond brooch costing two hundred and fifteen pounds. I paid the bill without saying a word. How-ever, now the girl informs me he's asked her to go away with him as soon as he's won the case. And I can't allow this lunacy to wreck his whole life. So I had to tell Rose—just before you came in—that the whole affair must cease."

I now began to see a reason for the Claimant's inattentiveness in the witness box. But a love affair wouldn't explain his apparent indifference as to whether he won or lost the case.

"She's a pretty little girl," I said. "How did you find her?"

"I took her on from kindness," Charlotte was saying—when the door opened and Tuke came in. Usually the man is quite self-possessed in an oily, cringing sort of way. But this evening he seemed wholly distraught.

"Where's James?" he asked. "Hasn't he arrived? I told him to wait for me outside the Court. Where is he?"

Charlotte glared at his untidy, greasy hair and his wild appearance. " 'Told him'?" she asked.

But Tuke was unmoved by her cold voice. "Yes, Lady Steede," he answered defiantly. "Told him."

"Isn't that going a bit beyond your instructions?" I asked.

Tuke swung round towards me. "You were in Court this morning. Have you ever seen such a performance? He must have gone out of his mind."

"The cross-examination was certainly a great disappointment from our point of view," I said. "But I'm sure when George Learoyd comes to re-examine, the position will change."

Tuke looked at me in astonishment. For a moment he was silent. "Then you haven't heard the news?"

"When I left the cross-examination was still in progress," I explained.

Slowly Tuke turned from me towards Charlotte. "Then you'd both better prepare yourselves for a shock," he said. "I hoped you'd have heard the news already."

"What news?" I asked him quietly.

"At one o'clock this afternoon," Tuke said slowly, "when the cross-examination was finished, the Judge adjourned the Court for an hour. When James left the witness box, he whispered to me that he wished to see George Learoyd urgently. As soon as the three of us were alone together, James dumbfounded us both.

He'd had a drink from his flask, but he was quite sober, so we had to listen to what he said. We had to take it seriously. Without a word of explanation, James told us he had no intention of proceeding further with the trial."

Tuke paused. Charlotte was gazing at him in bewilderment.

"After Learoyd had recovered from the surprise," Tuke continued, "he said that unless James was prepared to call Margaret Anstey, this was probably the wisest course to take. Learoyd made it clear he was now nervous that if we lost the case a prosecution might follow. I made a last desperate effort to make James see reason and call Margaret Anstey. But it was hopeless."

Tuke went to the window and stared out at the fog which was hanging thickly over the square. "At the time I thought James must have some secret reason of his own," he said. "But now I'm not so sure. I think he simply didn't care. He was tired of the whole business. So he just gave up—obstinate, careless idiot that he is."

Tuke turned round and faced us. "When the Court resumed after the lunch adjournment," he said, "Learoyd announced to the astonishment of all that he did not wish to proceed any further with the action. 'My client,' Learoyd said, 'submits to judgement against him with costs. He elects to be non-suited.' Then, of course, the Judge had a few words to say. 'Very well, Sir George,' said the Lord Chief Justice, 'I am sure you have taken the right course. Nevertheless, you will understand that I feel obliged to send the papers to the appropriate authorities, for there may be a case for criminal impersonation.' And that was an end to it."

"Impossible!" Charlotte said.

I moved towards her. I suppose I made some trite remark, but I doubt if she heard it. Her gaze was fixed on Tuke. "It's impossible," she repeated in a clear, strident voice. "Jamie must have gone mad. You must send for George Learoyd immediately."

Tuke shook his head. "Learoyd has finished with us."

"Then we must find another counsel," Charlotte announced firmly.

Tuke sighed, then he smiled at her in pity. "Our friend will certainly need a new counsel. And I'm afraid he'll need a new solicitor."

"So you're deserting us too?" I asked him.

"Regretfully," Tuke answered. "Yes, I am."

For the first time Charlotte seemed dismayed. "Why isn't Jamie here?" she asked in a fretful voice. "Where can he have gone to?"

"He'll turn up soon," I muttered.

"I hope so," Tuke said. "I have something rather urgent to tell him." Tuke seemed to have recovered his usual poise. He looked almost cheerful.

Charlotte glanced at him with distaste. Then she turned towards me. "Ned, can you find me new solicitors and counsel?"

"I'll certainly try," I answered. "In fact I'm sure I can. I'll go round to see David Agnew first thing in the morning. I know he'll do his best to help us."

Tuke had been watching me with interest. "I should remind you that George Learoyd with the full consent of his client elected to be non-suited," he said. "It's a peculiar feature of our laws. I hope your friend Agnew understands it." He turned gently towards Charlotte. "And I hope your son will be able to stand up to the strain of a criminal trial."

"A criminal trial?" I repeated his words in astonishment.

Tuke nodded his head. "Perhaps I should tell you that in my opinion Learoyd had good grounds for taking the decision in the way he did," he said to Charlotte in his smooth, oily voice. "He elected to be non-suited because that puts an end to an action without either a verdict of a jury or a decision of a Judge. It's little more than a formal record that the plaintiff—that is your dear son —elects not to proceed with his action and submits to pay the defendant's costs. Learoyd avoided a hostile verdict so that with any luck your son would probably escape prosecution."

Charlotte gazed at him in bewilderment. "Prosecution for what?" she asked.

"For perjury. Perhaps even forgery. That was the reason why

Learoyd decided to play safe. But then, unfortunately, as I told you, the Lord Chief Justice chose to say a few words. And he used the unfortunate phrase 'criminal impersonation'."

In the silence I heard the handle turn in the door. I looked round as the door swung open and the Claimant walked in. Strands of hair had fallen over his forehead. His face was red and gleaming. His eyes were shining yet strangely dilated.

"Good evening," he said. "Sorry I'm late." His voice was slurred.

"Where in heaven's name have you been?" Charlotte asked.

The Claimant smiled as he walked towards her. "Aren't you going to say good evening to me?" he asked. "Aren't you going to give your son a kiss?"

Charlotte turned away from him in disgust. "You're half drunk already," she said.

"No, I'm not," he laughed. "But I admit I did have a drink or two. I walked straight out of Court and crossed the river and drove through the fog to a place I used to know years and years ago—a public house in Lambeth."

Tuke was watching him sadly. "*Quem Jupiter vult perdere dememtat prius,*" he said.

"I never could understand much Latin. I told them that," the Claimant said. Then he smiled. "Poor Tuke," he murmured. "I have let you down, haven't I? But you didn't do too badly while it lasted. You had a good run for our money."

"Do you know what you've done today, you fool?" Tuke asked softly.

"I've lost a fortune," the Claimant answered. "And when I'm an old man I expect I'll look back and curse myself. But at this moment I reckon there are more important things in life than money. There's freedom, there's health and, of course, there's love—or what passes for it. I've started out with nothing before now. I can do it again." Once again he smiled. Then he moved to the side-table. "Will you join me in a drink?"

"I will not," Tuke replied. "And you've had enough to drink already."

"So one more won't matter," the Claimant answered, lifting the decanter.

"You won't forget our agreement, will you?" Tuke asked. "I mean you wouldn't be so foolish as to tell a lot of lies involving me? I can assure you it couldn't help you in any way. On the contrary, it would make your position far worse. Do you understand?"

"Don't worry," the Claimant answered. "You won't be troubled by me again."

As he spoke, the door was flung open, and Rose came into the room. She was no longer wearing her maid's clothes. She had put on a dark violet dress which I presumed she wore on her evenings out. Slowly she looked around at us, until her gaze rested on the Claimant.

"Go back to your room," Charlotte said.

The girl did not move. "No," she answered. "After all the lies I've been told, I want to get things straight."

Charlotte turned to the Claimant. "I must warn you," she said, "you'll regret this."

"Don't listen to her," Rose said to him. "She's plain jealous, can't you see? But she must learn she can't have everything her own way."

Charlotte turned to the Claimant. "Do you intend to allow that girl to stay in this room any longer?" she asked. "Surely the fact she's been your mistress for the last six months doesn't entitle her to insult me?"

The Claimant stared at her. "You knew," he said.

"I may be old," Charlotte answered, "but I'm not blind—or deaf, come to that."

"But she didn't object—because she thought you were safer at home." Rose's words seemed to tumble out in short rushes of bitterness. "She told me just now—she told me she'd rather you took me than a street-walker."

"I never used the expression," Charlotte said.

The Claimant took a long gulp of his drink. "Well, to get things quite clear," he said, "perhaps I'd better tell you I've asked Rose to come away with me."

"You poor fool," Tuke muttered.

"You planned to leave with that girl as your mistress?" Charlotte asked.

"Yes," he answered.

"You were living on my money and staying in my house. Every meal you ate, every bottle you drank I paid for. Your nights out drinking round the town were paid for with money I'd given you. Yet you didn't have the grace or honesty to consult me before making your little plan. Very well—you'll get no more from me. And you can leave tonight."

"Don't worry, Jamie," Rose said. "In a week or so's time we'll have all the cash we need."

Charlotte turned from Rose back to the Claimant. "Obviously the girl hasn't heard the news," she said. "Why don't you tell her?"

"I've chucked in my hand," the Claimant announced bluntly. "I've lost the case."

"Lost? I don't understand."

Tuke smiled at Rose malevolently. "It's all finished," he stated. "We're finished for good."

The Claimant went up to her. "That's what I was trying to warn you about yesterday. That's why I told you about the homestead we could have in Australia."

"Have we the money to get there?" Rose asked him.

"I've enough to get us to Sydney. There's a ship sailing next week—I saw it in the papers. We can stay in lodgings till then. I know a place we can go where they'll find us a room. It's not grand, but it's clean. I told you about it once—or at least I tried to. It's a public house in Lambeth. I went there this evening. Now do you understand?"

Rose's face was sullen. "I'm beginning to," she answered.

Tuke looked at the Claimant in silence for a moment. "I advise you to move as far away from London as you can tonight," he told him. "You'd better use a different name."

"Why the alarm?" the Claimant asked.

"Why?" Tuke cried. "After Learoyd's little speech, you heard the Lord Chief Justice use the words 'criminal impersonation'. You must know what the next step will be. Within twenty-four hours there'll be a warrant out for your arrest."

"He'll be arrested?" Rose asked. "What for?"

"For the misdemeanour of corrupt perjury," Tuke answered.

"He'll be tried?" Patches of crimson now stained the ivory colour of her face.

"Certainly."

"And if he's found guilty?"

"Penal servitude for seven years," Tuke answered.

The Claimant had been watching Tuke's expression, listening intently to make sure that Tuke was not trying to frighten him away for some private reason of his own. But Tuke spoke with obvious sincerity.

"How long a start have I got before they come for me?" the Claimant asked.

"They won't issue the warrant until morning. But you'd better clear out of London tonight, and don't leave any traces behind you." Tuke now turned towards Charlotte. "Lady Steede," he said, "when the police officers come in the morning, all you have to do is to say you have no knowledge of your son's whereabouts, and you'll answer any other questions they care to put to you in the presence of your solicitor."

Tuke walked with his quick light steps towards the door. Then he swung round towards the Claimant. "What a mistake you made!" he said. "You should have trusted your solicitor." He pulled open the door. "I did warn you," he added, then he waved his hand to us in farewell and left the room.

The Claimant moved towards Rose. "If you're still ready to leave with me," he said to her with a smile, "perhaps you should go and pack your things."

"I'm packed already," Rose answered. "I wasn't going to put up with any more insults."

The Claimant looked at her steadily. His smile now seemed to contain a slight trace of challenge. "Then shall we plan to leave in about an hour's time?"

"Do you think I'm still leaving with you?" Rose asked him.

"I'm not sure," he answered quietly.

"If I went to Australia with you, I know just what you'd do. I can tell you exactly. You'd find some other old woman to live off, and if you couldn't find one you'd try to live off me." Rose stared at him in sudden contempt. "You took me in once," she said. "I really did believe you were a baronet and a gentleman. But you won't take me in a second time—because you won't get the chance."

The Claimant nodded his head and smiled as if he had just heard an amusing joke. "You're wrong," he said. "But I expect you're quite right not to leave with me. I doubt if you'd really like it out there. You'd always be pining for what you might have missed in the way of a new brooch." He swallowed down his drink and crossed to the side-table. "I shall miss you all the same," he said.

"That's very kind of you," Rose answered. "I'm sure I should be flattered. I'm only sorry I can't return the compliment."

As she turned towards the door I saw the tears of rage in her eyes. There was silence for a moment after she had left the room.

"I found that girl in the poor-house," Charlotte said. "I trained her as my maid because I was sorry for her. After a while I found out she was a thief. But what else can you expect from that class?"

The Claimant poured himself another drink. "If she was a thief, why didn't you send her away?" he asked.

"Because of you—can't you understand?" Charlotte answered impatiently. "I knew what was going on. Why wouldn't you trust me? If you'd trusted me, we'd have won the case." She rose from her chair and moved over to him. "I knew there were gaps in your memory," she said. "I could have filled in those gaps far better than anyone. But you never wanted to be alone with me. You grudged every hour you spent in my company."

The Claimant was gazing at her over the rim of his glass. "Are you going to help me?" he asked.

"Of course," Charlotte answered. "I can save you, in fact. But you must do exactly what I say."

The Claimant frowned. "It depends what that is."

"You must stay here tonight," she said. "You must be ready for them when they come to arrest you in the morning. You'll be taken to prison, and soon after you'll be released on bail." Her large eyes were now glittering, and her strident voice trembled. "I'll then assemble the greatest array of legal talent the country's yet seen. You'll stand your trial," she continued. "We shall win, and you'll be a free man."

I had listened to them both in silence, but I now felt myself obliged to intervene. "Charlotte, do you realise exactly what you're saying?" I asked her. "Do you realise the position you may put yourself in?"

Charlotte's hand jerked out in impatience. "Please, Ned. Nothing you can say can change my decision. So please don't try. I'm sorry to be abrupt. But my mind is quite made up."

I decided I must be blunt. "Do you still believe he's your son?"

"Of course I do. Why should I doubt it?"

"And then?" the Claimant asked. "When I'm a 'free man'—as you put it?"

"I've always wanted to buy a farm in the west country," Charlotte answered. "You could manage it for me."

"Do you need a son so badly?" he asked.

"I've still money left. I'd naturally leave you everything in my will, so that on my death you could easily afford to marry."

"A few minutes ago you asked me to leave your house."

"I was angry, because you'd made a fool of yourself," Charlotte replied. "I wanted to bring you to your senses."

The Claimant took a gulp of his drink. "Well, I've come to my senses now," he said. "I'm leaving London tonight, and I'll get a passage to Sydney somehow."

Charlotte stared at him. Our minds can contemplate a prospect, however unpleasant, with a measure of detachment. Then, with some remark, reality strikes our hearts, and we wince from the pain. "You can't leave me," she said. "Not after all I've done for you. You're all I have left in the world now. You can't leave me, Jamie."

The Claimant gave her a strange smile. "That's the first time you've called me 'Jamie' since I came back from Court," he remarked. "I wonder what happened to make the name stick in your throat?"

Slowly Charlotte turned back to her chair and sat down. "You know I haven't been well," she said. "Ned knows all about it. The doctor says I haven't long to live. I only ask you to stay with me a few years. Surely, that's the least you owe to your mother. From the day you were born I've cared for you. As a child you were delicate, and when you were ill it was I who looked after you—because you refused to let anyone else touch you."

Suddenly the Claimant shuddered. Then he stared down at the glass in his hand. "I wonder when you first realised," he said. "Was it the very first time you saw me?"

I saw Charlotte's hands grip the side of her chair. "What are you trying to say?"

"I'm telling you I'm not your son," the Claimant answered. "And you know it."

Charlotte turned to me. "He's insane," she whispered. "He must be insane."

"Not yet," the Claimant answered. "But perhaps I'd have gone mad if I'd continued as your son for much longer."

"You *are* my son," Charlotte cried. "No one could so resemble Jamie and not be him. You're the image of my husband when he was your age."

The Claimant looked up from his glass. "Shall I tell you when I knew almost for certain you'd seen through me?" he asked. "It was the first time Learoyd came here. Learoyd asked if your son had any scar on his body. And you said that shortly before Jamie went abroad he'd been sharpening a stake when the knife slipped and cut his left forearm. 'Jamie still has the mark,' you said. Now the real Jamie—your son, that is—didn't have a mark on his forearm—as surely you must have known. But I did. Then I remembered you'd come into my room once while I was washing my hands and my sleeves were rolled up."

In silence the Claimant crossed the room and stood by Charlotte's chair, gazing down at her. "But I still wasn't completely certain you knew I wasn't Jimmy," he said. "You were so affectionate—and just as possessive as Jimmy had told me you were. I suppose by that time you'd almost persuaded yourself I was your son. But the truth was still lying at the back of your mind. So when I came in just now and you were furious with me, you never called me 'Jamie' once. Because at that moment it suited you to remember I was an impostor. Now you've decided that a fake son is better than none, so I've become Jamie again."

The Claimant moved away from her chair. "But I'm tired of it all," he said. "I'm tired of having to pretend any longer. So please give me some money, and I'll go."

As he spoke, Charlotte had covered her face with her hands. For a while there was silence. Then Charlotte let her hands drop from her face. Slowly she looked up at the Claimant. "When did you last see Jamie?" she asked.

"Will you give me enough money to reach Sydney and find work again?" the Claimant replied.

Charlotte nodded her head. "When did you last see him?" she repeated.

"Last winter," he answered.

"Was he well? Tell me. How was he?"

"Your son is dead," he answered.

"No," she said, with a little moan of pain.

"Your instinct must have told you your son was dead or you never could have tolerated me," the Claimant said. "You must have guessed I knew Jimmy well to have found out so much about him. If you thought he was alive, how could you ever have prevented yourself from asking about him? Besides, you saw me wearing his signet ring."

"You've told me so many lies—why should I believe you?" Charlotte asked. "How do I know you didn't steal that ring?"

"We've been living under the same roof for over six months," the Claimant answered. "Don't you know yet when I'm telling the truth and when I'm lying? I didn't steal the ring. Jamie gave it to me the night he died."

Charlotte was sitting in her chair, crouched and motionless, with her hands clasped beneath her chin. I could see the shadows of the firelight falling across her white hair. Her voice was hoarse when she spoke. "How did he die?" she asked.

"He'd almost burnt out his inside with drink," the Claimant answered. "He used to vomit blood."

While he talked the Claimant had been looking at us both. But suddenly he turned away, and he was silent, frowning as if he were remembering something of strange consequence. "On the evening he died I was with him in his room," he said. Then he was silent again.

Suddenly, to my astonishment, I saw a smile flicker across his face.

"I'd moved into his room that evening because the roof had leaked in mine, and the bed was damp," he said. Then he sighed, and his forehead now wrinkled as he frowned again. "So I was with him that night," he continued. "At about three in the morning, I suppose it was, Jimmy got out of bed and went over to the basin and started vomiting blood. Soon it made him so weak he could hardly stand. So I got him back to bed, and I put the basin by him, and I held his head. But I couldn't stop the blood. He was retching up whole pints of it. There was nothing I could do. He died just before dawn."

Charlotte was staring down at the fire. Her lips were trembling.

"You say there was nothing you could do," I said quietly. "But couldn't you have sent for a doctor?"

"There was no one to send. The two of us were alone there at the homestead."

In the silence I could hear the sudden crackle of a coal in the fire and the faint hissing of the jets in the gas lamps. "Why did he stay out in Australia for so long?" I asked.

"I reckon the life out there suited him," the Claimant replied. "He'd changed his name, of course. I was the only one who knew Jimmy was James Steede. He was happy out there, because he felt himself free of all that, I suppose."

Charlotte raised her head. The gaze of her dark, worn eyes

fixed on him. "Why didn't Jamie come home?" she asked. "You've still not told us the whole truth—I'm sure of it. Why didn't he come back?"

The Claimant stared back at her. "I expect for the same reason that made him leave home in the first place."

"I don't know what that means," Charlotte said. "I think you're pretending to know more than you do."

The Claimant jolted back his head and finished his drink. He walked to the side-table and put down his glass. When he turned I saw his face was stiff with anger. "Am I pretending?" he asked her. "Are you challenging me?"

For an instant Charlotte hesitated. Then her small, fleshless hands sprang together as if for mutual support. "Yes," she answered. "I'm challenging you—because I suspect you're not telling the truth."

"Right," the Claimant said. "Then you can have the exact truth." He leaned forward and spoke slowly and distinctly, pausing after each word as if he had knocked in a nail and were stretching out for another one. "Jimmy left England," he said, "because you told Margaret Anstey's parents he was diseased."

Charlotte made no movement. A vein had begun to throb on the left side of her neck. "You're lying," she said.

"You told them he'd caught the disease from a prostitute in Cambridge." Then he paused and glared down at her. "Now am I lying?" he asked. "When Jimmy heard what you'd done, he left Steede the very next day—you were spending that day at Lower Farm with Colonel Savage here, if you remember. Now am I lying? You ask me why Jimmy didn't come home to you. I'll tell you one of the reasons why. Because every evening when he was drunk, he'd curse your name."

"No," Charlotte cried out. "It's not true!"

"Night after night I'd sit there listening to him, drooling on about you and his life in England. That's how we got the idea. After he was dead—and the doctor had said he wouldn't last long —why shouldn't I go back to Steede in his place? So he began to give me more details. It wasn't difficult, because he liked to talk. Besides, long before I met Jimmy I knew half of it already."

Charlotte raised her head towards the Claimant. Her face was very white. Hair hung down over her forehead. "Before you met him?" she asked.

"You said just now I was like your husband," the Claimant answered. "What about him? I expect he found what he really wanted when he started his journeys in India. But before that, he'd found something he wanted in England. He'd found it in Lambeth, to be precise. The girl was fifteen when he took her away from the pub where she worked and got her a room in a lodging-house. A year later I was born. Now do you understand?"

Then, at last, I became convinced that the Claimant was telling the truth. For as he had spoken, suddenly the stray pieces of fact I had assembled for myself since the morning he had first appeared had come together in my mind and now presented a coherent and whole picture. As I glanced at Charlotte I saw that she too was convinced. Her face was stricken. When she spoke, it was in a voice close to complete despair.

"Did—did Jamie never think of coming home?"

"He used to say he never wanted to see Steede again," the Claimant answered. "And I'd sit listening to him raging against the life he'd led there, and I'd think to myself, 'You spoiled fool. What wouldn't I give to be in your place!' But now I understand."

"Did it never occur to him that I'd lied for his sake?" Charlotte asked. "He knew I was growing old. Couldn't he bring himself to forget?"

"Forget you'd ruined his life?" the Claimant asked.

As Charlotte watched him now, I saw that her face was contorted with bitterness, but she spoke so quietly I could hardly hear her words. "There was one quality made me fond of you," she said to him. "I used to think you were a kind person. Now I know you're heartless."

"You were determined to ruin his chance of happiness—just as you were glad to spoil mine with Rose. You can't learn, can you?" the Claimant replied. Then he shook himself as if he were shaking off some unpleasant dross. "Now give me the money you promised, because I must go."

Very faintly in the distance, for the sound was muffled by fog, we could hear a newsboy as he passed by the square. "Special edition," he was crying. "Steede Trial Result. Special Edition . . . Special Edition." Then his voice was lost in the deep fog.

"How much do you want?" Charlotte asked.

"Five hundred pounds."

Charlotte shook her head. I decided that once again I must intervene. "You told us you only wanted enough for your passage to Sydney," I pointed out to him.

"I've changed my mind," he answered. "I think my silence is worth more."

"In fact, it's a form of blackmail," I said.

"Exactly," the Claimant answered. Then he looked towards Charlotte and smiled grimly. "To use your own words," he said to her, " 'What else can you expect' from someone of my class?"

Charlotte's hands twitched, and she clenched them tightly together. "There's no more than thirty sovereigns in my room," she said.

Carefully the Claimant looked around him. I saw his gaze fix on Charlotte's diamond necklace.

"What you're wearing round your neck will do," the Claimant said. "I know where to get rid of it—even at this late hour."

"This necklace was a wedding present from my husband."

"Then isn't it only fair you should give it to his son?" the Claimant asked. "You could say it was mine by right of birth."

When I saw Charlotte's hand rise towards the clasp at the back of her neck, I felt I must try to help her—because I knew she was devoted to that necklace and had worn it almost every evening since William had presented it to her. "Give me an hour," I said to the Claimant, "and I'll bring you five hundred pounds."

But he shook his head. "I trust you," he said, "but I can't risk waiting here much longer. Besides, I'd like to have the necklace, since my father gave it to her. I'd like to feel I'd had some present from him in my life—even though I could only keep it a short while."

I turned to Charlotte. "Surely you can find something else he can sell to get himself some money?" I asked.

But Charlotte wasn't listening. She was staring down at the fire-place, her face wholly distraught, muttering to herself so incoherently I could scarcely make out what she was saying. "I could have done it," I heard her mutter. "I could have done it—if only he'd trusted me. And then Maude and Edmond would be back where they came from. But you lost it all—Jamie and you between the two of you. That's it. You lost it all. But why couldn't you trust me? Why couldn't you?"

The Claimant crossed the room and stood by her chair. "The police know I'm here, and I haven't much time," he said quietly. "So please be quick. Let me have the necklace. I need it. I've a long way to travel, and I must go now."

With shaking hands, Charlotte unfastened the necklace and put it down on the table beside her and pushed it towards him.

"Yes, you can go," she cried out suddenly. "You can leave me." Then she turned back towards the fire. "I'm old," she said. "I've got no children alive. I used to have memories I could look back on. But now you've taken even those away from me." With a weary hopelessness she shook her head. "I can't even think about Jamie now," she muttered, "because you say he never wanted to see me again. He hated me so much he cursed my name."

Suddenly Charlotte gave a low cry of pain, and bent forward her head and began to sob in misery. I moved quickly to her chair and gestured to the Claimant to leave. The hoarse sounds which seemed to rend her whole body were horrible to hear. I put my hand on her shoulder. "Charlotte," I said gently. "Please, Charlotte."

The Claimant picked up the necklace and walked towards the door. Then he turned back and looked at Charlotte, crouched in her chair, shaking with the anguish of her grief. For a moment he stared at her, dishevelled and twisting in her misery. Then, slowly, he put the necklace down on the side-table by the door and moved a few paces towards her. His voice was very quiet when he spoke—and rather hesitant.

"But Jimmy wasn't always like that—when he was drunk, I mean. He didn't always turn against you," he said. He paused for an instant and sighed. "Some evenings, for instance, some evenings he'd remember times when you were happy together—like the day you took him to buy his first pony."

Charlotte's face was hidden in her arms, so I could not tell if she was listening to him. But at that moment I only wanted to be rid of him. "Please leave," I said.

But he remained motionless, looking at her. For a second I thought of trying to turn him out by force. I dismissed the idea not only because he was obviously much stronger than I was and younger, but because the expression on his face had made me doubt if this was the time to make him leave. For the anger had now left his eyes, and as he gazed at her I could see pity in his look—perhaps remorse. So I kept quiet.

"He'd often tell me about the time he ran away from school. Do you remember?" the Claimant asked her gently. "He'd walked all the way from the station, and you met him in the drive and took him secretly to his room—because you knew that your husband and Colonel Savage here would want to send him back the very next day. But you brought him his supper, and later you came up and sat down by his bed."

Charlotte gave a little moan. "Please," she murmured. "I can't bear it. I can't any more."

But the Claimant's voice went on evenly. "You listened while he poured out all his fears," he continued. "And then you said —or so he'd tell me, and it was always the same—you said, 'You're small and you're young. You can easily be hurt. But don't forget that each day you're growing older and stronger. And never forget you've a mother who loves you more than anyone beneath the sky'. And you held him to you that night—as you used to when he was little. And he went to sleep in your arms."

Slowly Charlotte raised her head and stared up at him with her dark, watering eyes. But now her wet cheeks quivered with a slight hope, and her hands were clasped and a little raised as if in a prayer which she was ashamed to make.

"He remembered that?" she asked, her voice trembling in expectancy, yet half afraid he would take back the small coin of hope he had briefly held out to her. "He remembered that?" she asked again. Her expression reminded me of a child I had seen the previous day, begging in the street outside my hotel.

"Yes," the Claimant answered. "You see—part of him did love you."

Charlotte gave a long shuddering sigh and lay back in her chair. She was crying quietly. But there was no bitterness now in her grief, and I'm certain she was no longer aware of our presence in the room. For her mind was far away in the past.

The Claimant glanced down at her for a moment. Then he nodded his head slightly, as if he were agreeing to a remark which had been made to him. He went to the side-table and picked up the necklace. For a second he weighed it in his hand. Then he slipped it into his pocket, and I thought he would leave without another word. Indeed, he turned the handle of the door and opened it. But then he paused and swung round towards her. His manner suggested he had at that instant remembered a last duty he had promised to perform. His expression as he stared at her now was humble yet defiant. Suddenly he reminded me once again of Jamie when he was a young boy.

"You weren't the only one that loved him," he said to her.

For a moment his face looked worn in its sadness. Then he gave me a nod—an awkward, almost apologetic smile, and he walked quietly out of the room.

———

In the silence, we could hear his footsteps as he walked along the corridor. His steps were taking him, pace by pace, away from our lives. For we both knew we would never see him again.

But in our minds we could follow him down the staircase and out through the front door. Our minds could even follow him to London docks and to the ship which would take him on his way to the other side of the world. But our minds could accompany him no further. For he was returning—we realised when we thought about it later—to an existence so far removed from the security of the pleasant gas-lit room we were sitting in, with its stiffly elegant black-and-gilt Regency furniture, and its thick, dark-green velvet curtains with their heavy swags; so far removed from the fog covering the tall houses round the square, that he might be returning not so much to a different hemisphere, as to a world existing on another planet.

ABOUT THE AUTHOR

ROBIN MAUGHAM was educated at Eton and Trinity Hall, Cambridge, where he read English Literature and Law. During World War II he took part in some of the fiercest tank battles in the Libyan Desert and was mentioned in despatches for gallantry under fire. In 1945 he wrote his first book, *Come to Dust,* and was called to the Bar as well. The success of his book determined Lord Maugham—as he is more properly addressed—to devote his life to writing. Subsequently, he has written some sixteen books—novels and works of nonfiction—among the most notable being *The Servant, Somerset and All the Maughams* and, more recently, *The Second Window,* which was highly praised. ("A great, great achievement"—Alec Waugh; "Masterly"—*The Evening Standard.*)

The Servant, Line on Ginger, The Black Tent, and *The Rough and the Smooth* have all been filmed, and an adaptation of *The Servant* was recently performed on the stage in both Paris and Madrid.

Lord Maugham lives in the Balearic Islands. He is now at work on a new book.